Madison's Web

Randi-Anne Dey

Madison's Web

Disclaimer

This book is an Adult romance and contains implied fade to black bedroom scenes with a bit of spice that is consensual. Not recommended for children.

Reader discretion is advised for chapter fifteen - Bonds Unite. If you want the original writing of this chapter which is FULL spice, please message me on Madison's FB page and I will send it to you. (See back of book)

This novel is entirely a work of fiction. Unless otherwise indicated, all the names, characters, businesses, places, events, and incidents portrayed in this book are either the product of the author's imagination or used in a fictitious manner and bear no meaning to where they are placed within the book. Any resemblance to actual persons, living or dead, or actual events is purely coincidental.

Designations used by companies to distinguish their products are often claimed as trademarks. All brand names and product names used in this book and on its cover are trade names, service marks, trademarks and registered trademarks of their respective owners. The publishers and the book are not associated with any product or vendor mentioned in this book. None of the companies referenced within the book have endorsed the book.

Published in Canada
ISBN
Hardcover – 978-1-7382843-2-0
Paperback – 978-1-7382843-0-6
Ebook – 978-1-7382843-1-3

Dedication

This book is dedicated to the writing group 'The Four Muses' that posted the 2023 Build a Book, holiday edition challenge. Here's to you. **"Second chance with a professor at a winter festival."**

Thanks

Thanks to my parents, Dia and Rob, my neighbor Roger and my pups, Azlyn and Sandor.

Thanks to the Four Muses, for encouraging me to write this book.

Contents

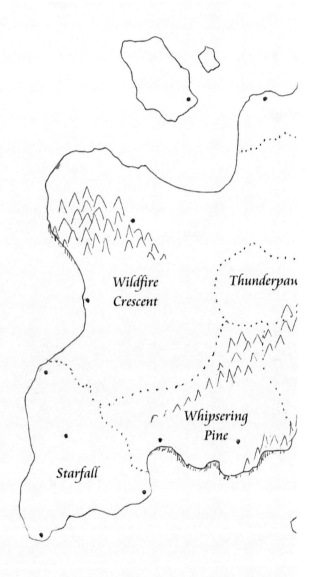

Wildfire
Crescent

Thunderpa

Whipsering
Pine

Starfall

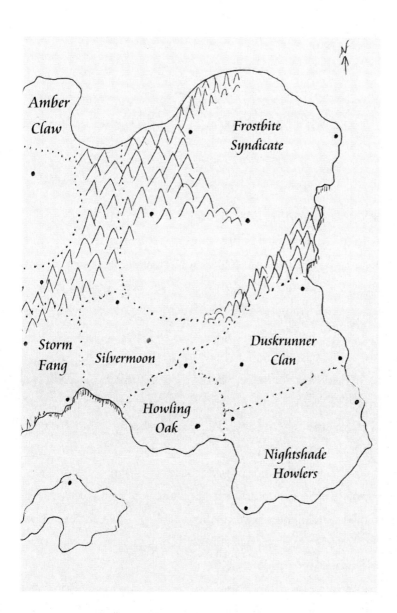

One

Reluctant Steps

M ADISON STARES OUT the window of the car, the hum of the engine in the background of her mind, the driver's off-key singing a minor distraction to her thoughts. She sighs heavily, not wanting to return home after she was driven out of town five years ago by her best friend. Or someone she thought was a best friend. Her hands tighten on the purse straps in her hands, twining them between her fingers as her mind drifts back to the past. Sasha set about destroying her reputation, all because she is a hybrid that got better grades than her in school. It didn't help that Aiden, the captain of the football team, had pushed Sasha away and compared them publicly, stating she would never be good enough for him. It wasn't as if Madison had intentions of dating Aiden, but that didn't matter to Sasha, who desired the pack to revolve around her. She was somewhat surprised that Sasha didn't set her sights on her brother Luke instead. Especially knowing he would be the next Alpha and she could be Luna. But then, Luke wasn't exactly interested in girls, nor boys for that matter, not unless they were his fated mate.

Madison's eyes wander over the winter wonderland outside, fighting the feeling of dread within as the signs of the pack appear. Her driver pauses when the guards stop him at the gate, asking their intent within the pack before continuing on their way. The Alpha of the Duskrunner Pack had called her home. An Alpha and pack she rejected when they banished her five years ago, but one that contained a man she called father for her life here. Also, one she hasn't spoken to since she left. In fact, she hasn't spoken to anyone from the pack, despite some of them attempting to reach out to her. She just placed them on ignore when their calls came in, but her father sounded desperate, especially as he left ten messages in a matter of a few hours. The strange part was it was a Monday night when normally his drunken calls came in on Saturdays. No, these calls contained fear within them, and she worried for her brother Luke, or she would have told him to go to hell, as she did the day he sided with Sasha.

She has to wonder what he wants and why he dared to call her. Had he heard that she built her own empire out west, richer and more powerful than his? Or has he figured out she is slowly buying out all his shares and assets under a hidden corporation? She doubts it because she's been careful in her acquisitions when dealing with him, not wanting him to find out until it was too late. Either way, she needs to be cautious and not let him anger her into giving away any information. One night is all she booked at the Regent hotel, and one night is all she is staying; in and out. The meeting with her father is early in the morning, but damned if she is staying in the pack house she grew up in. She owes the town nothing nor the people within it. They nearly broke her five years ago and would've if Victor and Clarice had not found her. A lot has changed since then, and she certainly is not letting them break her now.

She shifts her attention to her driver, Victor. One of the few that works for her that she trusts completely. He and his wife Clarice adopted her into their family back when she was struggling. She returned the favor by working with them and growing an empire around them, of which she is the figurehead. Her gaze meets his in the mirror, gentle brown eyes, wrinkles in the corners, framed with bushy brows. Sporting shaggy brown locks with hints of gray creeping in. She smiles his way, receiving one in return. "It will be alright, Maddie. We will be there in ten minutes, give or take. You do what you need to, and we'll have you home by dinner tomorrow."

"Thank you, Victor. I appreciate it."

Ten minutes later, Victor pulls up to the hotel, parking in the unloading zone. He pops the car into park and moves around to open the door.

Madison takes his hand and steps out, pulling her purse strap up and over her shoulder as she looks around, thinking not much had changed in the town she grew up in. She watches Victor move to the trunk and pull out her bag, rolling it over to where she stands. She nods in appreciation and takes the handle of her rollaway, turning to head into the hotel.

She pauses, a soft gasp escaping her as her eyes land on a taller man walking her way. Memories flood her as she stares into the piercing blue eyes, stepping back into Victor. His blond hair is longer than she remembered it, reaching his shoulders in waves. Her gaze drifts down his trim form, dressed in a black suit, with a silver embroidered vest peaking out beneath the blazer. "Professor Lucian Deplois."

"Miss Madison Evenstone. What a pleasure to see you again." He returns the once over, catching the recognition in her aquamarine eyes, pale skin, and a touch of freckles across her cheeks and nose. Her long brown hair tied back with a bow, reaching nearly mid back. He notices the elegant but simple attire: a black scoop neck top over a lavender flared skirt, down to the black boots, all covered with a black cloak.

She narrows her eyes as her hand tightens on the overnight bag. "Can't say the same, Professor. What are you doing here?"

"I heard my favorite student was returning. I came to say hello."

"Why?"

"Why wouldn't I? Are you here for the winter festival?"

She laughs coolly at the thought of staying in this town for the festival. Her voice fills with disdain as she answers him. "Right. No. I am here for one night to see what Alpha Davis wants. Then I will be returning to the airport. I have a flight booked out at three tomorrow."

The Professor's eyes soften a touch before returning to the intensity they were. "You should stay."

She arches her brow. "In a town that clearly doesn't want me? I think not."

"Madison, not everyone in the town feels the same way."

"They made it pretty damn clear when they drove me out." She glances at Victor, who stands silently behind her, a hand resting on the small of her back. "Victor, please park the car. I will meet you inside."

"Of course, Miss Madison." He hurries around and hops into the car, driving it to the underground parking beneath the hotel.

She turns back to the Professor, giving him a slight nod. "Do have a nice evening, Professor."

Professor Lucian steps forward, wrapping a hand around her wrist. "Madison, wait; not everyone wanted you to leave five years ago. I didn't."

Madison's attention snaps to the hand that dares to touch her, fighting the sensations he creates within her, and jerks her hand out of his touch. She lifts her gaze and glares at him darkly. "No, I suppose not, but NO one defended me, including you, Lucian. I left because you ALL sided with Sasha and didn't want the taint of a hybrid nearby. That much was clear. Now. Please leave. I have had a long day, and I am tired." She turns her back on him and stalks into the hotel, not daring to glance back, knowing if she did, she might run into his arms as she had years ago when she found out he was her mate.

Lucian's thoughts reach hers as she steps into the lobby. *I waited for you, Maddie. I stayed true to you, just as I know you have stayed true to me.*

'GO AWAY Lucian!' She draws her hands up and traces the pattern of a rune in the air, blocking communication from him. She can hear the whisper of her dragon within. *'That was not nice, Maddie.'*

'I am not ready to discuss it, Somoko.'

'He waited, Maddie, you know he did.'

'Somo, enough. I am not here for him. I understand you and Zuri want him, but he also could have come to us. It's not like we were hiding. But he didn't.' She feels sadness overwhelm her as her dragon retreats to mope with her wolf. She sighs softly. *'I'm sorry, Somo. I didn't mean to hurt you and Zuri.'* Receiving only silence from within, she approaches the desk, smiling politely at the clerk. "One room for Madison Martinez, please. I made reservations late last night."

The clerk clicks a few buttons on her computer and nods. "Yes, Miss

Martinez, master suite. I will have Luis bring you up."

"It's quite alright. Victor, my driver, will escort me as soon as he parks the car. I just need the key card."

"Right away, Miss." She pulls two cards out, swipes them, and hands them over. "Will that be everything?"

"Yes, thank you."

Madison moves to the side and pulls her phone out, glancing at the unread messages, placing it away as she feels Victor enter the lobby. She smiles his way and tucks an arm in his as they head to the elevator. "Miss Madison, he is still outside watching you. Should I be concerned?"

"I know Victor. It's fine. He's already reached his limit of hurt and can no longer do so."

They step into the elevator, watching the doors close. Madison presses the button for the 4th floor, staring at them as they light up.

Victor places a hand under her chin and directs her gaze his way. "Who is he, Miss Madison?"

Her eyes soften for the briefest of seconds before shaking her head as the doors open. "It doesn't matter, Vic."

Victor sighs, studying the woman he now considers a daughter of his, her back rigid as she steps out of the elevator and pauses before turning and heading down to their room. He follows quietly, stepping into the grand suite, noticing the twin beds, the lounge chairs, and the desk in the corner, along with a small kitchenette. The thought of the rumors of her sharing a room with a man brings a smile to his lips, knowing she did it deliberately, for she informed him before booking the room. He settles on the end of a bed, watching her throw her suitcase on the other bed and unzip it. She pulls out the laptop and sets it up at the desk in silence. She unfastens her cloak and drapes it over the chair. "Miss Madison. Something is clearly bothering you. Talk to me."

Madison turns and studies Victor. "Just Madison, Victor. You co-own the empire just as I do."

"You are the face. I am just the silent partner."

"But you are still a partner and don't need to call me Miss in private."

He chuckles. "I know, Maddie, but if I am to pretend to be your servant, then I need to stay in character. Now, stop avoiding my question."

She moves to sit on the bed opposite him, next to her suitcase, and smooths out her skirts. "There were a few things I left out when you found me, Vic, like the fact that my fated mate is here and sided with them."

"He's your mate then, this Professor."

"Yes."

"No wonder none of the wolves appealed to you in our empire. Did you not reject each other?"

"No. To be honest, it all went down so fast. I just couldn't take his rejection on top of everything else."

Victor moves to her bed and wraps an arm over her shoulders. "Living without your mate for five years. That's gotta be hard, Maddie. Especially with the pain of betrayal."

She shakes her head as she leans it on his shoulder. "I never felt any. Nor would I give it to him. That is why I put my heart into building the empire and keeping the wolves of Wildfire Crescent at bay."

"This Professor, I get the sense he is more than he appears, but I feel no wolf from him?"

She nods. "Yes, he's from another pack. Transferred here. His older brother is Alpha of the Frostbite Syndicate from up North, but no one knows it other than me. And now you do."

"Wait. Frostbite Syndicates are dragon shifters. He's a Silver dragon?"

"Yes. He's my dragon's mate. I found out when I turned eighteen and also discovered that I was a hybrid between wolf, dragon, and fey. Sasha, whom I thought was my friend, as you know, spread that really fast, along with the fact I was sleeping around. He would have felt the betrayal if I was, and didn't deny it, which hurt Somo and Zuri badly, for they both love his dragon Rhydian. He is just as bad as them in that regard. Honestly, I don't even know why I came back."

"Perhaps to put the old ghosts to rest. Sasha, your father, this professor.

You left in a hurry, Maddie, and were pretty broken when Clarice and I found you. You left loose ends, and that's not like the Maddie we know now."

She nods. "You're right. I left a lot of loose ends here. Loose ends that need tying. Thanks, Vic."

"Great. Now that it's settled. What do you want for dinner? I am starving."

Madison chuckles. "You are always starving, Vic. I don't know how Clary puts up with you."

He squeezes her gently. "Because she's my mate, and she loves me. Yours may yet redeem himself. He was here waiting and seems to have kept himself straight. Perhaps there is more to his side of the story than meets the eyes."

She shakes her head. "I would rather not discuss Lucian. Let's go down to the restaurant. Perhaps then you will stop pestering me."

Victor chuckles. "Never, Maddie. It's our job to pester you! That's what parents do."

Madison laughs, grabbing the nearby pillow and smacking him with it. "I should have run away back when you found me."

Victor grabs the pillow out of her hands and strikes her back. "Nah, you're stuck with us now, Maddie Martinez; ever since we adopted you and you took our last name. Come, let's go eat."

Two

A Fragrant Gesture

PROFESSOR LUCIAN REMAINS outside the hotel, watching through the window as Madison walked gracefully towards the front desk. He recalled the day she left town, tail between her legs, running from the people that had betrayed her, himself included. But it was something he needed to do. He had a job to do here, one that came before him and his mate, although he could have handled it better, he supposed. He smiled at her poise and grace, suspecting that not much could ruffle her fur now. Especially since he heard she was the Alpha of the Wildfire Crescent pack, absorbing smaller packs and rogues under her banner at a swift rate. It's one thing to be an Alpha, but adding that to the fact that she controls the strongest and second wealthiest empire in the Northwest speaks volumes. Someone backed her, and curiosity ate at him about who it was, and despite his research into her and her pack, he could not determine any benefactors. He narrows his eyes on the servant she smiles at, love in her eyes as she tucks an arm in his. He feels his dragon within challenging to come forward in jealousy. *'Chill, Rhydian. She hasn't betrayed us in five years. I doubt she will, with the old man.'*

'She's ours. And you just let her go. Twice now.'

'You know I had to.'

'You could have at least denied the rumors of her sleeping around.'

'Then people would know she's our mate. You know it was better we step back.'

'She is our mate, and you better not let her go this time.'

'I don't intend to Rhydian. We have less than 24 hours to win her over.'

'24 hours. We had five years to win her back if you had gone after her. There are planes that move faster than we fly.'

Lucian sighs. *'You know we needed to stay here to get our job done.'*

'Yah, yah, and yet, all this time and you still haven't completed it. You could have taken one week and gone to her.'

'Enough, Rhydian; I made a mistake. I will deal with it.' He turns and continues down the street, his mind contemplating how to win her back, suspecting by her cool demeanor that it is going to prove more challenging than he anticipated. Part of him hoped she would just jump into his arms, but the other part of him respects the glare she sent his way at their contact. He could feel the sparks of their bond at their touch and saw the way her aquamarine eyes flared when she jerked out of his grasp, knowing she did too. He also needed to figure out why she was back to see her father. Alpha Davis was very clear to everyone that he disowned her, and Madison retaliated by rejecting the entire pack. When Davis finally steps down, which he should have by now, her brother Luke would be next in line as it's the male heir in succession. Unless she was aiming to absorb this pack in hers, which made no sense. All the others bordered her territory, so it would be easy to control, but this one had several packs between them. There had to be another reason, and his curiosity ate at him.

Madison and Victor head down to the hotel restaurant, enjoying a meal together, talking low enough so as not to draw too much attention before returning to their room. Victor sprawls out on his bed with a book as Madison moves to her laptop. She searches through the news of the pack to prepare herself for when she steps into Davis's offices. She is certainly not giving her father any advantages by being surprised in the meeting. Her fingers type rapidly, clicking and sifting through the information. Noticing that recently, there were attacks on the pack by rogues and multiple offers to partner with Silvermoon that were declined for reasons unknown. She taps her fingers lightly on the table as she ponders this, shifting her attention to Silvermoon, searching through the information that she can find. She frowns slightly, picking up the pen nearby and chewing on its end, staring at the screen before her.

Victor lifts his gaze. "I recognize that look. What did you find?"

"Nothing. That's just it. Alpha D'andre of the Silvermoon pack offered a partnership to assist in the rogue attacks, but Alpha Davis declined. There is no reason to do that. It would have been a win-win situation for both packs."

"What were the terms of the agreement?"

"I don't know. I can't find them online. It's odd. We might have to make a trip over to Silvermoon, as I highly doubt Alpha Davis will tell me."

"He might, Maddie. He called for help. As you said, he sounded desperate."

"Perhaps, but I feel this sense of dread around me that indicates this is a trap. He wants something; I just don't know what. He was very adamant I was no longer his daughter. And it's not like Davis is my true father. What with having fey magic, a dragon, as well as a wolf. He's a pure wolf, and so was Mom. Somewhere, somehow, I ended up with another bloodline. I wish I could ask her, but she's been missing since I was ten."

"What about your brother?"

"I believe he's a pure wolf as well. He would have gotten it a few years after I left, so it's possible he has a dragon and kept it hidden because of what happened to me. Either way, I made everyone aware this pack is no longer mine when I severed ties and rejected it five years ago."

Victor rises and pulls a chair over, sitting next to her and swiveling the laptop around to look at the screen, flipping through the tabs she has open. "There must be something we are missing."

Madison rubs the temples of her head. "Yes, I think you are right. I am just not seeing it. Perhaps you can look. I am going to have a soak. I feel a stress headache coming on."

Victor nods. "Enjoy. I will continue searching for you. If I yield results, I will let you know. Don't forget to take your pajamas in there."

"Thanks, Vic." Madison laughs and rises, moving to the suitcase and pulling her pjs out, as well as her toiletry pouch. She heads to the bathroom and closes the door, setting her stuff on the counter. Pausing in front of the mirror, she studies the aquamarine eyes that stare back at her. Eyes that are unusual and ones she suspects came from her true father. She reaches out to touch the mirror, knowing it is a window to the soul, feeling the hurt and pain within that she keeps hidden from the world. Closing her eyes momentarily, she takes a deep breath before moving to the tub and setting the water on hot. She strips and settles into it, feeling the warmth wrap around her and ease some of her stress.

Lucian wanders down the street, resisting the urge to return to the inn as he formulates a plan. He looks down at his phone, knowing the dinner hour is upon them, thinking he could ask her to dinner, but suspects she will deny him. Likely having dinner with whomever her partner is. He steps into a cafe to have a meal, lost in his thoughts as he picks at his food. When he heard she was returning, he had hoped she would be here long enough to attend the winter festival. A smile crosses his lips as he recalls watching her just after she turned seventeen, enjoying the light displays and the music. He had known she was his mate well before she did, for most didn't discover it until they were eighteen. Lucian didn't dare tell her that her professor was already in love with her and had been for several years. He glances out toward the bustling town, with ninety percent of the people moving about being shifters and the rest being humans that were mated to them. As he steps out of the cafe, his eyes land on the flower shop, just about to close, and runs across the street. "A moment to buy flowers, if I may. I will pay you double."

The clerk narrows his eyes. "Do you know what you want, or are you going to take hours?"

"I know what I want."

"Right then, I am locking us in. I don't want anyone else thinking they can come in after hours. This way, please." He leads him back to the main counter. "Now, what can I get you?"

"I would like blue anemone."

"Blue what?"

Lucian chuckles at the clerk's expression. "Otherwise known as the blue daisy or poppy."

The clerk rolls his eyes, muttering under his breath. "You could have just said that in the first place. How many?"

"All of them."

His eyes widened in shock. "All?"

Lucian's eyes flash in annoyance. "Was I unclear?"

He shakes his head and steps back into the cooler, pulling out all the blue daisies and poppies and carrying them back out front. "What color paper?"

"Silver or White."

He nods and moves to the rolls, pulling a square of paper out and wraps it around the flowers. He ties a few ribbons in to secure it, taking scissors and running them along the edges to curl them. "How are you paying?"

"Debit."

"Right." He punches it into the till and hands over the pin pad. He shields his eyes as Lucian punches in his pin code while he completes the sale on his end. He picks up the flowers and hands them over. "Thank you, and have a delightful night."

Lucian accepts the flowers, seeing there are close to fifty in the bouquet, and gives him a nod as he heads outside. He strides back to the Hotel Regent and steps inside, catching the lingering scent of her in the lobby as he makes his way to the clerk. "What room is Madison Evenstone in?"

The receptionist looks through her computer. "I'm sorry, we have no one by that name registered here?"

Lucian frowns slightly. "I know she just checked in a few hours ago."

She rechecks her computer. "Oh, you mean Madison Martinez."

Lucian smiles. "Martinez huh? Long brown hair, the most amazing aquamarine eyes you have ever seen?"

"Yes, that would be her. Checked in for one night only."

"Indeed, she has a 3pm flight out tomorrow. Which room is she in? I have a gift for her."

The receptionist looks over at the flowers and smiles. "Room 411. Up the elevator, head left, last door on the right."

"Thank you." He heads towards the elevator, hearing his dragon muttering in his head. *'She better not be married to get that last name.'*

'Rhy, if she was married, we would have felt it. She's hiding the fact she's here. I would as well and am, in a way.'

Lucian steps into the elevator and punches the button. His foot taps impatiently as it rises, hearing the ding as the doors open and steps out onto the floor. He follows the lingering scent of coconuts down the hall and pauses at the door to her room. He knocks lightly, hearing a shuffling within and sensing movement.

Victor searches through the web, coming up just as blank as Madison has, suspecting she is right in that they probably had to go to Silvermoon. He shifts his searches to the Frostbite Syndicate. He scrolls through the information, discovering that the pack is a force to be reckoned with. Almost as strong as their own and ninety percent dragons, silver being the dominant color, but others are welcome. Also, if you wanted information on anything, they were the pack to go to, for they had an uncanny ability of gathering intel.

Glancing back at the bathroom door, he wonders what a dragon is doing in the Duskrunner pack and why he is still here five years later. He sighs, pinching the bridge of his nose, suspecting Madison is right. There were too many things not adding up. Thinking he needs to video chat with his wife, he pulls up Skype on the laptop just as he hears a knock on the door. Victor frowns, wondering who it could be as very few knew they were even arriving, let alone already here. He strides across the room and opens the door, quickly schooling his emotions as he stares at the professor standing there with a bouquet in his hands. "Can I help you?"

Lucian's eyes flare slightly when the man opens the door as he struggles to control his dragon. Rhydian roars in his mind at the fact that she is sharing a room with a man. One that is not them. Lucian stops to take a few calm breaths, pushing Rhydian to the back of his mind. "Yes, I am here to see Madison."

The man before him nods, the corners of his lips lifting a touch. "She is not receiving guests at the moment."

Lucian scans the room briefly behind him, seeing the suitcase open, the clothes scattered, and the room empty of his mate, hearing her voice coming from behind the closed door.

"Who is it, Vic?"

"It's just housekeeping, Miss Madison. Don't you pay no mind to what's happening out here. Enjoy your bath." Victor turns back to Lucian, hissing quietly. "I would suggest you leave, Professor. She doesn't want to see you right now. She's under enough stress, and she doesn't need you adding any more."

Lucian growls softly at the man in his mate's room. "Who says I am going to bring her stress?"

"You already have."

Lucian studies the man before him, sensing outward and feeling her in the bathing chamber. He gives a nod and hands over the flowers. "Tell her they're from Lucian and Rhydian. She knows where to find me if she wants to talk."

Victor takes the flowers and closes the door, leaning against it with a sigh. He knows Madison is going to be less than impressed her mate was here, or that he kept it from her. He places the flowers on the table and moves back to the laptop, and dials out, hearing the ring, then the sound of his wife on the other side. "Clary!"

Lucian stands at the closed door, fighting with Rhydian, who wants to push the door open and tear the man to shreds.

'Rhy, stop it now! Get your dragon ass under control.'

'He's in there with our mate, who's naked!'

'Yes, he is, but pay attention for once instead of letting your emotions overtake you. There were two beds, one with a book, the other with her suitcase. Now, while he smelled of our mate, he smells more of another I have never scented before. Third, he's wearing a wedding band, and she is not. Fourth, she's behind a closed door. If they were doing anything, do you think he would *answer the door in the same clothes he was wearing earlier?'* Lucian moves to the stairwell and slips inside, knowing very few people ever used them these days. He settles down on a step to sit. *'Now, I need you to watch our body while I dragon-step into the room and find out for sure because I just heard him video call someone.'*

Rhydian growls at Lucian. *'You better behave.'*

'I promise, I am just seeking info.' Lucian murmurs a few words as his spirit fades from his body and arrives in the room shrouded in invisibility. He shifts quietly to where he can see the screen of the laptop, but not so close that the wolf could sense a presence.

Victor smiles at his wife, her long blonde hair and blue eyes, with matching wrinkles in the corners and tanned skin from working outside so much. "How was the trip, Vic? How's Maddie taking it?"

"The trip was smooth, both the plane and the drive. Maddie's been quiet but taking it like a champ."

"I'm worried, Vic. I don't like that she's out there."

"Yes, she thinks it a trap, and I'm inclined to believe her."

"Then why did she go?"

"She is still seeking information about her mother going missing, Clary. And there are some loose ends out here that she needs to deal with."

"What loose ends? I thought she closed them all when she severed ties with her pack."

Victor glances back to the bathroom, hearing the soft music playing, before turning back to the monitor and shifting closer. "Her fated mate is out here."

"WHAT!!"

"Shhhh, Clary, she's soaking. She was getting a stress headache, and I don't need her hearing you."

"OMG! I can't believe she finally found her mate."

Victor shakes his head. "Clary, she found him five years ago, before she left the pack. He apparently sided with the pack."

Clarice gasps, placing a hand to her mouth as she shakes her head. "Oh, no! No wonder she rejected all the wolves that approached her."

"It gets worse. Clary. He's part of the Frostbite Syndicate. Alpha family."

Clarice grows silent as she ponders the information. "They are the only pack that rivals our own in power and size, Vic. They would make an excellent ally. If she's mated to one of them, she should use that to her advantage."

Victor shakes his head. "She doesn't want to have anything to do with him. I could feel her pain, Clary. There is also the fact that he's been here five years."

"Wait, how do you know he's still there?"

"Cause we ran into him on the way into the hotel."

"Do you suppose he is seeking the same information Maddie is?"

Victor shakes his head. "It's hard to say. Every lead on her mother has dead-ended. No one is talking. They all have the same story: that she ran away with a lover, but Maddie doesn't believe it. Her gut instinct is spot on, and it's telling her there is more going on in this pack than meets the eye, and I am inclined to believe her."

"You be careful, Vic; I don't want her going missing like her first mother did, you hear me?"

"She won't, Clary. I promise. I think I heard her moving in the bathing chamber." Victor turns as Madison opens the door, smiling at her dressed in her flannels. "Your mother's on video call, Maddie."

Madison moves to the desk and sits down, leaning her head on Victor's shoulder. "Mom! It's good to see you."

"Maddie darling, how are you holding up? Vic said you are getting a stress headache."

"It's fine, Mom, don't worry. We'll be heading back tomorrow at three."

"You make sure you're careful, and if you need more time, you let me know. I'm worried."

Madison smiles, her eyes drifting to the flowers on the table nearby. "I will be fi... Wait, where did those come from?"

"Where did what come from, dear?"

Victor frowns, glancing at his wife before he answers. "There was a delivery of flowers for Maddie."

"Ooh, do you have a suitor out there already, Maddie?"

"Not likely Mom. Probably delivered to the wrong room."

"If you say so, dear. What type of flowers are they?"

"Blue daisies."

"Someone knows your favorite flower."

"Yes, someone does... I am going to go for a run."

"You be careful, Maddie; I don't want to fly down there and turn you over my knee."

Madison laughs, blowing her a kiss through the screen. "I will. Remember, I have fey magic. I can just fey-step myself back here if I run into trouble."

"You do that. Have fun. I want to talk to your father now."

Madison leans over and kisses Victor's cheek. "I will be about two hours. If I am longer, call the search parties out."

Victor groans in dismay. "Did you really have to say that in front of your mother?"

"I love you, Vic, and I won't let Mom kill you. Love you too, Mom!" With that, aqua and silver lights float about her as she shifts into her wolf form. Her pajamas drop to the floor as she fades from the room into the forest behind them.

Lucian pauses when he hears the tone shift on the computer, his eyes landing on the petite woman behind the screen. "You better make sure you keep that promise to keep our daughter safe, Victor, because if something happens to her, the world will understand why our pack is called the Wildfire Crescent. I don't care who it is or what pack it is. I WILL burn them down and destroy them."

Victor nods. "I will be right by your side, Clarice. Our girl is strong, and we will keep her that way."

"Good. Now, how are you enjoying playing the part of a servant?"

"It's interesting, I think I..."

Lucian fades from the room and back to his body, intrigued by the information he just gained. He smiles at the thought that they were jealous of someone who had clearly adopted Madison into their family and made note to research her last name and the couple tied to it, though he suspects he knows damn well who they are now. Upon return, he can feel Rhydian flood his mind with questions, describing the conversation and just how adorable their mate looked in her flannel pajamas. He strides up the stairs to the roof and shifts to his dragon form. Taking to the skies, he seeks a clearing further into the mountains, arriving there in about twenty minutes. He settles in the snow and shifts back, lurking in the darkened woods to wait.

Madison arrives in the forest, her paws sinking in the snow, her white fur glistening with silver highlights beneath the moon. She retreats into her mind, allowing Zuri control as she runs quietly through the forest. After an hour, she slows, feeling the pent-up anger, frustrations, and stress wearing themselves out from the exercise, and wanders toward the clearing she spent a lot of time in as a teenager. It is a small patch where the blue daisies grow in the spring and stay in bloom throughout the summer. Blue daisies, her favorite flower, and only one person in the pack knows it. Lucian, because she told him. Zuri glances around before stepping out into the moonlight, snuffling through the snow for the flowers beneath it, watching as they sprout up beneath her fey touch. She hunkers down in the small patch, pawing at the snow around the flowers.

Lucian watches the silver wolf with black ears and paws step into the clearing, one of the largest he has ever seen. He growls inwardly at her beauty, having never actually seen her wolf or her dragon before she left town. Inhaling in shock as blue daisies rise from the snow, feeling her sadness emanate from her as she lies among them, knocking the snow off their petals. He steps out from behind the trees and into the edge of the clearing. "Maddie?"

Zuri snaps her head around as she stands up to face him, growling deeply. "Not Maddie. Zuri right now."

Lucian bows. "Zuri. It is nice to meet you."

Madison struggles within, fighting Zuri for control. *Back away from him, Zuri.*

Zuri stands her ground. *'He's our mate. The one you left.'*

'Yes, but he didn't come to find us, Zuri. Remember that.'

Lucian moves forward slowly, not wanting to make any moves to make her bolt. "Is Maddie in there?"

"Yes."

"Can I speak to her?"

"No."

Lucian nods, continuing his approach until he is standing right in front of her, reaching out to touch her muzzle gently. He can feel the bond instantly, sensing that Zuri can as well with how still she is standing. "Zuri. I need to speak with Madison. There is some stuff we need to discuss."

"No."

Three

Woodland Ambush

RHYDIAN GROWLS WITHIN Lucian's mind. *'Incoming wolves, fast, north side. I suspect they were tracking Zuri.'*

"Zuri, you need to let Madison have control. Rhydian just informed me we have company coming."

Zuri growls and flattens her ears, swiveling her gaze to the woods, seeing a small pack of wolves step out into the clearing. One larger black one, surrounded by nine smaller brown ones. Rogues from the scent of them. The large black one steps forward and shifts, standing naked in front of them, something wolves look past as it's the way it is when they shift. "Well, well, well. What do we have here? A human meeting with a wolf in the wilderness. The boss will be most interested in this. I'd suggest you shift, darling, so that we know who the white wolf is."

Lucian adjusts his stance, remaining next to Zuri as he studies the rogues before him. There is a glimmer of recognition, knowing he has seen the leader somewhere but can't place him. "It's none of your damn business who I meet and where."

"We make it our business when you are out in our territory after dark. The newcomer, I can understand not knowing, but you have been here long enough to know better. Now, you can come with us of your own accord, or we will take you by force."

"Do you have any idea who I am?"

"Ah yes. Professor Lucian Deplois from the Duskrunner College. No wolf. Teaches the sciences. Now her, we don't know, and we keep track of all the wolves in the area." Another ten wolves move out to flank on the backside.

Zuri spins to growl at them, narrowing her eyes on them, knowing there are now too many to fight. Listening to the words of the leader, she realizes they don't know Lucian is a dragon, so she steps back to allow Madison in to deal with it. Madison growls low and deep. "I am not shifting, nor am I going with you."

The leader's eyes widen. "The wolf can speak... Luna's blood. That explains the size of you. Which pack are you from Luna? The Silvermoon? Your coat is silver, so it would make sense. That makes you so much more valuable."

Madison snarls and steps closer to Lucian. "That's Alpha to you, of the Wildfire Crescent pack." She watches him pale slightly at the name, understanding it brings dread to many packs because of her ruthless takeovers. Or so word spread that she is. "To think, you can take us. Lucian, hang on." The second Lucian's hands grasp her fur, aqua lights surround them, fading them from the clearing back to the hotel room with one very shocked Victor.

Victor snaps the laptop shut quickly and rises. He pulls a blanket off the bed and stands between Lucian and Madison. "Don't you dare look, boy."

Madison shifts and pulls her jammies on quickly. She moves to place space between her and Lucian, adding the barrier of her father, as she narrows her eyes on her mate. "What were you doing there?"

Lucian's eyes follow her as she moves behind Victor, the corners of his lips lifting slightly. "Waiting for you. I knew my flowers would eventually bring you to the only place they grew out here."

Madison growls, mentally kicking herself for walking into that trap. "Dammit."

Victor looks between the pair. "Ok, what happened that you used magic to bring him here, Maddie? You know better than that."

Madison shifts her attention to Victor and moves to sit in the chair behind him. "Lucian knows about my fey magic, Victor, and rogues surrounded us. It was the only safe way out. You need to message Clary and let her know to be on the defensive, as I might have mentioned I was from the Wildfire Crescent pack."

"What the HELL, Maddie? We were keeping this under wraps. In and out, as you requested."

"I know Vic. They just angered me. There was something familiar about them. And they were confident they were going to take us with ease. They have done some research, but not enough, as they didn't know about Lucian being a dragon. I wasn't about to let him expose himself."

Lucian growls. "I kept my dragon hidden for years, Madison."

Madison scowls at Lucian. "He already knew Lucian, just like he knows what pack you are from and that you are my mate. One I left five years ago and one that DIDN'T come looking for me."

Victor sighs, putting his hands in the air. "Alright, you two, enough. There is more going on here, and we need to figure it out. Let's put the dragons away and talk it out like adults. Lucian, grab a chair and sit. I suspect this is going to be a long night."

Lucian returns the glare, turning his attention to Victor, knowing he is a father figure in her life, but wanting some sort of explanation from him and not a video call he watched. "And who are you, ordering the two of us around as if you own us?"

"Well, I'm her adopted father, and if you are her mate, that makes you my son-in-law. That's more than enough power. NOW, sit down, or Zion will step in and make you."

Lucian nods and moves to the vacant chair, his eyes drifting to Madison, who sits staring at the blue flowers before her. "You might want to put those in water. They will live longer."

Madison snaps her eyes to his. "They will be fine."

Victor looks between the pair, wondering how he ended up playing mediator, not a position he wants or desires. "Alright, you two. Explain what happened. Madison, you first. Then Lucian." He listens as they each explain what happened, catching that the leader seems familiar to both of them and that he knows she is not a wolf of the area. He moves to the laptop and opens it, waiting on the screen to boot, flipping to the tab he had open about the rogue attacks. "The attacks are not random. They are decisive and premeditated, Madison. How much are you willing to divulge to Lucian about why we are here?"

Madison scowls at Victor. "None of it."

Victor narrows his eyes. "Don't you give that look to me, young lady. The Frostbite Syndicate are skilled in their information gathering. It makes me wonder why Lucian is still here, especially as their reputation shows most of their tasks take no longer than a month or two."

Lucian glares at Victor. "There have been complications."

Madison sighs. "Sorry, Vic, I am just cranky."

Victor moves over and pats her shoulder. "It's alright, Maddie. But you need to decide if you trust him enough to tell him why you are here. Clarice thinks you should."

Madison groans. "Wait, you talked to Clary about this? Gawd, she is never gonna let me live it down."

"She is fine with it, but she will have questions when we return home. Now, yes or no?"

Madison shifts her gaze to Lucian, feeling the draw to him despite his betrayal five years ago. She averts her eyes, breaking the connection, and giving a slight nod. "Fine, yes."

Victor turns to Lucian. "I ask the same question of you. Are you willing to divulge information of why you are truly in the pack and have been for at least five years?"

Lucian mutters quietly. "It's confidential."

"So is Madison's. Yes or No? The decision is yours, boy."

Lucian shifts his gaze to Madison, slumped in a chair, looking defeated again, reminding him of the day he watched her throw her belongings into her car and drive from the town. Thinking that only a few hours ago, it seemed like nothing would break her, and yet here she sat, lacking the confidence she had earlier. "Yes."

"Good, now that it's settled, let's get to work. I would suggest you stick to public areas from this point forward, Lucian, especially since the rogues recognized you. Perhaps even stay here at the hotel with us until we determine what's going on."

Madison lifts her gaze to scowl at Victor. "And where exactly would he sleep, Victor? There are only two beds!"

"I am certain that two grown-ass people can share a bed and survive."

Madison narrows her eyes. "Fine. He sleeps with you."

"Not a chance, Maddie. Clary would be most upset, but we will deal with that later. Now, Lucian, Maddie is here because her father, Alpha Davis, who disowned her as you know, called her seven times asking for help."

"More like ten."

"Right, it doesn't matter. She sensed fear and desperation in the messages, but both of us suspect a trap. Silvermoon has offered alliances with Duskrunner to help with the rogue attacks, but Alpha Davis has rejected each offer. What is in the offers, we can't find, but we are hoping to head to Silvermoon after her visit in the morning with Davis. The secondary reason is to determine what happened to her mother, as she disappeared when Maddie was ten."

Lucian frowns at Victor's words. "I had not heard there were alliances offered, but I cannot get into the Alpha meetings. I can't even step foot into the clubhouse to be honest. In any of my forms. They have magics baring all non-wolves. I suspect, somehow, those rogues know that and assume I am wolf-less. Which, as you know, I am. I had not heard Maddie's mother had disappeared. Rumor has it she ran away with her lover."

Madison snarls. "Of course, that's the rumor, but that's not the truth of it. Mama felt the pain of Alphas Davis's betrayal often. She was hurting, but she would never leave Luke and I. Whenever I asked anyone about Mama, I could feel the magic compelling their answers, but I was not strong enough to break through it. Something happened, and I aim to find out what."

Lucian sighs. "I meant no disrespect, Madison. I was just stating what

I had heard. The reason I am here is along the same lines. Shifters have been going missing from many of the packs in the territory. A few here and there. The Lycan King suspects a trafficking ring, but we haven't been able to find anything. I have had several leads, but none of them panned out. Magic protects all the areas I need to get into, so it's making it all that much more challenging. The rogues gave me a fresh lead today in their comments about knowing all the wolves in the area. That means there is a tracking system of some sort. The shifters that are going missing are the ones lacking family. The ones others are least likely to notice. Not enough, but enough at the same time. We have informants in most of the packs in the area, but none of us have been able to find anything. The day you left, Maddie, was the same day I had meetings with others from my pack and the day a ten-year-old dragon shifter disappeared. The first one with a family. I know that's not an excuse, but I need you to know that."

Madison studies Lucian, feeling his sadness in the air at the loss, understanding but needing to ask the question. "Did you find them?"

Lucian shakes his head. "No, it's like he vanished. He wouldn't even have had his dragon yet. One minute he was there in the park; the next gone. No vans parked nearby. No one saw anything. Not even the local security cameras. It's suspected magic was involved, and there are several packs that have powerful magic within them. This one. The Nightshade Howlers, who we can't even get a spy into, and the Howling Oak clan."

"I'm sorry, Lucian. I didn't know."

"How could you, Maddie? I kept it from you. The second I saw you in my class, I knew who you were, and I kept that from you as well. I just wanted to protect you, but I went about it all wrong. But I also needed to just play the part of the professor. When Sasha turned the school on you, I was too late to stop it, and by then, you were packing your car. How I wanted to run after you, but I had a job to do. Still do, in fact. But I am not giving up on us. Neither Rhydian nor I will accept your rejection."

Madison pales slightly. "I never said I was going to…"

Lucian holds his hand up to stop her. "It's in your body language,

Madison. When you leave at three tomorrow, you will shut the pack down. Something you didn't do when you left five years ago. I don't want to be in that 'shut down.' It took time to find you on the side. Which pack you landed in, but then word spread about Alpha Madison. So I did research into your Wildfire Crescent pack. I know how ruthless you can be when you set your mind to it. I followed your uphill battle daily, building an empire stronger than most other packs out there and one that rivals ours." His eyes drift to Victor, recalling the video call, understanding now where her backing came from. "I suspected you had hidden backing, but I wasn't certain who until I heard Victor talking to one Miss Clarice Sylvanax. Daughter of the Lycan Queen herself. One who fell in love with a werewolf and disappeared into the pack system with ease."

Victor scowls at Lucian. "How did you hear that?"

"We have our ways, Victor Winterbourne, former Alpha of the disbanded Ironwood Moon pack. Clearly now using the name Martinez to stay in hiding, with Madison as the face of your business. I thought you looked familiar, but it wasn't until I saw the princess that I knew for certain. Does the Queen know where her daughter is?"

Madison looks over at Victor in shock. "Wait... Mom's a Lycan princess?"

Victor sighs. "You already knew she was a Lycan, sweetie," before scowling at Lucian. "I would appreciate it if this DID NOT get out. I don't need the Lycan Royals breathing down my ass for keeping their daughter in hiding all these years. How did you know it was her?"

Lucian chuckles. "I watched the video. She spoke like a Royal, especially when she threatened to wipe out any pack that harmed Madison."

Madison's eyes shifted from Victor to Lucian and back to Victor. "She did what?"

"Maddie. You know Clary is a touch protective. She was asking how the trip went and how you were. I said you suspected it was a trap. I probably shouldn't have, but you know I don't keep secrets from my mate."

Madison closes her eyes and rubs her temples, feeling the headache returning. "I know, Vic. It's just all a bit much and suddenly overwhelming."

Victor turns to glare at Lucian. "What do you mean, you watched the video?"

"Victor, there is a reason we are good at gathering information. We can step into rooms and remain unseen. When I dropped off the flowers, I heard your voice and was curious. Especially as my mate was nearby in the bathroom." Lucian rises and moves to sit beside Madison. "Here, let me."

Victor frowns, not liking that they could spy that easily, making a mental note that perhaps they should stay in character while in the room as well.

Madison feels Lucian moving, settling in beside her. The flood of his scent, the crisp clean snow mixed with a touch of pine surrounding her. She opens her eyes to his, staring into his blue ones a moment before averting her gaze, feeling his pull instantly and not willing to forgive him yet. She nods slightly, lowering her hands to her lap, resisting the urge to run as she had five years ago.

Lucian feels the conflict within her and reads it in her eyes, waiting until she accepts his presence within her space before reaching out to rub her temples lightly, using their bond to soothe her.

Victor studies the pair, knowing the mate bond was hard to resist. "Right, I am going to get us drinks from the bar. I will return shortly." He turns, picking up a key card off the table, and heads to the door, closing it after him.

Lucian feels him go, his focus on Madison as she relaxes beneath his touch. After a few minutes, he pulls her from the chair into his arms, breathing in her soft scent of coconut, wrapping her in his arms and holding her close. He strokes her temples lightly, twining his fingers in her long brown hair as he whispers softly. "Maddie, please forgive me for what I have done to you."

Madison curls up into his arms, feeling his warmth surround her, feeling safe lying there, knowing she should resist but is tired of fighting. Her voice is soft as she rests her head against his chest. "I don't kno..."

He places a finger to her lips. "Shhh, give me a week. Stay here for the winter festival this weekend. Let me prove it to you. I will pay for your flight changes and hotel costs. If, at the end of the week, I haven't succeeded, then I will accept your rejection." He can hear Rhydian growling in his mind. *'You better NOT accept Lucian.'*

'I don't intend to Rhy, but I need to say something to convince her to stay for the week.'

'Good.'

Madison ponders it, feeling the stress of the day sinking in along with the calm of the man holding her. She knew Clarice and Victor would be happy if she gave him a chance, as they were always trying to set her up, saying she shouldn't be alone. She sighs against him, her fingers twisting in his shirt gently, wondering if she could survive a week here. If she dared to risk facing a pack she cut ties with longer than twenty-four hours. "Fine, Lucy, one week, and then I am gone forever."

Lucian grins at her nickname, one she had given to him years ago and hasn't heard in five years. He feels her drift off to sleep in his arms, kissing her forehead lightly. "You won't be gone forever, Maddie. I promise I will win you over." He remains sitting with her in his arms, watching the rise and fall of her chest, the way her hair framed her face against him, not daring to move and break the moment. He lifts his gaze as Victor returns with two drinks, and frowns slightly.

Victor places his down on the table and moves one over to the desk. He looks at his daughter, curled up in his arms as he sits in the chair nearby. He keeps his voice quiet as he addresses Lucian. "Relax, boy, I know my daughter. I knew she would be asleep before I returned. Now we can talk."

He nods, looking down at Maddie again, before returning his attention back to Victor. "What do you want to know?"

"Why didn't you come after her?"

"I explained that."

"No, that's a piss poor excuse. Especially knowing the way she left. Do you know when Clary and I found her, she was in her car, starving, sleeping in the back seat, and beyond broken with no wolf or dragon. It took months of doctors and years to get her to explain what happened here, and even then, she left you out."

Lucian sighs, looking down at Madison in his arms. "I wanted to. I asked the Syndicate for a leave of absence, which was denied. They stated *if she was truly my mate, she would return.* I suppose they were right, but after a year had passed, I didn't know how to approach her. I knew I was at fault. Yes, I should have stopped the rumors, but I didn't know about them until the day before she left. Students don't always share stuff with their teachers, and I was focused on finding a missing child, so I wasn't paying attention to the classroom gossip."

Victor studies the pair carefully. "So, what's the plan now?"

"She has agreed to spend one week here, and if, at the end of the week, I don't win her over, I will accept her rejection without question."

"Your words, I am assuming?"

"Yes, why?"

Victor growls at Lucian, doing his best to keep his voice quiet. "You young people need a brick upside the head sometimes. Because she's never actually mentioned rejecting you. Don't you think she would have when she cut ties and rejected the pack? She even broke the bond with the family that raised her. What's one more? Three for three, so to speak, but she didn't. She waited for you to come to her. She rejected every wolf that attempted to court her in Wildfire, even the ones my wife set her up with. Why do you think that is?"

Lucian frowns, looking down at Madison at peace in his arms. "I...I guess I never really thought about it."

"Well, think about it! You have one week to win her over, and if that's what she said, she means it. In my dealings with her and the pack, Maddie doesn't go back on her word, and she never gives it unless she is certain of the outcome."

"I understand, Sir. I will succeed."

"Good, now, down to business. Madison is meeting with her father in the morning. We had hoped this would be an in-and-out ordeal. But searching the dark web, we found repeated rejections of the offered alliance, so I thought we could drive up to Silvermoon and find out the terms of the treaty before our 3pm flight. Now it seems we have more time if we are staying for a week. NO one is to know I am her second father and who we are. As far as this pack and everyone in it is concerned. I am her Delta, or a servant, who she is sharing a room with to incite gossip, and she's Alpha of the Wildfire Crescent. We are silent backers and intend to remain that way. Out in public, you will treat me as what I portray, and behind closed doors, you will treat me as her father. I know your pack rivals ours in strength, and we would rather not have you on the enemy's list. An alliance between us would be well suited." His eyes drift down to his daughter. "In more ways than one. Being Alpha Pierce's younger brother, you can make that happen. Now, until we find out what her father wants, our hands are bound in where we go, but we can offer what help we have to the disappearances. Clearly, it's intended to look like rogues are involved, but if they know who's in packs, my suspicion is they are pack members working with or for someone else. That's a scary thought when you think about it. They are betraying the very essence of a pack and how it works, and that needs to end."

"I will talk with my brother tomorrow. I am certain an alliance with the Wildfire Crescent will interest him, but it might be best to keep it under wraps for now."

"Agreed. Now, let's drink to it and hit the hay. It's late, and I, for one, am exhausted. Maddie has the right idea in finding sleep." Victor lifts his drink, savoring the taste of the whiskey as it soothes the edges of his anxiety about tomorrow. Not that he would ever let Madison know he was nervous about this trip.

Lucian nods, drinking some of the whiskey Victor returned with, enjoying the silence and the comradery he has in the moment with Victor sitting nearby and Maddie in his arms, knowing he can get used to it.

Victor sets his drink down and moves to Madison's bed, pulling the suitcase off it and placing it on the table. He rifles through it for his own pjs and tosses them on the bed with the book. He moves over and pulls the bedding down, making it easier for Lucian. "I'm afraid we have no extra clothing for you. We packed light. You are welcome to return home, but honestly, if those rogues recognized you, it would be better to stay here. Share the bed with her, but keep your hands from wandering. I don't want to explain to the police why there is a dead professor in our hotel room missing his hands."

"Understood. I will sleep in my clothes and keep my hands to myself." He lifts Madison as he rises, hearing her soft murmur of annoyance as he carries her to the bed and places her down gently. Crawling in next to her, he draws her into his arms as Victor shuts the lights out and shuffles to the bed next to them. Lucian can feel her softness in his arms, suspecting that she is going to be angry in the morning, but taking full advantage of it now. He props up on one elbow, his blue eyes glowing in the darkness as he watches her, counting each of the freckles across her face. He brushes her hair aside, hearing the muttering in the bed next to him.

"Go to sleep, boy; she's not going anywhere for a week."

Lucian chuckles and lowers himself down, his hold tightening on her, allowing himself to sleep with her.

Four

Betrayal Unveiled

WEDNESDAY MORNING, LUCIAN startles awake to the sound of an unrecognizable alarm, recalling rather suddenly where he is when he feels movement in the bed next to him. He rolls away quickly, not wanting to test her emotions this early in the morning, seeing Victor already awake at the laptop, a phone in his hand as he disables the alarm.

"Did you sleep alright, boy?"

Lucian sits up and watches her curl up in the spot he just left, wondering how she slept through that racket. "Yes, remarkably well actually. You?"

Victor arches a brow as he places the phone down. "Bah, I missed Clary, but you two looked peaceful."

"Did you sleep at all?"

"A little. I searched the dark web for clues but came up with nothing more than last night."

"I will call in favors later this morning as you meet with Alpha Davis, since I can't step into the pack house because of the magic barring non-wolves. Do you mind if I join you for the ride to Silvermoon? I would be interested in sitting in on those conversations."

"Do you not have a class to teach?"

"No, classes ended early this year for the holidays."

"So be it. Did you want to wake the lass, or shall I?"

Lucian looks down at Madison, her arms wrapped around his pillow now. "I will, even though I suspect it's better that you do."

"Good answer boy."

Lucian chuckles and places a hand on Madison's shoulder, shaking her lightly. "Maddie, it's time to get up."

She groans softly, pulling the pillow over her head, murmuring softly. "I don't want to. The bed is warm and smells so nice."

Lucian chuckles. "I can agree with that."

Madison opens her eyes in confusion, finding Lucian sitting on the edge of the bed next to her. Shock fills her as she realizes she can smell him all over the sheets, indicating they shared a bed. She bolts backward, away from his touch, finding herself rolling off the other side with a thud. She groans softly as she sits up. "WHY does my bed smell like you?"

"Because I slept in it with you last night, Maddie. Trust me, I kept my hands to myself. Your father already threatened my life if they wandered."

Madison frowned in his direction, turning her gaze to Victor. "Vic?"

"Don't worry, Maddie; he behaved. It was better that he stayed here last night. You best get ready. We are meeting Alpha Davis in an hour."

She nods, sending a scowl back to Lucian as she pushes herself up off the floor. "This does NOT mean things have changed."

"Understood."

"Good." She stalks over to her suitcase and pulls out her clothes for today, heading to the bathroom and slams the door behind her.

Lucian watches her go and turns to Victor. "I should head out. Perhaps it will put her in a better mood if I am gone." He moves over and writes his number down. "That's my cell if you need it, though Maddie already has it. Call me when you are ready to leave, and I will meet you out front. I need a shower, a change of clothes, and to make a few calls."

Victor enters the number into his phone. "Got it. See you shortly." He reaches out to grab Lucian's wrist. "Boy, she'll come around. Just be patient. The mate bond is hard to deny."

Lucian studies the old man for a moment, his eyes straying to the bathroom, hearing the shower start. "She denied it for five years, Victor."

"Yes, and so did you. You're clearly both stubborn. Yet, neither of you rejected the other."

The corners of his lips lift at the thought, giving Victor a nod and heading out the door. "I will see you later." Lucian wanders down the hall, his thoughts drifting to last night, feeling her softness in his arms, the fragile inside rather than the cool exterior. He groans, running fingers through his disheveled hair, finding himself wanting to explore more of that body, but not while her guardian is watching. He steps outside into the brisk air and heads home for a cold shower, for he certainly needed one. He slows down as he nears his small house set on the outskirts of town. His eyes scan the forest to his left, catching the scent of rogues in the area. He moves cautiously to the front door swinging wide open, wood splinters along the frame indicating someone kicked it. Pulling out his cell phone, he dials the local authorities, cursing under his breath about the fact that his morning just got filled with paperwork.

He remains outside as he waits, not wanting to contaminate the scene before they go over it for evidence. He debates calling Madison, but he knows she has enough stress, and he doesn't want her to worry. Within ten minutes, two cruisers pull up to his house, with the officers exiting the vehicle. "Professor? You called in a report?"

"Yes, it seems someone broke into my house."

"When did this happen?"

"My guess is, sometime last night."

"Were you not here?"

"No, I spent the night elsewhere. I came back to a splintered door. I have not stepped inside."

"Good. We will investigate. Stay here."

Madison fumes in the bathroom, dropping her clothes on the counter as she strips and steps into the shower. The nerve of him, thinking he could spend the night and share her bed as if he had not betrayed her. Who did he think he was? And why had Victor accepted him so easily? What the hell! It didn't matter that they were mates. She felt the hot water sting her skin, knowing Somoko didn't like it when she showered this hot, but it soothed her when she felt frustrated. *'Sorry, Somo, I will cool it down after.'*

'Are you bothered because you enjoyed sleeping with him, Maddie?'

'NO... Yes. Beside the point.'

'He's our mate, Maddie. Mine, Zuri's, and yours. You should just accept him. We would all be happier.'

'Five years Somo.'

'Yes, and he waited, just like you. He also had a valid reason.'

'I would rather not talk about it.'

Zuri chuckles in her mind. 'Somo, you know how she is. I loved his arms around us all night. His touch was so sweet.'

'Indeed, it was Zuri. I wanted his hands to wander, even if Victor threatened to cut them off.'

'Will you two stop?' Madison groans as she pushes them back in her mind, hearing their laughter and feeling their desire as the water runs over her. Placing her forehead on the cool tile, she can feel herself weakening to him and knows that she needs to stand strong. She picks up the soap and scrubs herself down quickly before stepping out and drying off. She pulls on a silken black top with lace edges along the neckline, completing it with a long turquoise skirt. Grabbing her pjs, she heads out of the room. Her eyes land on Victor, sitting at the laptop, one hand skimming as the other holds his phone. "Victor, we are staying the week."

"I know, lass. I already called the front desk and extended our stay. Perhaps while we are in Silvermoon, we can buy some clothes, as I am not wearing the ones we brought for a week straight."

"That sounds great." Madison laughs and moves to sit beside him, taking his hand in hers. "Thank you for understanding, Vic."

Victor squeezes her hand. "Just don't be too stubborn that you don't see what's in front of you, lass."

"Yes, I know. Zuri and Somo already spoke to me about it."

Victor chuckles. "Good. Let's get this meeting over with. Also, based on Lucian's words, I think we should try to stay in character in the room in case anyone is watching."

Madison nods. "I guess...When I first got Somo, she told me Rhydian was the only dragon in town. But things could have changed in five years."

"Still, I think it would be best."

"Agreed."

Madison slips some socks and boots on, then pulls her cloak over her shoulders and ties it closed. She picks up her purse and grabs her phone, stuffing it into her pocket. Taking a deep breath, she straightens her shoulders and steps out into the hallway. She waits until Victor closes the door behind her and tucks the key card into his pocket. They travel through the corridors, down the elevator, and step out into the street, smelling the crisp, clean air and seeing the fresh layer of snow covering everything. She watches people moving about and starting their day as she starts towards the pack house.

Victor steps in behind her, trailing her silently.

Fifteen minutes later, she can see the pack house looming in the distance. Her eyes drift to the wolves in training, recalling when she wanted to train in those circles. Now she trains with Clarice and Victor. As she approaches, a bitter smell fills her nostrils. She wrinkles her nose at the stench, turning to see Sasha approaching her with a smug smirk on her face. Madison stiffens, not wanting to deal with her best friend who betrayed her. "Sasha."

"So the prodigal hybrid and slut has returned. Pathetic. Groveling at your father's feet to be allowed back into the pack?"

Madison smiles coolly. "I think not. I am simply here because he called me and sounded desperate."

"Whatever bitch. I don't believe you."

"You don't need to... I know who I am and I know who you are now. I do have to wonder what your mate did wrong to be paired with someone such as you." Madison feels the reaction a split second before it happens. She stops the strike just before it hits her with her hand locking around Sasha's wrist. Her eyes glow with power as she glares at her. "You dare to strike the Alpha of the Wildfire Crescent Pack? I could demand your death for that. Show your respect and kneel." Waves of her Alpha power billow from Madison, causing everyone to kneel around her.

Sasha drops to her knees and bares her neck. She lowers her eyes despite her rage within.

Madison glares darkly at Sasha on the ground before her, resisting the urge to kick her in the face. "That's a good pup, Sasha. Now, tuck your tail and crawl back to your mate. If I see you again, it will not be pretty for you." She watches Sasha crawl away towards the fighting rings. She turns, finding Victor on his knees as well and reaches out to assist him. "Rise, Victor."

Victor bows and rises to his feet. "Yes, Miss Madison. Thank you, Miss Madison."

Just as he did, the door to the pack house flew open, slamming against the wall with a bang. "What the hell is going on out here?" Alpha Davis does a quick glance around, seeing his people kneeling out here too, before his eyes land on his daughter, standing straight and narrow, helping another up behind her.

Madison turns, seeing Alpha Davis glaring out into the courtyard. She smiles at him coldly. "Hello, Alpha Davis."

"Maddie!"

"It's Madison. Alpha Madison, actually."

Alpha Davis stares at her before giving a nod, "Right, please come in, Alpha."

Madison nods. "This way Victor."

"Yes, Miss Madison."

Madison's gaze drifts to Sasha, still crawling away, before following her father into the pack house. She glances around as she steps in, sensing the magic inside instantly. She can hear Somo and Zuri object as it dampens her fey powers. So, her father is dabbling in the art of dark magic, though it just adds more pieces to the puzzle. She follows him into his office, seeing four guards standing and waiting. She narrows her eyes on them, not recognizing them from when she lived here, feeling the darkness emanating from them, even with her magic dampened.

Alpha Davis gestures for her to sit as he settles into the chair behind the desk. "Please sit. Is tea still your favorite drink? I can have some brought."

"No thanks, I will stand. I don't intend for this to take that long. What did you want, Alpha?"

"There is always time for pleasantries."

"Not with you. If you recall, I rejected you and this pack. I am simply here to find out why you dared to call me so many times and check in on my brother Luke. Now, I ask again, what do you want?"

"You've changed, Maddie."

She hisses softly, her Alpha aura creeping out. "It's Madison."

Alpha Davis shakes under her aura as the guards around her drop to their knees. "Sorry, Madison. I need your help. It's widely known that you are the strongest pack in the territory and the richest. I had hoped my daughter would have mercy and help me financially. You see, I got into a bit of trouble with my gambling."

"How much?"

"Six hundred grand."

Madison stares at him. "To whom do you owe this debt?"

The door opens behind her as another steps into the room. Tall, sporting a trim beard and mustache, with feathered black hair and green eyes, dressed in casual clothes with an overcoat draped over his shoulder. "To me." He reaches out a hand. "Alpha Landon of the Nightshade Howlers."

Madison narrows her eyes and shakes the hand politely. She steps back and places space between them, understanding immediately that the guards in the room are his. "Alpha Madison."

"You mean Luna Madison."

Madison smiles coldly. "NO, I mean Alpha. Even your men recognize it."

His eyes move to Davis, still cowering behind the desk and his guards rising from their knees. "Your daughter is a female Alpha? That's even more impressive, Davis." He turns back to her. "Which pack are you from again?"

"The Wildfire Crescent."

Landon's eyes widened. "You're not serious?"

"Indeed, I am. Pull out your phone and google it. Madison Martinez."

Landon pulls his phone out and swipes a few times before typing on it quickly. Flickers of a frown cross his features as he glances at Davis before returning his gaze back to Madison. "Impressive M'dear. You have accomplished much in five years. I shall enjoy taking over that pack, but you would need to step down into Luna's position."

"Excuse me?"

"Well, part of your father's gambling debts included you, his daughter, as my Luna."

"Bloody Hell it did!" She snaps her gaze to Davis, seeing it written all over his expression.

Landon steps forward and takes her hand, kissing the back of it. "My chosen Luna. He clearly left out how beautiful you are. I shall enjoy our time together."

Madison jerks her hand out of his and levels a glare at the man twice her age. "Well, Alpha Landon, I am afraid the joke is on you. I am not his daughter. We do not share blood or genes in any way. If you had been paying attention, you would have noticed we have different auras and scents. He is all wolf. I am a hybrid. He also publicly disowned me as a daughter and part of his family five years ago. Along with that, I accepted his rejection and then rejected this pack as well. I severed ALL ties with his family and pack. So I guess if he offered you a daughter, you best be looking at all the whores he bedded. One of them might have a child of his loins. If not, then he better get producing. Lastly, I have a mate, and you are not it."

"WHAT?" Landon sniffs the air around her and narrows his eyes on Davis. "You lied to me?"

"No, Alpha Landon, she is my daughter; I raised her. My Luna Megan gave birth to her."

Madison turns to Davis. "You might have *helped* raise me, but you are not my father and my mother did the raising until I was ten. Then my brother and I pretty much fended for ourselves. You didn't care about us at all. You didn't even know I was a hybrid until I turned eighteen and that backstabbing bitch Sasha came running to you with that information." She turns to Landon. "You see, he couldn't have a hybrid in his family, as that would indicate my mother somehow had an affair. Not that he would even notice if she did because he was too busy screwing another. One of many he kept on the side. That being said, if Mom had two fated mates, then he would not have noticed cause the goddess willed it. Either way, Davis banished me, and I severed all ties, renouncing the Duskrunner pack as my own. You will not find any pack member that can mind-link me."

"You're lying."

"Why would I lie?"

Landon's eyes move over her, drawing on his Alpha power. "Remove your cloak."

Madison smiles, knowing he was trying to force her. "No, if you are looking for a mark, I am unmarked. You see, my fated mate is part of the Duskrunner pack. He didn't defend me, so I left him here, but neither of us has officially rejected each other. Now, since you tried to force me with your Alpha power, I am going to return the favor. *Kneel*." She watches as he fights it before eventually dropping to his knees. "That's right, Landon, I want to get one thing straight for all those in this room. I BOW to no one. I am the Alpha of the strongest pack in the northwest. If you want a war, I will face you head-on. If you want a battle of wills, I WILL win. I AM NOT anyone's pawn and dictate what I do on MY terms. Now, you will drop the debt against my father, or I will conquer your pack next. Understood?"

She watches Landon nod before turning to her father, anger raging in her at what he has done as the others in the room cower in fear. "If you gamble again, it's on you. IF I find out you are gambling with my name tied to it. I WILL destroy this pack and take Luke with me. Duskrunner will cease to exist, starting with you." She steps forward and places her hands on the desk, lowering her head to his to lock her eyes on him. Hers glow with deadly intensity. "IS that Clear Alpha Davis?"

He nods, his body shaking in fear at the woman standing before him, not recognizing her from when she left here five years ago.

"Good. Now I would suggest you remove my number from your phone and NEVER call me again." She turns, looking at her servant cowering in the corner with the other. "Victor, come with me."

His voice shakes as he steps forward. "Yes, Miss Madison."

She turns and strides out of the office, slamming the door behind her, anger and rage filling her at what her father had done. She pauses at Victor's mind-link. *'Calm yourself, lass. Find out what magic is here.'*

'It's dampening magic, Victor; I can barely feel my fey side.'

'That's not good.'

'No, I felt it as soon as I entered. I can still sense stuff, but I doubt I could cast.' She steps out of the pack house, seeing the eyes all turn to her, feeling them follow her and Victor as they stride away. Once they are back on the main road and out of sight, she breathes a sigh of relief, feeling a shake in her hands. *'The nerve of that bastard, bartering my hand in marriage like he owned me. To someone old enough to be my father no less. WHAT the hell is wrong with him?'*

Victor remains behind her. *'You be careful. Alpha Landon will not take it lightly that you embarrassed him and forced him to kneel in front of Davis's men.'*

'They were not Davis's men. The guards were Landon's. I could feel the darkness on them, matching the darkness on Landon. They have a dark witch working with them. We will need to find a white witch to combat that, as I am certain my fey magic will not be enough.'

'His men? Why would Davis have Landon's men around him?'

'I don't know, Vic. Something is going on that's not right. I also know where I recognized the lead rogue from. It's Landon's Gamma.'

'Shit.'

'Exactly. Somehow, they are marking themselves as rogues. I suspect the witch has a hand in that, as well as the fact that the Syndicate cannot place spies in Landon's pack. I have one more stop, Vic, then we can head to

Silvermoon.'

'*Your brother, I am assuming.'*

'*Yes.'*

Back at the pack house, Landon turns to Davis. "I want you to find what wolf is her mate and bring him here. He needs to reject her personally."

Davis nods and sends out a mind-link to all the wolves in the pack. '*Whoever is my daughter Madison's mate, answer me now.'* He frowns as he receives only silence back, giving a shake of his head. "There is no response."

Landon's Gamma Garrick enters the pack house and knocks on the office door, his eyes scanning the room and the anger within it. "What happened? Where is our Luna?"

"It seems Davis left some things out. Our Luna denied my claims to her and is, in fact, the Alpha of the Wildfire Crescent pack. She is also a hybrid and apparently has a fated mate somewhere in this pack."

"A hybrid?"

"Yes, more than just a wolf."

"Wait, a fey-touched hybrid?"

"She didn't actually clarify."

Garrick switches to mind-link with his Alpha. '*The white wolf was fey touched as she was standing in a field of flowers growing in the snow. She stated she was Alpha of the Wildfire Crescent pack as a wolf, which would make sense, as she was the largest wolf I have seen. But she was not alone. She was standing with Professor Deplois, clearly having a discussion. When we surrounded them, she took him with her when she shifted out.'*

'*So she's mated to a human?'*

'*It appears so.'*

'*He will be easy to kill, and when he's dead, I will take her for my Luna. I want her and her pack. Find him!'*

'*We tried Alpha. We went to his house but he didn't return home last night.'*

'*Check the hotel. That's where she will be staying. Search the room discreetly and report back to me.'*

Landon turns to Davis. "You have humans in this pack, yes?"

Davis nods. "A few. Most have mates within the pack."

"But there are a few unmated ones?"

"Yes."

"Perhaps one of them is your daughter's mate. Find out who? A non-wolf would not have a mind-link. Meanwhile, I have business to attend to. I will return."

Five

Whirlwind of Reckoning

M ADISON'S THOUGHTS ROAM as she turns to the left, taking her down a small dirt road. She stops at the cottage there, painted a pale blue with white shutters and a white picket fence surrounding it. Sensing movement inside, she moves forward and knocks on the door. As the door opens, Madison smiles at the woman who opens it, slightly shorter than she is, with short brown hair and hazel eyes. She recognizes her from school as a bit of a loner and mostly sticking to herself rather than the social crowd. "Rosa?"

"Madison? What are you doing here?"

"I am here to see my little brother, Luke."

Rosa looks over Madison, reading the confidence within her, giving a nod and stepping to the side. "He's in the kitchen feeding Aurora."

"Aurora?"

"Our pup. You've been gone a long time, Madison."

Madison blinks back the moisture in her eyes at missing out on her brother's pup and clearly meeting his mate. "Yes, it has been too long. I'm sorry. This pack was not exactly welcoming to me, but I should have stayed in touch with Luke."

"He tried Madison."

"I know he did, but I couldn't face it. I ignored all my messages, not just his. That's on me. I am here to make amends before I return to my pack."

Rosa smiles, taking Madison's hand gently in hers. "That's good. He will appreciate it. Come, this way." She leads her into a small kitchen, the cupboards a light oak with a pale green countertop. A table and chairs sit off to the side, with a small child in a highchair sitting in it. Her brown eyes sparkle as she giggles, watching the spoonful of food zooming towards her. "Luke, honey, someone's here to see you."

Luke pops the spoon in Aurora's mouth as he lifts his gaze to the doorway. "Maddie? Is it really you?" Rising, he moves over to stand in front of her, standing a good half a foot taller. He looks her over, her aquamarine eyes, her long brown hair free about her shoulders, the cloak draped over her. Luke grabs her suddenly and pulls her into a hug. "Gawd, I have missed you. Why, Maddie, why did you leave? We could have figured it out. It hurt sooo bad when you severed the connection to the pack."

Rosa places a hand on her mate's shoulder. "Luke, honey, One question at a time. Take her and…"

"My Delta, Victor."

Rosa nods. "…Victor to the living room. I will finish feeding Aurora and join you shortly."

Madison smiles. "If it's alright with you, I am happy to sit at the kitchen table and talk. This way, we don't need to repeat anything."

"If you wish." She gestures to the table as the rest settle in.

Madison watches the young child, her fingers in the bowl of Cheerios, trying to stuff them in her mouth and ending up with more of them in her lap. "She's adorable."

"Thank you, Maddie. So, what brings you back to the pack? I never thought I would see you again."

Madison sighs. "I wasn't planning to return, Luke. I'm sorry I never responded to our texts. It was… well, I was in terrible shape when I left here, and it took time for me to find myself again. The reason I am back is that Alpha Davis called me ten times, requesting me to return."

"Father, you mean."

"No, Luke, He's your father. He's not mine. First, he disowned me, and I accepted. Second, I am, in fact, a hybrid and not pure wolf. We do not share the same blood, but you are still my brother from Mom, even if I have a different father. Third, he just tried to sell me to Alpha Landon of the Nightshade Howler pack."

Luke growls deeply, his chair scraping back as he stares at his sister. "HE did WHAT?! He's as old as Dad! If he disowned you, what right does he have to sell you? Even if he hadn't, he can't sell you like a slave."

"Luke, Sit, please. I didn't accept it and told them both to go to H..." Her eyes drift to the child watching intently. "...To places I can't mention in front of your child."

Luke's eyes drift to Aurora. "Right. I thought people were just angry because you made them suffer when you rejected the pack. I already knew they were lying about you sleeping around cause I knew you better than that. So, are you saying Mom had an affair?"

Madison smiles slightly. "Actually, Luke. I don't really know. It's one scenario, but I am certain Davis would have felt it. The only other thing I can think of is Mom had a second fated mate, but I don't recall her being around anyone but Davis. Especially since he wouldn't let her out of the pack house. Third, some sort of magic was involved. Your guess is as good as mine."

"So Sasha wasn't lying about you being a hybrid."

"No, she wasn't. I have a wolf, Zuri, and a dragon, Somoko, as well as I can wield fey magics."

"Damn. And here I am, just a wolf." He nudges her playfully. "You always were one to outdo me."

Madison laughs, pushing him back. "Well, yes, isn't that what big sisters are for? Oh, and to add to that, I am Alpha of the Wildfire Crescent pack."

"What!! You're an Alpha?"

"Yes."

"How did you beat me to that position?"

"Well, because I might have challenged the old Alpha and won. Then, I grew the pack exponentially. Now, it is one of the largest in the Northwest."

"Damn, Maddie; now I know why you never came back. You've been busy. And this is your Delta, you said?"

"Yes, My Beta and Gamma are watching over the pack. Victor, meet Luke and Rosa. Rosa, Luke, meet Vic. My tried and trusted companion through this all. He and his mate Clary have helped me immensely."

"So is your mate a Luna?"

Madison hesitates, her thoughts drifting to Lucian for a moment. "I am unmated, Luke."

"You hesitated. Have you found your mate?"

Madison smiles slightly. "It's complicated."

"There is nothing complicated about it. They are your one and only. The one who is your destiny. You know that! If you have found him, or her, you should just accept it."

Madison shakes her head. "I can't. He was here when the sh... stuff went down and didn't defend me, therefore sided with them. He also never came after me when I left, Luke. Granted, I never contacted him either. As I stated to Rosa, I ignored all my messages for the first year. Hence, it's complicated."

"Damn... Who is he? I will talk to him. That is no way to treat my sister."

"No. We are working through it, Luke. Please don't interfere."

Luke studies her for a moment. "Fine. How long are you here for?"

Madison smiles wryly. "Well, I was supposed to fly out at three today, but he's convinced me to give him a week to win me over."

"Great! So we can hang at the winter festival and have dinner together."

"Luke, I will be a touch busy here. There is still stuff I need to sort out, but I promise, I will bring him to dinner, if you promise to behave."

He holds his hand out. "Deal!"

Madison accepts it and shakes it firmly. "Right, now I have business to attend to. I will be back late this evening, but I will stay in contact. Thanks, Luke, Rosa, for accepting me back and not judging me."

Luke rises and pulls Madison into a hug. "You are my sister! You definitely drive me batty at times, but I love you. I always have."

Madison hugs him tightly before stepping back. "I love you too, Luke. Stay safe. I will talk to you soon." She turns to Rosa. "Thank you for letting me in."

Rosa moves forward and hugs her as well. "Welcome back, Madison."

Madison returns the hug, happy to have part of her family back. She steps outside into the cool, crisp air and glances around at the forest. Victor moves up to walk just behind her, talking to her through their mind-link. *'So that seemed to go well.'*

'Yes, it went well. I sensed no magic upon him or Rosa. So the taint hasn't spread to him yet.'

'Please tell me you didn't just go there to see if he is working dark magic.'

Madison stops and looks back at the cottage. *'No, Vic, but that is one reason.'*

'Good, because he actually seems to care about you.'

'He does, and I will stay in touch with him this time when I return home.'

'That's what I wanted to hear, lass.'

'I know Victor. Let's get back to the car and head to Silvermoon.'

'You should text Lucian and tell him we are heading back to the hotel.'

Madison sighs and pulls her phone out. She scrolls through her contacts, tapping on the one marked Lucy. She hesitates a moment before steeling her resolve. Her fingers tap the keyboard.

> ♦We are heading back to the hotel. Perhaps fifteen minutes.♦

> ♦I will be there.♦

> ♦Perfect. See you shortly.♦

> ♦Looking forward to it Maddie <3♦

She tucks her phone away and turns to Victor. "He will meet us at the..." She hesitates, hearing Somoko in the back of her mind. *'Incoming. Seven of them, fast, heading directly towards you from the left side.'*

"What is it, lass?"

'*Thanks, Somo.*' She frowns as she turns towards the woods. "It could be nothing, but Somo sensed seven incoming. We should walk as if we don't know." She starts forward, not making it twenty feet before six rogues bolt from the woods, one remaining deep within the woods. Madison studies them carefully, recognizing some of them from last night, and hidden beneath the rogue smell, the scent of two of the guards in Davis's chambers. She backs up a step and mind-links Victor. '*I think they are about to find out you are not a servant, Vic. Some are from last night, and two are from Davis's chambers.*'

'*Use your Alpha aura, lass. Tell them to back down.*'

'*It won't work. There is a shroud of protective magic around them. I can feel it. They came prepared to fight.*' Madison glares at the six rogues in front of her. "I would suggest you let me pass."

The wolves lower their heads menacingly, the fur on the ruffs bristling in anger as the larger black one steps forward. "Surrender now, and you won't get hurt, little lady."

Madison arches a brow. "You want me to surrender to a bunch of filthy rogues? I think not."

"So be it. We do it the hard way." He lunges forward, snapping at her arm, only to find her arm is no longer there, but a silver-white wolf, towering over him, baring her teeth. She spins and lunges at his leg, her bite digging in deep as she pulls back, dragging the wolf off his feet and snapping the bone. Victor shifts behind her, his large black wolf unmistakable as an Alpha, amber eyes flashing in anger. Madison releases her bite to snap at another wolf launching at her, only to have Victor's wolf, Zion, collide with it, both rolling to the ground on the other side.

Madison withdraws into her mind, giving Zuri and Somoko full control as a third wolf charges in. Zuri growls low in her throat and springs straight up, landing on the wolf's back as he slides to a stop when he realizes where she went. Her teeth sink into his neck and, with a sharp twist, snaps it, killing him instantly. Landing on her feet, she spins to face the other two charging her. She inhales sharply as she feels their teeth piercing her shoulder, tearing herself from the bite as she latches on to the back leg of one of them. Madison twists her muzzle to break his leg as well while her breath heats up as Somoko joins the fight with the stench of burning fur and flesh filling the air. The wolf howls in pain, letting Madison go to bite at her face. The second wolf lunging at Madison yelps as Zion pulls him away by the tail. Zion's rage clearly emanates from him as the rogue spins to face the second Alpha. Finding he doesn't really stand a chance, he runs, only to find his life ending just as quickly as the other one did to Zion's anger.

Zuri's fury grows as she bites down on the wolf's ruff, frustrated that her grip was not enough to end him. But enough to fling him into the leader, as the pair of them roll in the dirt. They rise unsteadily to their feet, watching the white wolf glare at them. Zuri bares her teeth in almost a grin, her eyes shifting to a fiery glow, as Somoko comes to the front. Somoko inhales deeply and exhales in a breath of fire, ensuring she misses Victor ending the one he is playing with and getting the other three.

The black wolf, seeing three of his wolves dead, himself and another limping, calls for a retreat, only to feel the full force of a dragon's breath on the pair of them. They howl in pain as they bolt into the woods, their tails tucked with their fur on fire. Somoko turns her gaze to the woods where the seventh waits, her voice eerily cold and quiet as it echoes around her. "I see you, Alpha Landon. Watching and learning. Would you like to try your hand at the dragon, or the wolf? Since Madison has already shut you down. I think it's only fair that we each get a chance too as well."

Alpha Landon watches Madison shift instantly, her clothes landing at her feet, whereas other wolves need a few seconds and tear through their clothes. He is slightly shocked she didn't try her Alpha powers, but apparently, she could read situations well. His eyes stray to the servant, who is clearly more than he appears with an Alpha wolf. He makes a mental note to find out which pack this Victor is from, if that is even his name, and what their relationship is that he is pretending to be her servant. Both of them took his team down with ease, with what, two bites on her and one on him.

He backs away when he sees the dragon's breath landing on his gamma and the others. A hybrid of a dragon and a wolf? That is unheard of. Who the hell is she, exactly? Either way, she is going to be his Luna and bear his offspring, even if he has to keep her in silver chains to do that. Landon can just imagine how powerful their pups will be, and influenced by him, of course. Turning, he hears his name from the road and faces the dragon's eyes in the wolf's body. He backs away slowly, knowing one-on-one, he is clearly not a match for her, and bolts into the woods. Hearing her laughter following him, chilling him to the core, knowing somehow he will need to find out her weakness before attempting to take her again.

Somoko watches Landon leave before giving the reins back to Madison, who shifts back. She pulls her clothes on quickly and grabs the cloak. She turns away and holds it up, waiting for Victor to shift, feeling the cloak plucked from her grasp. "Thanks, lass."

"You're welcome, Vic."

She moves over to the wolves, her eyes glowing softly as she studies them, reaching down to pull a thin gold chain from around one of their necks. She hands it to Victor before moving to the other two, finding matching chains on them and removing them. "Right, these are clearly magical and have something to do with the rogue auras. When we find a white witch, we can ask them more about it."

Victor moves over to Madison. "Are you alright, Maddie? They looked like they latched on pretty tight."

"They did, Vic, but it will mend. I will need to wrap them at the hotel, as I can feel the blood dripping down my back."

Victor nods, looking at the gold chain in his hand. "At least we know the Nightshade Howlers are behind the rogues. If Davis knows and is in league with him, it would explain why he declined the agreement with Silvermoon."

"Yes, it's just another piece of the puzzle. Come, we need to go before someone finds these bodies."

"I suspect when we leave, they will come back for them, but you are right. We need to move."

The pair head down the road at a brisk pace, arriving at the hotel five minutes later than planned. Madison can see Lucian pacing out front, feeling his eyes lock on her before drifting down to her shoulder, suspecting he can smell the blood. He approaches quickly, but stops just before her. "You are bleeding. What happened?"

Madison shakes her head. "Not here; in the room."

Lucian nods, his gaze traveling to Victor, dressed in Madison's cloak, smelling the blood on him as well. He frowns, but follows beside Victor silently. Madison nods to the clerk as she passes her, heading down the hall to the elevator. She punches the buttons and waits as the door dings and opens. She steps inside, breathing a soft sigh of relief as she leans against the wall and closes her eyes. Lucian watches her, feeling the stress in her body, but knows he's still on probation, so he resists the urge to draw her into his arms. Once the elevator opens on the fourth floor, they head to the room and close the door. Victor moves to the suitcase and pulls out some clothes, muttering under his breath about packing light.

Madison smiles. "Vic, you know we were only gonna be here less than twenty-four hours."

"Better to pack extra, I always say." He closes the door after him.

Madison moves to the small kitchenette, opening the cupboards and searching for some cloth. She pulls out the paper towels and moves to the bed, pulling the shoulders of her shirt down. She tears off a piece and places it against it to stop the bleeding."

"Maddie?"

"It's fine, Lucy. Alpha Landon's rogues attacked us."

Lucian growls as he moves over to sit on the bed next to her. "What do you mean by that, exactly?"

She unwraps the necklaces from around her wrist and hands them to him. "Each of the wolves we killed had one of these. Three ran away, including his gamma, but not before I broke two of their legs. Landon watched the whole thing from within the woods."

Lucian frowns at the paper towel. "Maddie, you got bit."

"Yes, twice. It will heal. I just need to stop the bleeding until I can buy new clothes."

"Here, let me." He takes the towel from her and shifts to the back, placing it against her wounds and applying pressure. "What was Alpha Landon doing there?"

"It seems Davis had some gambling debts owed to him. About six hundred grand worth." Her voice fills with distaste. "And apparently me."

"Excuse me?"

"Oh, he sold me as part of the debts to be Landon's Luna."

Lucian growls deeply, his free hand clenching the necklace. "The hell you will."

Madison lifts her gaze to his. "I told him as much. Even made him kneel with my Alpha aura after he informed me I would need to step down to be Luna and tried to force me to remove my cloak to show him my fated mate mark."

Rhydian snarls inside at the thought of her with another as Lucian keeps him at bay, his voice coldly calm. "He's not going to like that, Maddie."

"No, I don't suppose he did, but as I stated to him, I am my own person. I decide who, when, what, and how I lead my life. I guess that's why he sent the rogues imbued with magic to ignore an Alpha's power. The aura of the necklace is to disguise them as rogues. Their bodies had an anti-Alpha aura. I would like to think that is how they are controlling Davis, but I suspect he's in on all of this, as it was Landon's guards in the room with him. Now, they didn't have that aura when I was in the room with them, so it means the dark witch is here, somewhere in this pack, and we need to be careful. They will figure out pretty quickly you are my mate because you were in the woods with me last night. They also learned that Victor is not a servant as he shifted and they saw Zion. It's hard not to miss an Alpha wolf."

Lucian sighs. "They already know. Instead of making the calls I needed to, I spent the morning dealing with the local authorities. Apparently, Victor was right. They broke into my house last night."

Madison snaps her gaze to his. "And you are telling me this now? What did they find?"

"There is nothing in there that would tie me to Frostbite or my reason for being here, but the picture I had of you is missing."

"Wait, you had a picture of me?"

Lucian's eyes soften. "Of course. You are my mate. It was on my nightstand."

Madison averts her gaze and blushes softly, trying to recall what picture he might have of her, not aware of his taking any when she was here before.

Victor opens the door, eyeing the pair sitting on the bed, a blush crossing Madison's cheeks, Lucian's hands on her back, with a paper towel soaked in blood. "Right, we will need proper bandages for your shoulders, Maddie. I will head downstairs and see if they have any."

"Thanks, Vic." She watches him head out of the room and close the door behind him, suddenly very much aware that Lucian was next to her on the bed. She twists her hands in her lap, at a loss for words now that they are alone without her chaperone.

Lucian watches her carefully, adjusting the paper towel as her wolf kicks in to heal the wounds upon her. He can see her hands twisting nervously, and places a hand gently under her chin, guiding her gaze his way. "Maddie, what's up?"

Madison lifts her gaze, aquamarine eyes meeting his blue, feeling the mate bond calling to her. Her mouth opens to speak but pauses, attempting to formulate some semblance of a sentence. "Lucy, I...."

"Shhhh Maddie. You don't need to be nervous around me. I will let you lead on everything. I just want to be around you."

Madison nods and shifts closer to him, curling up in his arms, resting her head on his chest. "Thanks, Lucy."

Lucian wraps his arms around her and holds her close. He doesn't like that they attacked her today, but knows better than to ask her to stay in. She is an Alpha, just as he is, and he needs to accept she will handle her own business, suspecting she will do the same for him. He can feel the soft scent of coconut surrounding him and tightens his hold on her, remaining there until the door opens and Victor walks in. Lucian catches the quick smile before Victor schools his face. "I brought gauze and tape, lass, to cover the wounds until they heal."

Madison jerks up and pulls away from Lucian, a blush staining her cheeks as she rises from the bed. "Thank you, Vic."

Victor hands over the gauze. "Once you get that taped on, we head up to Silvermoon. I am most curious now about the treaty, especially if Davis and Landon are working together to disguise pack members as rogues."

Madison nods, accepting the supplies, and races to the bathroom, closing the door after her. She strips off her shirt and looks over the wounds, already healing from her wolf. Ripping the seals on the gauze pads, she places them over the bite and tapes it down. She then washes the blood out of her shirt, drawing on her fey magics to dry it, knowing it would do no good for her to enter an unknown wolf pack smelling of blood.

Lucian watches her go, sighing as the door closes after her, his eyes lingering there until Victor draws his attention back to him.

"That seemed like progress, boy. Hers?"

Lucian nods, keeping his voice as quiet as Victor's. "Yes, she seemed nervous after you left. I told her I was leaving it to her to make any moves, but I don't know if I can keep that word. I want it all now."

Victor chuckles. "It seems you two are definitely made for each other. She is much like that."

Lucian rises from the bed and moves to sit at the table. "I don't know Victor. One minute, she's so confident, and the next, she feels like she is fragile and will break with the slightest touch."

"That's our Maddie for you. She is tough, trust me. You won't break her if you are honest. If you betray her again, well, it won't matter, will it, cause if I don't kill you, Clary will."

A wry smile crosses his lips. "Add my brother to that list. As much as he forbade me from taking a leave of absence, he was pretty pissed I let her go."

Victor laughs. "Good to know."

Lucian mutters under his breath. "That's right, laugh at my pain."

"As long as it's not Madison's."

Madison steps out of the room. "Not Madison's what, Vic?"

Victor smiles. "I was just threatening your mate, is all. How are you feeling?"

Madison smiles, her eyes drifting to Lucian. "He probably deserves it. Sore, but Zuri is fixing me."

"I do not!"

Victor chuckles. "Good, we should think about heading out to Silvermoon."

"Agre...." Madison stops, hearing her phone ring, and pulls it out. Seeing Luke's name on the screen, she swipes to accept. "Luke? Is everything alright?"

"No, Maddie. Davis is coming over. He wants to talk about why you were here. What should I say?"

"The truth. He will know if you are lying, and I didn't tell you anything that you need to hide."

"He's after something, Maddie. He has never been to the house; always makes me go to pack headquarters. I am gonna leave the phone on so you can hear, but be quiet so he doesn't know."

"Got it. I will place it on speaker for the others to hear."

She moves over to Victor and Lucian, sitting in a chair next to them, placing a finger to her lips. "Shhhh, no talking at all." They could hear some muffled movement and a door opening.

Luke opens the door and stares at his father, before bowing to him in respect. "Alpha Davis, Father. How can I help you?"

"I understand Madison came to visit you with her servant."

"She did, with her Delta, about half an hour ago or so."

"Delta?"

"Yes, that's how she introduced him."

"What did she want?"

"To reconnect and explain why she left here five years ago. She is trying to make amends for ignoring my calls."

"Did she say how long she was here?"

"Yes, she stated she had a plane out at three today, but her mate convinced her to give her a week. So they are staying for the winter festival."

"So she's not together with her mate?"

"No, she said it was complicated and that he has to win her back."

"Why?"

"Well, because I gather he was here when you believed that bitch, Sasha. He would have known my sister wasn't sleeping around but didn't step up and defend her, just like you didn't. She was pretty damn hurt about that as well as being betrayed by her family and her best friend."

"But she is a hybrid?"

"Yes, she confirmed that."

"Did she say who her mate was?"

"No, she just asked that I back down and not get involved. But she agreed to meet us for dinner at the festival with him."

"You know that she's chosen by Alpha Landon to be his Luna."

"No, I didn't. But fated mates outrank chosen any day. You know it's the will of the Moon Goddess."

"Of course, unless they no longer have a fated mate."

"What does that mean?"

"It means if a chosen mate marks them first, they become their fated mate."

"What the hell? No, it doesn't."

"We'll see, Son. I think it would be extremely beneficial for her to mate with Landon over a human. Let me know if she contacts you again."

Luke watches his father walk away before closing the door and heading to the bathroom. He turns a tap on before slipping the phone out of his pocket. "You better leave Maddie. DON'T come back. Rosa and I will make a trip to visit you. If your mate is human, take him with you, or I fear you won't have a mate."

Madison picks up the phone. "Thanks, Luke. I will not call you on this number again. I will see if I can get one with 1786 in the number."

Luke smiles at the number. "Got it, my favorite number of all time. Goodbye, Maddie. I am sorry we couldn't do dinner."

"We will one day, Luke. I love you."

"I love you too, Mads."

Madison hangs up the phone. "I think Luke is right. We can't stay here. Us being attacked by rogues in broad daylight. Lucian's house getting broken into. They are hunting, and we are the prime target." She turns to Lucian. "I am sorry, Lucian; I really had intended to give you the winter festival."

Lucian shakes his head, taking her hand in his. "Maddie. I understand. It's an unusual circumstance. We are still planning to head to Silvermoon. Perhaps they have a festival I can take you to. We can stay there for the week. I will call my brother and inform him of what's happening and that I *am* taking a leave of absence, whether or not he approves."

Madison nods and sets about packing the room, quickly stuffing all their belongings back into the one suitcase.

Lucian watches her hastily pack. "Can we stop by my house so I can grab an overnight bag as well?"

"Yah, it's fine." Madison nods as she does a last walk-through, ensuring that nothing is getting left behind. "Right, let's get out of here." She heads downstairs, stopping at the counter to check out. "I would like to check out, please."

The clerk nods, pulling up the info. "Oh, it looks like you have extended your stay. Is everything alright?"

"Yes. It seems there are issues at home, so we need to be on the 3pm flight."

"Very well." She sets about checking them out and charging the card Madison hands over. Once the purchase is complete, she hands the card back. "Have a nice day. Here is a survey you can fill in about your stay to win a free weekend here."

Madison smiles. "Thank you." She turns back to Victor. "Right, Vic, let's go home." They head down to the parking garage, Victor sliding into the driver's seat as Lucian and Madison climb into the back seat. Victor turns back to Madison. "You better call Clary. She's gonna want an update."

Meanwhile, the receptionist mind-links Alpha Davis. *'Alpha, they just checked out. Heading home on the 3pm flight.'*

Madison waits until they are out of the parkade before calling Clarice. She fills her in quickly on what happened as Lucian guides Victor to his house. She feels the car stop, and Lucian leave the back seat. Her eyes stray to the house he is walking up to, seeing the hidden fire surrounding the place. "NO! Lucian!!!" She tosses the phone to Victor and fades from the car, placing herself between Lucian and the house just as the building explodes behind them. She wraps her arms around him as the force throws them to the ground. A yelp of pain escapes Madison as flames burn her back, along with shards of glass embedding in deep as the windows explode outward.

Clarice can hear the explosion in the background. "Victor Martinez. WHAT the hell was that?"

"Clary, I can't talk right now. Lucian's house just exploded."

"I meant what I said, Victor. If Madison doesn't come home in one piece, there is going to be Hell to pay."

Madison struggles through the pain and draws on her fey magic. She steps them from the ground to the car and closes the doors behind them. "Get out of here, Victor, NOW!"

Lucian looked down at Madison's charred back and grimaces. He knows damn well that the explosion intended to kill him, feeling the car lurch forward as Victor steps on the gas. "Maddie, what have you done?"

Her voice fills with pain. "I couldn't let you die... Lucy... Somo's taking over. I have to go now."

"Maddie. No!"

Clarice heard Madison's voice. "Victor! You put her back on the phone...Now!"

Victor nods. "As you wish, Clary." He slips the phone back over his shoulder, keeping his eyes on the road.

Lucian reaches over and takes the phone as Victor passes it back. "Sorry, Miss Clarice, Maddie has retreated. It looks like Somoko has taken over."

"WHO is this?"

"Lucian."

There are fifteen seconds of silence before Clarice answers him. "Lucian Marzire of the Frostbite Syndicate?"

"The one and only, though, it's Professor Deplois here."

"Indeed, you are my daughter's mate. What happened?"

"It seems as I was entering my house, it exploded. Your daughter used her fey magics to protect me and took the brunt of the blast. I believe Somo took over to stop her from feeling the pain."

"So as I am to understand this, Landon and Davis are trying to kill you, to force Madison into another relationship."

"Yes, but we suspect there are other reasons for it. We just don't have all the pieces."

"I will kill them. BOTH Packs will be gone by the end of the week."

Somoko speaks quietly. "Clarice, Somo here. I know you can hear me. Let Madison do her job. If you kill everyone, she won't have all the parts to play with. And not everyone in the packs is involved. We need to take out only the key players and absorb the rest as planned. Look at the information she has attained in less than twenty-four hours. Give her time."

"Fine, Somo, but you and Zuri better bring her back here, or I will take it out on you as well. Lucian, you are now on that list with Victor. If my Madison doesn't return to me, you will find out exactly who you are dealing with!"

"Understood." He hears the phone line click, knowing that the Princess is right. His life is over if she doesn't survive this, so no matter what she does to him, he will accept it. As they approach the gates to the community, he shifts the unburned sections of the cloak over her back, trying to make it appear as if she is sleeping, rather than injured.

Victor stops as the guards step out, rolling his window down to talk to them.

"Heading out?"

"Yes, we have a 3pm flight in Newport."

The guard peers into the backseat. His eyes linger on Madison, covered in her cloak. "Thanks for coming by the Duskrunner Pack. Do visit again."

"We will. Have a good one." Victor rolls the window up and drives away, breathing a sigh of relief as the gates fade from their sight.

The guard watches the car drive out of sight, mind-linking their Alpha. *'Alpha Davis, they are leaving town. Said they had a 3pm flight in Newport.'*

'Damn, they checked out of the hotel as well.'

'She looks injured, Alpha. She was lying still across the back seat, her head in Professor Deplois's lap.'

'WHAT? What do you mean, injured?'

'It's hard to say, Alpha, but I could smell fire and blood in the back of the car. They covered her in a cloak, so I couldn't see anything, but her eyes were closed, and she was pretty damn still.'

'Dammit! That's all for now. If they return, I want to know immediately.'

Landon can read the rage in Davis as he turns to him. "That blast injured my daughter, and the professor is still alive, Landon. You guaranteed her safety."

"She was in the car. I didn't expect her to teleport out for a human."

"Why wouldn't she if he's her mate?"

"Well, now we know for certain, don't we? If she's going home, that could pose a problem, though."

Davis growls, sarcasm laced in his tone. "Geez, I can't understand why she would leave. Instead of waiting on me to gather information about her plans and lying low, you attacked her with your rogues, broke into her mate's house, and then blew it up, trying to kill him, all within a few hours.

Had you waited, we would have had more time because her brother Luke said she was staying the week. Now I won't be able to get her back here."

"Yes, you will. Keywords right there, her brother's here. She still has feelings for him. But first, I need a better plan before you lure her back here."

Lucian stares at Maddie lying still on the back seat. "She needs a doctor, Victor. There is a hospital in Newport."

"No, Somoko will keep her at peace until we get to Silvermoon. I would rather pack doctors to deal with her. Human doctors are going to ask questions, then look into the Duskrunner community and what actually happened. We don't need to risk exposing ourselves. Maddie would not want that. It's bad enough my wife might wipe them clean for what they have done to her."

He runs his fingers over her face gently, brushing her hair aside. "I suppose you are right. I just hate seeing her injured like this because of me."

Victor sighs. "It's not your fault. It's Duskrunner's. She opted to save you at risk to herself. That counts for a lot in my books. Now, stop feeling sorry for yourself; call your brother and tell him what's happening before my wife does or everyone's in trouble."

Lucian nods and slips his phone out of his pocket. He dials his brother's number, listening to it ring as he waits for him to pick up. After several rings, he hears his brother's voice on the other end, the slight edge of stress creeping out. "Lucian. What the hell is going on? I have a crazed Beta tearing my head off on the other line."

Lucian covers his phone and mutters softly to Victor. "Too late, Victor." He returns his focus to the call. "Pierce. That would probably be my mate's mother, Clarice?"

"Yes, I think that was her name. I told her I had another call and had to put her on hold. She sounded less than impressed."

"Well, you might regret that. She's the Lycan Queen's daughter. The one that disappeared about twenty years ago, but no one knows that, Pierce. Keep it between us."

"What the actual hell have you gotten into, Lucian?"

"It's complicated. This entire business with my mate has compromised my position in the Duskrunner pack. You will need another to take over, but they need to be cautious. Alpha Landon of the Nightshade Howlers has decided that my mate is his chosen mate. Landon's pack members attacked Madison in broad daylight today. Each one wears a necklace that makes them look and smell like rogues. They also had magic on them to withstand an Alpha's aura, so my mate and her Delta had to fight their way out of it. Three dead; the rest ran. It is uncertain if Alpha Davis is in on it, but my suspicion is yes. Especially since he's the one that tried to sell Madison to Landon. That is how they are taking the loners. They can track via pack mind-links and such. I suspect it means we have a spy in our pack as well. Madison figures a dark witch is involved and likely here at Duskrunner. It was magic that blew up my house, so they are trying to remove me from the equation. Unfortunately, it hurt Madison. We are heading to Silvermoon for the rest of the week. Then I will either go to the Wildfire Crescent with Madison or return home to you."

"As in THE Wildfire Alpha Madison Martinez?"

"Yes, that's her."

"Lucian, you be careful. Keep your mate safe. You are officially on leave until further notice. Now I need to get back to the other line and hope my eardrums stay intact."

Lucian laughs. "Good luck with that. She already lectured me."

"You couldn't have mated into a quieter family?"

Lucian looks down at Madison, his fingers twinning in her hair. "Clearly not. Good luck, Pierce."

"Take care, Lucian."

The phone goes silent as he tucks it back in his pocket, sitting in silence for a few minutes. He lifts his gaze, catching Victors in the rear-view mirror. "What did he say, boy?"

"Not much. He's talking to your wife right now."

"Oh, bloody hell. Damn, Clary is quick."

"I am certain my brother will calm her down. He can be very diplomatic when he sets his mind on it."

Victor nods. "Let's hope so."

Six

Silvermoon's Strays

EACH OF THEM slips into silence, with Victor focusing on the snowy road, watching for the signs and landmarks that directed him to Silvermoon. He hits the human city, wishing he could follow the airport signs to take them home. Instead, he takes the on-ramp to Highway 17, heading west to Bourke, knowing it would take an hour before they were safely over the borders of Duskrunner's territory.

Lucian remains still, keeping his eyes on Madison, his hands gently caressing her face, hearing Somoko purr slightly at his touch. "Somoko, you are not supposed to be enjoying it. You are keeping Maddie safe."

"Indeed, I am. Still doesn't mean I can't enjoy your touch. She does too. She just won't admit it, but Zuri and I are working on her."

He pats her shoulder lightly. "You are so bad, Somoko. I need to win Maddie over, all on my own."

"Ah, what's a little nudge here or there?"

Lucian shakes his head. "As long as you don't nudge her away from me."

"Trust me, another few nights of sharing a bed with her, and you will have her hook, line, and sinker."

He chuckles. "Well, it won't be tonight. I suspect she will be in the pack's hospital."

She purrs softly. "Tomorrow then. I look forward to it. You need to mark us so we can speak with Rhydian."

"I am not marking you until Madison agrees, Somoko. Do not tempt me."

"If you marked us, Landon couldn't get his hooks in Madison."

"I heard Madison was ruthless, but now I understand where she gets it from. I maintain my decision. I am not marking you until she agrees."

Somoko sighs. "Have it your way, then. Maddie's outnumbered in this. Zuri and I both want it."

"Shhh, I don't want to hear it." Lucian places a finger to her lips. "Rest. You need it to keep Madison out of pain."

Somoko growls and retreats within, focusing on the pain in her body.

Lucian sighs inwardly, rolling his eyes slightly, catching the smirk on Victor's face in the mirror. He scowls his way and pulls out his phone, placing his focus elsewhere while keeping a hand on Madison. Hours later, they arrive in Bourke. Victor slows the car, seeking the entrance to the pack camp, knowing it will not be on the main highway. He takes the next off-ramp and cruises through the town, finding the sign he is looking for after about thirty minutes. Turning left down a snow packed road, he travels slowly until the camp sign appears looming ahead of them. He rolls his window down as he stops the car, seeing the two guards approach, one on either side. "Are you lost, old man?"

"No, we are here to see Alpha D'andre. I am Victor Martinez, Delta to Alpha Madison Martinez. She is in the back seat, unconscious and injured. She needs to see a pack doctor immediately. Watching over her is her mate, Lucian Deplois."

The guards peer around the seat, seeing Madison lying still, her breathing shallow, the smell of fire and burned flesh filling their nostrils. "Lift her blanket."

Lucian nods, pulling the cloak off her, the burns clear across her back mixed in with the glittering of glass. "What the hell did that?"

"A dark witch tried to kill me. She intervened and took the damage."

The guard nods, his eyes glazing a moment. "Pack hospital is in the city center, right side. They are expecting you. Alpha D'andre will meet you there."

Victor nods in appreciation. "Thank you." He pulls away slowly, wanting to speed there, but knowing a few extra minutes would be worth it to make sure they stayed on the road. Twenty minutes later, they pull up to a small town, Victor's eyes scanning for the H. After a few blocks, he pulls up in front of it and hops out of the car. He opens the door to let Lucian out. The hospital staff wheel a gurney out as they lift Madison carefully off the back seat and place her on it. Lucian watches them take her away and moves to follow, only to feel Victor's hand on his arm. "Let them do their thing, boy. We will sit in the waiting room."

Lucian nods, his eyes following her until she is out of sight. "Right, and here I was so happy when I heard she was returning to town. Now I wish she stayed away."

"She's tough, boy. She will pull through this. If she doesn't, you and I will be on the run together, so I hope you know a good place to hide."

Another voice with authority speaks up from behind them. "On the run from who exactly?"

Victor turns, his gaze sweeping over Alpha D'andre standing there, taking in the fit build, suntanned skin, short brown hair, hazel eyes, and goatee. He offers a shallow bow. "Alpha D'andre. The one we are running from is my wife, Clary. She's quite upset that our daughter got injured, especially as I made a promise to her to bring her back in one piece, and I clearly failed."

He studies them for a moment, his eyes glazing over for a minute before he focuses. "It sounds like she needs surgery to remove glass shards. She's gonna be here awhile. Perhaps we can have a little chat in my office."

"Of course, Alpha."

D'andre leads them back to the pack headquarters and steps inside, waiting for them to enter. He arches a brow as Lucian hesitates. "Is everything alright?"

Lucian nods. "Sorry, I am from Duskrunner. The pack house has magic upon it that only allows wolves to enter it. All others cannot step foot inside."

"Interesting. I would be curious to hear more about it. There is no such magic in this building. You may enter." D'andre waits as they step into the main quarters before he leads them down the hall to an office on the right. Stepping in, he gestures to a couch that sits across from a desk. He moves to sit behind the desk, watching as they settle on the couch. "Did you need a drink? Soda, coffee, tea, something stronger perhaps?"

"Coffee, please. I could use one after the day I have had." Victor nods as he looks around the office, noticing it was simple yet elegantly furnished. A solid oak desk dominated the room, with a stained glass lamp sitting in one corner. A closed laptop sits in the center with a basket of papers on the right side of it. He shifts his gaze to the large plant sitting in the corner before turning it around to the other couch against the back wall.

Lucian smiles, giving a quick glance around the room but keeps his focus on Alpha D'andre. "Coffee as well, though at the moment, whiskey sounds mighty fine, but I want to be alert if Madison needs me."

"Coffee it is then." He withdraws to mind-link his Beta to bring coffee to the meeting. "Right. Beta Terrence will be here shortly. Then we can begin as to why you are in my pack and not your own."

The three of them sit in silence. Alpha D'andre studies the pair sitting in front of them, feeling the auras of them both, knowing there is more than meets the eye with them. It begs questions as well; why the woman is in his hospital, and how she is an Alpha. He lifts his gaze, hearing the soft knock before the door opens and his Beta steps in. Tall like his Alpha, but with lighter brown hair and green eyes. "Alpha, Maria has brought the drinks you requested."

"Thank you, Terrence. Maria, please place the tray on the table in front of our guests."

A shorter lady steps in, with her brown hair tied back in a ponytail, smiling gently at the pair sitting there as she sets the tray down. "Cream and sugar are there as well. If you need a refill, let Alpha D'andre know, and I will return." She bows and heads out of the room.

Victor leans forward and picks up the cup, taking a drink of the black coffee. "Oh... that is excellent coffee. Thank you, Alpha D'andre." Lucian, having a slightly refined taste, pours some cream in his and stirs it gently, eyeing the Beta who sits down on the couch behind them. He takes a sip and nods. "Agreed. It is good."

D'andre chuckles. "Well, now that you have praised my coffee, which, by the way, is the best, let's cut to the core of things. Who are you exactly, and why are you here?"

Victor laughs. "Well, the best coffee is debatable, but it is delicious. Now, before I go any further, I need your confidence that what we say will stay in this room."

D'andre studies the man before her, his eyes drifting to his Beta, but gives a nod. "You have my word."

"Good. I am Victor Martinez, Delta to Alpha Madison Martinez, my adopted daughter who is currently in your pack hospital. My wife Clarice is her Beta. This is Professor Lucian Deplois, her fated mate, but they are still unmarked. Both of us are investigating Duskrunner for different reasons. Madison's are because her blood mother went missing when she was ten. Then at eighteen, the pack rejected and banished her for being a hybrid, among other things, so she left and came to our pack. When Clary and I found her, she was pretty broken, but over the course of a year, we helped her get back on her feet. She challenged the former Alpha of the Wildfire Crescent and has become the strongest pack in the Northwest."

D'andre nods. "Yes, everyone knows of the Wildfire Crescent pack and their ruthless Alpha. How did she end up injured?"

Victor sighs. "Well. That's a bit more complicated. Apparently, Lucian is also investigating the pack for missing shifters. The Syndicate has narrowed it down to three. Duskrunner, being one of them. Monday night, Madison received calls from Alpha Davis, begging her to come home. We suspected a trap, but he sounded desperate, and despite the reputation Madison has, she really is a softy at heart. And DON'T you dare tell her I said that!"

D'andre laughs. "My lips are sealed."

Lucian chuckles. "Mine too. I know better than to mess with you and Clarice."

Victor scowls at them both. "If she finds out, I will know it's one of you.

But back to the topic. We arrived Tuesday afternoon, where she ran into Lucian. Madison was a touch emotional, so she went for a run to wear herself out, which she does in our pack, so I wasn't concerned. And being that she's a hybrid, she can return whenever she likes to my side."

"What sort of hybrid are we talking about?"

"She has a wolf, a dragon, and is fey touched."

"Damn, she's powerful. No wonder her pack is strong."

"It's strong because she worked her ass off to make it that way. While she was running through the woods, I guess she went to a clearing she frequented when she lived there. Lucian knew about it and was waiting for her. While they were talking about things, rogues surrounded them and demanded they come willingly."

D'andre shifts his gaze to Lucian. "Rogues are a problem in the area."

"Yes. There is more to that but I will get there. Both of them thought the leader looked familiar, but neither could place him. Either way, Madison used her magic to fey-step them back without a fight. Since they recognized Lucian, I felt it was best for him to stay in the hotel for the night." Victor runs a few fingers through his hair, trying to hide the stress in his body. "While he spent the night, they broke into his house, which we found out when we met up again. While he was dealing with that, we met with Alpha Davis. Apparently, he was begging for money because of his gambling debts, six hundred grand to be exact. Also, in that debt, he bartered Madison to be Alpha Landon's Luna."

D'andre growls slightly. "He did what?"

"She denied it, stating she had a fated mate. Landon tried his Alpha aura to get her to show him her mark, but she proved stronger than him. She stood her ground and then forced him to kneel before her, putting him in his place. When we left, she informed me there is dark magic protecting the pack house. It dampened her fey magic, but not her aura. She also let me know that two of the guards in the room were rogues that she saw the night before and that Landon's gamma is the leader."

"Wait, what?"

"It gets better, Alpha."

"How can it get better than that?"

"Well, after the meeting at the pack house, we went to her brother's house and visited for a short time. On our walk back to the hotel, six rogues attacked us, but Maddie sensed Landon in the woods watching. Wolves with magic to negate the Alpha aura and sporting magical gold necklaces that made them look and smell like rogues. Maddie and I fought our way out, killing three, and she broke the legs of two of them. We have three necklaces in the car to be examined by a white witch. We quickly decided it was not safe to stay in Duskrunner." Victor's shoulders slump as he takes a sip of his coffee. "Maddie had found out that you offered Duskrunner alliances, but not what was in them, so we had already decided to pay you a visit and perhaps stay a few days. When we arrived at Lucian's house to retrieve an overnight bag, Maddie must have seen something. She fey-stepped out of the car and wrapped her arms around Lucian as the house exploded. She took the brunt of the damage, but fey-stepped them back to the car. I got out of there as quickly as possible."

"So kill the fated mate before they mark, then force her to take a chosen mate. Damn. That's sick. It sounds like you have been through a lot in the past twenty-four hours. I will have rooms set up in the pack house for you to stay for as long as you need. There will be guards around you at all times to keep you safe as well. I don't like that they are disguising pack wolves as rogues. It means they are tapping into the mink-link network."

Lucian sighs. "Yes, it means it's possible they can have spies in each pack to find the ones they steal. So far, thirty are missing that we know about. Most of the targeted ones are ones with no family, loners, or quiet ones that stick to themselves. The first one to break that was a ten-year-old dragon shifter five years ago."

"How do you know that?"

"Because I am a dragon shifter. Alpha Pierce Marzire of the Frostbite Syndicate is my older brother. I have been undercover as Professor Deplois in the Duskrunner pack for the past eight years. It has been tedious as some sort of magic bars me from entering most places, and I suspect the info I need is contained in those buildings. When I casually question people, they all give the same answers. Madison told me it was the same when she questioned anyone about her missing mother. She could feel the surrounding magic, just wasn't strong enough to bypass it."

"Right. So two Alphas and a Delta at my door that I need to protect. Two packs nearby, wielding dark magic and pretending to be rogues... Anything else?"

"Three packs, actually. The other one we are investigating is Howling Oak."

"Oh, fantastic." He rolls his eyes as sarcasm laces his voice. "If Duskrunner is in league with rogues and dark witches, it would explain why he declined my treaties. I placed a stipulation within that all rogues we captured would be questioned and put to death if they gave us unacceptable answers. I have the treaties archived, but I will have them here in the morning. Now, I think you have had enough stress for one day. The maid will bring food to your quarters."

Lucian places his coffee mug down. "If you don't mind, I would prefer it sent to the hospital. I am going to wait there until Maddie wakes up."

Victor nods. "I'm with him. As you heard, my wife is expecting an update, as she was on the phone with Madison when the house exploded. If we are not waiting at the hospital, she will bring Wildfire Crescent down upon us, the Duskrunners, and the Nightshade Howlers."

"Damn, no wonder you were thinking about running. I will have food sent there and a contingent of warriors that I trust to guard the hospital. We will resume this in the morning."

They both rise and bow to Alpha D'andre. "Thank you, Alpha."

"You're most welcome. Your girl should be out of surgery soon." D'andre watches them leave and close the door, digesting all the information that was just spilled to him. He frowns slightly, not liking that there were potentially three dirty packs on his borders, but knowing at the moment, there is nothing he can do about it. He looks over at his Beta.

"What do you think, Terrence?"

"I don't think they were lying, D'andre. They seemed stressed, but I would be too if someone was hunting my ass the way they are. I can browse the Google bot and see what I can find."

"Do that. I saw the condition of her back. It was not pretty. I could also smell blood on both their clothing. It's intriguing and not in a good way. If the packs are running rogues to control the territory, it goes against everything the Lycan King stands for. He will need to be notified and brought here to speak with the three of them."

"I agree. How soon do you think he can get here?"

"Normally, I would say a week, but with dire news such as this... a few days, I expect. Perhaps quicker if he has a witch that can portal him."

Terrance nods. "I will have the maids set a suite up for them as well."

"Good idea. Now, on that note, I think I will head to the hospital as well. I want to speak with the hybrid before the others."

"To confirm stories?"

"Partly. The only way I can get a read on her is if I talk to her."

Seven

Awakening Truths

———

LUCIAN AND VICTOR walk back to the hospital in silence, each going to different places with their thoughts as a few guards follow them. As they enter, a nurse guides them to a waiting room. She informs them that Madison should be out of surgery in about ten minutes and they can see her soon. They settle in the uncomfortable chairs, Victor picking up a magazine to read as Lucian scrolls through his phone.

Alpha D'andre enters through the back, seeing the pair sitting in the waiting area, and moves through to the doctors' lounge. He nods to those there in greeting. "Is she out of surgery?"

"Yes, Alpha, they just wheeled her into a care room."

"Is she awake?"

"Not yet, but soon."

"Good. I would like to speak with her upon waking."

"Of course." She leads him into a small room with a bed, a small table, and a chair updating him on how the surgery went.

D'andre looks over at the sleeping woman hooked up to an IV and a monitor. Her breathing is steady as she lies propped on her side, with bandages all over her back. He pulls the chair over and sits beside her, brushing some of her hair out of her face, hearing her soft murmur. "Lucy." He frowns slightly, wondering if she is her missing blood mother, knowing that children who lost parents often suffer in silence. He takes her hand in his. "Not Lucy, D'andre."

Madison's brows furrow in the fogginess of sleep, not recognizing the touch or the smell of whoever is close to her. She knows she has heard the name D'andre before, but can't place it in her muddled mind. "I want Lucy."

"Shh, there is no Lucy here. You're in Silvermoon's hospital. There was an explosion."

Her mind digests his words slowly as a deep-rooted pain fills her. Her aqua eyes open to his, tears forming instantly and falling from them. "No, please, no, I didn't get... Noooo. Oh my Goddess." Her body shakes as grief overtakes her. "I tried to stop it. It just grew so fast. Vic, where's my father?"

D'andre realizes rather quickly he is not getting information from her at this moment. "Shhh, he's outside. I will get him." He rises and moves to the waiting room, feeling sympathetic for Lucian sitting there that she didn't ask for him. "She is awake and asking for Lucy and her father. I said I could get her father, but not Lucy. This seemed to distress her."

Lucian sighs, glancing sideways at Victor. "What did you say about Lucy?"

"Just that there was no Lucy here. Then she started sobbing."

"Damn, that would be why. I would be the Lucy she is talking about. I will go to her."

Victor laughs out loud, the magazine slipping from his fingers. "Her nickname for you is a girl's name?"

Lucian growls under his breath. "Yes, and I love it because she's the only one that calls me that."

D'andre chuckles. "Well then, Lucy, I suggest you get in there pronto cause I clearly made a mistake in saying you were not here." He leads them back to the room, both Victor and Lucian gasping in shock at Madison on the bed, her face wet from tears, the blanket clutched up to her face, her eyes staring vacantly at the wall.

Lucian walks forward, sitting in the chair before her. "Maddie, it's alright. I am here. Alpha D'andre didn't know you had a nickname for me." He reaches out to take her hand, watching her eyes refocus as they shift down to his touch and follow it up.

"Lucy? Are you real?"

"Yes, Maddie, I am real." He squeezes her hand gently. "I promise."

"So I saved you? The witch's spell didn't get you?"

"No, Maddie; you fey-stepped in time, but you took the damage. You shouldn't have done that."

"I had to. They can't know you are more than human. They were watching... Have to believe... if we are to win."

"I know, but you still shouldn't risk yourself for me."

She grows quiet, lost in her thoughts. "Will you stay with me tonight? Like last night? And hold me?"

"Of course I will. Victor is here too."

Her gaze drifts from Lucian, finding Victor nearby. "Vic... I am sorry I got you in trouble with Clary."

Victor moves forward, caressing her cheek lightly. "It's alright, lass. You're mother and I will duke it out when we get home. Just make sure you stand on my side so that I have a fighting chance."

Madison yawns, struggling to stay awake. "Deal... I love you, Victor."

"I love you too, Maddie."

Her eyes shift back to Lucian, squeezing his hand lightly, feeling sleep pulling her away. "My Lucy."

D'andre observes their interactions closely, clearly detecting the depth of love they share through their spoken words and the playful banter exchanged between her and Victor. Even in the midst of her drug-induced haze, Madison's fragmented conversations confirmed enough of their narrative that he knew he needed to make some calls. "I will have another bed rolled in here so that you may stay... Lucy. Dare I ask how you got that nickname?"

Lucian chuckles. "No, but I will tell you anyway. I was, until today, a professor at the Duskrunner tribe. I teach science. It's not an easy subject, and a lot of the class struggled with it. Madison was one of the top students. I already knew she was my mate, but she had yet to turn eighteen, so she didn't know it yet. But I suspect she felt a draw, as she often teased me in class about being so rigid. Her words, NOT mine, and No, Victor, I have not touched her in that way."

Victor growls slightly. "You better not have."

"I haven't. She was still my student at that point. Anyhow, it was nearing Halloween, and the class was talking about costumes for the local dance. They asked me what I was wearing, and I said I didn't have one yet. And so, we bartered a deal. If ALL my students aced my exam the week before Halloween, I would go in drag."

D'andre laughs at the proposal. "Oh no, let me guess, they all aced it."

"Yes, Thanks to YOUR daughter, Victor. She spent hours teaching the students out of class. The class even did their research and picked out sciencey drag names like Anna Phase and Ivy Profin, but the one that stuck was Ethel Alcohol, probably because it had alcohol in it. I was Professor Ethel for months afterwards in class. Madison was the only one who called me Lucy."

"That would be Madison for you. I am surprised the others didn't catch on to Lucy, with it being so close to Lucian."

"That's because she only ever said that when we were alone. I know it's a girl's name, but it's mine from her, and it tells me she cares."

Victor chuckles. "Well, Lucy, you won't ever hear it from me again."

Lucian mutters under his breath good-naturedly. "I think I will take Madison on a trip while you return home to face Clary."

"Hell no, I would not survive without my daughter's help. Don't think that after she trounces me, she won't come after you. Especially if you haven't marked our daughter yet."

Lucian laughs softly. "I expect she will. Remember, I heard her threats. I do NOT want to be on the receiving end of her anger."

D'andre glances between the pair. "Sounds like you have a hell of a wife there, Victor."

"Oh, she is, but you never want her mad at you."

"Does anyone want a woman mad at them?"

"No, I don't suppose they do."

"Alright, on that note, I have things to do. Dinner will arrive soon. When you are ready to retire, Victor, the guards will show you to your room."

Victor looks between Lucian and his daughter. "I will go back now. They need time together. I will just grab our suitcase out of the car. I would also like to know where to get a change of clothes this late. We packed for one day, and after the rogue attack earlier, the clothes I wore are pretty much in rags and on the road where I left them. I have yesterday's clothes on. In fact, we will all need a set in the morning."

"I am certain we can find some you can borrow. The shops open at 9am."

"Appreciate it."

D'andre steps out of the room with Victor, giving a glance back to Lucian still sitting in the chair beside her. He walks with Victor to the car, waiting as he pulls the suitcase and flowers out of the trunk. "Flowers?"

"They are Maddie's, from Lucian."

"I will have the maids place them in water and put them in her room."

Victor hands the flowers over. "Thank you."

"So honest answers here, Victor. If they are mates, why have they not marked each other?"

Victor sighs as he closes the trunk, his eyes straying to the hospital before following the Alpha back to the pack headquarters. "It's complicated. When Duskrunner banished Maddie, there were some pretty nasty rumors spread about her by her supposed best friend, Sasha. One of those rumors was that she was a hybrid, which is true. The other was that she was sleeping with the entire football team. All because Sasha wanted the captain, and he denied her. He said she didn't hold a candle to Madison, which pissed her off. Not that Maddie was interested in him but that didn't matter to Sasha. When the pack turned on her, Lucian did not confirm or deny she was sleeping around, so in her eyes, he stood with the pack when they banished her. That broke her the most, I think. When we found her, she was a mess. It took a year to get her to talk, and even then, in the five years she has been living with us, she never mentioned having a mate." He runs a hand through his hair. "And my wife tried to set her up, many times over. She rejected them all. When we returned to Duskrunner yesterday, we ran into him at the hotel. She was cold and closed down to him, which made me curious, so I questioned her when we got into the room. As I stated, the stress was enough to make her go for a run, heading to a familiar place. I guess Lucian was waiting for her. While they were talking, rogues surrounded them, ones who knew who Lucian was, but not her. As far as I know, no one from Duskrunner has seen her wolf or dragon. She ended up fey-stepping them to the hotel to avoid a battle. She agreed to stay a week and attend the winter festival with him, but that's not happening because it's not safe to go back."

"Do you want him to win her back?"

"Yes. A mate is your one genuine match. He made a mistake. Now he needs to make amends for it. I am giving them as much space as I can to make that happen but also to keep her safe, which I have clearly failed at."

"You didn't fail. She's here, she's safe. So you had a few bumps in the road. The doctor said her wolf is strong. She was trying to heal her wounds faster than they were removing the glass."

Victor nods. "I'm not surprised. She lost them both when they banished her and she rejected the pack. They have returned with a vengeance. Madison is slowly working on owning the Duskrunner pack undercover. It's another takeover of hers, but under wraps, so I would appreciate it if you kept it that way."

He stops at Victor's room, opening the door for him. "You have my word. Now, it appears I have two days to make a winter festival appear on the weekend. You will stay till Monday."

Victor laughs. "Is that an Alpha's order?"

"Well, that depends on if you want your daughter returning to Wildfire Crescent alone or mated."

"Monday it is. Thank you, Alpha D'andre. I know we have placed a lot on your plate. If you need anything, just ask, and I will try to help the best I can."

"I will. Have a pleasant night." D'andre nods and shakes Victor's hand.

He turns and heads toward the staircase, seeking his own Luna out, suspecting she is curious about what is happening. He pushes the doors to their suite open, seeing her curled up in the papasan chair, her blonde hair framing her face, an open book in her lap, and a glass of wine nearby. "Erica, my love. How was your afternoon?"

She smiles at her husband. "Lonely. You have been gone for most of it."

"Yes. I had a few surprises walk in the front door."

"I gathered. Good surprises, I hope?"

"Yes, and no. Two Alphas, and a Delta."

"A Delta here, without their Luna?"

"He's a Delta to one of the Alphas, actually. She's in the hospital. Someone tried to kill her mate."

The book topples from her lap, landing on the floor at a crooked angle as she sits up straight. "What?"

"She will be fine, my dear. The surgeons assisted her. She's resting, and her mate is with her. Her father, Victor, the Delta in question, is in the rooms I assigned him. I have guards watching all of them."

"If he's her Delta, why is he not with her?"

D'andre smiles as he approaches, picking up the book and straightening the pages before closing it and placing it on the table beside her. "I don't think he's really her Delta, my dear. I think that is just the title they are using. Victor is giving the pair time to bond as they haven't marked each other yet."

"I see, I think."

"I won't bore you with the complications of their relationship. But I do have a favor to ask. Apparently, Madison gave Lucian a week to win her back. Part of that week is attending a winter festival. Do you think you can make it happen for the weekend?"

Her gray eyes brightened. "I would love to make a festival happen. You will, of course, attend it with me."

"I will." He takes her hand and pulls her up, drawing her into his arms, holding her tight. "Thank you. Also, I will be inviting the Lycan Royals here. The trio brought disturbing news that needs to be addressed."

"Understood. I look forward to it!"

Victor closes the door, dropping the suitcase on the bed and pulls out the laptop. He moves to the desk in the corner and plugs it in, waiting as the screen boots up. Searching for the Wi-Fi, he finds guest access and connects. Victor stares at the screen before bringing up Skype and calling his wife. As the laptop rings, he taps his fingers lightly on the table, dreading this conversation. He jumps as the laptop buzzes, seeing Clarice's face appearing on the other end. "Clary."

"Don't you Clary me. You better have good news for me."

He sighs, running a few fingers through his hair. "We made it to Silvermoon. Maddie is in the hospital with Lucian. They had to perform surgery to extract the glass shards from her back, but they said she will be fine. Zuri was healing her faster than they could remove them, so she should be up and on her feet tomorrow."

"And Lucian?"

"He's fine. Maddie took the brunt of the damage. He had some burns and cuts, but they healed before we got here. Alpha D'andre has been an excellent host. She asked for Lucian when she first woke up, so that's a good sign."

"And you?"

"Tired, Clary. Stressed. Wanting to come home and curl up in your arms. It's a lot to process. We came out to talk to Alpha Davis, to find out he bartered her to marry someone else. Rogues attacked Maddie twice, ones that are, in fact, pack members of at least Alpha Landon. Possibly Davis, but no evidence on that yet. They broke into Lucian's house, and they tried to kill him by exploding his house with dark magic. You know, Maddie even apologized for making you mad when she woke up. I would love to pack up and return home right now, but I promised Alpha D'andre I would stay till Monday. How's your day going?"

Clarice leans forward and pretends to kiss the screen. "Better than yours, clearly."

Victor smiles half-heartedly. "Can I come home and have your day?"

"On Monday, you can, and you better be bringing a son-in-law with you."

He chuckles. "Well, that's why we are here till Monday. D'andre is apparently putting a winter festival on, just to hook them up."

Clarice claps her hands in delight. "Perfect! You will keep me posted, of course."

"I will." The pair talk until there is a knock on the door, and Victor signs off. "Come in."

A petite female maid enters, dressed in casual clothes, her blonde hair tied up in a bun. She offers a bow and places the tray of food down on the nearby table, along with several drinks. "The cooks did not know your preferences, so there is a bit of everything. When I return, I will have clothes for you and the two Alphas, though they are being placed in the room beside you when they discharge her from the hospital."

"Thank you."

"You are most welcome. I shall be back in an hour."

Victor watches her leave and moves to the food, his stomach grumbling at the smell because of skipping all their meals today. He lifts the lids, looking down at the stew, the fresh bread, and the cheese and meat platter. He sits and takes his time, consuming most of it before moving to the couch to relax, quickly nodding off to sleep. The maid enters, smiling at his dozing, and drops the clothes on the bed. She moves to the closet and pulls out a blanket and drapes it over him before collecting the trays and exiting the room quietly.

Lucian sits with Madison's hand in his, not daring to move until dinner arrives. And even then, he eats single-handedly, ensuring he stays in contact with her. When the nurses roll the bed in, he moves aside, hearing her soft murmur at the connection break. He kicks his shoes off and crawls into the bed beside her, as close to the edge as he can. Lucian takes both her hands gently in his, staring into her peaceful face, knowing that while she sleeps, she is not in pain. He allows himself to drift off to sleep, waking up several hours later with Madison in his arms. He smiles, and tightens his hold on her, shifting her so that she is fully on the bed before letting sleep take him once more. He wakes in the morning to the nurses muttering in dismay, scowling at the fact that she moved in the night. Lucian looks down at his mate, kissing her forehead lightly, before addressing the nurses quietly. "She came to me. I simply put her more fully on the bed."

"She could have done damage."

"I am sure she's fine."

"Well, you need to unwrap your arms so we can look at her back."

Lucian sighs and pulls his arms from around her, hearing her grumble and snuggle in closer. He chuckles. "Maddie, we are in a hospital. They want to look at your back."

She growls softly. "No, I don't want them to."

Lucian places his arms around her again and draws her close. "You can come back."

"Wait till the Alpha hears about this." The nurse scowls at the pair and stomps out of the room, mind-linking the Alpha as she does.

Twenty minutes later, Lucian can feel Victor and the Alpha approaching the hospital with his draconic senses. He sighs, looking down at Madison, knowing when she wakes up fully, they will be oceans apart in emotions again. He caresses her cheek gently. "Maddie. Your father is on his way. I should get up."

Madison opens her eyes to his, locking her eyes on his as she feels the draw of their bond, the call within, the desire to stay where she is. Her eyes stray down to his lips, wondering what it will be like to feel them upon hers, before drifting back to his gaze. Her body flares with heat at the thought of his hands wandering over her.

Lucian growls softly. "Madison."

"Lucy, please."

He groans, tightening his hold on her, as he leans in and kisses her softly at first, tasting the sweetness of her lips before deepening the kiss as desire fills him. His hands drift down her body, pausing at the cough, and the soft, "Excuse me?"

He breaks free from the kiss, his eyes shifting to Victor standing with his hands on his hips, glaring at him and Alpha D'andre with an amused expression on his face. "Right, hands that don't wander, or I will lose them."

"Lips there too, boy. Especially in a hospital when my daughter is supposed to be resting."

Madison blushes deeply, burying her face in Lucian's chest. "Vic, it was me. He said no."

"Madison!"

"Sorry, Vic."

Alpha D'andre chuckles. "Right, on that note, let's get the grouchy nurse back here to look at your back. If it's healed enough, you can leave the hospital."

Madison mutters softly. "Fine."

D'andre mind-links the nurse, seeing the door open and catching her scowl at the pair. *'Natalie, she is ready to have her back checked now.'*

Natalie moves over to the bed as Lucian pulls away, allowing her access to the back area. She pulls the bandages off carefully and looks over the pink skin. She studies some places that had deeper wounds before nodding. "Her back might be tender for a day, but overall, it healed up nicely. I will take the IV out, and she is free to go." She reaches for Madison's hand and pulls the IV out gently, tying the cords around the machine for cleaning later. "Thank you, Alpha." She gives a bow to D'andre and vacates the room.

Lucian sits up in the bed, groaning slightly at the stiffness of sleeping on essentially a gurney. Slipping his legs off, he stands up and stretches to loosen his muscles. He leans over and lifts Madison off the bed, and places her before him, keeping his gaze upward as he ties her gown tight behind her.

Victor growls lightly. "That's right, boy; you best be keeping your eyes from wandering too."

Alpha D'andre bursts out laughing. "I say, do what you want, Lucian. I suspect you are damned if you do and damned if you don't, so you might as well enjoy your damnation. Come, Alpha Madison, I have clothing for you in the bathroom. We will meet you out in the lobby once you are presentable."

Madison glances at Victor, blushing as she hurries past him to follow D'andre. She pads quietly beside him. "Thank you, Alpha D'andre, for having me mended."

"You are welcome. I believe your Delta wishes to do some clothes shopping this morning, but first, you are joining me and Luna Erica for breakfast. Luna's Orders." He stops at a door and opens it. "Here you are. Take your time; I will do my best to stop Victor from cutting Lucian's hands off."

Madison smiles, finding herself liking his carefree joking. "Thank you."

"Anytime. I enjoy having one of the most powerful Alphas indebted to me." He winks at her, humor within his voice as he heads back to where he could hear Lucian and Victor having a discussion about where, when, and how hands needed to be kept to themselves while his daughter remained unmarked.

"Alright, you two. It's too early in the morning. Victor, you want them to connect, yes? So let them do what they need to do. They are mates. It will happen eventually that they will mark each other. Let them have fun."

Victor turns and scowls at him. "And do you say that to your own daughter, Alpha D'andre?"

D'andre laughs. "Of course not. I am just like you. Think of me as the devil on your shoulder. Now come, I told your daughter I would have you both out in the lobby once she dresses, and she doesn't strike me as the type to linger."

Victor glares at D'andre. "Fine, but when your daughter comes of age, I am going to come back for a visit and speak the same words to her and you!"

"Of course you will. Come. Enough bickering. Luna Erica will not appreciate it." He leads them to the lobby, where he finds he is correct in his assumptions, seeing Madison enter the lobby shortly after them. He looks her over, dressed in blue jeans and a hoodie, her hair tied back with a ribbon to hang down her back and black ankle boots. "Great, now we just need your mate to change, and we are all set. His clothes are back at the house."

Lucian sighs, attempting to brush the wrinkles out of his suit and slip his shoes on. "My dry cleaners are going to have my hide when I take this in."

Victor mumbles under his breath. "They are not the only ones that will."

D'andre chuckles. "Victor, Behave."

The group head back to the pack out, where D'andre leads Victor and Madison to a dining chamber, settling them in. He then takes Lucian up some stairs to a room where he can change. "Right, I think I will have you moved to the other side of the wing after this, especially since I put Victor right next door."

Lucian steps inside, seeing a few sets of clothes for both him and Madison. "I am certain it will be fine...I hope it will be..." His thoughts drifted back to this morning. "Yes, I suspect you might be right... Another building perhaps?"

Laughter bubbles out of D'andre. "Well, I must say, with the three of you around, life is not boring! When you have made yourself presentable, come down to the dining chamber. I am assuming you can find your way back?"

"Yes, I can, thank you. It should only take a few minutes."

D'andre chuckles as he walks away, feeling sorry for the man, trying to win over his mate and having Victor breathing down his neck. He steps inside the dining chamber, seeing his Luna already talking with Madison and Victor. "Luna."

"D'andre! There seems to be one missing..."

"He's getting changed. He slept in his clothes last night."

Madison mutters softly. "And the night before."

"Two nights?"

"Yes, we never got to get him a new set. His house blew up."

"That explains why they were so wrinkled. He said a few minutes. Sit, have some tea and coffee. Breakfast will be out soon."

A few minutes later, Lucian knocks lightly and steps in. His gaze immediately moves to Madison, seeing her sitting between Victor and D'andres' Luna. He catches Victor's scowl his way, causing him to smile and move to the vacant seat on the opposite side with Alpha D'andre. "Luna, it's a pleasure to be joining you for breakfast. Thank you for accepting us into your pack."

Luna Erica smiles, her eyes drifting to Madison and back to Lucian. "You are most welcome. Now, enough formalities. I want to get to know the three that have my husband laughing to himself and willing to actually have a winter festival."

D'andre groans. "You were not supposed to tell them that, Erica."

"Oh, come now, D'andre. They walked the streets. There is no signage for a festival, and now one is happening. They are going to figure it out." She turns her gaze back to her guests, catching the soft blush crossing Madison's cheeks as she looks down at her lap. She smiles. "So the festival is for you, Madison."

Madison glances to the side at Victor, giving a nod. "Yes, I suppose it is. I didn't mean to put you out. It was supposed to be the festival in Duskrunner's territory, but we had to leave..."

"And why would you need a festival? I am curious."

Madison's blush deepens as she drops her gaze to her lap. "It's complicated."

"It can't be that complicated, my dear."

Lucian watches Madison shift uncomfortably beneath the Luna's gaze. "It's because of me, Luna Erica. I angered Madison five years ago, and she gave me a week to win her back. Part of that agreement was that we attend the winter festival together."

Confusion flickers across her gaze as she shifts it to her husband. "But

D'andre said you are mates."

"Yes, but I betrayed her trust, and I am working to earn it back. I won't mark her until I have done so."

Victor smiles. "Good answer boy! I am glad to hear that!"

Lucian rolls his eyes. "Of course you are."

D'andre laughs. "See! What did I tell you, Rica? They are fun even after all they have been through. I cannot wait to meet your wife, Victor!"

"What do you mean?"

"Oh, apparently she called this morning. She's on a flight out tomorrow first thing. She placed her eta at my front door about 10:30 in the morning."

Victor mutters under his breath. "I'm surprised she isn't showing up today after what happened yesterday."

"I think she wanted to, but she said she needed to make certain the pack was safe from any attacks it might face." He turns to Madison. "Who would dare to attack your pack?"

Madison groans. "That would be my fault. When the rogues attacked us, I kinda let slip I was the Alpha of the Wildfire Crescent. I suspect they could figure out easily enough that I have not returned to my pack, which would make it prime time to attack."

Erica arches a brow, turning her shocked gaze to her husband momentarily. "The Ruthless Madison Martinez?"

D'andre places a hand on his wife's. "The one and only, but she's not here to take over our pack. Are you Madison?"

"No Alpha D'andre. Though, I believe we should draft up an alliance of some sort when this is all over."

"Great! I'm in! Now, breakfast is arriving. If there is anything I am missing, let me know, and I will have the cooks prepare it." At that moment, several maids enter, carrying trays of food that they set on the table before them, ranging from bacon and eggs to waffles and pancakes. Diced fruit sits on platters with a variety of cheeses. The group sits and eats together in gentle comradery, getting to know each other as they banter back and forth. At the end of breakfast, D'andre rises. "The shops should be open for clothes now, though you are welcome to wear what's offered for as long as you are here."

"Thank you, Alpha. It's very generous, but we will need some of our own clothes to travel back in."

"I understand. Enjoy your shopping." D'andre watches the three of them offer bows and leave the dining area, suspecting that shopping will keep them busy for a few hours. He smiles at his wife. "So, what do you think?"

Erica laughs, patting his hand gently. "I like them. You may keep them."

D'andre laughs. "Yes! I finally found some strays you approve of!"

Erica nudges him gently, kissing his cheek. "Indeed, you have. Now I need to get a festival organized. I want to see a marked Alpha before she leaves here."

"Don't tell Victor that. He's still protective of her."

"Yes, I can see that. I will talk to his wife tomorrow, and we can both work on him."

"Good plan. Now I have to make some calls regarding the information they brought me yesterday." He kisses her gently. "You know where to find me if you need me."

"Yes, in your office."

Eight

Unspoken Tensions

A FTER A FEW hours of shopping getting enough clothes to cover them for the week, Madison, Victor, and Lucian have lunch at a nearby restaurant to eat. They get some coffee to go as they make their way back to the pack house with bags of clothes and another suitcase.

Victor pauses at his door, watching Madison automatically move to his side. "Lass, I believe they placed you with Lucian in the room next door."

Madison's eyes snap to him. "What?"

Victor takes her hand and squeezes it gently, giving her a hug and whispering in her ear. "Stick to your guns, but don't be too stubborn or go too easy on him. I will see you at dinner." He kisses her cheek lightly and steps into his room, closing the door behind him, leaving Madison standing in shock, staring at the door.

Lucian watches her, seeing her frozen in place, feeling the uncertainty of sharing a room alone with him radiating off her. "Madison, I promise to behave."

She turns, studying him for a moment, and moves to his room, seeing the four-poster king size bed in the center of the room with dark blue bedding. Her gaze moves to the black couches with two end tables facing a fireplace, where a large screen TV sits on the mantle. A dinette sits in the corner near a window, her flowers sitting in a vase upon it, with pale blue lace curtains framing the window beside it. Dropping her packages on the bed, she moves to the door to the right of it and opens it, seeing a large bathing chamber with a full-sized soaker tub. She stares at the tub, finding herself wondering if two could fit in it, feeling a heat fill her as a blush crosses her cheek.

"Madison." Lucian groans slightly at the shift in her scent and moves over to the table and chairs to sit and place distance between them. "If you don't stop thinking that, I will join you in that tub."

She mumbles under her breath at why her thoughts were going there when she was still mad at him. She moves back to the packages, searching for her pjs to lounge in for the afternoon, realizing they are probably in the suitcase with Victor. "I will be right back."

Lucian watches her. "What are you after?"

"My pjs and phone charger."

He nods and rises. "I will get them for you."

"Thank you."

Lucian heads out of the room and shuts the door, taking a deep breath to stop the shake in his body as he leans against it. He closes his eyes for a moment, resisting the urge to go back in there and kiss her as he had this morning or better yet, join her in that bath she is planning on having. Groaning softly, he pushes off the door and knocks on Victor's, knowing he will be the splash of ice water he needs to get his thoughts back on track. "Victor, Maddie needs her pjs and charger."

Victor opens the door and looks Lucian over before laughing softly. "Are you scared to be alone with her, boy?"

Lucian chuckles. "I am more scared of you, Victor, but she wants her pjs. I suspect she wants a bath, and if she comes out of there without them, I cannot guarantee what may or may not happen."

Victor grumbles under his breath. "I don't want to hear that. Fine, come in. They are still in the suitcase."

Lucian moves over to the small carry-on and unzips it. He riffles through the few articles of clothing and pulls out her pjs, charger, and her small toiletry bag. "Thanks."

Victor watches Lucian carefully as he goes through the suitcase, carefully avoiding the underthings. He chuckles as he moves over to him, patting his shoulder lightly. "Alright, boy. I can see your intentions are true. Just don't break her heart again, alright. Or I would like to say I would break you, but I think Clarice will break you first."

Lucian's grip tightens on her pajamas. "I don't intend to, but one minute, she is soft and inviting, and the next, she's cool and indifferent and has a definite space aura about her. It's a hard read to know if it's something I have done, or something another has... Or if her mind has wandered into the past where I was an idiot."

Victor chuckles. "Well, I think just keep doing whatever you are, and it will work out. I have never seen her kiss anyone besides giving her mother and I a quick kiss on the cheek, let alone a kiss like that. I will admit, it was a bit of a shock to walk in on that this morning."

"Sorry. I will try to behave, but she made it so hard to resist that I failed."

Victor leads him back to the door. "Lucian, you are a good man, and the mate bond is hard to fight against. I know. Been there, done that. I have Royals pissed at me, remember? I will be happy to have you as a son-in-law, but it will not stop me from being protective of her. Now, get back in there. You need time alone together without me breathing down your neck."

"Thank you, Victor." He heads back to his room, seeing the bathroom door closed, hearing the soft sounds of music playing within. He lays the pjs on the bed and moves to the couch, pulling out his phone to scroll through it before texting his brother to give him some updates. He can hear some water splashing and the soft voice of Madison singing behind the music, smiling at her off-key notes. Twenty minutes later, he can hear her phone shut off and the door open. He closes his eyes as the scent of coconut, mixed with the lavender soap that she has clearly used, overwhelms him.

Madison steps into the main room, seeing Lucian on the couch keeping his gaze pinned to the phone. She slips quietly over to the bed where her pajamas are and picks them up, allowing the towel to drop around her feet.

Lucian senses her progress across the room, hearing the whisper soft drop of the towel at her feet. He groans softly as his hand clenches on his phone, resisting the urge to turn around and face her. Feeling Rhydian struggle to break free, wanting to pounce on her and mark her. "Maddie, you are killing me here."

"Sorry Lucy, I didn't...."

Lucian closes his eyes, mentally counting to ten as he follows her movements. "Just get dressed. Rhydian is going nuts."

She quickly pulls her clothes on and grabs her toiletry kit, running back to the bathroom and closing the door.

Lucian exhales as the bathroom door clicks shut and relaxes his hold on his phone, thinking he needs a shot of a good stiff drink. He isn't certain how he is going to survive the afternoon alone with her until dinner time. Rhydian growls in his mind. *'I know how you can spend the afternoon with her.'*

'Rhy, stop. I am not doing that.'

'But you want to. We both do, and she did too this morning. I could feel it.'

'Rhydian! I don't want any regrets afterwards. Understood. Until I can guarantee that, I am going to do my best to keep my hands to myself.'

'Suite yourself.' Rhydian retreats into Lucian's mind, his soft mutterings filtering through. *'Stuck with an honorable prude is what I have.'*

Lucian chuckles, answering in his mind. *'Yes, you have. Deal with it.'* He catches the door opening again, feeling Madison pause a moment before following her steps to the bed. "Is it safe?"

"Yes, Lucy, it is. Sorry, I ..."

Lucian turns on the couch, taking her in as she stands near her packages, her soft flannel pjs looking warm and inviting, the dampness from her hair creeping into the flannel and clinging them to her shoulders and upper body. "Shhh, it's fine Madison. I understand it's the nature of werewolves and that nudity is not something you are concerned with. What with shape-changing and losing your clothes. Dragons absorb their clothes and gain them back upon change. But I made a promise to your father to behave, and you standing behind me naked made it very hard not to jump over this couch and drop you on that bed you are next to."

"I understand." Her fingers play with the bags on the bed, feeling the tension between them in the air.

"Right. Sorry, I think I am going to have a shower now. Then perhaps we can see what movies they have and watch one?"

Madison breathes a soft sigh of relief. "That sounds good. I will look through and pick a few out."

"Great." Lucian rises and moves towards her, stopping a foot in front of her. He leans down and kisses her cheek. "I want no regrets between us, Madison. I will wait until we are both certain." Looking through the bags, he grabs one and collects the towel that remains on the floor before heading to the bathroom. He breathes a sigh of relief as he closes the door behind him and focuses on pushing her scent out of his mind, even though it fills the bathroom. He places the bag down on the counter and steps into the shower, feeling the hot water washing over him.

Madison's gaze follows him to the bathing chamber till the door closes. She once again wonders what a shower would entail with him in it. She groans and snatches a book out of the bag, along with her phone charger, and plugs her phone in. *Zuri, stop. I am not going in there. I know it's you planting those thoughts in my mind.* She pauses, looking at the bare couch, and pulls the folded blanket off the end of the bed, dragging it over and dropping it on it. She glances through the movies, picking out a few that look interesting, and lays them on the table before collecting her book and curling up beneath the blanket.

Zuri huffs in response. *'It is not, but I wouldn't be opposed to it. It's Somoko. She likes Rhydian's presence, a lot. And that kiss this morning, man, oh man, we want more of that, Maddie! Make it happen.'*

'Gawd, how am I supposed to make reasonable decisions in my mind with the two of you pestering me?'

'We wouldn't pester you if you just gave into the bond that's already there.'

'You heard him, Zuri, Somo. No regrets, and I am not certain I am there yet.'

'We are Madison. Get with the program and deal with it so we can get it on already.'

Somoko pipes into the conversation at this point. *'Yes, I can't wait to romp with Rhydian. I bet he's stunning. He sounds it; his voice causes shivers to run through me.'*

Madison shifts on the couch and runs a hand through her damp hair wondering how she is going to make it through the next few days of sharing a room with Lucian and not succumbing to his touch. Both Zuri and Somoko chuckle in her mind and retreat as the bathroom door opens. Her eyes lift to his, the rich blue drawing her in, as the book flips closed. Her voice is soft as she runs her eyes up and down him, slightly damp, clean-shaven, and dressed in jeans and a dark blue Henley. "I picked out a few movies. They are on the table."

Lucian smiles, seeing Madison curled up on the couch, a book in hand and a blanket wrapped around her. "Good book?"

Madison looks down at the book and turns it over. "I don't really know. Zuri and Somo were pestering me."

"Let me guess. The same pestering Rhy is giving me. That we are taking too long to commit." Lucian moves to the table and looks over her choices, seeing a couple of comedies, one romance, and one crime drama. He picks them up and reads the back of each before deciding on the romance.

Madison blushes. "Yes. That about sums it up."

"Right, so let's make them happy and watch *Love Actually*. I hear it's pretty good and a holiday movie."

"Yes, a few of the pack members were talking about it. I never really had the time to see it."

"Let's remedy that, shall we?" He plunks the movie into the DVD player and picks up the remote, moving to settle on the couch with her. He clicks the TV on and drops the remote on the table, taking Madison's book and placing it beside it.

Madison chews on her lips a moment before lifting the blanket. "Did you want under?"

"Are you sure?"

"Yes, I'm sure."

Lucian smiles and shifts under the cover with her, drawing her into his arms and tucking the surrounding blanket around him. He can feel her settle into his arms as the movie starts. He brushes a few stands off her face and kisses her forehead lightly. "Thank you, Maddie."

"You're welcome, Lucy." She smiles, feeling his aura wrap around her, bringing her comfort as she snuggles into his arms.

Two hours and fifteen minutes later, neither one of them dares to move as the credits roll across the screen until the DVD shuts itself off and the screen lights the room with its blue glow. Lucian's eyes shift down to Madison in his arms, knowing he should make the first move and pull away, but finds his hand running along her cheek, pushing the strands of hair aside as he moves down her jawline. Feeling the call of her lips that were ever so slightly parted and wanting to taste them again.

Rhydian whispers in his mind. *'Do it.'*

'Shut up, Rhy.'

Madison closes her eyes momentarily at his touch, feeling it stir something deep within. A soft gasp escapes her as he trails his fingers down along her neck. She lifts her gaze to his, feeling the desire within his gaze, and reaches up to pause his hand at the base of her neck, barely above where their marks would go. Her voice is quiet, a hint of pleading for the unknown laced within it. "Lucy..."

Lucian growls and pulls her close, unable to fight his desire to kiss her, his hands cupping the side of her face, his fingers lightly caressing her cheeks and down along her jawline. He lowers his head, nibbling on her lips tenderly. "Gawd, Maddie, how many times I have wanted to kiss you? How many times have I woken up from you in my dreams to nothing but an empty bed beside me?" He stops nibbling and kisses her, gingerly at first, as if she would disappear on him as she has in his dreams, before an arm slips down around her waist and pulls her close as he deepens the kiss.

Madison gasps as he pulls her in, feeling his lips upon hers, the heady scent of him filling her as she responds to his touch. She could feel the light nibbles, each one sending shockwaves of delight through her, hearing his whispers in the back of her mind, but finding it a struggle to even speak. She feels a wave of heat moving through her as his hand travels along her body to her waist, feeling herself pulled closer as his kiss deepens. Her hands roam softly, wanting to explore him, wanting to uncover that which is hidden to her.

Lucian sighs as her hands wander, his desire swiftly overriding any good sense in his head. He kisses along her jawline and up to her ears, tasting and exploring, her soft gasps further enticing him as he moves back to take her lips once more in his, this time demanding that she succumb to his touch.

Madison's hands pause as Lucian kisses along to her ears, gasping at the fires and the strange sensations it creates, feeling her body arching closer to his, but not understanding why. She closes her eyes as her fingers tighten in his shirt, pulling him close, submitting to what he is creating with her. She could feel him back at her lips, his tongue testing, teasing, and pushing its way in, demanding that she respond. Her head spins rapidly at his touch, finding herself breathless as he breaks the kiss.

Lucian groans as her body arches and presses against him, feeling her responding to his touch. Shifting her slightly, he places her across his lap, straddling him. He mentally curses himself for wearing jeans and not pajama bottoms like she did as he stiffens beneath her. He feathers kisses along her jawline, moving back to her earlobe and sucking on it gently, feeling her body arch once more against him. His hands roam gently down her body, lingering on her hips as he tightens his grip there.

Somewhere in the back of her mind, Madison registers him shifting her, blushing deeply at the position she is in, before feeling her body once more react to his as his lips find her earlobes. A strange warmth fills her as she wiggles to get closer to him, hearing his groan of delight, only to have his hands stop her. She whimpers softly, her hands drifting down to find the bottom of his shirt and slipping them under to touch bare skin.

Lucian kisses down her neck, pausing in spots to nibble before finding the spot at the base of her neck where mates mark each other. Kissing her gently, he sucks lightly on the skin, feeling the fires within challenging him to sink his teeth in and just do it. He denies them and continues to kiss across the hollow of her throat before returning to her lips once more, tasting the sweetness there.

Madison's body trembles as his lips move down to the marking spot, shaking in desire, in want. The fires jump through her as he moves down her neck to the hollow at her shoulder. She gasps in delight; a soft *please* spills from her lip only to have his lips take hers once more, silencing her requests.

Lucian groans as he feels her body moving on his, his body practically quivering as her fingers find his skin beneath his shirt. "Gawd, Maddie, you are so...." He pauses, recognizing somewhere in the back of his mind there is a knock on their door. He buries his face in her neck, breathing deep of her scent to stabilize himself, before pulling back and cupping her face. "I love you, Maddie, but we need to stop. No regrets." A second knock sounds, and he answers. "Who is it?"

"It's Vivian. Alpha D'andre said to let you know dinner will be in the main hall in fifteen minutes."

"Understood. We will be down there."

Madison struggles to focus on what Lucian is saying, her body filled with strange sensations and wanting more of what he is doing to her. She blinks as she recognizes he is speaking with another. A deep blush floods her face as she scrambles off his lap, pulling the blanket with her to wrap around her as she backs away unsteadily on her feet.

Lucian resists stopping her as she springs off his lap and places distance between them, adjusting his jeans slightly with a soft sigh. He sees the blush creeping across her cheeks and recognizes her flight pattern, opting to remain seated. "Maddie, I didn't mean for it..."

Madison places herself on the other side of the bed, closing her eyes at the warmth that still fills her. She fights the desire to crawl back into his arms and continue, knowing she shouldn't. She could hear both Somoko and Zuri purring in delight in the back of her mind, not helping in her struggle to regain clear focus. Her eyes find his, and she tightens the surrounding blanket, seeing that he hasn't moved towards her. She can feel the concern emanating from him and shakes her head. "It's fine, Lucy; I should have stopped you."

Lucian winces at the slight pain inside at her words, knowing she didn't mean it the way she worded it. He rises slowly and turns to face her. "Did you want to stop me, Maddie?"

She backs against a wall, her eyes still laced with passion as she shakes her head. Her voice is barely a whisper when she finally answers. "No, but... but I have never done that before."

Lucian nods, having tasted the innocence in her reaction and her kiss. "I'm sorry, Madison. I went back on my word to let you lead. If you wish, I can have Alpha D'andre put us in separate rooms."

Madison feels the loss within at the thought of him sleeping elsewhere, at him not being here with her. "Do you want that, Lucy?"

"No, Madison, Gawd no, I want to stay here with you. With you in my arms, on the bed, the couch, hell, even the floor. I don't want to leave you, but I also don't want to overstep your boundaries again. I cannot guarantee that I could have stopped or what might have happened if the maid had not knocked on the door."

The corners of her lips lift at the thought of curling up on the floor before her eyes move to the bed. She holds them there a moment, recalling how well she slept with his arms around her. No dreams, no nightmares, just peace and sleep. "I don't want you to go, Lucy."

Lucian breathes a sigh of relief as he approaches her. He takes her hand in his and kisses the back of it, pulling her into his arms and holding her tight. "Thank you, Maddie."

She nods as she closes her eyes, tears creeping from them as he holds her, her body shaking gently as she struggles with the overwhelming emotions that flood her. "I'm sorry Lucy."

"Shhh, Maddie, Don't cry. I am not leaving you and will always be here for you. I just don't want to do something that will make you run from me again."

She sniffles against him, clinging to his shirt. "I can't help it. They just started."

He chuckles softly, kissing her forehead as he brushes the tears aside. "Well, please make sure they stop before you see Victor, or I'm a dead dragon."

She giggles against him at the thought. "I don't think he would really kill you."

"Damn right, he would. You were asleep when he threatened my life."

She looks up at him, her eyes glistening from the tears. "I wouldn't let him, Lucy."

"That's a comforting thought. Now, I would suggest you wash the tears out of your eyes and put real clothes on. Dinners probably in five minutes and would do no good to me for you to have puffy eyes or lips..." He traces a finger over her lower lip gently. "...when we see your father."

Madison blushes lightly. "Right. I will be right back." She steps out of his arms and moves to the bags, grabbing one with her clothes, and runs for the bathing chamber.

Lucian groans as she leaves the room, thinking that is the most difficult thing he has ever done. *'DON'T even go there, Rhy.'*

'What? I said nothing.'

'You forget, we share a body. I can feel your thoughts.'

'Yes, but she felt nice, didn't she? The way she moved on us so naturally. Bloody maid... Vivian... I think we should eat her for interrupting us.'

'Rhydian! We are not eating the staff. Now get your mind off what we just did. I would like my jeans to fit again. Thank you very much.'

'Hey, you're the one that put jeans on. Next time, put on those casual pants. More room to play with them on.'

'Bloody Dragon.'

'Bloody Prude.'

Madison closes the bathroom door and leans against it. She closes her eyes, still feeling the emotions spinning inside her at a rapid rate, from the feelings he creates, to the fear of loss at losing him. Walking over to the mirror, she stares at herself, seeing red rimmed eyes and puffy lips. She runs a finger softly over her lips, thinking how gentle his kiss was, yet taking full control of her lips. Madison shakes her head and turns the cold tap on, grabbing the washcloth from nearby and soaking it. She places it to her face, feeling its bite against her warm eyes and holding it there, repeating the process a few times.

'Maddie, I am impressed. I thought it would take us days to get to that point.'

'I don't want to discuss it, Zuri.'

Somo chuckles. *'But it felt so good, didn't it, Maddie? His lips, his touch, the fires within us.'*

Maddie hangs the towel up to dry and strips out of her pajamas. *'Alright, fine. It was nice.'*

Zuri coughs slightly. *'Nice, you're calling that... just nice.'*

'Ok, it was better than nice.' Madison can feel Somoko smiling inside her.

'That's my girl. Let the dragon out to play.'

'I would rather not be discussing this.' She pulls on a pair of patterned tights and an oversized t-shirt before dragging a tan hoodie overtop. She steps out of the bathing chamber, a slight blush staining her cheeks. "Right, ready to go."

'We are happy you enjoyed it, Maddie. Just keep in mind, it gets better. That's just the foreplay.'

Madison's blush deepens. *'Enough, you two!'*

Lucian turns as the door opens, having taken the time to calm his fires inside and adjust his clothing. He turns as Madison steps out of the bathroom, meeting her gaze as her blush deepens. He moves over to her side and takes her hands, whispering softly in her ear. "Bloody dragons."

She bursts out laughing. "You have no idea!"

"Oh, I think I do. Shall we find Victor and get dinner?"

She smiles up at him, resting her head on his shoulder for a moment. "I think that's a great idea." She loops her arm through his as they leave the room and knock on Victor's door. They can hear movement along with his muttering. "Yes, yes, I'm awake."

"Victor, no napping. It's dinnertime. You can nap after, all the way to the morning."

Victor growls a few things under his breath about daughters disturbing his peace as he opens the door. Frowning slightly at her, he immediately notices the swollen lips and swivels his gaze to Lucian, who stands stoically beside her. His gaze drifts down to their linked arms. "Maddie, are you and Lucian getting along better?"

She smiles. "Yes, we watched a movie and cuddled on the couch. Now I know why you and Mom do it. It was fantastic."

Victor's frown deepens, knowing where he and his wife's cuddling often ended up. "What movie and how long was it?"

"Oh, a romance called *Love Actually*. It's about two and a half hours. It's based in Britain and follows several couples and their relationships. I liked it when the president had to sing yule carols in the dodgy end of town."

Victor's gaze shifts to Lucians, catching the barely perceptible shake of his head. "That's good. Perhaps I will watch it with Clary. Come, I am certain D'andre and his Luna are waiting."

The trio arrives at the dining area, seeing the Alpha and his Luna already sitting. Madison moves forward. "Sorry we are late, Alpha. We got caught up in a movie."

"Just D'andre, Madison. We are all friends here. Please sit. What movie did you watch?"

"Love Actually. It was pretty good." She settles in the chair at the table, smiling as Lucian and Victor sit on either side of her.

D'andre shifts his gaze to Victor and Lucian, smiling at the different tensions radiating off them. "Victor, are you looking forward to seeing Clary tomorrow?"

"If I survive the initial meeting with her, yes. I will need to watch from an upper balcony or something to gauge her mood as to whether I go into hiding."

Lucian mutters. "I certainly hope you warn me if you are going into hiding. I don't want to face her either."

"Hell no, boy, you are on your own!"

D'andre laughs. "I cannot wait to meet this Clary that has two grown-ass men scared of her."

Madison sighs. "I will protect you, father. It's my fault anyhow, so just stand behind me."

Victor chuckles. "You might be right, actually. The best place to hide would be behind you. Clary clearly favors you over me."

Madison pushes his shoulder gently. "She does not!"

Lucian smiles. "Having watched the video call, I do believe she does Maddie."

Madison scowls. "Fine, I will ask her tomorrow. When is she arriving?"

"10:30 in the morning. I have a few others coming in, including a white witch, to examine those necklaces you said you have, Madison."

"Right, they are in the suitcase in Vics' room. I will bring them down tomorrow."

"I also pulled the three separate treaties from my files so we can go over them tomorrow. Since we didn't do it this morning, as previously discussed."

Victor nods. "Right, sorry about that."

D'andre smiles. "No worries, Victor. You all looked like you needed a day to just relax without business and meetings."

"Appreciate it."

"Now, let's continue the day of relaxing. We have dinner, and afterwards, if you like, we can hit the games and movie room."

Lucian breathes a quiet sigh of relief at having a distraction for the evening. "That sounds great, D'andre."

D'andre chuckles, his eyes finding his wife for a moment as platters of food arrive. "Indeed, now, let's eat." After dinner, D'andre leads them to the games room, where other pack wolves sit playing games. A snooker table dominates the main room. Along the far wall, several gaming consoles and TVs sit with plush couches. Some are vacant, others have pairs duking it out. An air hockey table sits in a small alcove, with a group of five cheering on the pair playing. An archway opens into another room, with several tables mixed with card games and board games.

Madison smiles in delight. "Alpha, this is fantastic! Victor, we need one of these!"

"We can look into it, lass."

A few heads turn as they enter, nodding in greeting to their Alpha and eying the others curiously. D'andre smiles at Madison's excitement. "Everyone, this is Alpha Madison and her Delta Victor. With her is her mate Lucian. I trust you all to show them a good time."

Madison turns to D'andre. "Wait, you're not staying?"

"Oh, I am, but I will be at the poker table. Correct me if I am wrong, but you don't look like a poker girl. Now, Victor, I would peg as a poker player."

She laughs. "Nah, I want to play those video games."

Victor chuckles. "Indeed, I am."

"Lucian, poker or video games?"

Lucian watches Madison bound over to where two wolves are playing, her eyes on the screen, watching and learning the game. "Games."

D'andre winks. "Good answer. Rica?"

"You know me, dear. I am going to take the boys' money at snooker."

He kisses her cheek. "Good. Make them broke enough that they want more work."

She smiles. "That's the plan. I have a winter festival that needs staff."

The group splits up, with D'andre and Victor making their way to the poker table to join a few that were already gaming. Luna Erica sets up the snooker table, encouraging a few warriors to set their stakes on the table, enlisting them to work the festival when they lose to her skill. Lucian gravitates towards the gaming consoles where Madison is, each of them battling it out against each other. Hours pass as laughter, conversation, and competition fill the air. Madison reverts to watching the console, her head resting on Lucian's shoulder. When they kill his character, he looks over at her, noting her eyes are half closed. "Are you tired, Maddie?"

"Yes, a bit."

"Well, you were in the hospital last night. Shall we let Alpha D'andre know and call it the night?"

Madison covers her mouth and yawns. "That sounds good, Lucy...ian."

Lucian chuckles at her near slip and rises. He lifts her into his arms as she curls up against his chest. "Thank you, everyone, for the games. It was a lot of fun, and I look forward to a rematch, but it seems my mate needs to sleep. Have a good night." He carries her over to the poker table, seeing the studious crowd staring at the cards on the table. "Victor, Alpha, I am taking Maddie up to bed. I will see you in the morning."

Victor looks up, seeing a half-asleep daughter in his arms. "Sweet dreams, Lucian. Remember, NO wandering."

D'andre laughs, patting Victor's shoulder, giving Lucian a wink. "I will keep him here all night. Wander away, my boy."

Victor growls at D'andre, earning a surprised look from the others at the one daring to growl at their Alpha, who, in turn, didn't seem to care. "That's it. I am taking all your money now."

"You certainly can try!"

Lucian chuckles and gives them a bow. He leaves the game room and heads back to their chambers. He shifts Madison slightly to enable him to open the door. Once inside, he kicks it closed and moves to the bed, placing her on it gently. "Maddie, you might want your pajamas on."

She murmurs and pulls her hoodie off, moving to her shirt next, only to have Lucian's hands stop her. "Maddie? Perhaps in the bathroom?"

She looks up sleepily into his eyes. "I'm too tired."

Lucian smiles and kisses her forehead gently. "Alright, just give me a minute, alright." He moves the bags off the bed, placing them on the dresser, and pulls out his own pajama bottoms. Grabbing the bag of toiletries, he moves to the bathroom, leaving her the room to change in. He opens the door ten minutes later and sighs, seeing her curled up on the bed in her t-shirt and leggings, sound asleep. Moving to her side, he caresses her cheek lightly. "Oh Maddie. To fall asleep as fast as you can." He shifts her on the bed and pulls the covers out from beneath her. Taking a moment to debate whether to put her on her pjs, he opts to leave her be. He slips in beside her and draws her into his arms, hearing her soft sigh of delight, and allows himself to drift off to sleep with her.

Nine

Clash of Loyalties

L UCIAN WAKES FRIDAY morning to a soft knock on the door, his eyes moving to the clock flashing 9:15 on the night table. "Alpha said to bring some food since you missed breakfast. He said to let you know the meeting will be at 10:30 in the large dining hall."

"Thanks. You may enter and place it on the table."

"You're welcome."

Lucian watches her keep her gaze from the bed, and moves to place a small platter on the table. "If you need housekeeping in the room, just place this on the door." She lays a blue ribbon beside the tray and heads out of the room, closing the door after her. He looks down to Madison curled up in his arms, her expression peaceful, a slight smile on her lips, finding himself a touch jealous of whoever or whatever was bringing a smile to those lips in her dreams. "Maddie. It's time to wake up. We have a meeting to go to in an hour and a bit. We apparently missed breakfast."

Madison grumbles in her sleep-fogged mind. "I don't want to. I like it here."

Lucian chuckles. "I do too, but that doesn't mean we can stay. Come, we should eat."

"Lucy... why are you so professor like in the morning?"

He kisses her softly, whispering against her lips. "I don't have to be, but I suspect your father will kill us both if we miss that meeting."

Madison wakes up suddenly at his lips on hers, her hands moving to push against him and finding bare skin. She pushes back in shock. "You slept with no shirt on?"

"I never sleep with a shirt on, Maddie."

"Oh my!" She blushes and scrambles out of the bed, placing some distance between them.

Lucian chuckles and rises. "There's the Madison I know. Food is there, you should probably eat. I am going to have a quick shower and will eat after."

Madison watches him collect his clothes and head to the bathing chamber. She moves to the table and lifts the lids, noticing it is more of a cold-cut breakfast, with meats, cheeses, fruits, muffins, and croissants. She sits in the chair and eats some of the food, the shower running, humming in her ears. It reminded her of a time in her past, when they were heading into school and a sudden rainstorm caught them. The way his blazer clung to him and wanting to know what he looked like beneath it. She blushes at the thought of knowing, as she had seen it, or not. Suddenly regretting averting her gaze too quickly. Shaking her head, she forces her mind off her mate and onto the meeting. Recalling they need the necklaces, she moves over to her phone and unplugs it, scrolling through it as she mind-links Victor.

'Vic, we need to remember to bring those necklaces down to the meeting.'

'Maddie, do you know what time it is?'

She turns to look at the clock in confusion. *'Yes, it's twenty after nine in the morning. Meetings in about an hour. Are you alright, Vic?'*

He mumbles softly in her mind. *'Yes, that damn Alpha kept me up till three in the morning, and I owe him my adopted child, I think.'*

Madison laughs at the comment, knowing that even being miserable, he could make a jab at her old Alpha. *'Oh Vic, go have a cold shower. I will meet you downstairs. Bring the necklaces.'*

Lucian opens the door as Madison laughs, seeing her phone in one hand and a chunk of cheese in the other. "Maddie?"

Madison turns, doing a once-over of a still-damp Lucian, dressed in casual dress pants and a tan blazer over a gray henley. "Victor is grumpy cause he lost at poker last night."

Lucian rolls his eyes. "Great, I think I will do my best to avoid him today."

She rises and moves to his side, rising on her tiptoes to kiss his cheek. "I will keep you safe. It's my turn now; the food's pretty good." Grabbing some clothes, she skips to the bathroom with a dance to her step. She places her music on and steps into the shower, singing to herself as she readies herself for a new day. Dressing in a pale lavender top, she pulls on the long flowing black skirt and ties a wide sash around her waist, with a matching ribbon in her hair, pulling it back off her face. Once she is done, she leaves the chamber, moving to Lucian's side. "Ready."

Lucian glances at the clock. "We should be just in time."

Meanwhile, downstairs, Alpha D'andre greets the Lycan Royals and their guards who arrive at his door. "King Caden, Queen Paige. Welcome to Silvermoon." Each of them imposing in their own right. Caden is tall, dark blue eyes, wavy brown hair to his shoulders with a solid build that is not hidden beneath the suit he is sporting. His wife, with paler blue eyes and long blonde hair that hung to her waist in waves, dressed in more casual attire than her husband.

King Caden nods. "Thank you Alpha D'andre, Luna Erica. This is our witch, Brittany. She will examine those necklaces you spoke about."

D'andre eyes the white witch that arrived with him, from her light blonde hair to piercing green eyes that glowed, standing barely up to the King's shoulder. He meets her gaze, feeling the power behind it, and offers her a nod, doing his best to quell the nervousness that arose in her presence. "Perfect. The others should be downstairs in about thirty minutes. It seems they all slept through breakfast. Did you want to retire to your room until then, or meet with us in the dining chamber?"

"Dining chamber."

"So be it." He bows to them and leads them to the dining hall, knowing it would be best for a meeting with this many people. A long wooden table dominated the room that would easily sit thirty around it. Dark blue velvet covered the wooden chairs with matching curtains hanging in the window. He gestures to the two chairs at the head of the table.

Caden moves around the table and settles into a chair near the head of the table, but on the right side, opposite the door. Two of his guards circle around after him and back up against the wall, while two remain at the door to the room. Brittany settles in next to Queen Paige, her eyes drifting around the room as she listens to the conversation. "Head table is yours in your domain, Alpha D'andre."

"Understood, Sire. Thank you." He leads his Luna over and places her in the seat on his right at the head of the table.

"I look forward to speaking with these three that you spoke of. Are you certain they are telling the truth?"

"Yes, I am certain. I had my doubts as it sounds fantastical, but Alpha Madison confirmed it. Usually under the influence, you are not alert enough to lie. She even spilled her mate's nickname, which is a girl's name."

"So what happened that they all slept in?"

"Well, Madison just got out of the hospital yesterday morning, so I suspect she overdid it. Her mate Lucian is not willing to leave her side, and her Delta was playing poker with me till three in the morning."

The King chuckles. "Did you win?"

"I did, but he gave me a run for my money." D'andre looks up as his Beta enters the room.

"They are all moving, Alpha. They should be here soon. The Delta's mate also drove through the main gates about ten minutes ago, so we will be on time for the meeting."

"Perfect."

Terrence bows to the King and Queen and settles in the seat across from them, pulling out his iPad to take notes of the meeting.

Victor stumbles out of bed, his head pounding from lack of sleep, eyeing the trays sitting on the table. He staggers over to it and lifts the lid that says, *open first*. He smiles as he sees a bottle of Tylenol, a glass of water, and a note from D'andre.

You might need these before your wife arrives. I don't want her thinking I am a terrible host. I heard this rumor; you don't want her mad at you.

Victor chuckles and cracks open the bottle, taking two and washing it back with the water. He lifts the other lid, seeing a variety of cold breakfast cuts. He eats a bit, glancing at the clock, knowing he has time for a quick shower. Damned if he is seeing his wife in yesterday's clothes. He readies himself, grabs the chains, and heads down to where the meeting is. He walks in and freezes, the necklaces falling from his hands, as his eyes land on Caden and his wife. "Bloody hell." He backs up, only to hear the King's voice booming across the room.

"Victor Winterbourne! Where the hell is my daughter?"

D'andre glances between the pair in confusion. "Winterbourne?"

Victor's face flushes, and he narrows his eyes on D'andre. "You should have informed me you were calling the King in."

"He needed to know."

Caden launches across the table and grabs Victor's shirt, lifting him up and slamming him into the wall as he lands a punch to his face. "TELL ME!"

Victor's eyes darken as Zion comes forth to fight back, blocking the next strike from hitting and returning the favor. He hisses in anger. "If your daughter wanted to see you, SIRE, she would have contacted you. Clearly, she did NOT!"

"You Bastard! YOU Dare to speak to me like that?" Caden lands a second punch to the face, followed by a third as Victor struggles to land a punch against someone twice as strong as he is.

Madison walks in with Lucian at her side, shock filling her at Victor being pummeled by the King. Her eyes glow in fury as she glares at him. "NO! Leave my father alone." Aqua lights surround her as a wave of power slams into the King and throws him across the room.

Victor slides to the ground with a groan. "Maddie... don't...."

Caden rights himself and glares at Madison. "You dare to interfere?"

Alpha D'andre grasps the table to steady himself as a gasp escapes his lips at the fact that Madison just flung the King across the room as if he were a stuffed toy.

Lucian moves to Victor's side quickly, helping him to stand. "Victor?"

Madison straightens herself slowly, squaring herself off, and levels a glare at Caden. "I Do! You have no right to beat my father."

"I AM the Lycan KING!"

"Do I Look like I give a Damn? You're not touching him!"

He bares his teeth and growls at her. "He stole my daughter."

She returns the growl as she shifts to stand protectively between her father and him. "That's BULLSHIT, and you know it."

"Step aside, or I will make you."

"I'd like to see you try."

Caden shifts into a large black wolf with amber eyes and charges toward Madison, finding nothing but a pile of clothing and a shimmering of aqua lights.

Madison shifts and fey-steps behind the King, allowing Zuri full control as she latches onto his tail, her teeth digging in past the fur to the skin below and pulls back away from her father.

Caden feels a sharp pain in his backside, only to find himself dragged back away from Victor, disbelief in his gaze as he has yet to encounter a wolf as strong as he is. He spins suddenly, dragging her a few steps with him, taking in the silver wolf with black ears and feet, nearly rivaling him in size. He snaps at her shoulder, feeling his wolf, Sterling, resisting him. *'NO, don't hurt her.'* Only to find she is no longer there. *'She's mine, Sterling; stop fighting me and back down now!'* He can feel her teeth sinking into his shoulders and down his spine, the pain flaring through his body as he rises on his hind legs. He backs up into the wall, slamming her between them, feeling her hold loosen and catching the ever so quiet whimper in pain.

His delight is short-lived as a deep growl emerges, and the body behind him pinned to the wall shifts. He can smell the fear in those around him, watching his wife and Luna Erica scramble from their chairs and back against a wall. Confusion fills him as claws dig deep into his body, knowing wolves didn't have claws, seconds before he is sailing through the air and slamming into the wall on the far side. He groans slightly, wondering what the hell this Alpha is, rising to his feet to glare at the white wolf. Only he isn't looking at a white wolf, but a silver dragon with aqua eyes and a stream of flame coming right at him. His nails dig into the carpet as he propels himself forward, feeling the fire on his backside, smelling the burn of wood mixed with the burning stench of his fur. "What the HELL?"

Somoko's eyes stalk the King as she launches from where she stands, landing on the table, her claws digging deep into the charred wood. "You will never hurt my father again." Her tail swishes angrily, her rage growing at him and what he has done. The muscles in her hind legs tighten as she prepares to launch herself on the large black wolf, only to hear her mother's voice commanding the room.

"SOMOKO! BACK down now!"

She turns to growl at her, meeting Clarice's gaze, feeling her Lycan power rolling over. "I WILL NOT! HE was beating on Dad."

"Somoko, I should not have to tell you twice."

Somoko glares at Clarice in a battle of wills, feeling her Lycan Lycine threatening to break forth before backing off the table.

Caden, seeing his chance, charges the dragon, only to have Clarice step in the way. "DO it, and I will publicly disown the Royal family... Father."

Caden growls, his amber eyes locking on his daughter that he has not seen in nearly twenty years. "You wouldn't?"

"Wouldn't I? I disappeared for twenty years. Would you like to challenge me with that?"

Victor stumbles over to her side with Lucian's help, one eye swollen shut, and both his lips split. "Clary."

D'andre turns to the woman that entered as the pieces connect in his mind. "Wait, Clary... Clarice, the Beta? Is a Lycan Princess. Are you saying that you are married to the Lycan Princess and Madison is her daughter?"

Victor takes Clarice in his arms, having missed her the past few days, feeling her aura soothing him. "That is mostly right. We were in hiding until you called him here. Had I known, I would have just sent Lucian and Madison in."

Caden backs up a step at the word daughter, shifting his gaze between them. He watches the one that helped Victor take his jacket off to cover the dragon as she shifts back to mortal form. He pulls his blazer around her and buttons it up, drawing her into his arms. Caden narrows his eyes on the aqua-eyed brunette. "She will be punished accordingly for attacking the Lycan King."

Clarice's face hardens as she glares at Caden. "She will NOT. YOU were the one that stepped out of line because of your temper. WHY do you think I left, Father? Victor didn't kidnap me. He didn't steal me. I LEFT freely because you couldn't accept the fact that he wasn't a Lycan. What was it you said? *He's just an Alpha.*" Disgust fills her voice at her father's behavior. "You already beat him to near death once. I wasn't about to let you succeed on a second try. I can just imagine what would have happened if he was a human... He would be dead right now. It shouldn't matter what status our mates are, be they Lycan, wolf, human, or dragon, like Maddie's mate is."

D'andre arches a brow, trying to piece this all together. "Wait, Victor is an Alpha too? Damn, three Alphas knocking on my door. You kept that one hidden well under a Delta title, Victor."

Queen Paige, who remained silent during this, moves forward to the table in disbelief. "Caden, is that true? And don't you DARE lie to me!"

Caden shifts his gaze to his wife and then back to his daughter. "He's not good enough for her. She needs to be with a Lycan."

"Caden Sylvanax. I am ashamed of you. There will be NO punishment and, by the Queen's orders, I protect the four that just entered this room. You even so much as lay a finger on them, and I will ensure you sleep on the couch for a year. DO you understand me?"

Caden growls but backs down from his wife.

"Good! Now shift back and sit your ass down."

D'andre looks around the room. "Well. Now I see where the Ruthless Alpha Madison gets her tenacity from. I also understand why you would need a place to hide, Alpha Victor."

Victor groans, muttering softly. "Don't tell her that."

"A place to hide? Victor?" Clarice scowls at Victor as she leads him over to a chair and sits him in it.

Victor squeezes Clarice's hands. "It was said in jest, my love."

"It better have been." Clarice eyes the charred table before her as she stands next to him. "Alpha D'andre, we will pay to replace your table."

D'andre laughs, delight twinkling in his eyes. "Oh, hell no! I am going to have resin poured over the top of it. This is one hell of a conversation piece, about when the Lycan King and the hybrid Alpha Madison had a fight, right here in this very room. I must say, Madison, if I didn't love my Luna and you didn't have a mate, I would want you as a Luna as well. Both your wolf and dragon are beautiful and clearly one hell of a fighter that they can take on the Lycan King. Seeing him sail through the air twice is not something I will ever forget. Gawd, I wish I had that on camera!"

Lucian tightens his hold on Madison, glaring at the Alpha. "She's not yours either."

D'andre chuckles. "Simmer down, Lucian, your mate is safe from me." His eyes drift to his Luna backed against a wall. "I love my Luna Erica with everything I have. She is my mate in every way. Come, love, I think it's safe to return to the table."

The King shifts back as a servant appears with clothes. He dresses in them quickly, keeping his dark gaze on the one that attacked him. "You are a hybrid. Wolf, dragon, and witch?"

Madison lifts her gaze defiantly. "Fey."

"That would explain your instant travel. You have mastered the fey-step well. Who taught you?"

"Clarice did."

Sterling sits smugly in the back of Caden's mind. *'I told you. Family. I could smell it.'*

'I don't want to hear it right now, Sterling.'

'Fine.' Sterling retreats but hovers just close enough to hear the conversation in the room.

"Come here, child."

Madison narrows her eyes on him coldly. "I am not your child. I am Alpha Madison of the Wildfire Crescent pack."

"Yes, I recall. What I don't recall is seeing my daughter and her mate there."

"I glamoured them."

His eyes darken dangerously. "Are you saying you lied to me about who was in your pack?"

Madison matches his gaze from within Lucian's arms. "It's not my fault you were not smart enough to catch the names Vic and Clary."

Caden growls deeply and rises, his hands clenching at his side. "Why you insolent litt....."

Clarice slams her fists on the table. "SIT DOWN, father! She never lied to you. All she did was disguise us at *my* request. The reason we gave her was we were not on good terms with the Royals because Victor dissolved the Ironwood Moon pack, and you were unhappy about it."

Alpha D'andre looks between the pair. "Wait, Winterbourne, that's where I have heard the name from. Alpha Victor Winterbourne of the legendary Ironwood Moon pack. Him and his pack disappeared about twenty years ago. The stories of the warriors that came out of that pack are legends themselves and what many strive to achieve this day without success. The rumor is, even the King had his warriors trained by them." His eyes move to Madison's. "Damn, girl. No wonder you have the balls to take on the Lycan King."

Victor shakes his head, slumping into the chair. "It's all in the past, Alpha D'andre. Yes, I trained some of the King's guards. That's how I met my mate and retired with her. Dissolving the pack was the best option that would allow us to go into hiding. And we stayed there happily until we found Madison and knew we had to help her."

Queen Paige shifts her gaze to the pair still standing. "Found Victor?"

Victor turns his attention to the Queen. "Yes, her pack banished her when she turned eighteen and was in rough shape. We adopted her and took her in as our daughter."

Queen Paige turns her attention to Madison, her voice soothing. "Come closer, Madison. I promise Caden will behave. You can have your mate with you." She waits patiently as Madison approaches slowly, studying the young lady before her, focusing on the color of her eyes. "What pack were you from?"

"Duskrunner."

"Who are your parents?"

"Clary and Vic."

"No, your Duskrunner parents."

"Well, I am not entirely certain who my father is, but my mother is Luna Faeloria."

"What do you mean you are not cert...Wait, Faeloria? Are you certain that was her name?"

"Pretty certain."

"What did she look like? Do you have a picture?"

"Yes, I have a tiny one in a locket, but it's easier if I just glamor myself." She focuses on her memories of her mother, the way her eyes light up when she smiles at her. Madison's hair color lightens to an ash blond, her height a touch taller, and her eyes very much bluer, closer to that of the queens. She holds the glamor for a few seconds before fading it away.

Paige gasps as Caden pales. "No, it can't be."

"What?"

"That's our daughter."

Clarice snaps her gaze to her parents. "Daughter?"

"Yes, Clarice. You were probably too young to remember your sister, Faeloria. She was two years older than you. We were having a picnic when your father received a mind-link of rogues attacking the palace. You and your sister were playing nearby. A rogue came out of nowhere, picking you because you were younger. But your sister defended you and pushed you out of the way. He latched onto Faeloria instead. I couldn't shift because I was pregnant with your brother Felix, or I would have lost him. In the end, we lost Faeloria instead. Your father gave chase, but the rogue ran too close to the cliffside and lost his footing. He fell into the ocean below, taking your sister with him. We found the rogue days later, washed up on the beach, but never found our daughter." She looks back to Madison. "I am certain we would have recognized her during our pack visits."

"Well, no, cause she had a glamor on her. You would have seen that, but I can see through the glamor, like the one your witch is currently using."

Paige arches her brow and looks at Brittany. "Our witch has a glamor?"

"Yes, over her eyes, to make them look real. They are actually chrome silver."

"Interesting. It begs the question, why didn't she recognize us and reach out? She was old enough when we did our pack visits."

"I am uncertain, unless she couldn't or didn't know. Perhaps Davis had something on her that stopped her. Magic? Or he threatened our lives? Although he would have seen her glamored appearance and not her real one, so I don't know if he knew she was your daughter. I know he called her Luna Megan while we were growing up. Mom told me she felt her real name was Faeloria, but I don't think she told anyone else. It's just another piece of the puzzle I am trying to solve."

"So you're saying our daughter's alive?"

Madison shakes her head. "Well, I don't know. She went missing when I was ten. It left me and my brother to deal with Alpha Davis."

"You have a Brother. Is he a hybrid as well?"

"He's a pure wolf, like Davis is. I am the only hybrid."

"No, your Great Grandmother was a hybrid. She was very much like you, in fact. And your mother was fey-touched. It's possible she was a hybrid, but since they took her as a child, we never saw her shift."

"I never saw Mom Faeloria with a dragon. Only a wolf, and even then, Davis didn't allow it much."

Alpha D'andre shakes his head and chuckles. "So...now she's a Lycan princess as well?"

Paige nods. "It would seem that way. We have a Granddaughter and a Grandson."

Madison mutters under her breath, sending a scowl the King's way, noticing he is still glaring at her. "You have more than that. Clary and Vic have four pups of their own."

D'andre's eyes move back to Madison. "Damn, that would explain why her wolf is as large as the Kings and how she healed so fast from the surgery."

Paige snaps her gaze to D'andre before returning to Madison's. "Surgery?"

Madison nods. "Yes, we had some issues in Duskrunner with them trying to kidnap me and kill my mate. Apparently, it's a thing when Alpha Landon of the Nightshade Howlers wants you as a chosen mate, and you decline, saying you have a fated one."

Paige ponders it as she studies the pair. "But you are neither marked, nor bonded to him?"

"It's complicated, and it doesn't matter. I have a mate. End of story."

Paige turns to Clarice. "Did you know she was Lycan?"

Clarice glances at her daughter before nodding. "Yes, I could smell it. I didn't know she was royal, though. We told everyone her wolf is the size it is because she's an Alpha and encouraged that belief. Along with spreading the rumor with just how ruthless she is."

Madison scowls at her mother. "Wait, you knew? And you didn't tell me?"

"Maddie, you had enough emotional trauma. I wasn't adding anything to your plate."

Madison's eyes turn to Victor, seeing the bruising on his face. "Did Dad know?"

"He knew, sweetie."

Madison nods, her eyes straying to Lucian's as she steps back into his arms and rests her head on his chest, suddenly feeling overwhelmed that she was not just a hybrid, but a Lycan princess.

Lucian draws Madison into his arms, holding her tight as he rests his chin on the top of her head, his fingers lightly caressing along her back. "It will be alright, Maddie; we will work it out."

Paige shifts her attention to the tall blonde man standing before her, his arms wrapped around their granddaughter. "Now, I understand you are her mate, but who are you beside that young man?"

Lucian lifts his gaze, meeting the Queen's before drifting over to the King, seeing him in an entirely new light now. "I am Lucian Marzire, brother to Alpha Pierce Marzire of the Frostbite Syndicate."

Caden snaps his attention to Lucian. "You are one of my spies?"

"Was. It seems Maddie being a target, compromised my position. Especially since they tried to kill me and got her instead."

Caden's eyes darken to coal black as Sterling pushes himself forward. "Someone tried to kill my granddaughter. I will end them."

Clarice scowls in his direction. "If there is anything left over after I get through with them, Sterling. They are mine, and don't you dare touch them."

Paige pats her husband's hand. "Sterling, hun, let Caden come back."

"No, he's miserable and cranky right now. He's not ready to accept this. I am. I want to get to know my granddaughter and her mate. And see Lycine again. And perhaps even Victor and his wolf Zion."

D'andre watches the interactions, running his fingers through his hair. "Damn, I never expected the three strays arriving at my door would have so much power. A hybrid, a Princess, and three Alphas. This just gets better and better."

Victor glares at D'andre. "Perhaps for you, pup, but not those of us who were deliberately hiding."

"You're just cranky because I took your money in poker last night... Wait, are you gonna resurrect the Ironwood Moon pack now that you are out in the open?"

Victor chuckles. "I don't have to. The Ironwood Moon pack never dissolved if truths were to be told. We rebranded it as the Wildfire Crescent."

"No wonder her pack grew so quickly. Impressive Victor. You made an entire pack disappear. To have that kind of loyalty from your pack is what most Alphas only dream of."

Sterling turns his jet-black eyes on Victor. "You have been living just below our gazes this entire time?"

"Yes, I suppose we have. We only stepped more into the open these past five years with Maddie."

Sterling turns his gaze to his granddaughter. "Maddie. I like it. "

Madison growls slightly. "It's Madison. Alpha Madison Martinez to you. You need to earn the right to call me Maddie."

Sterling arches a brow and starts laughing. "Alpha D'andre is right. You are packing a pair. Fine, Alpha Madison it is. Can I meet your wolf officially? I know your dragon's name is Somoko, as Clarice called her that. I would like to see her after, without a breath of fire burning my backside. That still stings, I might add. So does my shoulder, for that matter."

Madison stares at the King, or rather his wolf who has taken over, mentally debating whether she trusts him. She decides that, so far, he seems the cooler of the two. "Her name is Zuri." She steps back in her mind, allowing Zuri forward. "Sterling. Is there a reason you wanted to meet me?"

"Damn, I know her dragon's sporting kahunas, but clearly her wolf is too. No wonder you dared to fight Caden. I am impressed with how you handled yourself. Clarice taught you well. I just wanted to say, I do not have the same temper that Caden does. He never had a temper until the rogues kidnapped his daughter. It's not an excuse, but I need you to know that. Perhaps you can convince my granddaughter to get to know me better. Yes?"

Zuri's aqua eyes stare at him, unblinking. "I will think about it. Somoko is not ready to talk to you."

"Understood. You may allow Madison back."

Madison feels Zuri retreat into her mind and steps forward once more. Her eyes glance around the room, noticing quite a few watching her. "Please tell me Zuri behaved."

Clarice smiles at her daughter. "She did. Perhaps a bit cool, but that's understandable."

Madison sighs and closes her eyes a moment, feeling Lucian's heart beat against her, grateful that he was supporting her through all this.

Alpha D'andre smiles at the fact it seems like the tempers seemed to have calmed down somewhat. "So, now that it seems like most of us have a level head, shall we get down to why we are all here?"

The group nods and moves to sit in the chairs around the charred table. D'andre at the head, with Luna Erica to his right side. King Caden, or rather Sterling, returns to his seat next to Luna Erica with his Queen beside him. The silent witch who watched the entire fight without moving remains where she is. Clarice pulls the chair out beside Victor and sits down next to him at the far end of the table. Lucian guides Madison over to sit beside her mother and settles her in. He moves to the door to pick up the three gold chains and Madison's clothes. He drops the chains in front of the King before returning to settle next to Madison, handing over her clothes.

Ten

Sibling Turmoil

MADISON HUGS HER clothes tight, covering her lap with them, knowing she probably should get dressed, but she isn't about to do it now. She works on folding them when her cell phone rings. She pulls it out of her pocket to glance at it quickly, a frown crossing her features at the caller ID. Her hands shake slightly, feeling a terror creeping into her heart. "I have to take this. I am sorry." She swipes the phone to answer, knowing it was improper manners to answer a phone in a meeting, so, put it on speaker for all to hear. "Hey Luke, what up?"

The others look over at her to reprimand her, just as both Victor and Lucian place fingers to their lips.

"Maddie. How are you?"

"It's been a rough twenty-four hours."

"Yes, I heard there was an explosion at Professor Deplois's house. It burned so bad that they couldn't even find his body. They also found three dead guards on the road, close to my house."

"Really, that's interesting."

"Hey, you know that the 17th just passed and... Hold on, Maddie... Rosa, 86th that, she is watching you... Sorry, you know how it is, Maddie, they are always watching... Don't need her to learn bad habits."

"It's all good, Luke. Kids are like that."

"Yes, hey, speaking of kids... you know that gold locket Mom gave you?"

"Yes."

"Do you still have it?"

"Of course." She reaches up to her neck, fingering the locket gently.

"I was wondering if I could get one made for Aurora. I just remember how magical it was the day Mom gave it to you."

"Yes, I can have one made for you. I have a larger framed picture of her. It might be better."

"Nah, I think that's the one. It's special."

"Sure, I suspect it will take a few days to get it made. Perhaps I can drop it off next Monday or Tuesday?"

"Great. Tuesday would be better. I gotta get Aurora down to sleep. She likes to wake up between nine and ten while I am on the laptop. So I have to be careful about what I am looking at or searching for. I don't need her to see anything on the interweb beyond her learning levels, if you get what I mean."

"She's a child, Luke. She won't remember till she's older."

"Still not taking any chances. It's not worth the risk. I gotta run, Maddie; Rosa needs my help. She keeps forgetting her password and gets it mixed up with the one used in high school and her pet's name. It's only been a week, and I need to reset it again and find something she can actually remember. Take care. I love you."

The phone grows silent as Madison stares at the blank screen while the others watch her. Her voice is soft and filled with a slight edge of anger at what Davis and Landon are doing. "Luke's in trouble, and we are being spied on."

Victor frowns, feeling the pain in his face, having heard the conversation and replaying it in his mind. "How do you know that, Maddie?"

"He told me. Our safe word, or danger word, so to speak, is a number. 1786, to be exact. He said the 17th just passed, and then to his mate, he said 86 that. Its code for one of us is in trouble. He said she was watching and then asked about the locket and how magical it was when Mom gave it to me. Mom never did. I found it in her room in the jewelry box. So the locket is what they are using to scry on with. He mentioned his daughter likes to wake up between nine and ten to watch him on the laptop. My guess is, that's when the dark witch is using her magic to spy on us." She reaches up and pulls the locket off her neck, placing it on the table before her.

Victor chuckles. "You are far too clever, Maddie; I would never have gotten that."

Madison smiles, a sadness crossing her features for a moment. "Luke and I learned to speak in code like that. Alpha Davis was... is not a nice man. Mom Faeloria put up with a lot for us before she disappeared. I was actually hoping she had run away, but then she would have brought us, and she didn't. So something else happened. After that, our conversations were much like that one. Hidden messages within normal speech."

Lucian reaches over and squeezes her hand. "So if I am to read that right, we are going back to the pack on Monday or Tuesday of next week."

"Yes, and we have a way into the Duskrunner database now. Luke gave me the passcode within that message. Or close. It might take me a few tries. Also sounds like they change it weekly. Probably Tuesdays. So we need to determine what's going on and make a plan fast. I will also need a phone with 1786 in the number to call him from because my guess is, there is a guard monitoring his calls, and my number is recognizable. Luke won't answer unknown numbers, but he will if there is 1786 in it."

Alpha D'andre nods. "And that's our cue to get down to business. But first, let's lock that necklace up. Shall we? Do no good to have them watching us now."

Madison nods, sliding it down the table to him, watching as a guard takes away her cherished possession. "You should keep it in a jewelry store. Especially if they were listening to his call and know that I am getting another one made."

The group spends most of the morning going over what each of them knows, as well as the treaties. D'andre hands over paper so they can write things down, creating graphs and timelines of the events, trying to see if there are any clues or links they missed.

At lunch, they take a break. Madison slips into another room to get dressed again and hands Lucian's blazer back to him. He pulls the blazer on and smiles at her scent all over it, knowing he is not washing it anytime soon. After food and coffee, the group reconvenes at one, with an additional pack member. Each of them is much more amicable to the other, with Sterling withdrawing to let Caden back into the meeting, who remains silent and broody, but his anger seems to have subsided.

"Madison, this is Nathan. His cell has 1786 in it."

She smiles. "Can I borrow it?"

"Of course, Alpha Madison. That's why I am here."

"Great, now pay attention. When someone calls you back, you need to play along. Understood." After he agrees, she moves her gaze to D'andre. "I will need a laptop as well, though Vic can get the one from our room."

D'andre nods, and within a minute, they place a laptop in front of her.

Madison's fingers click across the keyboard with ease as she studies the screen, chewing softly on her lower lips as she ponders the password. She makes a few attempts and finds success on the fourth try. Scrolling through, she searches the database for a Nathan living in the Stormfang Pack. She picks up his phone and swipes it on, editing the one in the file to match the one in her hand.

Lucian carefully watches her. "What are you doing, Maddie?"

"Editing. And you're going to finish it, depending on how this conversation goes. Put in searchable details that they will need to confirm. Like addresses, relations, anything they have listed there. I will try to keep most of it the same, but in case it changes, the updated information needs to be there if they search it." She slides the laptop his way as she calls her brother's number on Nathan's phone. She places it on speaker and waits, counting five rings before it's picked up.

"Ya?"

"Luke. It's your friend Nathan Wilson, wife Diana, address 1546 5th street, Oaklands, located in Stormfang. He wants to talk to you about the birth of his new pup, Zoe."

"Oooh Hey Nathan! Long time so see! Yes, you and Diana have a new pup! That's awesome. How's she doing?"

"Are there guards there, Luke?"

"Yes, Rosa and I were thinking about possibly having three pups, but you want five; that's crazy!"

"Are they Davis's guards?"

"Nah, we are uncertain when we want another just yet. Perhaps a year apart or something."

Madison ponders it for a moment. "Have they threatened you, Luke?"

"Cool. Yes, I remember when we met at the winter festival. Do you have them in Stormfang? We were thinking about taking Aurora to her first one this year, but it might be overwhelming for her."

"Is Landon still there?"

"Yes, I think she would really enjoy it. Hey, Zoe might be a touch young, but Aurora really enjoys reading."

Madison frowns at the sudden switch of topic, looking at the others. "What are you trying to tell me, Luke?"

"I was at the bookstore in town as they have some exceptional kid's books, even if there is a crank-pot running the store. She practically chased me out when I took too long to decide."

Madison smiles. "Oh Luke, I love you!"

"Yes, no, books are outstanding. Aurora loves *Hiding in Plain Sight*. We feel it will help her understand we are wolves living in a human world as she grows up. I also placed an Amazon order for one that will teach her what wolfsbane looks like and how to avoid it. Don't want my pup injured."

"Wolfsbane? Are you saying the pack ordered some?" She glances at the laptop screen, wanting to flip through the database to look.

"Yes, you can't be too sure, especially when it can grow like a weed in certain areas. Hey, I was thinking, Aurora's old enough to travel; perhaps we can come visit. I am sure Aurora and Zoe will become fast friends when they meet. Rosa wants to stop in Silvermoon on the way and look around for a few days."

Madison pales slightly at his words, her eyes drifting to the windows that were open. "Hold on a sec Luke."

"No worries! Babies man, when they puke, it's everywhere."

She rises quickly and closes the windows. Everyone else, realizing what his words meant, followed suit, and within seconds, the room was closed off and the drapes drawn.

Alpha D'andre watches the windows close and sends a mind-link to his trusted warriors. *'I want you to surround the pack house and fan out. ANY wolf you don't recognize, capture alive if you can. If they look like they will escape, shoot to kill. NO ONE is to leave these grounds.'*

Madison returns to the table. "I am assuming Landon is still lurking about. Where is he staying?"

"Yes, I gotta head up to the pack house in about an hour. Duties, you know. Hey, did Alpha Landon come to your pack? Apparently, he is in the market for a Luna. He's even got a sizable dowry offered for the right one. Yes, like the old days, except I think it was usually the woman with the dowry. I get it! He's clearly desperate."

"That's not good Luke."

"Yes, I don't know why he's not waiting for his fated mate. Perhaps she rejected him, not that he would tell anyone. There's gotta be a story there, I am sure, but he definitely is going for a chosen mate. Alright, Nathan, I gotta go! We will touch base in a month or so after the holidays. Byeee!"

The phone goes silent, matching the silence in the room as Maddie turns to the laptop Lucian is typing on. She scans it carefully before pulling it from him and jumping through a few pages. Her frown deepens as she sees the pack house ordered a pound of wolfsbane and had a history of ordering it for the past thirteen years. She sighs under her breath. "Bloody Hell."

D'andre watches Madison carefully, seeing her expression change to one filled with anger and dismay. "You really are ruthless. I can't believe you just pulled that off."

"I haven't succeeded yet. There will be a call coming in from a strange number to Nathan's phone." She turns to him and hands his phone back. "I hope you were paying attention cause you are about to get tested."

Nathan nods and pockets it, moving to sit at an empty chair around the table. He pulls a piece of paper his way to write what he can remember. He pauses at the address. "Addy?"

"1546 5th street. Oaklands. The dodgy part of town."

"Victor...Can you get the... Never mind." She pauses at his condition, suspecting he was still very sore from the beating. "Lucian, can you get my laptop out of Vic's room? There are things I need on it."

"Of course." Lucian rises and runs from the room, returning with it a few minutes later, and places it in front of her.

D'andre arches a brow. "Ours is not good enough?"

Madison smiles. "It is, but it's not attached to the dark web like mine is."

"The what?"

"The web no one knows about, where underhanded dealings and rogues hang out."

Caden growls. "There's a web for that?"

"Yes, and I have access to it." Her fingers fly across her keyboard, bouncing back and forth between the two. Aqua lights filter from her fingertips on D'andre's and back to her own. Her frown deepens as she types more into hers, sifting through the information as she pulls more tabs up before jumping back to Duskrunner's database."

Lucian watches the tabs open, her gaze scanning quicker than he can before another tab opens. Knowing she was his top student, he is still unprepared for how fast she flips through the tabs and apparently absorbs information. He smiles inwardly, watching her work, suddenly understanding why he dressed in drag on that one Halloween. "What are you looking for, Maddie?"

"Shhh, Lucy; I am busy."

The rest watch in silence, seeing the concentration in her expression, knowing there is something she is seeking. Each slowly realizing just how dedicated she is to her pack and her obligations, and how she got to be Alpha. After about five minutes, her fingers tap the counter, muttering a curse under her breath.

Victor looks over at Madison, recognizing the tapping fingers as done.

"So what's the general gist, Maddie, cause between last night's drinking and poker to the pounding I took this morning, I am finding it hard to think straight."

"Well, there is a drawback to the coded speech and how it works, as I might not assume or guess correctly, but here is my take. They have spies here in Silvermoon watching us, so they know I haven't returned home. Landon is staying at the pack house with Davis, and there are five guards at Luke's house, three inside and two lurking in the woods outside. He is uncertain whose guards they are. They have threatened to take his pup Aurora away if he doesn't comply with their demands. The dark witch we seek is currently hiding in plain sight as a clerk at the pack bookstore. They have placed a ransom out for my capture, and I suspect they will try to capture me at the winter festival, probably using wolfsbane. Something happened to Landon's fated mate, but Luke couldn't get the info without getting caught, so, he bailed on the mission."

Caden growls, low and deep, the room feeling the power of his Lycan anger. "I can't believe this is happening in my kingdom. I will end those packs."

Madison turns to scowl at the King. "NOT until I find my mother. If we want to find the missing wolves, we just can't storm in there and take them all out. We need to play this smart."

"Are you, an Alpha, daring to tell me what to do with my kingdom?"

Queen Paige places a hand on her husband's. "Lycan and Princess, my dear, and apparently she is. NOW shut up and listen, or let Sterling return. She's right. We need to lay a web down to catch those daring to cross its fibers, and it can't just be vibrations upon it. I want a secure capture. We don't want any innocents caught in the middle when we step in to take them down."

"Agreed, now, my searches. This is where it gets scary. Duskrunner and Nightshade have been ordering wolfsbane along with granulated silver regularly since my mother disappeared. Recently, they have added other stuff to their purchases, like powdered iron and a few runes. It looks like

Howling Oak is the principal supplier for both of them, among other things, dark web wise. Like moon crystals, which paralyze supernaturals. Chronoshift marks which stop any magical movement, from fey-steps and teleports to a witch's portal. Right down to the shadowbind rune that binds all magic and takes shape-shifting away."

"How the HELL do you know about this Madison?"

Madison scowls at Caden. "Because I do my research before I walk into any situation. And I have rogues in my pack that want to be there. They helped me learn how to navigate the dark web in exchange for being sworn into my pack. As to why? Well, I want to know what the pack contains before I take it over, and I AM in the process of taking Davis's pack from him. He just doesn't know it yet. Now, back to what I was speaking about. Near as I can see, and I can't be certain I found all the names, Lucian can confirm that later, but each time Howling Oak sold product to either Duskrunner or Nightshade, a wolf went missing within the week. Also, it also looks like a family in the Howling Oak raised Mom as their own. They said she was nine, but you said she was eight. So they have the age wrong, which means they forced her into a chosen mate marriage with Davis."

The King rises and slams his fist into the wall behind him as the Queen tries to pacify him. D'andre stares at the two computers in front of Madison, an expression of disbelief written on his face, while Luna Erica sits silently, shaking her head back and forth as if it's not happening.

Victor groans. "Fuck Ducks!"

Clarice scowls at him darkly. "Victor! Language!"

"Clarice, Madison is old enough to hear a curse word. She's probably thinking it, but she doesn't dare say it in case you have soap hiding in that pocket."

"Mom, Dad's right, this called for it."

Lucian pulls the laptop forward, reading through the tabs at a slower rate, unable to believe that she found in a matter of minutes something he had been searching the past eight years for. "Well, I would say I need to call my brother so that he can report to the King, but I guess I will just report to the King." He looks up at Caden and points at Madison. "What she said... And what Victor said."

Madison places a hand on Lucian. "Sorry, Lucian, I didn't mean to take your job away."

Lucian shakes his head. "No, I am glad we finally have a lead. And it's a hell of a lead."

"It looks like both Duskrunner and Nightshade ordered about a hundred gloomshroud runes. With enough of them, they can create a magic dampening field. If they have access to witches, which they clearly do, they can imbue them with species-specific magic... So to speak. From what I gather, Duskrunner set theirs to only allow wolf-blood into the pack house. I would hazard a guess that Nightshades are the same. That's why I felt my fey magic suppressed when I entered the pack house and you couldn't enter the building."

Brittany speaks for the first time, her voice quiet, yet filled with power. "That is why they are taking them."

Madison turns to her in confusion. "You lost me."

"The ones missing. In order to make those runes and crystals, a dark witch needs to drain the essence of the creature in question. To make anti-wolf charms, you need wolf's blood and essence. They won't care if they drain them, as they can just get a new one, for wolves are a dime a dozen." She lifts the gold chains that sit on the table, forgotten. "They made these necklaces with a rogue's blood and essence, but no one notices when a rogue goes missing."

Paige frowns, her gaze turning to her witch. "Are you saying they kill them?"

"Likely. If they survive, they leave behind the shell of a human without a wolf. They will wander around lost, end up in a mental institute or hospital labeled as delusional, or, in medical terms, have dissociative disorders. Fey are difficult to catch, so they will be cautious with a highly sought-after commodity. At least until they have another fey in their possession." Brittany turns her gaze to Madison. "Dragons are another that are coveted for such magic. But they are difficult to contain as they are stronger and more volatile than wolves, so they will seek younger ones. Madison is a walking beacon of delight to dark witches."

Lucian growls softly. "Yep, again, what Victor said."

Madison pales considerably, understanding why Landon placed a bounty on her head. "That would be why they took the dragon child... D'andre, can we access these to the pack printer and get those tabs printed before they disappear? The dark web has a way of shifting."

"Yes, I will get the printer turned on, and you can connect to it. Get that done fast." D'andre runs from the room, heading to his office. He powers his printer up and fills the tray with paper. He quickly returns. "Good to go, Madison."

"Lucian, you start on D'andre's laptop. I will work on mine. Print all the tabs."

They each work on sending the information to the printer as fast as they can while the King paces the room angrily. Once they are certain they have them all, they nod at each other. "All are in queue, D'andre."

D'andre shakes his head and starts laughing. "My god, Madison, you are truly amazing. And to think I almost told my guards to deny access to the two strange wolves and a human at my gates. You have definitely earned your position as Ruthless Alpha Madison. So, what do we do now?"

"Well, we need to figure out a plan, I suppose. If Howling Oak is making the charms, then they must be keeping the captives there. We need to free any still alive and stop all three packs."

"By Tuesday?"

"Yes, but I owe a winter festival to Lucian and your Luna."

"So today and Monday then, because you need to return Tuesday, and it's a three to four hour drive."

"Correct. I can fey-step with a few people to Luke's house, but they should see us drive in, which will cause the guards at the gate to start the chain reaction to us arriving."

Queen Paige returns to her seat, leaving Caden to pace. "Right, and they clearly want Lucian dead, so Caden will take his place. Lucian will stay here."

"What? No! I am sorry, my Queen, I think they might recognize the King."

"Not if you glamor him to look like your mate."

Madison frowns, turning her gaze to Caden standing beside her. "They will smell his wolf! Lucian doesn't have a wolf. They think he's human."

"Brittany will assist with that. She can mask our wolves if we need to. We will send our Lycan guards with you, glamoured to look like D'andre's, as they may or may not know we arrived."

D'andre frowns at the implication that his guards are not skilled enough to protect Madison and the King. "My guards are quite skilled, my Queen. You need not send yours in."

"D'andre, I am not saying they aren't. Those of us that remain will need protection here. Clearly, they are on your lands somehow; likely the dark witch has portaled them as Brittany does with us. It's possible they will try a strike here while Madison is in their pack. You aligned with her, so in their eyes, their enemy now." She looks at Brittany beside her. "I think you should go disguised as Victor. They might need a witch, though I will say, Madison, your fey magic is quite strong. It surprised me at how easily you threw my husband across the room."

Victor growls. "I am not leaving my daughter unattended."

Paige smiles patiently. "Victor, she won't be. She will have Caden, Brittany, and four of our strongest guards. Don't you agree that perhaps you and Caden should NOT be traveling together just yet?"

Victor narrows his eyes on Caden. "You better bring her back in one piece."

Clarice whispers in Victor's ears as he lowers his head. "Of course, Clarice." Clarice turns to her father. "They have strong magic, enough to explode a house and put my daughter in the hospital. As much as I am furious with you, Father, I know that at least Sterling will keep our daughter, your granddaughter, safe. So if he fights to get free, Caden, YOU

Let him, do you understand me?"

Caden glances between his daughter and granddaughter. "Understood."

Lucian glances at Madison sitting beside him, listening to the conversation. "You realize I am not human and have a dragon. I can take care of myself."

Queen Paige shakes her head. "Yes, and with all the cameras and cellphones out there, wolves are natural if accidentally caught in a picture. Dragons are not."

"My Queen, I do not think I can sit here and wait as Madison places herself in danger."

"Get used to it, Lucian. I have heard the stories about Ruthless Madison Martinez. You are in for a rough ride if you think she's going to be the angel sitting perfectly at your side."

Madison blushes, shifting in her seat as they talk about her exploits. "I will be fine, Lucian. If all else fails, I can fey-step us back and out of danger."

Just then, Nathan's cell rings, causing them all to jump. He places it on speaker-phone as he answers it. "Hello, Nathan Wilson speaking; I don't recognize this number. Who is this?"

"This is Martin from the Duskrunner Pack. We are updating our database. We just have a few questions for you."

"Martin who?"

"Martin Lopez."

"Right. What questions do you have?"

"Can you please confirm your address and which pack you reside in?"

"Sure, it's 1546 5th street. Oaklands, Stormfang Pack The dodgy part of town."

Martin chuckles. "Dodgy part, huh?"

"Yes. Diana and I want to move, especially since we just had our first pup, but we don't have the finances yet. One day soon, though."

"Who is your presiding Alpha and Luna?"

Madison quickly jots names down on the paper and slides it over.

"Alpha Darian and Luna Willow. Ravenwind is their last name if you need it."

"Perfect. Now we have you in our database, but we have no connections for you within the pack."

"Oh, that would be Luke. We ran into each other a few years back at the winter festival when Diana and I were there."

"Do you happen to know Luke's last name?"

Madison quickly pens the name and slides it across. "Yes, I think it was Eveningstone or something. It's on my phone, but I can't look while I am on the line with you. I am bad at disconnecting people."

"Evenstone?"

"Yes! That sounds right. It's funny cause I called him earlier to tell him about our new pup, Zoe! But he had to go, which worked out cause Zoe vomited milk all over me, and I wanted a shower. You caught me just as I stepped out."

"Great, that's all we need. Probably talk to you next year when we go through the system again."

"Hey, no worries! Have a wonderful holiday." He hangs up the phone and looks around. "Did I do good?"

Madison nods. "You did great. Now we need to make a plan."

D'andre heads to the office, bringing the stack of printed tabs and slides them across the table for others to look over in case Madison missed anything but doubted it. They continue to hash out ideas until five, when D'andre calls the meeting for the evening, each of them feeling mentally exhausted and needing a break. "Alright, I think we are about done. We are overtired and struggling. Let's take the weekend, enjoy the festival my wife planned, and return to this Monday morning. Your Majesties, you are welcome to stay."

Paige shakes her head. "As much as I want to spend time with my newly found family, it's better that we return home and not be tied to you yet. Afterwards, Madison can count on the fact that we will be spending time in her pack. A LOT of time. Isn't that right, Caden?"

Caden sighs, his eyes wandering to Victor. "Of course, my love."

Paige smiles and rises. "Good, now come here and give your grand-mama a hug before we teleport out."

Madison rises and moves over to give her a hug, finding herself liking this woman much better than the man she was married to.

Paige hugs her tight before pulling her back to look into her eyes. "We will make this work. Somehow, I promise. Now, I wish to speak with Clarice and Victor before we leave. I will see you Monday, and I guarantee Caden will be in a better mood."

Madison smiles. "If he leaves Vic alone, I will leave him alone."

"He will, honey, I promise."

"Good. I will see you on Monday. Alpha D'andre, thank you again for hosting us. I think we will have dinner in our room tonight, if that's Ok."

"Of course, Madison, and it's just D'andre! I will have food sent up."

She smiles and turns to Nathan. "Thank you for doing that. Just so that you are aware, you may or may not get another call."

Nathan chuckles. "I now have my notes tucked in my phone case."

"Good thinking."

Finally, she moves to Clarice and hugs her, holding her as tight as she can. "I missed you, Clary! I am sorry I made you mad at Vic."

Clarice draws her in her arms, feeling the stress in the way she clung to her, knowing she was riding on the edge of emotions. "Shh, sweetie, it's gonna be ok. You know I can't stay mad at Vic for very long."

She sniffles slightly. "I know, I just didn't...."

"Hey. Vic and I will come upstairs after I talk with my mother and father. Does that sound good?"

"Yes, that sounds great."

"Perfect, say thirty minutes. Let's have dinner together. I want to have a chat with your mate."

Madison laughs. "You should talk to Vic first. Apparently, he's threatened his hands, eyes, and lips."

Clarice arches a brow. "He has, has he?"

Victor groans. "There you go, lass, getting me into trouble again."

Madison moves over and kisses his cheek gingerly, noticing that a lot of the bruising was already healing. "You know I love you, Vic. I won't let anything happen to you again."

Victor takes her hand and squeezes it. "Thank you for earlier."

"Your welcome, Vic." She turns to Lucian, who stands silently watching her. "Come on, Lucian, let's go upstairs and relax before dinner."

As Madison turns to leave, Alpha D'andre stops her. "Madison, wait. It appears my men have caught a rogue outside. Your Majesties, I suggest you stay here and keep yourself hidden. I want Madison to see if she can identify him."

Madison glances at the others and nods. "Lead the way, D'andre."

He jogs out to the front door with Terrence, Madison, and Lucian following, Clarice and Victor behind them in the doorway. Each seeing a group of four warriors dragging one trussed up rogue. Madison stands back slightly, studying the one struggling, his eyes holding a wild look to them until they land on her. He stills suddenly and smiles. "The Luna we are looking for finally comes out of hiding."

D'andre glances back at Madison before glowering at the man. "That's Alpha to you."

He laughs a maniacal laugh. "Not for much longer! Luna she will be!"

Madison approaches, hearing Lucian's objection, but continues anyhow. She watches as the guards tighten their hold on him. "A rogue that knows Landon wants a Luna. What's the bounty on me?"

He hisses quietly. "I am not saying."

"Rogues like to think they are special, and yes, some of them are, but most are pack wolves who don't like rules. There is a unique aura when the rogue truly is a rogue, than one part of a pack, wanting a pack, or being forced out of a pack." She reaches out to his shirt collar and pushes it aside, seeing the gold chain there. Her fingers loop through the metal, seeing the man's eyes widen in fear seconds before she rips the necklace off him.

"NO!"

Madison looks at the chain in her hands. "Just like the other magic imbued chains." She lifts her gaze to the man standing before him as the rogue smell fades from him, and darkness shrouds him. "He's from Landon's pack, D'andre. Do what you want with him."

D'andre nods. "Take him to the dungeons and lock him in silver chains." He watches the warriors drag him away, hearing his curses before his words strike a chill in all their hearts. "I hope Landon gets you, bitch! He will teach you a thing or two about learning your place. NO one will see you ever again, just like your mother after she rejected Landon and he sent her away."

The chain slips from Madison's hands as the color drains from her face, feeling the pain deep in her heart at it being confirmed her mother didn't run away. She steps back, finding Lucian right behind her, placing hands on her shoulders.

"Shh, Maddie, He's not getting you."

Alpha D'andre immediately links more of his warriors. *I want perimeter patrols around the pack house at all times. Effective now.'*

Eleven

Darkness Descends

M ADISON'S EYES FOLLOW the man being dragged to the dungeons, feeling her world collapsing about her, the shadows of when the pack banished her creeping through the edges of her subconscious. The floor beneath her gives way as she tumbles down into the darkness that calls her, her eyes staring at the vacant space long after he disappears from sight.

Clarice pales, recognizes her look and runs to her, placing her hands on either side of her face, shaking her to get her to focus. "Madison, DON'T you go there, you hear me? YOU get back here right now!"

Somoko's voice is quiet as she answers Clarice. "She's already gone, Clarice. She fell before they took the guard away."

"GET her back!"

"Zuri is trying, but she's struggling in the darkness. It's got tendrils and is pulling her in, so we might lose her, too."

Clarice looks up to Lucian. "Get her inside now! Up to her room."

Lucian nods and lifts her up, cradling her in his arms, feeling her body slump against him as he hurries inside with her, taking the stairs two at a time.

Clarice follows, opening the door for him and trailing behind as he lays her down on the bed. Clarice sits next to her and draws her into her arms. "Maddie, please fight this."

Victor's body shakes, a pained expression on his face as tears slip from his eyes. He takes Madison's other hand in his as he sits opposite his wife, rubbing the top of it in small circles. "Gawd, I should have never allowed you to come back, Maddie."

D'andre collects the chain and heads into the pack house, bounding up the stairs to Lucian and Madison's room with the King and Queen following. "We'll keep her safe. I promise. I have extra guards set up, and we will question Landon's man for the rest of the evening."

Caden growls. "I am sending Lycan guards to patrol as well. NO one is touching my granddaughter. You can expect them within the half-hour."

D'andre nods, understanding better than to refuse the King. "Understood." His eyes sweep over Madison, staring at the ceiling, a confused Lucian, and two terrified parents. "Now, what's going on?"

Clarice lifts her gaze to D'andre, her eyes filled with unshed tears. "It's difficult to explain, as I don't really understand it, but she was like this when we found her. Unresponsive. Lost in her own mind. I guess it's somehow tied to her fey-step, where she just leaves. When we retreat to allow our wolves forward, we are still there in the background, just as the wolves are when we are front and center. Her presence is gone, somewhere else."

Lucian studies Madison on the bed, her vacant eyes, the shallow breathing. "It could be fey, but I suspect it's tied to her dragon. We can leave our bodies and put them in stasis. It's what makes us excellent information gatherers, but usually we train to use that ability."

"Perhaps... The patrols notified us of a rogue in our territory. The current Alpha Gregory told us to do away with her and be done with it. He had zero tolerance for rogues. When we arrived, we could smell that she was a rogue, but she didn't have the odor of wild rogues. I figured it had something to do with a pack rejection, which is often no fault of the recipient. We took her in as part of our family. It took four months of doctors, tests, and patience before we saw a reaction from anything in her and another year before she opened up to us about what happened. Clearly, she still kept things hidden, like her mate being part of the pack rejecting her. It was near the year's end that Alpha Gregory found out we betrayed him and kept the rogue instead of killing her as commanded. He tried to kill her himself, but she proved stronger and defeated him. Because we didn't know the trigger, the doctors warned us she could slip down the slope again."

Lucian sits on the bed. "But I didn't reject her. I have been trying my best to win her over."

Clarice reaches out to caress his cheek gently. "This is not your fault, Lucian."

Victor grumbles. "NO, it's mine. I should have said no when she said we were coming back. Especially since it was Duskrunner that put her in that condition in the first place."

"Vic, it's not yours either. It's pure circumstance. Think about it. She gets numerous calls from Davis and feels dread, knowing she has to return to a pack that hates her and that she rejected. It is also one she left her mate behind in that she feels sided with them." She holds her hand up to silence Lucian. "Shh, I am stating this from her side. You return, and she finds out Davis sold her to Landon. Then you get attacked by rogues twice, learning they are actually pack members. They try to kill Lucian, and she ends up in the hospital." She faces Lucian for a moment. "Now, she is struggling with whether to accept you in her heart, which she has, because she saved you... or reject you because her mind is hanging onto the betrayal. Add that to what we learned today. Her mother is my sister, which explains why I have an overprotective bond over her, and she's a Lycan. Which I kept from her, so another betrayal in her mind. And she's a Princess of the Royal family. That alone is a shock to the system. She's not just Alpha Madison anymore in her eyes. She lost her identity today. Plus the father that raised her, is either kidnapping himself or assisting in the disappearances of all those innocents, her mother included. Her brother with his new pup, and mate, that she missed out on because she left, is in trouble, and it's all resting on her shoulders to fix it. Not including the battle with her grandfather over his beating on Victor."

"Damn, I never really looked at it that way." Lucian brushes his fingers over her cheek. "That's a lot to deal with in a few days."

Caden looks between the three sitting on the bed with his granddaughter, feeling his wife beside him. "How do we fix it?"

Clarice shakes her head, the tears freely falling now. "I don't know, Father."

Somoko whispers quietly. "Lucian marks her."

Lucian jumps off the bed in shock. "NO! I am not marking her without her consent."

"Then you will lose her. Rhydian can bring her back. The bond will be an anchor to this world, as well as the anger at being marked without consent will bring her back."

"EXACTLY! NO Somoko."

Somoko growls, the aqua in her eyes glowing as she pushes herself forward, struggling against the darkness. "Lucian, Maddie is gone, Zuri is gone. The darkness is reaching for me, and soon I will be gone. Enough with your damn morals and MARK your bloody mate, or you won't have one."

Clarice smiles, swiping away her tears. "Yes, that would work. If she has not marked you, a full moon will erase your mark, so it's a win-win."

Lucian growls. "It's not, though. It's me she's going to be pissed at! I have worked hard at winning her trust back, and this is going to throw it out the door."

Caden growls under his breath, his Lycan aura radiating off him. "You better mark my granddaughter Lucian Marzire, or I will make life HELL for the entire Frostbite Syndicate. Is that clear?"

Lucian glares at the King, struggling to resist the command. Feeling the aura strengthen against him, he bows and moves back to the bed. He looks over Madison's vacant eyes, caressing her cheek lightly before pulling her shirt away from her neck. He leans in, whispering in her ear as his fangs elongate. "Please forgive me." He closes his eyes and sinks them into the marking spot, feeling her body arch as Clarice and Victor hold her down. Removing his fangs, he watches the blood spill from the bite and murmurs a few words. He runs his fingers through it and draws a pattern as a silver dragon tattoo burns into her neck.

Madison sinks into the darkness sobbing, feeling her world spiraling out of control. She curls up against Zuri and wraps her arms around her wolf, burying her face in her fur as she struggles with everything that has happened. She lifts her head, hearing a soft whisper echoing around her in the shadows. "Lucy?" Seconds later, she feels a burning pain in her neck as fires roll through her body. She cries out as a flood of emotions overtakes her, a mix of fear, concern, and love. Zuri fades from her as the darkness recedes from her mind. "No, Zuri, come back!" She turns, feeling a new presence, and finds herself face to face with a silver dragon. "You are not Somo. Who are you, and why are you here?"

The dragon curls his tail around her, urging her closer as he lowers his head to look at her closely. "No, I am not. Rhydian at your service, my dear."

"Rhydian? How are you here?" She can feel his love emanating through her and mending her brokenness within.

"Lucian sent me. He felt it was safer than coming himself."

"Why would he... Wait just a moment..." She reaches up to her neck and rubs the tenderness there as anger floods her. "Did he bloody well mark me?"

Rhydian eyes sparkle in mischief as his body starts to fade. "You will only find out if you come back."

"Dammit, Rhydian. Get your ass back here right now and answer the question!"

"Na ah a Madison." He grins as he pulls away completely and returns to the light, his voice echoing around her. "I will see you soon... mate!"

Madison glares at where he stood, fighting the darkness as her rage grows within, one directed at both Rhydian and Lucian. Her fey magic lights up the shadows around her as she returns to the room. Her eyes flash with fire and lock on Lucian sitting next to her. She hisses softly as her fists clench at her side, oblivious to the consecutive sighs of relief that surround her. "YOU Marked me!"

Lucian nods. "I'm sorry, Maddie, I know I said…"

She swings her hand around and slaps him in the face, hissing in fury. "You said on my terms. You lied to me!"

Caden growls deeply. "Alpha Madison! CONTROL yourself. I commanded him to. Your mother and father agreed with it."

Madison shifts her gaze to the room as she pushes herself up in the bed away from Lucian, her eyes flashing dangerously on everyone else before landing on the King. "You all had NO right!"

Clarice reaches for her hand, seeing the pain Lucian was in. "Madison, honey. Listen to me. You were gone. You were dragging Zuri and Somoko away with you. We couldn't lose you again, sweetie. It was the only way."

Madison's eyes fill with tears as she turns her gaze to her Mother, feeling an overwhelming despair inside at what has happened. She crawls into her mom's arms and cries against her, her hand moving up to the mark upon her neck.

"Shhhh, it's alright; I am here." She mind-links Victor as she holds her daughter tight. *'Get everyone out.'*

Victor nods. "Right, then, let's go. Maddie needs time with her mother. Lucian, that includes you." He ushers everyone out of the room and closes the door after him. "I don't know about you, D'andre, but I could use a stiff drink right about now." He pats Lucian on the back. "It's alright, Lucian. She will forgive you."

"Let's hope so." Lucian closes his eyes, feeling her sorrow and pain, thinking perhaps Victor was right in needing a drink.

D'andre leads the group down to the games room and past the other wolves, who gawk or bow as the King and Queen pass them. He settles them all at one of the round card tables and moves to the nearby bar. He collects glasses and a variety of drinks on a tray and sets them down. "Help yourself. I don't know what you all like. My Queen, Brittany, if you want a lighter drink, I have a selection of wines and can mix drinks."

The Queen shakes her head as she reaches for the spiced vanilla rum. "Thank you, but no. I'm with the boys. I want the hard stuff."

The group sits and drinks, each of them finding a small measure of solace in the bottle from the stress of the day. All but Lucian, whose stress only grows the longer he doesn't hear from either Clarice or Madison. Food arrives and is placed before everyone, and soon, the group is eating in silence, waiting for a report.

Upstairs, Clarice holds her daughter tightly, letting her cry out her pain, feeling it radiating off her. She caresses her gently as she waits patiently for her to be ready to talk, having gone through this many times in the first year they found her. Half an hour later, Madison clutches her mother's shirt. "How could he do it, Mom?"

"Who, sweetie?"

"Lucian."

"The King ordered him, Maddie. Few can withstand his power."

"Lucy could have. I know it."

"Even if he could, Maddie, he threatened Lucian's pack."

Madison drifted in thought about her mother's words. "I don't like him anymore."

"Sweetie, Lucian loves you. You are just mad, and once you get past that, you will like him again."

"No, the King. I thought I might, but I don't."

Clarice laughs and tightens her hold. "He is.... Perhaps a bit rough around the edges, but I am certain you will accept him one day."

"No, I won't. Lucy was supposed to mark me tomorrow, after the festival. Not with everyone here."

"Was that the plan?"

Her voice was quiet. "No, he didn't know. I didn't tell him that. He said on my terms. It was supposed to be special between us only."

Clarice kisses the top of her head. "Maddie, he marked you. You still have to mark him. And how many people can say the King demanded it. Hell, he told me your father was NOT to mark me, and when he found out he had, he nearly killed him."

"How did you deal with him?"

"Life will not always be easy. Sometimes the world is going to crash down upon you, like it did today. But that's why you have mates. Someone that is made to stand beside you through thick and thin, your perfect half. Lucian sacrificed his trust in you to bring you back because you were slipping into a coma again, and we needed you here. He was the only chance of getting you back quickly. He didn't want to break that trust, but did for you. As for Caden, he decided Victor was not good enough because he wasn't a Lycan. How I dealt with it, well, we went into hiding. Until we found you. I should have told you that you were a Lycan, but you were already so fragile. I didn't want to add to that."

"I know, Mom, I am not mad at you. Really. I should have figured it out. Zuri is the same size as you, and you are a Lycan. Vic is alpha, and he is smaller than us. I just didn't want to put that together."

"And that's fine, Sweetie. You didn't have to. We love you, no matter who or what you are. Your brothers and sisters do too, and we will work through this. Although, it sounds like they intend to get more involved in our lives. I wonder if we dissolve Wildfire Crescent and pop up as a new pack if they will notice. Perhaps the Rebellious Moon pack?"

Madison giggles. "Considering we confessed it downstairs, they might look closely at new packs appearing now, especially one with that name."

"Yes, you might be right. You will forever be glamouring our asses to keep us hidden."

"Right, just use my powers, Mom. I see how it is!"

Clarice teases her gently. "Why do you think we rescued you, dear?"

Madison smiles and snuggles back into her mom's arms. "Thanks, Mom." She sits and talks with her, sorting out her emotions, asking her questions about what is happening between her and Lucian and the strange feelings inside. How Somo and Zuri both tease her about her reactions to them. She listens to her explain how the bond works and what she should expect with the first mating, feeling a blush cross her cheeks at some of the discussion. Their topic drifts to the winter festival, knowing it is something she promised Lucian, hearing that she is going to be surrounded by the King's guards. She sighs, thinking it is not entirely the romantic time she envisioned with her mate.

Clarice chuckles. "Just pretend they are not there. Trust me, you get used to it. If you want to kiss him, do it. They will look away. If they don't, blast them in the face with a snowball. Then next time they will."

Madison laughs quietly. "Let me guess, you did that."

"More often than I can count on one hand, my dear."

"I would have loved to have seen that."

"Oh you might tomorrow, Vic and I are joining you at the festival. And if they so much as look the wrong way at you, they will find out just how good of an aim I am."

"I can't wait."

"Alright, are you ready to face the crowd?"

Madison shakes her head. "No, but you can send Lucian up."

"Alright, Maddie. Remember, I am always here or a mind-link away. Talk to me. Talk to Vic. We have gone through a rough road. We know what it's like, and we don't want to see you spiral downhill again. Lucian loves you; that much is clear. Give him a chance, sweetie."

"I will, Mom."

Clarice rises and heads to the door, watching as Madison rolls over and grabs a pillow, holding it close. She steps outside, her eyes landing on the two guards at the door. "Where are the others?"

"In the games room drinking. We will have a guard from downstairs take you. We are under orders not to leave this door."

"Understood." Clarice heads downstairs, arriving at the landing where a guard steps out of the shadows and leads her to the games room. Her eyes move over the group, leftover food sitting on the table, most stirring their drinks in silence. She nods in thanks and approaches the table. "Lucian, she has asked to see you."

Lucian's gaze snaps up from his drink. "Did she say why?"

"Yes, but I am not at liberty to say, as everything we discussed was in confidence. You want information; you talk to her."

"Thank you... Night everyone." Lucian downs his drink and runs from the games room.

Victor mumbles under his breath. "That boy is already whipped."

"Now, Victor, leave Lucian alone." Clarice sits down in his now vacant seat beside her husband.

"Right, sorry, Clary. I am not interfering."

D'andre laughs. "Speaking of whipped!"

"Shut your mouth, boy."

Erica places a hand on D'andre. "D'andre, hun."

D'andre turns to his wife and sighs. "Dammit, we are all whipped."

Caden laughs for the first time since arriving. "You know what, D'andre? I think Paige and I might take you up on your offer to stay this weekend. This is going to be fun."

D'andre dares to roll his eyes. "Of course, Sire. I will have rooms prepared for you."

Lucian pauses at the door and lifts his hands to knock but hesitates. He catches the slight smiles crossing the guards' lips as they maintain their gaze on the wall across the hallway.

Rhydian chuckles in his mind. *'Chicken shit, just knock.'*

'That's right, laugh. You're not the one she's pissed at.'

'Oh, I wouldn't say that exactly. She was pretty damn feisty in the darkness. Even told me to get my sweet ass back to her.'

'She did not!'

'Well, perhaps not sweet, but she was demanding my ass to return when I left her. I was hoping she was angry enough to follow, and she did.'

Lucian rubs the side of his face. *'Yes, and who did she take it out on? My cheek still smarts from that strike.'*

'Bah, it was worth it. She came back, and now she's asked for you, so knock on the damn door already. We marked her. Now she's gotta mark us.'

Lucian sighs and knocks on the door. *'Like she's going to let that happen now.'*

Madison lifts her gaze from the pillow she is hugging, recognizing

Lucian's scent from behind the door. "Come in, Lucian." She watches as he opens the door seeing the hesitation and fear in his eyes as she pats the bed beside her. "Sit with me?"

"Are you going to kill me?"

She smiles, a tiredness laced within her voice. "No Lucy, I am not."

Lucian closes the door and moves over to sit on the bed next to her, noticing the exhaustion written in her eyes, and reaches out to take her hand in his. "I really am sorry. I didn't want it to happen that way."

She crawls over and curls up in his arms, closing her eyes as she listens to his heartbeat. "I know Lucy."

Lucian stiffens as she curls up against him before relaxing and wrapping his arms around her, tightening his hold as he kisses the top of her head. He can feel her breathing level out, his fingers lightly running through her hair. He whispers softly. "I will make it up to you... somehow. I promise."

"Lucy, I am sorry I slapped you. I didn't mean to... I was really mad and didn't understand how you could do that... I won't do it again... Ever."

Lucian places a hand under her chin, his gaze meeting hers. "Maddie, if you don't want it, you know you can clear it under a full moon. As long as you have not marked me."

The color drains from Madison's face as her hand reaches for the mark on her neck. "You don't want me to have it?"

"Gawd no, I want it there forever more, but I know you were resistant to us being marked."

She breathes a sigh of relief and slumps against him, feeling his scent surround her and soothe her. "Good, cause I am keeping it, though I am gonna give Rhydian an ass whooping when I see him next."

Lucian's shoulders shake with laughter. "He might have mentioned you threatened his sweet ass."

"He is anything but sweet, and I will teach him a lesson in the fighting rings when we return home."

Lucian's voice trembles as he realizes just what she has confessed to. "Does that mean I succeeded? That you will accept me as your mate?"

Madison yawns as the emotional exhaustion creeps through her body. "Lucy, I accepted you when I saved you from your house. Now sleep. I am tired, and you are talking too much."

Lucian smiles as a strange warmth fills him inside, feeling his dragon dancing around in delight. "Maddie. You should get into your pjs. We both should, actually."

"Right, in a minute..." Her eyes close as she drifts off to sleep. Lucian remains seated for an hour, just watching his mate sleep in his arms, the energy within buzzing that she accepted him and his mark. He wanted to run outside and tell the world that she is finally his, but doesn't dare move from her sweet embrace. He heard the soft knock on his door, answering in a quiet voice so as not to wake her. "Come in."

Clarice smiles and enters the room while Victor peeks his gaze around the door, both seeing their daughter asleep in his arms. "You are going to get uncomfortable sleeping like that, Lucian."

"I won't. I just wasn't ready to move."

"So she accepted you then?"

Lucian's eyes alight with happiness as his grin grows. "Yes, she has."

She pats his shoulder. "Welcome to the family, Lucian. Now Vic and I are going to crash. It sounds like the festival will be fun tomorrow, and I look forward to it. You can let Maddie know the King and Queen will be joining us tomorrow."

Lucian caresses Madison's face lightly. "Thank you, Clarice. I know you had something to do with her acceptance."

Clarice smiles and leaves the room, pausing at the door to glance back, knowing they will both be fine. "I don't know what you're talking about. Sweet dreams, Lucian."

Lucian adjusts Madison, hearing her mumble slightly in her sleep as she clung to him, causing a chuckle to escape him. Slipping down in the bed, he pulls a pillow over and curls up, drawing her into his arms. He kisses her forehead softly, "I love you, Maddie, I always have." Lucian closes his eyes, the scent of coconuts enveloping him as he drifts off to sleep with her.

Twelve

Boundaries Tested

M ADISON MURMURS SOFTLY, feeling a weight over her, pinning her to the bed, the soft scent of pine surrounding her as she tries to roll over. She blinks in confusion, seeing an arm wrapped tightly around her and following it up to Lucian's face. Her hand moves up to her neck as memories from yesterday and last night fill her, tracing the mark she knows is there. His mark. One that was forced upon her against her consent, yet one she wasn't willing to part with. She blushes softly, recalling that everyone watched him give her that mark, something that is supposed to only be between the two mates themselves.

Lucian wakes as he feels her move, watching her hand move up to the mark on her neck and trace it lightly, noticing the blush crossing her cheeks. His arm tightens around her as he whispers quietly into her ear. "Do I want to know where your thoughts are this early in the morning when a blush is crossing your cheeks, Maddie?"

She looks back towards him, her blush deepening as she meets his gaze, chewing softly on her lower lip. Her gaze travels down to his lips, recalling the kiss they had in the hospital as she shakes her head. "No, probably not."

Lucian shifts, bringing an arm up to caress her cheek lightly, traveling down to run his thumb over her slightly parted lips. Desire fills his eyes, knowing exactly where her thoughts were straying to through their bond, recalling just how sweet her kiss is. "I think I might. I can feel your heart rate increase, Maddie."

Madison closes her eyes, feeling the sparks from his touch fill her, working their way through her system and weakening her willpower regarding him. She inhales sharply as his thumb caresses her lips, a soft groan escaping her. "Lucy…"

He cups her face in his gently, his thumbs running lightly over her cheek. "Maddie, my love. If I start, I cannot guarantee I will stop. I have waited five years for this, and I will not rush it, and I'm pretty certain they will call us for breakfast soon."

As if on cue, there is a soft knock at the door. "Breakfast is in twenty minutes. Alpha D'andre has requested that you join him and Luna Erica."

Madison mutters under her breath about having some sort of hidden camera in the room as she rolls out of the bed in dismay.

Lucian chuckles, watching her sit up on the edge of the bed. "Well. They might, but I doubt it. Come, let's go have a shower."

"Together?"

"Why not? We have twenty minutes and seem to be in the bad habit of sleeping in our clothes."

Madison blushes deeply. "Lucy, I have never done that before."

"Madison, you see naked men all the time when you shift. How is it any different?"

She rolls her eyes and twists her hands together, feeling a heat within her at the thought of a steamy shower with Lucian. "Oh, I don't know. The fact that it's You! And involves hot steamy water pouring over us."

He arches a brow, scenting the desire on her as she shifts before him. "I will keep my hands to myself… mostly."

Madison scowls at him. "Fine, I am gonna hold you to that."

"Deal." He takes her hand and rises from the bed, leading her to the bathroom. He twists the taps on and sets the temperature. "How hot do you like it?"

Madison feels the heat creep across her cheeks again. "Fairly hot, but Somoko hates it, so I need to cool it off for her afterward."

Somoko purrs inside her. *'For him, Maddie, I would take it hot and spicy.'*

'SOMO! I don't want to hear it.'

'But I don't care. I saw Rhydian when he came to you last night. I'd do him too, in an instant.'

Zuri giggles. *'I may not be a dragon, but damn, yes, and the way his tail wrapped around her and pulled her close.'*

'Oh gawd.' Madison places her palm to her forehead. *'You two, stop already.'*

Lucian chuckles. "Let me guess, the hotter the better suddenly."

Madison shakes her head. "I would say you have no idea, but I bet Rhydian is pulling the same shit on you."

"Indeed he is, though I am certain he's a bit more crass. After all, he has referred to me as a prude several times for not pouncing on you."

Madison laughs, her eyes roaming over Lucian. "A prude? You? That's priceless. At least you only have one of them hounding you."

Lucian undresses, dropping his clothes in a pool on the floor. "You have me there. Rhydian is enough. I don't know how you deal with two of them."

"Some days, Lucy. Most of the time, I think they talk to each other and plot against me." She sheds her clothes, dropping them with Lucians. She pauses, seeing him drop his boxers, and averts her gaze, feeling her body fill with heat again.

Lucian groans. "Madison! Time's-a-ticking, get in here, or Rhy will jump you."

Madison nods and finishes undressing. Stepping into the shower with him, she feels the warmth surrounding her as the water strikes her and runs down her body. She closes her eyes as Lucian's presence and scent overwhelms her in the small shower stall. Feeling his touch at her hands, she looks down and sees the bar of soap in his. "Thanks."

He nods, watching her struggle with their proximity, feeling the same struggle himself, wanting to turn her to face him and kiss her under the water. To run his hands over her and slowly lather every part of her body. He groans, thinking perhaps this was not such a good idea.

Madison's eyes lift to his, hearing his groan, and steps closer. A smile teases her lips slightly as heat fills her cheeks. She lathers the soap and places a hand on his chest, running it gently across his skin as the bubbles wash off with the stream of water. She catches the subtle stiffening in his frame, hearing the sharp intake of his breath, even above the showers thrumming.

"Madison!" Lucian growls and grabs her hand to stop her. "You keep doing that, and my hands will start wandering the same way yours are."

Madison blushes and looks down at the bar of lavender soap. "Right, sorry, it was just...."

"I know Maddie...I know. It is taking every ounce of my willpower not to lift you up and take you right here, right now. I want it to be perfect, and that's what's stopping me, but you are making it very hard to do."

"Sorry, Lucy." Madison turns away slightly, studying the shake in her hands, not understanding what exactly has come over her, in that she wants to touch him, to caress him, and to have him do likewise. She sighs softly and works on scrubbing herself down, doing her best to avoid touching him in such a small space. Once she is certain she has soaped everywhere, she spins around to rinse off, allowing Lucian more access to the water. Her eyes travel over him, feeling the warm flush from yesterday fill her again at the sight of him with water running down him. "Oh gawd. I gotta get out, Lucy." Madison pulls the curtain aside and steps out, stopping to look at the bar of soap still in her hand. She reaches back in quickly and drops it into the dish. Snatching a towel off the rack, she runs out of the bathroom as she wraps it around her. She moves to the balcony and opens the doors, feeling the cold air from outside quell the flames within her.

Lucian groans, his eyes watching her backside as she runs from the shower, resting his forehead on the cool tile. His hands clench at his side as he resists the urge to chase her, pick her up, and drop her on the bed. He closes his eyes and focuses inward, regulating his breath, in and out, driving his desire away. After a few minutes, he picks up the soap and scrubs himself down and rinses off. He shuts the water off and steps out, drying himself and wrapping a towel around his waist. He moves out into the room, seeing her standing in the open door. "You're gonna get a chill,

Maddie; it's snowing out there."

Madison turns, her eyes traveling over him momentarily, noticing the broad shoulders tapering down to a narrow waist, stopping at the white towel around his hips. Shifting her gaze to the floor, she mentally berates herself. It's not like she hasn't seen naked men before, including some warriors more buff than he is. She smiles, recalling the she-wolves clinging to the fences around the fighting rings and swooning over them as they spar. But Lucian, he is hers, and perfect, leaner than them, but fit, with a strength that holds her tight against him yet gentle in his touch, and soft in ways she never expected him to be.

Somoko chuckles. *'But not soft there.'*

'Somo, behave!' Madison slides a glance his way and closes the door. She moves to her bags of clothes, pulling out her last set of clean clothes, wondering if she could go hide in the laundry room for a few hours.

'Hmmm, I think I am beginning to side with Rhydian about both of you being prudes!'

'We are not! We just have limited time, and he wants it perfect.'

Zuri purrs inside her. *'I think even a quickie would be puurrfect.'*

'Gawd. What's gotten into you two?' Madison turns her back and pulls her bra and undies on before dressing just as quickly in a pair of black tights and a blue T-shirt. She moves over to the hoodie and drags it on before sitting on the bed and pulling fuzzy socks on.

'Nothing yet, Maddie, but soon, and we look forward to it.'

Madison blushes deeply, covering her face with her hands and groans, mumbling under her breath. "GO away."

Lucian watches her dress, knowing he should dress as well, but finds her backside most enduring, especially in the neon pink panties with black writing sprawled across them. *'When in doubt, Vodka.'* As soon as her tights are on, he moves to pull on some casual khaki pants with a black Henley. He leans on the couch and pulls black socks on before slipping his feet into some runners. He grabs the matching blazer, her scent still lingering on it from yesterday, and pulls it on, turning at her muttering.

"Maddie, is everything alright?"

She lifts her gaze and shakes her head, knowing somehow she needed to shift her mindset, but they were not helping. "Just Somo and Zuri." She rises and pauses at her damaged cloak draped over a chair, fingering it gently as she studies the damage, knowing it was beyond repair. "I guess my cloak is toast."

"It is." He watches her carefully, sensing the unsettled feelings within her. "We can always see if they have a seamstress here."

"I suppose, but I am pretty certain we won't be here long enough. Especially if we are returning to Duskrunner on Tuesday."

"Well, you are. Apparently, I am staying."

She rolls her eyes at the thought of who is potentially going with her. "Not sure how I am going to pretend to like the King." She steps over to her boots and pulls them on.

He chuckles. "I don't want you liking him either. Is that bad?"

Madison giggles as she moves over to his side and loops an arm through his. "Probably. On that note, I suppose we should go down and have breakfast. At least we are not seeing him till Monday."

"Right... There was a change of plans. They are staying the weekend and joining us at the festival."

She groans softly. "Seriously."

"Afraid so."

"Damn, can we have breakfast delivered?"

"Afraid not."

Madison sighs as she follows Lucian out the door to their room, seeing two guards standing on either side. She watches Lucian close the door and loop the blue housekeeping ribbon over the handle. A frown crosses her face as she glances back at the guards falling into step behind them. "Were they there all night?"

"Yes, and below your balcony."

"WHAT! I was standing in the doorway in just a towel!"

"I know Madison, trust me. I wanted to pull you from the door instantly, but I doubt they saw anything. There is a deck in the way, after all."

Madison blushed softly. "You could have warned me."

"I did. I said it was cold outside."

"That is NOT a warning."

"What did you want? Oh, by the way, Maddie. Two of the King's guards are standing beneath you, that may, or may not, be able to see up your towel? That would definitely cause them to look up. I think not."

Madison sighs. "Right, I didn't think..."

Lucian stops and turns her to face him. "Maddie, you didn't know. I did, hence the gentle warning. Now, I think we are definitely late for breakfast."

Madison looks up into his eyes. She reaches out to touch his cheek gently. "Thank you, Lucian. For being patient and staying true and just everything."

Lucian envelopes her into his arms and holds her tight. "I love you, Maddie. I have since the day you stepped into my classroom."

She sighs against him. "I thought you were the cutest guy there, but you were my teacher and way off limits."

Lucian chuckles. "Good thing I am not your professor anymore."

"Yes, it is! Come, I want to go to the festival! It's been years."

They head down the stairs, finding more guards at the bottom, standing on either side. A staff member rushes out and leads them to the dining hall. She opens the door for them and steps aside. Madison's eyes sweep over the room, talking in the group sitting there chatting amongst themselves, with coffee or tea already in most of their hands. Madison's eyes land on her parents first, before shifting to D'andre and Luna. "Sorry we are late, Alpha, Luna."

D'andre smiles, his gaze running over them, reading the happiness in Madison's eyes and seeing her arm looped through Lucian's willingly. "Just D'andre, and it's quite alright. We were taking bets on whether Lucian would survive the night or whether his body would go out the front door in a body bag."

A blush stains Madison's cheeks at their teasing. "If I was to kill him, D'andre, you would need to replace the glass doors on the balcony, as his body would have gone sailing through them."

D'andre laughs. "True. I saw how well the King flew across the meeting room. It would have been a frosty night for you if you had."

Caden chokes on his coffee, fighting the laughter bubbling up within as Paige pats him on the back. "Damn. I guess those rumors are true about how ruthless you are."

"Oh no, I would have invaded my parents' room." Her eyes drift to the King, her voice cooling slightly. "I earned that title, Sire. It's not a rumor."

Clarice lifts her gaze to her daughter. "Not a chance, sweetie. You made your bed; you would have had to live with it."

"MOM! ... Dad?"

Victor shakes his head. "Not going against your mother, Maddie. You know that."

"Fine... So, who won the bet, and what was it worth?"

Victor sighs, rolling his eyes. "Your mother and five hundred dollars."

Madison's eyes light up as she moves over and kisses her mom's cheek. "I need a new cloak!"

"Buy your own sweetie. This is my spending money."

Madison sighs and plops down in the seat next to her, pretending to pout. "You don't love me anymore."

Clarice pats her hand gently. "Of course I do, just not enough to buy you a cloak. Get your mate to do it."

Madison laughs. "He's already offered."

Lucian arches a brow. "I did?"

She giggles as he sits next to her. "You did."

Luna Erica smiles. "If you want a new cloak, Madison, I can have a seamstress make you one. It would take a few days."

"It's alright, Luna. Lucian will have one made when we return to Wildfire. Thank you, though. I am looking forward to your festival."

Lucian mutters under his breath. "Considering you were just discussing my death, I don't think I should buy you a cloak, my dear."

"Thank you. It might not be as grand of a scale as Duskrunners since D'andre only gave me a few days to make it happen."

"I am sure I will love it." Madison turns and takes Lucian's hand in hers, caressing it gently. "Hey! I wasn't the one placing bets on my killing you. They did."

He chuckles, squeezing her hand gently. "True. I have to say, I am glad you didn't."

Caden observes the pair, knowing he forced a mark on his granddaughter, grateful that she isn't taking it out on Lucian too much. At the very least, she should blame him, and judging by the way her tone cooled as she addressed him, she did. That being said, he pounded on her father, which put them on a grim note to begin with. Caden turns his gaze to Victor, the one who stole his daughter away. Correction, the one mated to his daughter, that he himself drove away. Something he was reminded of last night by his wife and the hours of lectures she gave him over his actions. He sighs inwardly, grateful Victor's wolf healed him and removed the bruising, unlike his, who refused to after the way he treated the pair. He shifts uncomfortably, feeling the bites on his backside still smarting. Not that he would ever admit to that to any in this room. His granddaughter clearly had power behind her, for he couldn't recall anyone ever coming close to defeating him as she did. He knew if Clarice had not stepped in, if she had been even a minute later, he very well might not be standing here. Caden found himself hoping that one day, she will accept him enough to train together in the warrior's ring and discover just how formidable she is. His gaze drifts back to Lucian, reading the same love in his eyes for Madison as Victor has for Clarice. Hearing his wife's mind-link within his thoughts, he lifts his gaze to her.

'Caden, honey. Perhaps a little less concentration in your gaze. It might give the wrong impression of glowering at Victor and Madison with the way you are staring them down.'

'I am just thinking.'

'I know you are. I recognize the look, but they don't, and Madison is already warily watching you. D'andre might love it, but I don't care to see you have flying lessons again.'

'Just be grateful no one had their cells on and were recording. I would definitely need to place a ban on that video. Don't need the Kingdom knowing my granddaughter trounced me.'

'Well, she is the Ruthless Alpha Madison Martinez and currently runs the elite Ironwood Pack. It explains how her pack grew at an alarming rate.'

Caden laughs, causing those in the room who were already not watching him to turn and look in his direction. He shakes his head, meeting Victor's gaze, before they return to Madison and her airs of indifference towards him. "Sorry. Apparently, my wife seems to think I am glowering at the pair of you, when really I am not. I was, in fact, lost in thought. She informed me she doesn't want to see me flying across the room at the same time I was thinking, or rather hoping, that Alpha Madison would accept me enough to hit the training rings with me one day."

D'andre chuckles. "I would love to be there for that one, Sire."

He scowls good-naturedly. "Of course you would. At least this time, I will be prepared for what I am facing." He turns back to Madison. "You kept your abilities well hidden, my dear. I just assumed you were a pure wolf, like all the other Alpha's out there."

Madison offers a half-smile his way. "Clary taught me that a skilled tactician keeps some strategies in the shadows, revealing only what is necessary, reserving the full arsenal for the perfect moment. That and hybrids are not always welcome."

"And did I see the full arsenal?"

"No, Sire, you did not, but I will admit, you came close, and certainly more than others have."

"Good to know. So, Alpha Madison, do you think it's possible?"

Madison's hand tightens slightly on Lucian's, studying him carefully before her eyes find her father's. "Only if you apologize to Victor for beating on him."

Victor shakes his head, warning laced in his eyes and voice not to go there. "Maddie..."

"No, Vic. If he wants to accept me, then he has to accept you. That's the way it is. And part of that means he needs to apologize for how he treated you. No apology, no acceptance. It's as simple as that."

Caden chuckles, nodding her way. "Deal. You are indeed ruthless." He turns to Victor. "I apologize for how I treated you and should not have let my rage get the better of me or attack you the way I did. In the future, I will attempt to control my temper better so that it does not happen again. I also accept that you are the chosen mate of my daughter, Clarice, and are now part of our family."

Victor's eyes drift to his wife's, seeing her smile. "Thank you. I am certain that will make Clary very happy."

Madison smiles, resting her head upon Lucian's shoulder, feeling his arm wrap around her. "Now my mom."

"Damn, girl. You know I am the King, right?"

"Yes, and you are not above apologizing."

He growls under his breath, but the humor dancing in his eyes gives him away. "Clarice, my daughter. I am sorry for the way I treated your mate. It will never happen again. You and your mate are welcome at the castle anytime you wish."

Clarice smiles at her father. "Thank you. I have wanted that for a long time now."

Madison looks between them, ensuring the apology is sincere. "Perfect. Now, I want to see the lights and trees and the vendors and the bonfire with roasted marshmallows!"

D'andre chuckles, loving her enthusiasm and grateful that his wife planned a festival, even if it was short notice. "First, breakfast. You need it if you are going to be running around in the fresh snow."

The food arrives shortly, and the eight of them sit and talk about what they may or may not see at the festival, keeping the topics light. Each understands this is their weekend off of life and what is going to happen during the upcoming week. During this time, they bond closer to each other as D'andre, Erica, Caden, and Paige learn more about the Wildfire Crescent and the family bonds between Clarice, Victor, and Madison. After breakfast, they bundle up, along with both D'andre's and the King's guards and head out into the town center.

Thirteen

The Winter Festival

MADISON BOUNDS FORWARD, aware that some of the guards follow her, but ignores them as she moves through the flickering lights beneath the snow and woven through the trees. She reaches up to touch one of the purple ones, giggling as the snow falls from the tree upon her head and shoulders. Her eyes brighten as she turns to Lucian. "I love the sparkling lights. It's the best part."

Lucian gently brushes some of the snow off her. "I remember."

"What do you mean, you remember?"

"It was the first year you were in my class. I was out about the town and saw you, staring at the lights in wonder. You were seventeen. Far too old to be fascinated by them, and yet, I found it adorable that you were. I followed behind as you bounced through the festival in wonder, bypassing the booths and the entertainment only to stop at the clusters of glittering lights beneath the snow. Almost all of them actually."

Madison blushes, averting her gaze slightly. "I didn't know anyone was watching me."

Lucian takes her hand gently in his and kisses the back of it lightly. "I don't think you needed to know that your old professor was watching you."

"You're not old, Lucian."

"Older than you, Maddie, and old enough to be your teacher."

Victor growls protectively. "Just how old are we talking, Lucian?"

"DAD!"

Clarice moves forward and pats Victor's shoulder. "It doesn't matter,

Victor, they are mates, and you leave them be." She takes Madison's other hand. "Come, sweetie, let's go shopping. I want to see the market. The boys can go to the beer gardens."

Madison giggles, giving a nod, her gaze lingering on Lucian for a moment before following Clarice to the market with Paige and Erica. Half the guards follow the ladies, while the others remain with Lucian, knowing that Duskrunner also wanted him. Madison strolls through the market slowly as a few hours pass, looking at all the wares in wonder. Her eyes land on a white crocheted dragon. She picks it up and turns it over, falling in love with it instantly. Her fingers caress its horns lightly, feeling the soft wool beneath her fingers.

"What did you find, Maddie?"

She turns, holding the white dragon out to her mother. "Rhydian."

She laughs softly. "Is he as adorable as that one is?"

"Not even close. He and I are going to have words when we meet, but it still reminds me of him. I'm gonna buy it and give it to Lucy."

"I am certain he will love it."

She nods and pulls out her wallet. She pays for the dragon and accepts the bag to drop him in. "Thank you." She twists the handles around her wrist, happiness dancing in her eyes as she faces Luna Erica. "I love your festival, Luna. It's amazing. Thank you for this."

"Just Erica, Madison. And I am glad that you do. Come, we should find the boys and hit a food stand. I am certain they are probably enjoying their drinks far too much. After lunch, we can enjoy some of the theater shows, and later, there is a bonfire with some music. I am afraid it's a local band, but they cover a lot of the pop songs you youngsters listen to."

"I will listen to pretty much everything. Is there dancing?"

"Yes, there will be dancing."

Clarice nudges her. "Are you looking forward to dancing with your mate?"

Madison fidgets with the bag around her wrist. "I have never danced with him. It will be something new."

Erica and Paige glance at each other. "Never?"

Madison shakes her head. "No, he was my professor when I was in school. Very much off-limits. Then, when I found out he was my mate, Alpha Davis banished me for being a hybrid."

"Well, they were wrong about that, and Caden will rectify that with you on Tuesday."

"I know. I just want to enjoy the day, have fun, and not think about it."

Paige turns her gaze to the left, seeing the group heading their way, a few of the frolickers clearing a path for the King and his men. "And that we can do. Look, it seems they have come looking for us. Lucian appears to have only eyes for you, Madison."

Her hand tightens on her bag as her gaze snaps to his, feeling the draw within it. She reaches up to touch the mark at her neck that feels like it is calling to him. She catches the hesitancy within him as he pauses in front of her and takes his hand in hers, feeling the sparks at their touch. After glancing down momentarily, she lifts her gaze, finding his eyes once again and swiftly becom lost in their blue depths as she whispers quietly. "Are you hungry, Lucian?"

"Always."

Paige chuckles, nudging her husband as she watches the interactions between the pair. She can feel the bond emanating from them and realizes they have clearly forgotten about the rest of them. She smiles at Victor's protective scowl, showing that while they didn't give birth to Madison, they obviously love her deeply. Grateful that Madison at least found some peace with her banishment in the arms of her daughter, Clarice. A daughter her own husband had all but banished. Paige shakes her head, not wanting to go down the path of resentment, knowing she will do her best to make up for lost time. Especially as Madison is the firstborn of their firstborn, and therefore, in line for the throne. She has proven she can handle it with the way she has grown and managed the Wildfire Crescent pack. Her eyes drift to Clarice, wondering if she figured that out when they found out she was Faeloria's daughter. She steps forward. "Alright, you two, let's find a food stand and find a place to sit and eat."

Madison blushes, realizing she is staring, and nods, her hand tightening on the bag at her wrist. She follows the others, keeping her eyes down except for the occasional glances to Lucian. Each time, she finds him watching her, bringing heat to her cheeks, wondering at his thoughts.

'You can always ask me, Maddie.'

'Are you reading my mind, Lucy?'

'No, it's written all over the quizzical expression on your face, with the light blushes appearing here and there.'

'I don't want to know... Well, not right now, at least.'

He tightens his hand on hers. *'But later... Yes?'*

Her blush deepens as she mumbles under her breath. "We should keep up."

'Alright, Maddie, you can escape me now, but you will not escape me tonight.'

'We will be at the bonfire tonight.'

'After that, Maddie, when we are alone in our room.'

She places her hands to her face, feeling the heat rising within at the thought of being alone with him. "Oh gawd. It was so much easier when I hated you."

Lucian turns her to face him and pulls her into his arms, resting his head against hers. "I never hated you, Madison. Just hurt and angry that you fled, but I understand why." He kisses her cheek lightly, whispering softly. "And I don't think you hated me either, or you would have rejected me when you rejected your family and your pack."

She snuggles into his arms, a subtle shake within her. "I thought I did."

"I know, and I respect that you did. Come, the others are ordering food."

Madison glances around, realizing suddenly it is just them and the guards. She scans the fair, seeing her parents in a lineup at the food booth. She moves up with him to catch up to the others, stepping in behind at the end. Victor grumbles under his breath about the smooching and finally catching up, which earns him a sharp elbow to the rib cage. Madison giggles. "Thank Mom."

"Anytime, dear. Your father has forgotten what it was like when we first met."

"I have not."

"Really? It seems like it with the way you are grumbling about them being together, only to contradict yourself in that they are not moving fast enough. Make up your mind, Victor."

Victor huffs slightly. "I just don't want his hands wandering over something that is not his yet."

Clarice rolls her eyes at her husband. "But she is. If you go by that logic, Vic, then Madison needs to keep her hands to herself."

Victor turns to scowl at his wife a moment, hearing D'andre's chuckle behind him.

"Oooh, this is where I get to play devil's advocate... Madison, let your hands wander all you want!"

Victor growls at D'andre. "Just you wait till your pups are old enough, D'andre."

A deep blush crosses Madison's cheeks, her eyes catching Lucian's out of the corner of her eyes before landing on D'andre. "I think you are just a shit disturber, D'andre."

"Damn rights I am, and you, my dear, cannot back out of the treaty you agreed to."

She laughs, winking his way. "Ah, but we haven't agreed to the terms of the treaty. I will definitely add a clause to some effect regarding your antics and the consequences of it."

"I look forward to what you might come up with, Madison. I dare say, with your skill at computers, I might need to get a hundred lawyers to look it over for any loopholes in your favor and add some in my favor."

"You think a hundred is going to be enough, D'andre?"

"Damn! Is it wrong to say I'm glad you came to my pack and that I can hold the *you have to be nice cause you owe me*, over your head."

She shakes her head, a devilish smile playing on her lips. "Not at all,

D'andre. You need to use what you have, and I will take that into account."

"Why does that sound so ominous?"

Madison arches a brow and gives him her best innocent expression. "Oh, I don't know, D'andre. Perhaps because you are entering into a contract with the Ruthless Madison Martinez of both the Wildfire Crescent and Ironwood Moon pack."

"Damn girl, you are good. Come on, I see a table free over by the heaters. Let's grab it for the others and discuss terms."

Lucian chuckles at their conversation. "I will order you a burger and a coke, Maddie. Anything else."

She shakes her head. "No, that's good, Thanks Lucian." She bounds over to the table, placing her bag off to the side, and settles in, bantering with D'andre about the contract she is going to draw up.

Lucian's gaze follows her, watching her relaxed appearance, the happiness dancing in her eyes as she laughs with D'andre. Erica moves over and loops her arms through Lucian's, teasing him lightly as she guides him forward. "Lucian, dear, I would like a husband to sleep with tonight. Now stop shooting daggers his way. It's clear Madison only has eyes for you."

Lucian looks down at Erica and sighs. "Sorry. It's hard because she was gone for so long. It feels like a fight to get her to laugh that way with me."

"Lucian... She has a nickname for you. You two have gone through a lot of stress in just a few days. D'andre is safe for her. He's not stress. He's simply a friend that has helped her. You are an emotional tie and past pain. From what we understand, one she's still sorting out. I guarantee, once this is over, the two of you will be just like my husband and her, but with a mate bond connection."

"I know, but patience does not come easy to me."

Erica chuckles. "Well, that's what I am here for. I have plenty for both of us. Now, let's order food and get over to them." She turns to the others and leads Lucian past them. "Sorry, one hangry mate here. We need to order food so he can get back to her."

The rest chuckle, moving Lucian and Erica to the front of their pack as they order food before the others. They stand to the side, talking with the King, Queen, Clarice, and Victor. Once their lunch is ready, they each grab the trays and wander over to the table. Erica moves to D'andre's side as Lucian settles beside Madison. He pulls her plate off and sets it before her, along with her soda.

Madison smiles up at Lucian as he sits next to her. "Thank you, Luc...ian."

D'andre chuckles at her near slip, wondering if she realized she called him that yesterday in the meeting. "Still can't get over the fact that you call him a girl's name, and he accepts it."

"How do you know about that?"

"Cause you asked for Lucy in the hospital room and called him that yesterday in the meeting. Not that I think anyone really caught it with everything else that was going on. He explained how you tricked him into dressing up in drag and that everyone else called him Professor Ethel."

Madison blushes softly, looking down at her food, and mutters softly. "Well, Lucy seemed to fit him better."

Lucian reaches out to take her hand. "And I explained to D'andre, who is teasing you, that I love my nickname and only you call me that, so it's special. I don't care who knows it, Maddie."

Madison looks up to him cautiously, her fingers fidgeting with the tray her burger sat on. "Are you certain?"

"I am. Now, eat your food before it freezes."

"Thank you, Lucy." Madison laughs and digs into her burger.

D'andre sighs. "Ah... Young love."

Erica nudges him gently. "Leave them alone, D'andre, and eat your lunch."

The rest settle at the table as they receive their food, eating in silence and enjoying the winter day from beneath a tent with propane heaters around them. They can hear the chatter of others at the festival, the laughter of children as they run through the winter wonderland, followed by their parents. Madison watches the people moving around, lingering on the sparkling lights as they flicker beneath the snow, going back in her memory, trying to recall Lucian following her the last time she was at a festival. She shivers slightly and glances around, feeling suddenly like someone is watching them. Lucian feels the shift in her, reaching his thoughts to her. *'Is everything alright, Maddie?'*

She continues to scan the fair, drifting to the woods nearby, suspecting that whoever is watching is lurking in there. *'No, I feel as if someone is watching us.'*

'Well, we have the Lycan King and Queen at our table.'

'No, they are watching us. Not them.'

Lucian places an arm over her shoulder and pulls her close. He kisses her cheek gently. *'We stay in the group and don't separate. I doubt whoever it is will try anything at a festival of people.'*

'They took a dragon away in a park full of people, Lucy.'

He growls softly, drawing the attention of the others. *'They are NOT getting you.'*

Caden looks over at the pair, seeing the protective arm around Madison with her gaze focused elsewhere. He follows it to the woods, seeing nothing in the darkness. "Is everything alright?"

"No. Maddie feels like someone is watching us."

Madison sighs, leaning her head on Lucian, her eyes drifting from the woods to the King. "It's fine, Lucian is right. They are probably looking at you, Sire. We stay in the middle of the group and enjoy the festival."

D'andre frowns and mind-links his pack warriors. *'I want a team of eight to scour the south woods right now. Circle around and catch them in a web if you have to.'* He smiles at Madison. "We will not let them get you, Madison. I just sent a team of my best warriors into the woods. If someone is there, they will catch them."

"Thank you, D'andre."

Deep in the woods, a few wolves watch from within the shadows, following them throughout the day and gleaning information as they all meet up again for lunch. They back up a step, further into the shadows, when their target's eyes seem to lock onto their location in the woods. Being too far away to mind-link, one of them pulls out a cell phone and texts Landon.

♦We need the witch to bring us back.♦

♦I Think the Luna saw us but I am not certain now.♦

Landon reads the text and growls under his breath, not wanting his men to take their eyes off their target. He texts back.

♦Issac and Caleb will remain to watch. Garrick, you will return with a report.♦

♦Understood.♦

Garrick turns to the others. "You are to remain and watch."

Landon turns to his witch. "Vespera, bring Garrick back."

"As you wish, Alpha." She chants a few words and summons the Gamma back to the room.

Garrick gives a nod to Vespera. "Thanks." He turns to his Alpha. "Landon... We have some problems. We were at the festival, trying to steal our Luna away, but the Lycan King and Queen are in Silvermoon. Both his and D'andre's guards are protecting our targets and patrolling the pack house they are staying in. Noah has not checked in since yesterday. It's possible they have detained or captured him. Our inside man, Alaric, is looking into it and where he might be, but it seems many of them are close-lipped about what's happening in the pack house."

Landon's fists clench at the fact that the King is in Silvermoon. He didn't recall reading that he is doing a pack tour, which means that Alpha D'andre called him. He growls, knowing it is an inconvenience for sure, but they could work around it with magic. They have before and could again. "What the hell are they doing there?"

"I don't know Alpha, but they are certainly protective of our Luna. Also, there is one more thing."

"What?"

"The Luna's servant Victor. The one with the Alpha wolf."

"Yes.. what about him?"

"He is married to one of the King and Queen's children. A daughter who looks a lot like Luna Megan, as a matter of fact, when Vespera removed her glamor."

"WHAT!"

"Here, I took a video. Give me a minute." He scrolls through his phone to the pictures and brings the video up, handing the phone over to Landon.

Landon watches the video of the group eating lunch together, frowning at the resemblance he can see in the Queen, her daughter, and Megan. His anger grows at seeing Madison looking up at the Professor and leaning against him when he drapes his arm around her. A Professor that should have died in the explosion. Landon smashes the desk with his fist, sweeping the lamp and trays off in his rage, hearing them crash to the ground. Anger that he didn't see Megan for who she was before he shipped her off to the witches. Instead, he should have forced a mate bond on her when he took her from Davis. He could have had a royal under his control. But then, no one knew who she was. Davis had said she was from the Howling Oak pack, so how is it possible that she's related to the King and Queen? If only he had only seen that Megan's daughter had the same fey magic, he could have stolen her before his puppet Davis banished her. Idiot, kicking that power out of his pack because of some tramp who couldn't keep her mouth shut. But now, she has shown her power, and it is one he aims to control in both her and their offspring. He glares at the phone and hands it back to his Gamma. "This is NOT going as I planned. Go back and watch for an opening. Even if I just get her. Once she's marked, she's mine."

"What if she's already marked? They seemed pretty close?"

"Then we shoot to kill him. Set one of Davis's men to take the fall."

"Understood."

"Vespera, send him back. You and I are going to pay a visit to Davis. I want to know how he managed to be mated to a royal and kept it from me. Also, how she ended up in the Howling Oak pack and not in Whispering Pines where the Royals live."

Vespera nods, creating a portal back to the woods where she took him, waiting until he steps through to close it and reopen one to the bookstore's basement. Landon steps through into the darkness, followed by her, as she closes it behind her. "Did you want me to wait here, Alpha?"

"No, today you come with me. I will use magic if needed to get that information out of him."

"What if he doesn't know? He didn't know she had a glamor spell on her."

"Then we find out what he does. We also put pressure on the brother because he would have Royal blood as well. In fact, he will definitely be of use to us now."

Back at the winter festival, the group finishes their meals, placing their plates and trays on the racks to be cleaned, and head off to the afternoon performances. The six of them keep Madison and Lucian between them at all times, with the guards forming a box around all of them. Everyone of them on edge and wary about her being stolen. Especially after D'andre receives a mind-link from his warriors, that indeed, there are tracks in the snow, both wolves and boots, at the location he directed them to. D'andre glances at Madison, hand in hand with Lucian, not wanting to concern her in any way that her feelings were correct. *'How many?'*

'Looks like three, Alpha.'

'Take a team of twelve and see if you can catch them. They might have magic at their disposal, so be careful. Also, I want you back at the pack house before dusk, so time it accordingly.'

'Understood.'

'Report when you return. We will probably be at the bonfire.'

Erica leads the group to a large tent covering a stage. Propane heaters sit between the benches as they settle in to watch the show. Madison sits next to Lucian, with Clarice on the left side of her, and Victor directly behind her with D'andre right beside him. Two guards slide in and sit on either side of them while the rest of them space out around the outside edges, their eyes trained on any that approach the group of eight. Erica and Paige sit to the right of Lucian, with Caden right next to them.

Fourteen

Frosty Showdowns

M ADISON SHIFTS CLOSER to Lucian as she sits, placing her hand in his as she draws her bag into her lap. She watches the theater in delight, forgetting all about the guards that protectively surround her. She giggles and laughs at their antics on stage, loving the outfits and the storyline they told. After an hour, there is a fifteen-minute break in which Victor and D'andre run back to the food vendors to bring back teas, coffees, and hot cocoa for the group. They remain there for another three shows before calling it and heading back to get dinner before the bonfire. Madison skips alongside Lucian, her hand holding his tightly, as she pauses every so often at the shiny lights. Enamored by the twinkling beneath the snow.

Lucian smiles at her delight, pausing every time she stops to look at the lights, feeling amazement at how she finds wonder in such a simple thing. Most walk past them, ignoring the dancing lights beneath the snow, looking instead to the vendors and that which money could buy. He knows her pack is one of the wealthiest out there, after Frostbite, of course, but money seemed to be a means to an end for her. Even on their shopping trip, the clothes she chose were for comfort, and yet, her aura screamed of power, wealth, and status. Enough so that no one questioned her wearing a forty-dollar hoodie rather than a three-hundred-dollar one. He squeezes her hand gently, drawing her aquamarine eyes his way, feeling the warmth of her smile filling him. It was a smile he missed every hour of every day that she was gone, and he made a mental vow never to lose her again.

"Lucy?"

Lucian pulls her close, drawing her in for a quick hug. "It's nothing, Maddie. I was just lost in thought."

Madison smiles, rising on her toes to kiss his cheek lightly. "That's allowed. Just don't get too lost. It might get you marked."

He arches a brow, a devilish grin gracing his lips. "Is that a promise?"

Madison blushes and looks away, feeling the sudden wash of heat and uncertainty within her at his gaze.

Lucian reaches out and places a hand beneath her chin, guiding her eyes back towards his. He studies her aquamarine gaze, the surrounding lights that dance off them, the pink spreading across her cheeks. His voice is quiet, meant only for her. "You didn't answer my question, Maddie."

She reaches up to her neck, her lips parting slightly as she whispers. "Lucy...I."

Lucian cups her face in his hands and leans in, kissing her gently. He groans at her soft sigh of delight, feeling her body responding to his touch, finding himself wanting the day to be over so he can take her up to their room. He pulls away, catching the yelp behind him, his eyes shifting to the spectators and one guard with a face full of snow. His brow furrows in confusion at the guard, only to see another snowball sail through the air at another guard, hitting him square in the face. He shifts his gaze to Clarice, a frown upon her face, with a third snowball in her hand. "Anyone else that stares will join the two guards in white-washed faces."

Madison blushes deeply at the people who had stopped to watch Lucian and her, not missing Victor's scowl as she buried her face into Lucian's chest.

Lucian chuckles at the expressions of both the guards as they wipe the snow off their faces, keeping their gaze averted from the pair. "I understand completely why you are a force to be reckoned with, Clarice."

She turns her gaze to Lucian. "I warned my daughter that if any of the guards stared at her kissing you, they would eat snow. And so they are."

Caden burst out in laughter, gathering a snowball and throwing it at his daughter. "Clarice, you have not changed at all."

Clarice gasps in shock, feeling the snow strike her shoulder, and turns to face her father. She throws the one in her hand at him, face-planting him with her accuracy. "Of course not."

Paige lifts her hands and backs up next to Erica. "Just so you know, Caden honey, you are on your own. I will just spectate with Luna Erica here."

Lucian squeezes Madison before pulling her away, kissing her cheek lightly. "Clarice is defending you, Maddie. You may want to step in and help her."

Madison's eyes travel to Clarice, watching Caden toss a second snowball her way, breaking apart in her hand as her mom reaches out to catch it.

"You never could throw snowballs, Father." Clarice chuckles as she quickly gathers another two, tossing one back at her father, striking him solidly in the chest despite his trying to dodge it.

Caden growls in humor and grabs another snowball, turning to toss it at her, only to have her duck. It sails past her and strikes D'andre square in the face.

D'andre wipes the snow off his face and arches a brow at the pair. "Oh, I see how this is gonna go."

Madison giggles at the sight, only to have her mother's second snowball strike her. She looks down at her hoodie in shock. "Mom?"

"Stop laughing, Maddie, and start attacking, or I will think you are on the King's side."

Madison could feel the humor rising in Lucian and grabbed the snow that still clung to her, throwing it at his face. "You're laughing at me!"

Lucian puts his hands up. "You can't prove that, Maddie."

Madison reaches down and collects a couple of snowballs, only to see Lucian running to hide behind Victor. She tosses one his way, hitting him in the back as her second goes toward the King, sailing wide of him and ending up striking a guard's arm.

Within a few minutes, the entire festival was in a giant snowball fight, with the guards doing their best to keep watch on those they needed to.

Twenty minutes later and soaked through from the snow, they make their way back to the pack house to change and have dinner. Upstairs, Madison drops her bag on the table and moves to the stacks of folded clothes on their bed. "Yes! Laundry day." She grabs a pair of jeans, one of Lucian's Henley's, and runs to the bathroom to change.

Lucian arches a brow, seeing her grab one of his shirts, his gaze following her backside to the bathroom. He smiles as he strips out of his wet clothes and pulls on dry ones quickly. Picking up the damp ones, he drapes them over the chair to dry out before moving to plug his phone in to charge while they eat. He growls softly in delight at seeing her in his shirt, one corner tucked into her jeans. "Gawd, that's even better than a hoodie and tights, Maddie. Raid my wardrobe any day."

She blushes softly, pulling at the shirt nervously. "They always looked comfortable."

Lucian moves to her side, caressing her cheek lightly before dipping down and kissing her softly. "They are. I prefer them over button-down shirts and beneath a blazer, you can't really tell."

Madison closes her eyes, feeling her head spin at his kiss, wrapping her fingers in his shirt. Her voice was soft. "I could."

Lucian draws her into his arms. "I suspect not much missed your gaze, my dear Madison. After all, I was a drag queen for Halloween because of it."

Madison laughs softly. "I don't know what you are talking about."

Lucian smiles, caressing her cheek lightly. "I saw you on those computers, my love. It's very clear, having seen you actually at work, why you were my best student. I can only say I am glad it was only a drag queen outfit and not something more drastic."

"I don't know Lucy. You looked pretty fine as Ethel Alcohol. I still have the pictures saved to my favorites on my phone."

"Please tell me you are joking about that?"

"Nope, and don't even think about deleting them. One of them is my screen saver on my desktop at home."

Lucian groans and mutters beneath his breath. "So Victor has seen it?"

Madison giggles, kissing his cheek lightly. "You will have to ask him. Come, let's go get dinner. I am starving. And I want to roast marshmallows at the bonfire. I love them." She leads him downstairs to the dining chamber, her gaze moving to the table, a nice shiny coat of resin overtop of it. She runs her fingers along it, catching D'andre's chuckle, and lifts her gaze to his. "That was quick, D'andre."

"Yes. My only regret is that it isn't signed."

"Perhaps we can remedy that." Madison moves over to stand beside D'andre, her eyes slitting to dragons as she allows Somoko forward. Aqua lights filter around her fingertips as one finger elongates to a claw. She draws on the table, burning past the resin, deep into the wood beneath it. 'Somoko was here.' Somoko recedes, allowing Madison back, who gazes at the words on the table and laughs. "Oh, Somo, you better hope no one with magic walks in here."

D'andre looks down at the words with a mixture of delight and confusion. "Am I missing something?"

Madison waves her hand over the words, magic filtering into the words for a few moments, allowing D'andre to see the true words written there. 'Somoko was here and would have defeated King Caden if Clary had not stepped in.'

D'andre laughs out loud, running his fingers over words as they fade. "Damn, too bad they can't stay."

Madison smiles and pats his shoulder gently. "Find a faerie stone."

"A what?"

"A natural stone with a hole through the center. Look through it, and it will show what is beyond the fey magics."

"Where do I get one of those?"

"Usually along a river's edge, but some of the metaphysical shops have them. They may or may not work, especially if it's manufactured. You need a natural one."

"Right, I am adding it to my shopping list."

Madison smiles and moves to sit down near Lucian. "If I find one in my travels, I will send it here."

The rest filter in as the group enjoys a dinner of stew and fresh baked bread. A peaceful calm settles around the table as they laugh and banter with each other, realizing that in a matter of days, a bond of sorts has formed between them. At the end of dinner, D'andre receives a mind-link from his warriors.

'Alpha, we caught two. We suspect one teleported or portaled away as his tracks just stopped in the snow.'

'Right, bring them in. We are just finishing dinner.'

'Already there, Alpha. As we didn't know exactly how the third left, we thought it best not to linger. We are about ten minutes away.'

'Right, I will meet you out there.' D'andre looks over at Madison. "It appears you were right, Madison. There were three in the woods. My guards caught two of them, but it looks like one just disappeared. His tracks end, so probably a portal of some sort. Would you like to question them before the bonfire or in the morning?"

"Before, please."

"Wise plan. Apparently, they are ten minutes away. Once they are secure downstairs, we will pay them a visit."

Madison nods and grows thoughtful. She suspects they are Landon's men because, so far, every one of them has been. It makes her wonder what his hold on Davis is, because clearly there is one. And it isn't the six hundred grand. She is pretty certain that it is just part of the ruse in saying that he bid her away with that debt. She sighs inwardly, not understanding Landon's sudden obsession with her. She vaguely recalled seeing him at the pack house growing up, but why now? Why have his sights set on her, after she left? Is it because of her rise to power? Not that he could have known she was Madison Martinez. And it's not like she's the only Madison in the world. Unless somehow they saw a picture of her on the internet. It would have to be Landon, as she doubted Davis would even look for her. He was extremely clear the day he rejected her as a daughter and banished her from the pack. Though Landon did seem surprised when she introduced herself as Wildfire's Alpha. She feels a nudge interrupting her thoughts, looking up to Lucian studying her carefully.

"Earth to Maddie."

"Sorry, Lucy. I was lost in thought."

"That much was clear. Anything I should know about?"

Madison shakes her head. "No, just thoughts."

Flickers of a frown mar his features before he hides it with a nod. "Later then?"

She smiles and rests her head on his shoulder. "Yes, later."

D'andre chuckles. "Well, now that Madison is back in the land of the living, let's go downstairs and have a chat with some spies, shall we?"

"That sounds great."

The group of them rise as D'andre leads them out of the pack house. He walks beside the King, chatting as they travel through the guards' barracks, catching those around bowing to the King as they pass. He gives a nod to them and stops at the dungeon doors, waiting as the guards unlock them and let them in. Down into the darkness they descend, with dim lights lining the walls. It levels out below surface level, as medieval style cells line either side of the passage. Some with cots, others with chains; most of them empty. Guards wait near the end of the hall, bowing to the group. "Alpha, these are the two we caught. As stated, a third is still out there. We will return in the morning to see if we can scent them out."

"Agreed. I do not want any out there after dark. Too many rogues running free." He turns to the two in the cell and looks them over carefully. "Did they have the necklaces?"

"No, Alpha, they did not."

D'andre turns to the King and Madison. "Do you recognize them?"

Madison shakes her head. "No, but they bear Landon's darkness like the other one did."

Caden steps forward, letting his aura roll off him, watching as they bow in submission. "Who are you, and what do you want?"

"Caleb."

"Issac."

"What pack?"

They answer in unison. "Nightshade Howlers."

Caden growls, causing them to drop to the ground and quiver at his power as D'andre's guards all drop to their knees. Madison struggles against the aura, knowing that he intended it to be only the prisoners. "Caden. Perhaps I should question them."

Caden's eyes flash as he turns to Madison. "I am the King!"

"Yes, and you are making everyone bow in submission. There are ways to get info without that aura."

Caden looks around, seeing almost everyone on their knees, and lowers his aura. "Right. You might have a point."

Madison smiles and turns to the two in the cell. She lifts her hands as aqua magic glows upon her fingertips and into the prisoners, wrapping around them like a blanket. "Right, now you and I are going to have a talk. You will tell me what I want to know as you will find my magic stronger than your will to resist it. Tell me about Landon's plans."

They nod and relinquish the information. "There is a bounty on your head, Luna. He wants you by his side and will do whatever it takes. He sent us to retrieve you, but we were not expecting the King and his men to be here guarding you. It made our job more difficult, so Garrick texted Landon about it. His witch Vespera called him back but left us to watch. Then we saw the warriors, so we ran. Landon will not be happy that Alaric had not passed on that information."

"Who is Alaric?"

"He's our spy in this pack. He's supposed to send updates, and that is a pretty major one to miss."

"And do you have spies in every pack?"

"I think so. We were just aware of this one, as he's our contact here."

"Does this Alaric have a last name?"

"Probably, but I am unaware of what it is."

Madison turns to D'andre, catching the shock in his gaze at the talking guards. "Do you know who he is?"

"Yes, I know. How is it you can get them to talk like that, Maddie?"

"Fey truth magic. They cannot lie. It will only last about five minutes, though."

Caden growls softly. "Impressive. I did not know it had this power."

"Yes, it does, but it's visible, so I cannot use it in the mortal world." She turns back to the prisoners. "Do you know what Landon's actual plan is?"

"Actual plan? He wants you as Luna."

"Yes, but why?"

"Cause you are his mate?"

"Wrong. I have a mate, and it's not him, so there is another reason. If you had to guess, what would be his reason?"

Issac frowns. "Power then. If he has you, he owns Duskrunner and Wildfire."

Caleb shakes his head at his co-conspirator. "Nah, she is beautiful, powerful, and unattainable, and he doesn't like it. There was a rumor he had her mom, and she denied him a mate bond, too. That's why he sent her to the witches. With her, he intends on keeping her and having his witch force her to mark him. Then he can control her pup's power when they are born."

"How do you know that?"

"I overheard him talking to Vespera."

Madison grows thoughtful, neither feeling like a valid enough reason, but then if the man was not sound in the mind, it didn't matter on the reason. And clearly, he wasn't, with trying to force a mate mark on her and control any pups that arose out of it. She bristled slightly as a soft growl escaped, knowing if she had pups, they would be Lucian's, and he was not laying a finger on them.

The two men in the cage pin themselves to the back wall in fear at her growl, feeling the power in it despite the softness of it. "Sorry Miss Luna. We didn't mean to offend you. Just stating what we feel."

Madison refocuses on the men. "Alpha, it's Alpha. Do you know when he plans to take me?"

"Well, he was going to try here, but there are too many guards. Perhaps if you return to Duskrunner. He doesn't tell us his plans until he needs us."

She nods, switching tactics. "How many of the rogues out there are Landon's?"

"Most of them, I believe. It's his way of controlling the area."

"Have you been rogues?"

"Yes, it's part of our pack duties. We have to put a necklace on and make sure everyone is in after dark. We bring those who aren't to Landon in the cellblock."

"And these cells? Where are they?"

"It depends. He has some on Duskrunner, Howling Oak, and his own lands. None of them are close to the pack houses. He keeps them in remote areas."

"And you know how to get to them?"

"No... Yes. Only when we wear the necklace."

"When you place these necklaces on, what happens?"

"What do you mean?"

"I mean, do you still know who you are, or are you controlled by the magic in the necklace?"

Lucian growls softly. "You're NOT putting one on Madison."

Madison turns to Lucian and smiles. "I never said I was. I am simply asking questions."

"Yes, and I can see where this line of questioning is going."

"Lucian, I don't even have them. Caden's witch has them."

"Right, still... DON'T even think about it."

She turns back to the men and arches her brow. "Well?"

"No, it doesn't control you. It makes you smell like rogues and you get stronger than you normally are. You also automatically know where to take the people when you find them."

"So you are willingly kidnapping people, then?"

"No, that's not...." Both men pale as they realize suddenly where her questioning led to, not that they can resist answering with the magic surrounding them forcing them to tell the truth.

D'andre inhales sharply. "You are ruthless. I didn't even see that coming."

Madison offers him a wry smile. "It's all in the knowhow. Hence why I suspect your hundred lawyers will not be enough, my friend."

"Damn, I am so screwed!"

Madison laughs, patting his shoulder lightly. "Indeed you are. Good thing I like your mate!" She turns to King Caden. "They are yours. They freely admitted to kidnapping innocents without magical control, with plans to take me and force me into an unwilling mate bond. That should be enough to convict them. As for the spy, leave him active. We will feed him false information."

Caden looks between them and Madison, shaking his head at what she had just done. "You should have been a lawyer, my dear."

"Bah, lawyers are boring. Besides, I used magic to force the truth. That doesn't fly in a court of law, but it does in the supernatural world. Now, I want to roast marshmallows. I hope you have them, D'andre, or I will ensure I add something regarding that to our contract."

D'andre chuckles. "My wife has them. Does that count?"

Madison laughs. "Indeed, it does. Come on, Lucian, let's go find the others." She heads back down the passage, leaving the King and D'andre to watch them walk away.

"Damn, Sire, you have one hell of a granddaughter there."

Caden nods, seeing the lightness in her step, amazed at how carefree she looks with Lucian, especially when someone is hunting for her head. "Yes, she is. Come, she's right. We have a bonfire to get to. We can discuss this more on Monday." Caden strides forward, following Madison and Lucian out of the pack jail, smiling at the fact that she stopped to watch a few of the warriors spar. He steps up beside her, resting on the wood fence, his eyes taking in their stances critically. "So, do they compare Madison?"

She looks up to Caden a moment, then over to D'andre, who steps in beside him. "No, they have weak points they leave open. I could take them both on at the same time and win."

D'andre turns to his guards, watching them spar. "Where?"

"I will show you." Madison smiles and hops over the fence, striding casually towards the fighters. "Boys, how would you like to spar? Two on one."

They look her over before glancing at D'andre, who shrugs his shoulders. "Alright then, little lady. Let's see what you have." They back up a step and set their casual stances, clearly not expecting a challenge from this petite woman standing before them.

She laughs at their posture. "I will give you a fighting chance. Treat me as a threat, or you will be on your back in less than three seconds."

They chuckle softly at her words. "Someone is certainly sure of herself."

Madison nods and moves, reacting faster than they can. Grabbing the one's wrist and yanking him forward, she ducks under his arm as she lifts him up and over her shoulder. She pivots, sweeping her leg out to trip the second while dropping the one over her shoulder on him, both flat on their back before they know it. She looks down at them, smiling at their shocked expression. "Lesson number one. NO matter who it is, you treat them as if they are your equal or better than you. Fight as if your life depends on it. In our scenarios, you are both considered defeated."

Victor, who walked up as Madison stepped into the ring, laughed at the two lying in the muddy snow. "Oh lass, are you beating on the boys again?"

"Of course."

They both rise sheepishly, brushing the snow off. "You caught us off guard, is all."

"Really, and yet, I warned you. Want to try again?"

They look at each other, stealing their expression and stepping into a stance. "Right, this time we take you down."

Madison nods and positions herself, waiting for them to make the first move this time. They circle around her, testing her defenses as she watches them carefully, monitoring their moves. She studies the way they roll on the balls of their feet, leading with their intents and giving away their movements. Her lips tip at the corners as she feints to the left before spinning around his swing suddenly, taking out the feet of one next to him. She then elbows the one behind her in the ribcage, watching as buckles in pain. She continues her spin again and kicks him hard enough in the backs of his legs to drop him, smiling as he, too, falls to the ground. "Defeated again, boys. You give away your intent to strike in the way you dance on the balls of your feet. You should change that." She smiles as they groan before sprinting back to the fence and vaulting over it. "D'andre, your men need work!"

D'andre sighs, seeing his men on the ground twice in less than five minutes. "Did you have to beat them so easily, Madison? It makes me look bad."

Madison laughs, her eyes returning to the men struggling to their feet. "Sorry, D'andre. The challenge was there, and they were easy compared to Ironwood's elite."

"That's just great."

"You bring those marshmallows, and I will come back to train your men. How does that sound?"

"Deal."

Madison loops her arm through Lucian's and heads back towards where her mom, Paige, and Clarice were talking.

Clarice smiles at her daughter's approach. "I am assuming you trounced them?"

"Of course."

Paige looks at Madison in confusion. "Trounced who?"

"D'andre's warriors fighting in the ring."

Caden chuckles as he moves to stand in the group. "I don't even think they knew what hit them."

Paige arches a brow. "You fought them?"

Madison nods. "If you could call it that. They ended up flat on their back twice before even landing a strike. Right, D'andre?"

D'andre sighs. "I would rather not discuss it."

Clarice laughs at D'andres discomfort. "If it makes you feel any better, Victor trained her."

"No, it does not. Come, I believe they are lighting the fire now."

Erica leads them to a large clearing in the woods, with a stone ring in the center, surrounded by benches. A few warriors stack wood in the center of the ring from a nearby woodshed, while another tucks fire starter and newspaper between the logs. Off to the side behind the benches is a small table, where bags of marshmallows sit, along with long stakes for roasting them. Behind them, in a valley of sorts, sits a small amphitheater where a band is working on setting their equipment up.

Madison lets Lucian go and runs over, grabbing a stake and a bag, hearing their chuckle as she holds it close. She moves to sit on the bench with Lucian as she anxiously awaits the fire.

The rest of them settle down as D'andre moves forward, pulling a box of matches out of his pocket. He waits until the warriors back off and surround the area before lighting the fire. Flames lick at the paper and burn through it swiftly as ash floats in the surrounding air. The dry kindling catches fire, the sound of crackling wood fills the clearing. The fires continue to grow, lighting the damper wood as a stream of smoke reaches for the sky. Within a few minutes, they can feel the heat on their faces as the bonfire roars.

Madison rests her head on Lucian's shoulder, watching the flames dance as she hugs the marshmallow bag close to her heart. She shifts her gaze to the others, each also watching the flames as they sit in peace around it. Smiling up at Lucian, catching his eyes watching her, she feels a happiness within that she agreed to give him the winter festival. She blushes softly, feeling where his thoughts are going through the mark on her neck.

She focuses her attention on the bag of marshmallows and the stake in her hands. Opening the bag, she plucks one out and places it on her roasting stick. She dips it into the fire, rotating it until it's golden brown, and pulls it back to inspect it. Giving a nod of approval, she hands it over to Lucian. "Marshmallow?"

Lucian chuckles, taking the marshmallow off the stick. "I don't get to do it myself?"

Madison giggles as she reaches for the marshmallow. "Fine, I will eat it if you don't."

Lucian pulls it away and holds it out of her reach. "Nope, it's mine. Go roast your own!"

She leans forward, kissing his cheek. "I can do that!" She pops another one on her stake and sticks it in the fire as Lucian enjoys the first one. A few minutes later, she pulls the second one out and pops it in her mouth, moaning in delight at the heavenly taste. She glances at the others, also roasting their own, thinking they needed to do this at her own pack, cause this is heaven. An hour later, and on a sugar high, Madison pulls Lucian down the slope to where others are dancing. A nervousness fills her, not because she hasn't danced before, but because it hasn't been with him; her Professor that chaperoned the dances and was always off limits.

Lucian smiles and draws her into his arms. He holds her and whispers softly to her. "Forget I was your Professor, Madison. Just dance as I saw you dancing at school."

Madison sinks against him for a moment and steps back with a nod. A smile lights her face and her eyes as she dances with him, flirting lightly for the faster songs and holding him close for the slower ones. The others join in for a few of the songs before returning to the bonfire and the hot cocoas that Luna Erica has delivered.

At the end of the dance, they moved back to the fire, singing off-key shanties with the others and enjoying the evening's close. As the fires die down, they bask in the glow of the embers before dousing them and heading back to the pack house, each with a happiness in their heart.

Fifteen

Bonds Unite

———

LUCIAN AND MADISON walk together quietly, following the others as they leave the bonfire, each drifting in their thoughts about the festival and what the evening will bring. As they arrive at the pack house, Madison hugs Clarice and Victor goodnight, giving a nod and a smile to the others. "Thank you all for a great time today." She takes Luna Erica's hand and squeezes it gently. "You put on the best festival ever. I had so much fun."

"You are welcome, Madison. Sweet dreams, and we will see you tomorrow."

"You will." Madison turns and bounds up the stairs, heading to her room, knowing Lucian will follow. She opens the door and kicks off her shoes. She pulls off the borrowed jacket and drops it over the chair, followed by her hoodie. Once she is comfortable, she moves to the bag that is sitting on the table, where she dropped it off before dinner. She opens it just as Lucian enters and closes the door behind them. Her fingers toy with the handles of the bag nervously as she roams her gaze over him, feeling the draw despite the apprehension of being alone with him.

Lucian studies his mate, seeing the nervousness in her, "Madison? Is everything alright?"

She nods and glances back down at the stuffie in the bag. "Lucy, I bought you a gift from the fair."

"A gift?"

"Yes, but now..."

Lucian chuckles. "Is it that bad that it's making you nervous?"

Madison smiles, relaxing a bit. "Well, it might be." She pulls out the white crocheted dragon and holds it up in his direction. "It reminded me of Rhy and you."

Lucian moves forward and takes it from her gently, turning it over in his hands. "It is beautiful. Thank you, Maddie."

"Are you sure you like it? I mean, it's a stuffie."

He chuckles, reaching up to caress her cheek lightly. "Yes, and I have a girl's name for a nickname. It's from you, Maddie. I love it, just as I love my name."

She smiles, stepping into his arms and resting her head on his chest, his scent of pine and fresh snow mingling with the wood smoke of the bonfire soothing her. "I had a great day today, Lucy. Thank you for convincing me to stay for the festival."

Lucian places the dragon on the table and wraps his arms around her, tightening them momentarily. "Thank you for not flying back on Wednesday and giving me this chance."

Madison nods against him, closing her eyes and just listening to his heartbeat, not willing to release him just yet.

He kisses the top of her head, feeling her emotions within. "I know Maddie. I know."

After a few minutes, Madison pulls away and steps back. "I suppose we should get some sleep."

"If that's what you want, Maddie."

She lifts her gaze to his, feeling his draw, her eyes drifting down to his lips as hers parted slightly. Her voice barely whispers. "I don't want to sleep yet, Lucy."

Lucian reaches up, tracing a thumb over her lower lip as his eyes darken in desire. "What do you want, Maddie?"

Madison closes her eyes, feeling the sparks and the heat within at his touch. "More…"

Lucian smiles, removing his thumb from her lips and places a hand on the small of her back, drawing her in close again. He kisses her lips, tasting gently, feeling the desire within at her request. He supports her as he feels her sink against him before whispering against her lips. "More of what Maddie."

She whimpers softly as he breaks the kiss, hearing his question in the back of her mind. She lifts her gaze to his, placing her hands on his chest and twining her fingers into his shirt. "This... Whatever it is that you make me feel."

Lucian groans at her innocence and lifts her into his arms, carrying her over to the bed. He places her down gently and crawls beside her. He caresses her face lightly, brushing a few strands of her hair off her face. "Are you certain, Maddie? I don't want to pressure you."

"Lucy, stop talking..."

"You are truly amazing." Lucian chuckles, his hands caressing her cheek lightly before cupping her face and kissing her again, hearing Rhydian in the back of his mind. *'Yes! It's about time! Make her ours for real.'*

'Go away Rhydian.'

'Hell no.'

Lucian pushes back in his mind, doing his best to block out his dragon. He tastes the innocence in her kiss and in her reactions, knowing to take it slow despite Rhydian wanting to jump her. He deepens the kiss, feeling her body respond to his touch as he caresses along her jawline and down her neck to her body.

Madison registers in her mind they are moving, only to feel the soft bed beneath her and the partial weight of Lucian on top of her. She closes her eyes, feeling the delight inside at his touch, hearing both Somoko's and Zuri's purring. She smiles inwardly at their happiness, feeling a heat fill her as Lucian's hands drift along her body.

Lucian breaks the kiss with a groan, feeling his desire ramp up inside him, and pushes it down. He kisses along her jawline, to her ears, nibbling on her earlobe, before moving down her neck. His fingers find the bottom edge of her T-shirt and slides it slowly up her body.

Madison sucks her breath in as his fingers caress across her bare skin at her hips, arching slightly to get closer to his touch as the fires within demand of her. Her fingers grasp his shirt, wanting it off as she pulls on it gently.

Lucian chuckles at her impatience, assisting her in removing his shirt as he pulls it over his head, his body tingling as her fingertips graze his skin. He returns to her shirt, lifting it up and over her head, and tossing it aside. Kissing down along her neckline, he nibbles on the mark on her neck, his mark, and one she accepts despite it being forced upon her. He groans as she wiggles and arches beneath him, feeling his desire grow as he kisses along her shoulder, his hands wandering down to her waist. His fingers linger at her jeans. "Maddie..." His words are both soft and gentle, yet carried a warning stating that if they did not stop, then there would be no turning back. Wanting to make sure she is certain before stepping past his point of no return without a fight.

Madison sighs at feeling his bare skin against hers, tracing along his muscle lines, exploring every curve with her fingertips, only to dig her nails in as she feels his teeth nip at her mark. She gasps in delight, wanting and needing him closer as fires flare through her body. "Lucy... please."

Lucian smiles at her response, knowing that tonight, after all the years of nothing but dreams, she was his to claim, to be his mate and wife in all ways. "Shh Maddie, just relax and let me treasure you." His hands caressing along her cheeks as he cups her face, as he returns to her lips, kissing her deeply, feeling the fires grow within at her hands roaming over his shoulders now. "You have no idea how truly beautiful you are Maddie and now, you belong to Rhydian and I."

Madison closes her eyes, the love that she has for Lucian emanating from her, his touch bringing a well of emotions and fires she could not explain, knowing in the back of her mind that she has always loved him, from the first day she saw him in class. She sighs softly, no longer resisting the emotions that she struggled to deny and accepts the fact that she is, as he said, his.

Lucian peppers kisses along her body, spending some more time there as he lowers himself on top of her, resting on one elbow as he idolizes her, taking his time exploring and learning her as she succumbs to his touch, each of them soon lost in an evening of bliss with Madison claiming Lucian as her own, and placing her mark upon his neck where it belongs.

Later, as they curl up together, wrapped in each other's embrace, each with a happy warmth within, Lucian kisses her cheek softly. "I love you, Madison."

She snuggles in close as he draws her into his arms, her voice a breathless whisper. "I love you, Lucy... That was epic."

"Epic, huh?"

She breathes in his scent, feeling a peace settle over her. "Yah... epic." She closes her eyes, drifting in the warmth of his embrace, and allows sleep to steal her away.

Lucian smiles, caressing her cheek lightly before drawing the covers over them as best as he can. He whispers in her ear as she drifts off to sleep. "Yes, my dear Madison, it was." He rests his head against hers, feeling the mark vibrating on his neck, allowing sleep to take him away as well.

Madison stretches lazily as she wakes up Sunday morning, with a weight over her body. She blinks in confusion before a deep blush crosses her cheeks as she recalls what she did last night.

Lucian chuckles softly at her blush, knowing exactly when her subconscious left and her waking consciousness kicked in by the blush staining her cheeks. He caresses across them lightly. "Good morning, Maddie."

Madison sighs softly at his touch, feeling a stirring within as her gaze meets his for a moment, traveling down to the mark on his neck. She reaches up to touch the tattoo there, seeing a pair of wolf and dragon eyes staring back at her. "Morning, Lucy."

Lucian inhales sharply at her touch on his mark, feeling their connection through it, along with a happiness that they are finally together, as one. His voice is soft as his gaze finds hers. "Yes, you placed it there last night, Maddie. No undoing it now."

"I don't want to undo it, Lucy." Madison blushes again, running her fingers down along his chest, feeling Zuri in her mind.

'Yes, gurl, I told you it would be fantastic. You can tell him that Somo is talking to Rhydian. We already talked now that the two of you finally admitted you love each other and marked one another.'

'Zuri, you know it had to be on our time. I was not letting you pressure me.'

'Yes, but look at what you missed out on. We could have been doing that nightly.' She purrs softly.

Lucian cups her face in her hands and kisses her gently. "That's good because now you belong to me and Rhydian, who is strangely quiet."

Madison giggles softly. "That's cause he and Somoko are talking. Zuri just told me."

Lucian groans. "I can just imagine what they are saying."

"Probably the same thing Zuri is lecturing me on. That we took too long to admit our feelings."

Lucian travels a finger down along her neck and over to the hollow of her throat. "We? I already knew I loved you even when you were a student of mine, my dear Madison. But I will accept the blame in the 'we' because if I wasn't such an idiot back then, we could have been together five years ago."

Madison sighs, closing her eyes at his touch, the sparks of heat filling her. "It's not your fault, Lucy. I ran too fast to give you a chance. And then I just drove until I could drive no more. I recall gassing up a few times, but the rest was a blur until I stopped. Next thing I knew, I woke up in the hospital."

"I'm sorry you had to run, Maddie. Teachers are often the last to hear the rumors, and I would have stopped them had I known sooner."

"I know that now, Lucy. It was just circumstance and a bad best friend."

Lucian kisses the top of her forehead. "If it makes you feel any better. Her warrior mate, Mathew, was not impressed with her behavior and the situation. He made her publicly apologize to the football team as it wasn't just your reputation she tarnished with that rumor. It was all of theirs as well."

Madison snaps her eyes open to his. "Really? I guess I never really thought about that."

"I understand why you didn't. You were just rejected and banished by your father. The football team was the last thing on your mind. Mathew keeps her in line the best that he can, but she's tainted for sure."

She sighs, recalling her visit back. "Yes, I kinda feel sorry for him being stuck with her. I was truly naïve thinking she was my best friend, when all she wanted was to bring me down, and she succeeded in that."

"Only temporarily... You grew strong from it. An Alpha of your own pack."

"Yes, I did, and I already had words with her when I arrived. She accused me of coming back to grovel at Davis's feet and thought perhaps she could slap me when I denied it. I caught her hand and forced her to kneel at my feet, informing her I could have her head for striking an Alpha. I guess she didn't do her research like you did, Lucy." She smiles coolly. "Even made her crawl back to her mate."

Lucian chuckles. "I would have loved to have seen you put her in her place." He caresses the strands of hair off her face. "I will admit, you were difficult to find, Maddie. It took me a year and a half to track down where you landed, but after that, I checked on you daily."

"Clary said I was in the hospital for four months before I woke up. I remember being in a tiny cave with darkness all around me. It felt comforting, and yet it seemed to watch me with an intensity that made me nervous. Shadows seemed to dance at the edge of my vision, but I could never lock my gaze on them. Then, somehow, I was in a hospital. It took time before they let me out of there, and even then, I hid inside Clary and Vics' house, rebuilding myself."

"Yes, Clarice told me when you slipped back into darkness and I sent Rhydian to find you. She figured it was your fey-step, but I suspect you dragon stepped, leaving your body in stasis. Though, usually, your dragon remains as a guardian of your body. It is something that is trained to do and difficult to accomplish. And to be gone for more than a few hours is a feat in itself. My brother Pierce will want to talk to you about that, and I can teach you how to use it properly."

"Thanks, Lucy." Her voice was soft, a sadness filled within. "Zuri and Somo ran away during the drive. It was too hard for them to deal with, being rejected and then rejecting the pack back. I was on my own for the drive, lost in my pain with my support system gone when I had just found them. I couldn't deal with it and eventually broke. Thank you for sending Rhydian to find me this time, even though I still owe him an ass-whooping."

Lucian chuckles. "As long as it's his ass and not mine."

"Never yours, Lucy."

He kisses her gently. "I'm glad. So now what happens?"

She sighs under his kiss, pulling him close and snuggling against him. "Now, I guess I'll take you home with me."

"What if I had plans to take you home to Frostbite?"

"Na ah Lucy. I run Wildfire. Your brother runs Frostbite; therefore, I have Alpha seniority! You come home with me."

He laughs softly, nibbling on her neck, teasing her gently. "But I have a home in Duskrunner, waiting on my mate to return and a job to do…"

Madison pushes his shoulder gently, rolling her eyes in amusement. "Had! It's gone now, remember? But if you want, I will rebuild it when I take over Duskrunner."

Lucian sits up and looks at her. "How are you going to manage that, Maddie? It's not attached to yours on any borders, and there are other packs between it. It would be extremely difficult to maintain."

Madison reaches up to caress his cheek lightly. "Well, there is Luke, who, by rights, should be the next Alpha. To be honest, it is not something I had thought about, other than the slow takeover of Davis and finding my mom. Now that I see what's going on, I might cleanse all three packs, Howling, Nightshade, and Duskrunner and offer them to D'andre. But I need to talk to Luke about it, as I don't want to take his position away in doing that.

Perhaps Howling to D'andre and Nightshade to Luke."

"That would be a wiser plan. But it is possible Luke might happily move to Wildfire to be with you."

"If he does, D'andre gets them all."

"Well, I think he's earned it by putting up with all of us."

Madison laughs, her fingers tracing lightly over his chest. "That's right. So much for his quiet holiday."

Lucian closes his eyes at her touch, grasping her hand to his chest. "Indeed. Now, I do believe we have had enough to talk. I feel the desire to explore my wayward mate."

Madison blushes softly. "You do?"

Lucian's eyes alight with desire as he drifts his hand to the sheet that covers her, pushing it down slowly. "I do, now. What did you say to me last night? Stop talking, Maddie." He leans forward and kisses her gently, teasing, nibbling, before deepening the kiss as his hands roamed over her. Each of them soon becomes lost in the sensations their mate bond and each other's touch create.

Meanwhile, downstairs, D'andre sits having breakfast with his wife, Caden, Paige, Victor, and Clarice. He smiles at the fact that they seemed to be missing a certain young couple from the table, one that didn't even acknowledge the knock on their door this morning. He laughs suddenly at Victor's third scowl directed at the empty chair and door, causing them all to snap their gaze to him. "Sorry. Victor's scowling has made my morning."

Victor directs his scowl to D'andre. "It's not polite for them to miss a host's breakfast. Madison knows better."

D'andre shakes his head. "Victor, it's fine. You and I both know why they have missed breakfast. I will have food sent up. I highly doubt they will leave that room today. It's pretty safe to assume Lucian is now sporting a matching mark on his neck."

Victor's chokes on his coffee and glares at D'andre. "I don't want to know."

Caden chuckles. "Now you know how I felt, Victor, though I will admit, you have far better restraint than I did, and for that, I apologize. I should not have beat on you... both times."

Victor growls softly. "Even if I wanted to, I'm pretty certain both Clarice and Madison would flatten me."

"Yes, my granddaughter is strong enough. I certainly would not want to add my daughter to that."

D'andre laughs at their antics. "Darn. And here I was hoping to see more flying lessons. I really do need to get cameras installed in the pack house."

Clarice smiles at both her father and D'andre. "What Victor is not telling you, Father, is that Maddie already has proven her worth in the training rings against the Ironwood elitists."

"So I was right in thinking that if you had not stopped Somoko, I would not be standing here."

"Correct. I recognized her movement. She was about ready to pounce on you with four sets of claws and teeth. Victor is very important to her, and she is protective of those she loves. You threatened that. She reacted."

D'andre picks up his coffee and takes a sip. "Damn, that girl really can fight if she can hold her own against Ironwood's finest."

Clarice chuckles. "I didn't say hold her own, D'andre; I said proved her worth. She defeated them all... All except Vic, but I think that's because she holds back when facing Vic."

D'andre coughs, placing his coffee down so as not to spill it. "Good thing I already agreed to sign a treaty with her then."

"Indeed, it is."

Sixteen

Strategic Deception

T HE GROUP EATS breakfast, enjoying light banter when D'andre gets a mind-link from Nathan. *'Alpha, I just got a text from Luke, the Alpha Madison's brother. I think she needs to see it.'*

'She's kinda busy right now.'

'I think we need to make her unbusy. I am on my way to the pack house with my phone, as I am uncertain how to answer it.'

'What does it say?'

'Hey, Nathan! Did you take Zoe to the winter festival as we discussed? We were at the theater here, watching a play in which the frost father took the snow bird. Have you seen it? Apparently, it's based on an old Lycan myth. I messaged coordinators about getting a copy but haven't received a reply.'

'Dammit, I will get them out of their room.' D'andre rises. "If you would all excuse me, I think I need to get the two lovebirds downstairs now."

Victor asks. "What's going on, D'andre?"

"I'm not sure, but Nathan just got a cryptic message from Luke. He's on his way now."

Victor sighs, muttering under his breath. "I will go get her. You meet your man." He turns and strides from the room, heading back upstairs. He knocks at the door and listens, receiving no response.

The guards chuckle. "They won't hear you. They are in the shower."

"Great." Victor rolls his eyes and mind-links Madison. *'Maddie, get out of the shower pronto. We have an issue.'*

Madison's hands pause on Lucian, turning towards the door, knowing Victor wouldn't disturb her unless there is trouble. *'What is it, Vic?'*

'Just get downstairs as soon as you can, lass.'

'Understood.' Madison pales and glances up to Lucian, who is watching her intently. "Somethings wrong. We are being called downstairs."

Lucian nods and rinses off with her, both of them vacating the shower within a minute. Maddie towels herself off and pulls on clean clothes, running a quick brush through her wet hair.

Lucian pulls on a pair of khakis and a black Henley, feeling the stress radiating off Madison. He dresses quickly and moves over to give her a quick hug. "Whatever it is, we will face it together."

"I know. Victor just sounded concerned." Once she determines she is presentable, she moves to the door with Lucian, seeing the guards avoid her gaze as they move to step in behind them. She blushes and looks down at the floor, forgetting that they were standing outside her door all night and probably this morning.

Lucian squeezes her hands. *'It's fine, love; they won't say anything to you.'*

She groans inwardly, her blush deepening. *'But they were there and probably heard.'*

'Yes, I very much suspect they did. And the flush on your face is a dead giveaway to where your thoughts are.'

'LUCY!'

He chuckles and leans in to kiss her cheek. He whispers softly in her ear. "They will just know we love each other."

Madison shakes her head, struggling to compose herself as they head downstairs, seeing Victor waiting for her at the bottom. She smiles as his eyes move to Lucian's neck, catching the corners of his lips that tip up at the mark that sits partially visible beneath his collar.

Victor reaches out to Lucian to shake his hand. "Welcome to the family, boy. I hope you are ready for organized chaos."

Lucian chuckles, taking Victor's hand, glancing briefly to Madison beside him. "Is it going to be more chaotic than this past week?"

He laughs. "I guess you are going to find out. Too late to back out now. Maddie, Nathan is in the dining room waiting for you."

She frowns, knowing there was no way they should have been able to find out about him. Giving a nod to them both, she runs to the dining room. Her eyes land on the serious expressions of the group there before finding Nathan's, his hands turning his cell phone over in his hand nervously. "What is it, Nathan?"

"I got a message I think is for you." He hands over the phone, set to the message. "I wasn't sure how you wanted me to answer it."

Madison looks down at the text, reading it carefully as the color drains from her face, and she sways slightly. She closes her eyes to steady herself, feeling an overwhelming fear and anger within.

Lucian moves up behind her, resting his hands on her shoulders. "What is it, Maddie?"

"They have taken Aurora from Luke. They know she's tied to the Lycan King."

Caden's deep growl breaks the silence in the room. "Are you saying they took my great-grandchild?"

"Yes. Enough planning. We go in today. We need to find her. I will not have my brother's family pulled apart because Landon wants me as a mate. Clary, I need the Ironwoods elites on their way. I know you set them up. Lucian, you need to get Alpha Pierce to send his forces here to D'andre. You, Vic, and D'andre will direct them. Caden, Brittney, and I head in by car as planned within twenty minutes. D'andre, I need you to mind-link your pack asking for volunteers to travel with us. Include your spy in that link. Also add that Wildfires warriors are incoming and allowed through the gate."

Clarice nods and pulls out her phone, texting her son Cole, the Gamma they left in charge. "I will text them. I left them ready to board a plane at my notice. They can be here in about three hours."

"Clary, I want them to hit Howling Oak. They will probably have the highest concentration of witches because Howling Oak is selling the charms. The captives will need to be nearby, as they need access to them to drain them. Ironwoods are elite enough to defeat any guards that they have placed to secure the prisoners."

"Understood Maddie."

Madison's gaze shifts to the King. "No offense, Sire, but I know my men. I don't know yours. Your forces can strike Duskrunner with us and Frostbite Syndicate because they can fly on their own, Landon's pack. I suspect all three packs will have witchcraft, so if they have anyone to combat that, bring them."

Paige glances at Caden. "You WILL bring Ironwood trained guards with you. Brittany will go get them now."

D'andre sighs, noticing she omitted him. "And what about my forces, Madison? They are perhaps not as skilled as Ironwood, but are quite skilled."

Madison smiles at D'andre. "Yes, and they are protecting my mate, my mother, my father, and my queen, as well as you and your Luna. They have a job, and they better do it." She turns to Nathan, who remained silent during all this and hands his phone back to unlock his screen. "Text him back. We have seen the play and can look into getting you a copy. We just need to find it first. Mix it up with some comments about Zoe and perhaps the library."

Nathan nods and starts texting the message back.

"I need to grab my phone and put traveling clothes on. They will expect us to go right for Luke, but we will check into the hotel first. There, the King can mind-link Luke." She turns to Caden. "I am assuming you can link with anyone in your kingdom. I cannot, not since I rejected the pack."

Caden nods. "Yes, if they are within range. If he is still within the pack, it should not be a problem."

"I suspect he and his mate are, but not Aurora."

Lucian frowns, pulling Madison back into his arms. "I am not liking this, Maddie; it's too rushed. You know it's a trap. You knew the last one was, and look what happened."

"Yes, I know it's a trap, Lucy, but I am walking in knowing it, rather than suspecting it. I am also going in with an army this time. It's something I have to do. I need to save Aurora and all the others that Landon has taken."

"I understand Maddie. I am just concerned. I lost you once, and I don't want to lose you again."

"Lucy, you won't. Now that I have seen it, I can fey-step us all back here if I need to."

"This far?"

"Yes, I could have taken us back to Wildfire if I wanted to. I can carry everyone that's going with us, plus Luke's family." She looks over to D'andre. "Once they discover I glamored Caden to look like Lucian, shit's gonna hit the fan, and it's possible you are gonna have them coming straight here."

Paige meets Lucian's gaze, feeling his concern. "Brittany can also carry people with her teleports, or even create a portal to run through. She and her sisters made protection charms while we were at the festival against what they suspect the group will potentially be facing. One will go to Madison, the King, and one of the guards along with herself."

Madison turns to Lucian. "Lucy. Please trust that I will come back to you."

Lucian sighs, pulling her in for a tight hug. "I do, Maddie. I am just scared, terrified, in fact."

"I know, Lucy. I am too. He wants you dead and me as his mate. He's clearly crazy, and we need to stop him, but we need to have proof. We also need to handle it quickly and efficiently, with as little damage as possible."

Lucian kisses her cheek. "Come back to me, Maddie, in one piece."

"I will, Lucy." She turns to the others. "Right, I will glamor the King and Brittany so that the spy sees them leave with me. Vic, Lucian, DO NOT go near windows or see anyone. I don't need him texting you are still here. The spy needs to send the confirmation text that you left and that the armies have arrived here. After that, D'andre, you can place him in the dungeons."

D'andre nods. "Understood. I have some men watching him. As for Victor and Lucian. I will lock them upstairs on the third floor. That is our personal quarters. We will reconvene down here once the armies arrive."

Madison laughs. "I hope it's a good lock, D'andre."

D'andre arches a brow. "Is there something you're not telling me, Madison?"

"Not at all, D'andre." She winks his way before moving to hug her mother and father. "I love you both so much. Take care, and Victor, behave!" She turns to Lucian, caressing his cheek lightly. "I love you, Lucian Marzire. I can't wait to take you home. Now, I need to get my purse, phone, and jacket. I will be right back." She bounds upstairs, collecting what she needs, and returns downstairs.

Upon return, Brittany is there, handing each of them a pin and a necklace. "Put these on. They will help to combat some of the magic they will be using."

Madison nods, slipping the necklace on, reminding her of her locket. "I should probably take the locket as well, D'andre. You wouldn't happen to have an extra gold chain I could borrow, would you?"

Erica smiles and rises. "I do. I will get it for you, Madison."

"Thank you." She pins the pin to her jacket, catching the slight shake of Brittany's head. *To your bra, where it can't be seen. As soon as we get in the car.*

'Got it.'

Erica returns with her locket and a golden chain. Madison nods and tucks them in her purse. "Thank you. I will return it, I promise."

"You're welcome, Madison." She moves forward and hugs her. "Take care of yourself. I don't want you returning to this pack the same way you arrived."

"I won't. This time, I am ready for them."

"Good."

Once they are ready, Madison murmurs a few words, weaving her spell over both Brittany and the King, watching their appearances morph before everyone's eyes.

Lucian stares at the King, having never seen such magic, and moves forward, studying the King carefully. "Impressive Maddie."

Victor chuckles. "You will get used to it. Maddie is an expert at glamor. At least we don't need the glamor anymore for the impromptu visits from the King. I will admit, it's unnerving to look at yourself in the mirror and see another face."

"It's unnerving staring at a living moving version of myself and two Victors."

Madison laughs and drapes her arm over the King's. "At least they like you. Imagine two Vic's trying to cut your wandering hands off."

Lucian chuckles. "One is enough, thanks. Stay safe, Maddie. I will await your return."

Victor laughs. "Alright, boy, let's you and I go hide. D'andre, let the way."

Madison watches them leave before turning to the others. "That's our cue. Let's go." She walks out with the King, hand in hand, with Brittany following behind them. As they step outside, Madison can see the army of the King's guards posted around, with four of them surrounding a car. He leads her up to the car and opens the door.

Madison buckles up and leans back, moving her pin from her jacket to her bra. Once that is done, she pulls out her phone and notices the texts that are waiting from her brother. She reads through them, blushing as she realizes that she didn't even hear them going off this morning. She taps the edge of her phone as she ponders all that has happened, before messaging him back.

> ♦ Luke, the necklace is done. Lucian, Vic, and I are on our way back to Duskrunner today. We should be there in about 3-4 hours. Thinking we can stay for dinner, but then we need to crash, have a 9 am flight out in the morning.♦

> ♦Great! I will see you later tonight then Maddie ! Thanks♦

She looks at the two guards sitting silently beside them, turning to glance at the King sitting beside her, mind-linking him. *'Do they know it's you?'*

'No. Only those in the room know. Paige and I thought it best.'

'Good.' She shifts closer to him, resting her hand on his thigh as she leans against him.

'What are you doing, Madison?'

'You are my new mate. Play the part, Sire.'

'Right.' He drapes an arm around her, playing with her hair softly.

'Victor should scowl every so often, too.'

The King chuckles, kissing her forehead lightly, earning an honest scowl from Brittany, who sits across from them. *'How's that?'*

Madison giggles, twining her fingers through his hand. *'Perfect.'*

'Madison, you realize Lucian is not going to be happy with you. Hell, my wife and daughter are going to skin me alive.'

'Sire, it has to happen, and Clary knows already. I warned her about what is going to happen.'

'Just Caden, Madison, or Gran-Pappy. And she let you leave?'

Madison smiles, knowing she isn't quite ready to call him Gran-Pappy, but he is growing on her. *'Caden then... Yes, I earned my name, and Clary knows better than to stop me when I've made my mind up. You know it's also the only way we will find the other captives.'*

'I know; doesn't mean I like it.'

'So have Brittany find me fast. I won't have Zuri, but I am hoping Somo will still be with me.'

'We will, Madison. Trust me, we will.'

'Good.' Madison closes her eyes, feeling the stress of what's happening drain her and allowing herself a few hours of sleep in the car.

Caden feels her body relax against him, shifting his gaze to her as he brushes her hair aside, hearing Brittany's huff of dismay. He chuckles and lifts his gaze to her. *'Brittany, I am not cheating on my wife, but Madison has a point. We are supposed to be mates, so we need to act it out. You are playing Victor perfectly, I might add. She's also my granddaughter.'* His gaze drifts back down to Madison. *'And she's risking herself to save strangers and rogues. I just hope Paige can keep a handle on the situation at D'andre's if Madison suffers any pain because Lucian will come undone.'*

Brittany's gaze moves to Madison, sighing softly. *'Understood Sire. I will keep scowling and huffing. As for her mate, my sisters are there. If they have to bind him, they will. Thalia has an earth binding on Madison. Even in a suppressed magic zone, as long as Madison's feet are on the ground, we can find her.'*

Caden nods, glancing at the guards that travel with them, knowing when this is all done, there is going to be a lot of explaining needed. He only hopes it goes off as planned and that there are no hitches in that plan.

Seventeen

Bittersweet Homecoming

THREE HOURS LATER, they approach the gates of the Duskrunner Pack. Caden wakes Madison up with a gentle shake. "Maddie dear, we are here."

"Already?" Madison lifts her gaze sleepily, the brief flicker of shock registering that she is snuggling with the King before recalling she deliberately curled up against him as her waking mind kicked in. She sits up more fully and stretches, hiding the yawn that escapes.

"Well, you slept the whole way m'dear."

"Right, I must have been tired. Hopefully, Vic was good to you."

"Yes, only the odd scowl here and there."

Madison laughs, feeling the car slow down and hearing the guards speaking up front. Their windows rolled down as another peers inside. "Who is back here, please?"

"Alpha Madison, Professor Deplois, my Delta Victor, and two guards."

"The guards' names?"

Caden mind-links her quickly. 'Orion and Atticus. The ones up front are Jasper and Adrian.'

Madison narrows her eyes at the one looking in, her Alpha aura rolling off her. "It's none of your concern. Last time we were here, someone tried to kill my mate. This time, I have come prepared. If you will not let us pass, then I need a necklace delivered to my brother, Luke Evenstone. That is why I am here."

Caden keeps his face passive despite the disapproving tone in his mind-link. 'Madison, we need to get into the pack.'

She watches the guard back out of the car window, her mind touching the Kings. *'He won't deny us. He wants me in the pack.'* A minute later, the guard allows the car to roll through the gates. She settles back down beside Caden. *'Told you.'* She turns to the window, watching the surrounding snowscape, recalling her visit here less than a week ago, the dread she felt within, once more feeling it but for different reasons. She sighs softly, feeling the King's hand on her shoulder.

"We will be fine, Maddie. Trust me. We prepared for this."

She turns back to Caden, studying him for a moment, the corners of her lips tipping up slightly, finding her anger subsiding around this man that is her King and Gran-Pappy. She knows Somoko is still angry with him because she can feel it, but suspects that in time, her dragon might get over his beating on Victor. Especially on the day that they finally meet in the fighting rings, and she lets Somo out to play with him.

"What are you smiling about, Maddie?"

"You."

"Why does it not feel like a good smile?"

Madison laughs, her eyes glancing at the guards as she curls back up against him, earning a growl from Brittany. *'I was thinking when we do finally get to face each other in the fighting rings, I will let Somo out to play first. It might help her get over her anger with you.'*

"Damn, you really are ruthless."

Each of the guards snapped a quick look at the pair, earning a smile from them both, neither willing to explain why that comment came about. Ten minutes later, they pull up to the front of the inn and stop the car. The three of them wait inside the car as the guards do a thorough scout of the area. Once they are certain it's clear, they exit the car and stretch, each of them doing a quick glance around as they enter the inn. Madison approaches the desk, asking for two rooms with two queen-sized beds.

"And who is it for?" She eyes the guards surrounding the three of them warily, feeling the power and strength rolling off them.

"Madison and Victor Martinez, along with Professor Deplois and my guards."

She nods and enters it into the program. "Oh, I see you in our system. We have two on the second floor. Room 204 and 205, across the hall from each other."

"That's acceptable."

She enters more into her computer, swipes the cards, and hands them over. "Enjoy your stay."

"Thank you. Could we please request a wake-up call at 6am? We have a 9am flight out in Newport and need to be there at 7:30."

"Of course, Miss Martinez. I will enter it now."

"Thank you." She reaches over to take Caden's hand, walking with him to the elevators up to the second floor. Once there, she looks down the hall and heads to room 204. She slides her keycard in the lock and enters, three of the guards moving in with them as the other parks the car. She scans the room, noticing it's similar to the one upstairs, two beds, a small table and chairs, and desk. One lounge chair near the window. She pulls her jacket off and drops it on the end of the bed, along with her purse. She then sits next to them and pulls out her phone to text her brother.

> ◆Luke, we just checked in. We are going to take a rest from traveling and head over for dinner. Are you still good with that?◆

> ◆Sounds great, Maddie; see you at dinner.◆

Madison places her phone back into her pocket. "Alright, it's set. Dinner with Luke later this evening. Now we get to rest for a few hours." She moves over to the guards and hands them the key to 205. "You guys can take a break, too. We will be safe enough inside the room."

The nod and bow. "We will rotate shifts, Alpha Madison. One of us will remain at your door at all times. When we go to dinner, all four are to be with you. King's orders."

Madison mutters under her breath. "Of course it is. Fine."

Caden moves over and places an arm over her. "It's no different from Alpha D'andre's, my love."

"Sorry, Lucy, you are right. I am just stressed and cranky." She nods to the guard. "I'm apologize. I didn't mean to take my crankiness out on you. Do what the King has required of you. I think I might curl up and read a book for a few hours." Madison pulls a book out of the bag and sits on the bed among the pillows.

The guards nod and leave the room. One remains outside the door while the others move into their room. Brittany and Caden sit on the bed with Madison, finalizing their plans with Luke.

Meanwhile, the clerk downstairs mind-links the Alpha. *'Alpha Davis, there is a note in our system that you wanted to be informed if Madison Martinez checked in again. She did. She's in rooms 204 and 205. Arrived a few minutes ago with Victor Martinez and Professor Deplois along with three guards, but someone was parking the car, so I am uncertain how many there are.'*

'Thank you, Stephanie. Did she say anything?'

'No sir, just asked for a wake-up call as they have a flight out at 9am tomorrow.'

'Perfect. Let me know if they leave the inn.'

'I will. Alpha.'

Back at Silvermoon, Victor and Lucian pace around the third floor while the others sit and wait. Paige glances occasionally over at Clarice, who keeps checking her phone. *'What's up, Clarice?'*

Clarice glances at Lucian and Victor. *'Nothing yet. Soon, I think.'*

'You and the King, you have an alternative plan, don't you?'

Clarice shifts her gaze to Paige. *'I don't know what you are talking about.'*

'Clarice, darling, you are my daughter. I can feel your emotions. I can feel them all actually, but yours is a different nervousness than theirs.'

She sighs, looking at her phone once more, wishing the text would come in. *'Madison is allowing herself to get captured.'*

Paige rises to her feet in shock, shifting to her outside voice as she glares at

Clarice, drawing the attention of the others in the room. "WHAT? Caden allowed this?"

Clarice shakes her head, glancing at the others in the room. "Not right now."

"Oh, I think right now is perfect. They deserve to know. We all do."

Victor looks at his wife seeing her hand tighten on her phone. "Deserve to know what? Clary?"

Clarice closes her eyes at the others' questions, knowing they are going to be mad but also knowing she needs to keep them contained. At the very least, for an hour or so after capture. "All I can say is I will tell you soon. Brittany has set stuff up downstairs."

"Brittany went with Maddie!"

"Yes, but her sisters are downstairs, following her commands."

D'andre lifts his gaze. "Yes, I gave them a closed conference room at Brittany's request, with guards posted at the doors."

"When they are ready, we will go downstairs. D'andre, is your spy contained?"

"Yes. I had him removed from play as soon as Frostbite's army got here and put him in the dungeon with the others. We will question him after this is over."

"Good."

Paige narrows her eyes on her daughter. "Clarice, You WILL tell me everything."

"I can't, Mother."

"YOU can; I will make you."

"Sorry, Caden overruled you. I can't."

"Dammit. Caden and I will be having a talk about this."

Victor growls. "What's going on?"

Clarice shakes her head, sliding a glance Victor's way. "Please, Mother. Don't."

Paige levels a glare her way, weighing out the responses and consequences of what might happen if they all knew. Suspecting that perhaps Caden and

Clarice are right in not letting the others know. "Clarice will tell you when she's ready." Paige moves to sit down, pulling out her phone and sending a barrage of texts to Caden about what they have done.

An hour later, Brittany and Caden leave Madison alone in the room, each of them doing their best to quell their nervousness. They give a nod to the receptionist as they head into the bar attached to the hotel and order drinks. After downing a few of them, Brittany and Caden argue about Madison. Brittany tells Caden that his daughter deserves better and what is he going to do to step up? Caden argues the fact, saying Madison says they belong together, no matter what... whatever that means. Each of them keeping their voices just loud enough to draw attention but not overpower the bar.

The receptionist lifts her gaze toward the bar, her wolf's hearing catching the conversation, reaching to contact the Alpha again. *'Alpha, the two men are in the bar arguing about Madison. I am guessing she is still in her room. They seem unhappy with each other after a few drinks. I guess her father is questioning her choice of boyfriend, and he's arguing back.'*

'That is great news, thank you, Stephanie.' Davis turns to Landon, sitting in the chair across from him with his witch Vespera, having texted him as soon as Madison crossed through the gate. "It seems my daughter is at the inn, 204 or 205, with her Delta and mate in the tavern downstairs. She arrived with guards, but I doubt they will be in the room with her. If you can magic step in, she is ripe for the taking."

Landon smiles in delight, a darkness alighting in his eyes at how easy those idiots have made this by leaving her alone. He looks at his witch. "Are you ready?"

"Of course, Landon."

"We can deal with the others after we get her. If they are in the bar, it will draw too much attention. I am certain once she goes missing, they will head to the streets to look for her. We will take them down then."

Vespera smiles. "Understood. I can manage an Alpha wolf with ease."

Landon rises and moves to shake Davis's hand. "Pleasure doing business with you, Davis. I will let you know when Madison is my Luna. You can come visit."

Davis returns the shake. "Luke gets Aurora back now, right?"

"Once Madison is bound to me, and not before." Landon turns to Vespera and takes her hand, both of them fading from the office and landing outside the hotel. "Right, rooms 204 and 205. Figure out which one, and let's get in there and get her."

Vespera closes her eyes and draws on her powers as a small floating eye hovers before her. She floats it up to the second floor, peering in the windows, and soon determines which room Madison is reading in. Seeing no guards inside the room, she slips out into the hallway. Noticing one leaning against the wall, she continues to the room across the hall. Retracting her spell, she turns to Landon. "She's alone, one guard at her door, three in the room across the hall. We need to take her silently and quickly."

Landon pulls the needle out of his pocket and nods, uncapping it and taking Vespera's hand. She teleports them into the room next to the bed Madison is reading on. Landon jumps on her quickly, the needle sliding into her neck before she can even react.

Madison feels the prick in her neck, her wolf's eyes flaring to the forefront, throwing Landon off the bed just as a bright light flashed in them. She growls in pain, blinking a few times, feeling darkness creep into her vision as she struggles against the wolfsbane and magic, slipping into the bliss of sleep.

Landon groans, his eyes turning to the door as it opens, the crash drawing the guard's attention. He runs to the bed, taking advantage of his shock. He grabs Madison and throws her over his shoulder as both he and Vespera teleport out. The guard roars, drawing the attention of the other guards, who race into the room. "What happened?"

"Get the two downstairs drinking. This is not good. An Alpha and a witch took Alpha Madison. I could smell it rolling off them." One guard bounds down the stairs, sliding to a stop at the bar, taking in the two acting as if they were drunk, knowing that as a wolf, it is difficult to accomplish. "You are needed now."

Caden and Brittany see the pale guard standing before them, the shake in his stance, understanding exactly what has happened. They rise and follow the guard back to the room at a run, finding three guards staring in shock at the book on the floor, the empty bed, and an overturned chair.

"I'm sorry, I heard a crash. When I opened the door, she was unconscious on the bed, and they took her."

Caden ushers them into the room and closes the door behind them as Brittany moves around the room, studying the magic that was used. She turns to Caden. "They used wolfsbane, Sire, and blinding light. It knocks even the strongest Alphas out."

The guard's frown at her comment. "Sire?"

Caden smiles. "Sorry Atticus. We felt it better that only the three of us knew what was happening. Madison glamoured Brittany and I to look like Lucian and Victor. We were expecting them to take her. That's why we were downstairs drinking and acting drunk."

"I don't understand. The King...You told us to protect her at all costs."

"Yes, because we knew that Victor and Lucian would lose their minds if they knew the true plan. We have tracers on Madison with the hopes they will take her to the same place the others are being held captive. Brittany's sisters are magically watching her so she will be safe'ish. Wolfsbane is always a risk, but a risk that is necessary."

"So, are we going after her?"

"Yes, and No. We need to give her time to wake up from the wolfsbane and figure out where she is. I estimate that about the same time we arrived here, Madison's and Lucian's armies will have arrived in Silvermoon. Upon arrival, Clarice will give them instructions on where they are to lay siege. Madison will fight from within, with the aid of Brittany and her sisters, who are already watching her, assuming they haven't found the tracking pin on her."

He sags against the wall, breathing in a sigh of relief. "So you planned this?"

"Yes."

"Gawd, I thought I was never seeing my mate again. That you would kill me."

A wry expression crosses Caden's face. "Well, it's possible both Madison's and Lucian's packs will, especially if we don't get her back in one piece. But it will be all of us, not just you."

"That is not comforting, Sire."

"I suppose not, but Madison is strong and will return to us. Now, because people are listening, we should fight in this room to make it look like Victor and Lucian are upset that you lost their girl."

"Understood. I finally get to put my acting class to good use."

"I didn't, but I am King. It's ingrained in us." He pauses and raises his voice. "WHAT do you MEAN you lost her!! I left you to guard her!!!"

"I was guarding her, OUTSIDE her door, where she commanded me, Professor. It's NOT like I can ignore an Alpha's order."

"WHERE were the others?!"

"In their room, Resting... Also as she commanded! ONE of us had to drive all the way here. Besides, it's not entirely our fault. PERHAPS if you had NOT been drinking downstairs and still in the ROOM with her, this wouldn't have happened."

"You DARE to speak to me like that!! JUST wait until she hears about this."

Brittany steps in, her voice the calmer of the two. "Perhaps, instead of yelling like we are, we should get out and find her?"

"And where would we go, Victor? I worked in this town and can't get into half the buildings here. You know that. I have no bloody wolf!"

"Then you wait outside with the guards, and I go in."

The guard growls. "DO You really think it's a wise idea to separate? We already did that, and look what happened."

"Fine, we contact the King and see what he recommends."

"Yes, LET'S do that. YOU tell him YOU LOST the girl and NOT us!"

They grow silent, nodding to each other, as Caden pulls his phone out, seeing the barrage from his wife. He swipes past them and texts Clarice five words.

♦We lost her, you're up.♦

He looks up and whispers. "Now we wait."

Lucian paces alongside Victor, each of them scowling at Paige and Clarice, knowing something is going on that neither is relinquishing information about. D'andre remains silent, watching the dark looks between mother and daughter, suspecting he knows exactly what is happening. He glances at Lucian and Victor, reading the stress within the pair, understanding how they loved the girl the way they did, for he, too, found he adored her charm and wit. They all jump when Clarice's phone bleeps, every eye in the room turning towards her. She reads it quietly, unable to hide the color draining from her face. At the same time, Lucian staggers, feeling a weakness flood his body and a burning pain at his wrists. "Madison's hurt."

Clarice nods. "Yes, likely with wolfsbane and silver cuffs. This is our cue to send in the teams to position themselves. D'andre, please take us to the room with Brittany's sisters."

Victor growls as he assists Lucian to stand properly. "What the HELL is going on, Clarice?"

"Victor, please. Just come downstairs."

D'andre rises and leads the group down into one of the conference rooms. He opens the door and guides them in. The scents of patchouli and sandalwood from the incense around the room bombard them. On the table is a large map of the continent, with laptops sitting at four of the corners. Each of the laptops appears to be connected to a conference screen, due to the screen savers matching the displays on them. Wrapped around each laptop is a woven silver chain leading to a crystal lying on the map. White candles burn in bowls sitting beside each of the laptops and around the map. And in the middle of all this, four sisters chant softly and work diligently, each dressed in robes that seem to match the element on the laptops. They look up and nod to those they have not met. "Clarice. Is it time?"

Clarice nods. "It is."

"Greetings. I am Sister Thalia. I represent earth if you haven't figured it out." She turns to the others. "Those with me are Fiona, who is fire, Dallas, who represents spirit, and Iris, who favors water. Brittany is air and will not be joining us here, though is assisting on her end."

Lucian and Victor growl at the same time. "What's going on?"

"As you know, dark witches are in play, draining the lives of innocents, and they need to be stopped. As with any witch, we can magically shield our whereabouts, so it makes it hard to track us. The only way to find them is to run into them, or trick them, and so that is what we have done." She moves to the laptops and clicks a few of the keys, bringing up Caden, Brittany, the guards, and Madison on the screens.

Lucian feels a rage fill him, seeing Madison locked in chains, hanging limply from a wall. "WHAT the FUCK? Why is she in silver chains?"

Thalia turns to Lucian. "Please remain calm. She chose this path."

"What do you mean she chose this path?"

"Lucian, we cannot find the dark witches or where they are draining people. She opted to get captured, hoping they would take her to the same compound. It looks like by the cages we can see, they have. Now we track her, but first, we wait until her signal."

"Are you saying she KNEW about this?"

"Yes, Caden, Brittany, and Clarice knew, along with us. Now, if you cannot stay calm, I will have D'andre lock you up. You stay and watch, or suffer downstairs. The choice is yours."

Clarice moves over to Lucian and places a hand on his arm. "Lucian. Madison is tough and wanted to do this to save the others. Please don't make us lock you up. You know our armies are moving into position as we speak. She will be home before you know it."

Lucian's jaw ticks as he grits his teeth, feeling Rhydian struggling to break free against him, wanting to shred all those that put his mate in danger. He closes his eyes and clenches his fists, struggling not to give in to the urges. He breathes in deeply, forcing his mind to think of Madison, her soft smile, her aqua eyes, the light scattering of freckles on her cheeks, finding her presence in his thoughts calming. He opens his eyes to glare at Clarice, stalking to a chair to sit in as his gaze focuses on his mate. "Fine. We will leave it to you."

Clarice exhales a sigh of relief, catching Victor's scowl her way, and mind-links him. *'NOT you, Vic. You had to know Maddie would do this.'*

'Yes, but you let her!!' He stalks over to sit beside Lucian.

D'andre sighs and moves to stand between Paige and Clarice. "So how does this work?"

Thalia smiles and turns towards the screens. "Think of these like security cameras, real time, except it's magic. I suspect Madison is no longer wearing the necklace, but they were simply a distraction anyhow for the dark witches to find and not look further for the tracking token we gave each of them. Only one guard has a pin, so if they separate from either themselves, Caden, or Brittany, we will not be able to track them. At the moment, though, the plan is to stay in the room until we hear from Madison."

"And how do we do that?"

Thalia laughs and moves to the laptops, turning the volume on. "It's the 21st century, we have sound. Now, sit, be quiet and watch."

Eighteen

Undercover Gambit

LANDON STRIDES DOWNSTAIRS, past all the cages that contain the captured fuel for the witches. Hear their cries and moans delights him, loving that he is one in power. He moves to where Madison hangs limply on the wall, still under the effects of both the wolfsbane and the spell. Standing silently, he places a hand beneath her chin, lifting her head to study her features as she sleeps, desire filling him as his gaze travels along her body. A cruel smile graces his lips at the thought of all that he would do to her once they were mates. He revels in delight that she will fight. In fact, he counted on it, and just thinking about pinning her down and taking her against her will, over and over, brings his member to attention. He can hear her breathing shift, glad she is finally returning to the land of consciousness. "Well, my dear. You cost me a lot of time and investment, but you are finally mine."

Madison groans as she wakes up, first aware of the pain in her wrists from the silver chains. Registering that Landon is speaking to her in the far reaches of her mind, she struggles against the drowsiness. Cracking her eyes open, she blinks a few times as the three of him solidify into one. She snarls softly, feeling the wolfsbane coursing through her, knowing Zuri is suffering far more than she is. "Let me go, old man, and you might live."

Landon laughs and steps closer, breathing in deep of her scent. "I don't think so. I am going to mark you, and you WILL mark me, just like Davis forced your mother to mark him. Then you will be mine to do with as I please."

Madison schools her expression into one of disdain despite the rage burning inside her at his words. "Well then, I hate to spoil your plans, but you can't mark me, and my mate will find me."

"No, he won't, Maddie." He runs his fingers down her cheek to her throat, grabbing it firmly as he glares at her. "I will keep you here chained to a bed where you will pay back your debt in services to me."

Madison growls, pulling against him and the chains. "Like Hell, I will. I owe you nothing."

Landon pulls a knife from his boot and places it against her neck. "You are not in a position to defy me, Maddie." He slices through her hoodie at the neckline, stopping to stare at the dragon tattoo that is there. "WHAT the fuck is that?"

Madison lifts her chin in defiance, the cool steel on her skin as he slices her clothes and takes advantage of his distraction. She brings her knee up and slams it into his groin. The knife clatters to the ground as he grabs his manhood and mewls in pain. "That's my mate's mark, you bastard. And it's Alpha Madison to you."

Landon stumbles back out of her reach and struggles with the pain for a few minutes. His rage grows at the woman in chains before him. "How the hell does a human mark a mate?"

"Cause he's not human, you asshole. He's a dragon shifter from the Frostbite Syndicate, and he's going to find me."

Landon glares at her and approaches, slapping her across the face. "Then I will have to kill him, but I will have you as mine, Maddie. In fact, I think it will weaken him to feel the betrayal pains of you bedding me tonight." He turns and leaves, stopping at the guard nearby. "Knock her out again and get her fastened to the bed in the back room. I aim to have her tonight. Tomorrow, I want her mate hunted down and killed. Spread the word."

Madison feels the burning in her cheek from his slap as her head snapped under its force. Her tongue traces along her lips, feeling the split he caused. She smiles and starts laughing as he turns away, jerking on her chains as hard enough to rattle them. "You're going down, Landon. This pack will be dust in a matter of hours."

Landon pauses and turns to face her. "I don't think so, my dear."

She hisses softly, rage billowing out from her. "DO you even know what you have done and who you are dealing with?"

Landon stalks back to her, staying just out of reach of her legs. "Of course I do. Your mother Megan is somehow related to the Lycan King and Queen, cousin perhaps? Still working on that. Either way, that places you with Royal blood, along with your brother and his child, though the child will be of weak lineage. It's you I want. I will add your Royal heritage to the power of owning not only Duskrunner but Wildfire Crescent as well. You will be my Luna, and if I have to use magic to control you, I will. And when we have offspring, I will control them too."

Madison smiles coolly, her eyes dancing in delight at taking Landon down a notch. "So you don't know."

Landon scowls at her darkly. "I just stated I did."

Madison pulls forward, as close as she can get to him, her eyes flashing in anger as she meets his gaze. "My mate is Lucian Marzire, the little brother of Alpha Pierce Marzire of the Frostbite Syndicate. My Delta is Victor Winterbourne..." She waits for the name to register, and when it doesn't, continues. "The Alpha to the elite Ironwood Moon pack, currently residing under my banner of the Wildfire Crescent." She smiles as she sees the color draining from his face. "I am the princess of the firstborn of the King and Queen. Their entire army, trained by my Delta, has arrived via magic, and are waiting on the signal to advance. Wildfire's elite warriors will have arrived in Silvermoon as well. I am certain you know the stories about them, along with Alpha Pierces' Syndicate army. All of them are now under Alpha D'andre's and my Delta Victor's command."

"But Victor was with you when we stole you."

"Was he though? You do know there is such a thing as magic. Your witch has it, as well as your rogues. You are not the only one with a witch in their pocket... or five."

Landon smirks. "They still have to find you first, Madison. We took the magical necklace off you and tossed it in the ocean."

Madison chuckles, her aqua eyes flaring in humor at his stupidity. "Indeed, they do. You think that because I am not on Nightshades grounds, they won't find me? I already directed Ironwood to take down Howling Oak first. That is where I am, right? I mean, Howling Oak is the principal supplier for charms against supernatural's, and witches need supernatural's to make those charms. Charms, both you and Duskrunner have bought a lot of these past thirteen years. It was a witch who took me from Duskrunner, so it only makes sense I am here. I want you to know that the witch that was with me, disguised as Victor, is currently tracking me."

Landon glares at Madison as if weighing the truth of her words before turning and stalking out of the dungeons.

"There is nowhere to hide, Landon. They will find me." Madison watches him leave, pulling on the chains as she struggles against them. *'Somo, are you there?'*

'Yes, Maddie, I am.'

'How is Zuri?'

'She's sleeping in the darkness from the wolfsbane in our system.'

'How are you? I can feel the dragon wards.'

'Yes, but they're weak, like a child's ward. They won't affect me much.'

'Wait, like a 15-year-old child?'

'Possibly. It's hard to say.'

'I can't fey-step us out of here, Somo. They have the anti-step wards up. We are going to have to fight our way out.'

'We can do that, Maddie. Whenever you are ready.'

'We wait... Until Ironwood is close. Then we take them down.' Madison eyes the guard warily approaching her with a needle in hand, suspecting that whatever is in there will knock her out fast, and she didn't aim to have that happen. She presses herself against the wall, placing as much distance between them as she can, waiting for him to get close enough.

In the conference room, Lucian feels his rage grow at the treatment of his mate, envisioning the many ways he is going to tear Landon limb from limb, making him suffer. He can feel Victor's calmness beside him, not understanding how he is not just as mad as he is anymore. He hisses softly to him. "How can you not be furious?"

Victor places a hand on his shoulder for a moment. "Because I know Madison. Just watch Lucian. As much as I am unhappy about being left in the dark, this was the right call to make."

He turns his gaze back, watching the guard approaching with a needle, adding another to his list of destruction as he watches Madison cower away from him. Pain rips through him at seeing her fear, knowing it is not something he ever wants to see again. "She's clearly scared, Victor."

"She's not. She's Ironwood's finest."

Once he is within range, Madison wraps her hands around the chains, ignoring the burning on them, and pulls hard. She lifts her lower body off the ground and wraps her legs around his neck, twisting her body as much as she can suddenly and snapping it. She watches as he slumps to the ground, the needle dropping from his hands rolling across the floor.

Lucian jumps up in shock at her lightning speed, much like a cobra striking her prey, realizing the guard did not even have the chance. "What the Hell?"

D'andre mutters under his breath. "Extra glad right about now that I have an alliance with her."

Victor chuckles, looking at the pair. "Madison trained and defeated Ironwood's best. Part of that training was in shackles. She will be out of them soon."

"Are you saying she can get out of shackles anytime she wants?"

"Yes, and without her fey-step. Just watch the show, boy, and learn who your mate is and why she's earned her title."

Landon stalks up stairs, going over in his mind what Madison has said below, as a shiver runs through him. If, in fact, she is telling the truth and not spouting lies, then they are in a whole heap of trouble. He didn't care about the Lycans or the Frostbites. It was Ironwood's reputation. Every shifter of every class knew how deadly they were, but they all disappeared twenty years ago. He turns to his witch who is waiting for him. "Vespera, we need to see Xandor; take me to his pack house, please." He waits until she creates a portal, and steps through it, landing on runic pattern drawn upon the floor. Leaving her in the arrival chamber, he works his way to Xandor's office. Landon knocks and enters before receiving an answer, seeing him sitting in his usual position. In front of a laptop lost in thought, as he stares intently at the screen, chewing on a pen. "Xandor. Could you do a search for me on the shifter net?"

"Of course, Landon. What were you looking for?"

"The Ironwood Moon pack."

The pen drops from Xandor's hands as he shifts his gaze to Landon's. "Why are you asking about them? That name brings dread to even the best warriors."

"Just curious, more specifically, their Alpha and a picture of him."

Xandor frowns slightly, suspecting an ulterior motive, knowing his friend well. He turns to the screen and types into it, spending a few minutes sorting through the limited information on them. "Alpha was Victor Winterbourne. It is written that he even trained the King's forces. But something caused them to go dark about twenty years ago." He spins the laptop around, brown hair, brown eyes, looking very much like a younger version of the Delta that Madison has.

"Shit!"

Xandor turns to look at the man on the screen. "You know him?"

"He's Madison's Delta. She threatened the Ironwood pack with me in the cellblock."

Xandor rises from his seat, feeling the sudden shake within as fear engulfed him. "You get her out of my pack NOW!!! I don't have the guards to defend against them. Dammit, Landon. Give her back and grovel at her feet and hope she forgives you cause they are going to tear us apart."

"No, I can't. She's the firstborn princess of the King and Queen. That means she will inherit the throne one day, and I intend to be her King. Can you imagine the power? I just need to get rid of her mate, Lucian Marzire."

Xandor stares at his friend in shock. "WHAT?!! Did you just listen to what you just said?" He slams his laptop closed and tucks it into a drawer, pulling out a key and locking it. "I gotta get my Luna out of here. I do not want her caught in the crossfire."

"There won't be a crossfire, Xandor; you are worrying about nothing."

He rolls his eyes and grabs his keys out of the top drawer. "That's right, because there will be nothing left of us. Frostbite Syndicate is no joke in their fighting skills. Ironwood trained the King's men. We are as good as dead. How long do we have? My Luna is innocent in all this, and I will not have her die because of a stupid mistake you made."

Landon growls in anger and stalks towards Xandor. "It was a mistake not doing research, perhaps, but not stupid. She is immensely valuable, and I WILL claim her as mine."

"So get downstairs and claim her then."

"I can't. She's already marked. I need her mate killed."

"Then I suggest you get on with that. I am going to work on getting my Luna on a plane to visit her sister in Stormfang." He leaves Landon to ponder in his office as he stalks from the room and heads to the bedroom. He reaches out to find his Luna with their mind-link. *'Monica, sweetie. Where are you?'*

'In the library, Xan.'

'Great! It's a good time to go visit your sister.'

'I can call her and ask, I suppose.'

'I mean, now. I am heading to the bedroom to pack for you.'

'Wait, what? Why?'

He sighs, glancing back towards his office as he heads upstairs, knowing he kept her in the dark about his dealing. *'Cause darkness is coming, and I want you out of its path of destruction.'*

'Xan, honey, you are scaring me. Is everything alright?'

'No, I NEED you to leave Monica. As soon as you can.'

'I will be right there.'

Xandor heads into the bedroom and pulls a suitcase out of the closet.

He lays it on the bed and unzips it, tapping his foot as he waits for his wife and mate. He turns as she enters, smiling at the love of his life, dressed in jeans and one of his button-down shirts. Her brown hair pulled back into a ponytail. Her reading glasses pushed up onto her forehead like a headband. He moves over to her and hugs her tightly. "I love you, Monica. Always remember that."

She hugs him back, feeling the desperation in his hug. "What's wrong, Xandor?"

"Please. Just pack. Take four guards and drive. Quickly."

"This has something to do with Alpha Landon and those witches he hangs out with, isn't it?"

"Yes."

"I knew he was bad news, Xandor."

"I know, and now is not the time. Please. Monica. I really need you to leave."

"Alright, for you, Xandor. Text me when I can return." She places a hand on his chest, lingering it there a moment, before moving about the room, quickly packing. Within ten minutes, she is in the backseat of a car with four guards, waving goodbye to her mate, a sinking feeling creeping within as they drive away.

At the hotel in Duskrunner, they sit and wait for the recommended hour before leaving. Caden and Brittany head to the bookstore first, finding it dark inside with the door locked. Brittany draws on her magic, hearing the click of the lock as the door opens. Caden enters first, taking a moment to allow his gaze to adjust, and scans the store. Sensing no one, he steps further into the darkness, moving to the counter to search, looking for any indication that a witch works here.

Brittany moves in behind him, her hands weaving magic through the air, watching as silver beads of light float to a back door. She moves over to it, glancing at Caden sorting through papers. "This way." She leads him through the door and down some stairs to what clearly is a storage or cellar for the bookstore. The boxes are all pushed to the side, and a pattern of runes adorns the floor. "It's a travel pad."

Caden growls softly. "So, what do we do with it?"

"We destroy it by marking it up. If we break the runes, the pad becomes unusable. This is good! It means the witch in question has limited teleports and needs pads to travel to conserve her magic. Easier to catch that way. Drawback is, if destroyed, the witch in question cannot get back here, so we need to hunt her elsewhere if she is not already here."

A wide grin spreads across Caden's lips, his fingers elongating into claws as he rakes them deeply across the first rune. "Elsewhere it is. If she is here, there is no escape. If she is not, she cannot warn Davis or rescue him."

Brittany remains silent, watching Caden destroy the circle, knowing that being air magic, there was little she could do to the runes in question. Her eyes land on an open book with magic radiating off it, flaring with power at each rune destroyed. She moves towards it, knowing it is one of the witch's books of power, a grimoire, so to speak. Brittany smiles at how careless this witch is, first placing a travel rune in a public store and second leaving her tome here with it. She magically closes the book, not daring to touch its darkness, and chants a few words, fading it from sight to be destroyed later. "Sire, I think we have completed what's needed here. We need to go find Davis."

Caden smiles coldly. "I can't wait."

In the dungeons, now that Madison is alone, she glances around, feeling the darkness cloying in the air. The smell of mold fills her nostrils, along with other rank smells. She turns her gaze to the other chains, immediately noticing they are empty, but senses people in the cells beyond the solid door. *'Somo, it looks like others are down here. Are you ready?'*

'Yes.'

Madison shifts against the wall, wrapping her hands back around the chains, hissing in pain at the silver burning more of her skin. "Fucking Silver. Whatever Mom, I know. Besides, by the stench of this place, there is no bloody soap down here." She continues to wrap the chains around her hands until they are taunt with no room to move.

Her comments earn a chuckle in the room watching back at Silvermoon. Those that have not seen her technique are curious as to what she is doing. Victor chuckles. "Ah, Maddie, not that you can hear this, but she will have soap when you return."

"What is she doing?"

"You will see. Ironwoods' best."

Madison tests the chains a moment before suddenly spinning her lower half of her body up and over her head, planting her feet on the wall. Somoko growls deeply as both of them push away from the wall, feeling the brief resistance before tightening her body and dragging the pins out of the wall, landing on the dead guard with a thud. She rolls over and springs to her feet, cuffs still attached to her arms, with chains dangling from them. She brushes herself off and pauses, knowing pins ripping from the walls will have caused enough noise that any nearby guards would hear.

"Damn, she broke those like they were nothing."

"Yes, no matter how hard we drove pins into the walls, she broke them all and then held her own against the warriors in the field, even with heavy shackles on her wrists. It is a trick we keep close to the heart along with others you might see her use today."

D'andre turns to look at Victor. "Wait, are you saying you had training scenarios that involved escaping dungeons?"

Victor laughs. "Yes, among other things. Ships, castles, labyrinths. It's not just fighting in a ring. Other factors often come into play. The Ironwood elites know how to deal with ANY factor that comes their way. I recall the day she taught us that trick. Normally, we used iron shackles as they don't harm wolves, but for Maddie, being fey touched, we had stainless steel ones made. She and a few others were prisoners, and one group needed to get into the building and free them. Three groups. One captured. One defending them and one rescuing them. They all get thirty minutes to plan. The defenders entered the building and positioned themselves accordingly. I hit the start timer, and the rescuers entered the building, only to find the defenders already disabled by Madison and the other prisoners. We initially suspected she used her fey magic, despite it being a skill only mission, but the others said no. They watched her free herself, and they did the same. Now we teach that skill to all our Ironwood elites."

"Damn. You even time them." D'andre turns his attention back to Madison, now moving cautiously through the cavern.

"Missions need to be quick and efficient. Any delays can cost a life. As well as lack of attention. Having them timed teaches both. Afterwards, we go over each scenario in fine detail, on pros and cons, and how to improve it. The winners in each instance design the next challenge and either sit out on a break, or be the prisoners while the other two groups compete. It gives everyone motivation to win. Madison's team, even though she wasn't supposed to be competing, won that day, so they got the break. It was the first time that the break team got a back-to-back rest."

Madison pauses at the first door, peering inside to see a wolf locked up. Her voice is soft. "Hey. I am here to free you, but you need to remain quiet and stick with me." Seeing the gray eyes lift her way and nod, she steps back and studies the lock. A smile graced her lips, mentally thanking Victor for being wise enough to keep their secrets hidden. She hisses softly as the silver burns her fingers, as she laces the chain dangling from the cuffs on her wrist through the lock and tightens it, ensuring it's solid. Using her body for weight and power, she twists suddenly, the chain snapping through the bars on the lock under its pressure. Pulling the broken lock off, she opens the door quietly, all the while sensing for Landon to return. Moving her way through the cages one by one, each one burning her hands from handling silver as she breaks the locks. Near one of the final cages, she peers in and inhales sharply. She stares inside, seeing the ten-foot tall Shadow Walker bound in iron. She moves to loop her chain through the lock as another prisoner places her hand on hers. "No, it will kill us."

Madison shakes her head. "He or she is a prisoner as well. We save them all."

Victor growls under his breath. "Turn the view. I want to see what she's freeing."

Thalia nods and moves to a laptop. She types a few things in and switches the perspective, each of them gasping in horror at who she is releasing. "Dammit, Madison, DON'T!!"

Madison breaks the lock and steps into the room cautiously, but stays out of reach. "Alright Shadow Walker. I know your reputation. I have no desire to die this day, and I suspect you have no desire to remain chained here. So let's make a deal. I will free you, and you don't drain my soul." She meets his red gaze, feeling them pin her down emotionally as he searches within her, shivering at the sudden chill encompassing her. Her nerves are tight, waiting, the prickling of her skin as anxiety sweeps over her before catching the glint of white teeth and a barely perceptible nod. "Great. Its a deal then."

Madison moves forward, looking over the chains that bound them, muttering under her breath at the fact that they are cold iron. "Another bloody metal. What the hell, silver burning my wolf and iron for my fey? I hate this place." She looks over the clasps on the lock, realizing these will need to be picked and not broken. She reaches for her locket, muttering a curse under her breath, realizing it's still at the hotel. A locket that concealed a tiny wire for picking locks. "Hold on." She runs out and searches the guard for keys, suspecting the witches and Landon had the cage keys, but he should have house or car keys. Once she finds his personal ones, she collects the needle and carefully empties the wolfsbane out of it. She returns with the keys and finds one that slides into the slot loosely. She then bends the tip of the needle and works its way in, searching for the tongs to unlock it.

She takes a deep breath, understanding she is in a time constraint, and closes her eyes, drawing on her training. She can feel the Shadow Walker's gaze studying her intently and struggles against the shake in her hand as she knows the rumors about them. She closes her eyes, taking a breath to stabilize herself before refocusing on the task. Hearing each tumbler click, she removes the lock and slides the chains off the creature, stepping back as he billows out in freedom. The creature's eyes glow as he reaches out, grabbing Madison's wrist, who stares in shock, feeling the immediate coldness in his touch, the drain on her very soul. "YOU agreed." Panic fills her as she tries to pull away from his tight grip.

"Prinncesss..."

The other wolves cower and whimper at his voice, low and gravelly, bringing a chill to the surrounding air.

He reaches forward with his other hand, caressing Madison's cheek as she trembles in dread, still struggling to withdraw her wrist, but finding the wolfsbane limiting her strength. His touch follows her skin down her neck, pausing at Lucian's mark. "Hmmm, mated Prinncesss..." He trails his claws down along her arm, stopping at her wrist, and draws a symbol there, a tiny rune of darkness, burning it into her skin. He smiles, a devilish smile, and fades from the room.

Madison shivers, reaching out to rub the rune off her skin, finding it permanently burned into her skin. She hisses angrily, knowing he can lurk in the shadows. "What the hell? You fucking marked me."

Lucian growls deeply, his fists clenching in rage at her comment. "I will end it."

Thalia shakes her head. "You cannot end it, nor remove it. Madison will need to find out the reason, as I have never seen a Shadow Walker mark anyone, let alone leave them alive."

Madison turns to the others, feeling their fear radiating off them, and smiles reassuringly. "It's fine. I am still alive, and it's gone. I will figure it out... Somehow." She moves to the last two cages, breaking the locks and releasing another two wolves. Her heart sinks as she scans the area, not seeing any more cages that would house her mother or a dragon, instead finds the wolves looking at her expectantly. "Have any of you seen a dragon teenager? Or even a wolf pup. They stole my brother's child."

One of the smaller ones nods. "Yes, the dragon. Down the passage over there. I have seen it leave and come back. Him and a wolf, but most do not. It's safer to remain in the back corner and hope they forget you are here."

"Right, that's the way I am going. You are welcome to join me, or head up those stairs, as I suspect that's the way out. If you run into warriors, tell them Madison freed you, and they won't cut you down, as my army is currently advancing on this pack."

They look at each other nervously and continue to follow Madison.

Madison nods and heads down the dark passage, allowing time to adjust to the darkness. Dampness clings to the air around her from the water dripping off the rocks, the wet slime coating the walls that she keeps a hand on. Hands that burn from handling the chains around her wrists. She wished the wolfsbane would dissipate so Zuri could mend her, knowing she is going to have to take her for a long run after this and feed her a lot of steak as an apology. Holding up her hand to stop the others, she pauses at a glowing light in the darkness ahead of her. Pressing herself against the wall, she moves forward to a room with a portal hovering in the middle of it. She curses softly, instinctively knowing she is going through that portal.

Clarice growls softly. "DON'T you do it, Madison! WAIT for Ironwood's army."

Madison glances up towards the ceiling. *'Somo, you still with me?'*
'I'm here Maddie.'
'I suspect we will need to go into fight mode the second we step through that.'
'Looking forward to it, Maddie.'

Madison smiles as she turns back to the others. "I am not forcing you to step through this portal where I expect a battle is waiting. I am a trained warrior and can handle myself... Hopefully. But you, you have been captives here, and I will not judge you if you decide to stay here. The choice is yours. Just be aware, Landon is still out there and may come back."

Clarice clenches her fists at hearing Madison's words. "If you step through that portal, I WILL turn you over my knee, Madison Elara Martinez. You are not too old to do that!!"

Lucian matches her growl. "You won't be the only one."

Madison pauses right before the portal and looks back. "I can hear those thoughts, Clary... My full name? Really? And you have to catch me first."

Victor narrows his eyes. "Don't you worry, lass, I will catch you for your mother."

Madison smiles. "I love you, Vic!"

"She should not be able to hear you." Thalia frowns at the three of them cursing her, carefully looking over the magic radiating off the map to the laptops, showing them her location.

Clarice mutters angrily. "She probably can't. She just knows me well enough to know what my reaction is."

With that, Madison turns before her doubts get the better of her and steps through the portal. The smell of death surrounds her, blending with the salt water of the ocean. Winds blow through her hair as she crouches low immediately, feeling Lucian's anger through their bond right now. She scans the grounds before her, expecting a flurry of activity, but sees only dead people lying around, scattered among the runes. Off to her left are five cages, three of which contain figures lying slumped on the bottom. She moves forward cautiously, the darkness in the air bringing a sense of foreboding to her.

Goosebumps prickle her skin as she stops at the first body on the rune. She brushes the black hair aside, her eyes white, with a face frozen in terror. Skin shriveled around her bones as if bled dry, and yet, blood still dripped from the slice in her throat. Madison shivers and moves to the second one, rolling her over, seeing her in the same state. She shifts cautiously over to the remaining two, each also very much dead.

Glancing around nervously, her skin crawls as if something is watching her, and suspects that whatever did this might still be around. She rubs the mark on her wrist, a feeling of dread creeping over her, knowing exactly what killed these witches, and she didn't want to be next. She quickly approaches the cages and peers in, a gasp escaping her at her mother, lying near death. "Mom?" She moves around the cage, seeing a complex series of locks, and stares at it in dismay, realizing it's beyond her skill level.

She chews on her lip as she ponders how to get past it as her eyes land on the witches. Moving over, she searches each of them, revealing a set of keys. Running back to the locks, she plunks the keys in, turning them as the dark purple shroud leaves the bars and the door opens. She reaches in and pulls her Mother out of the cage, feeling her stir in her arms. She carries her over to a small grove of trees and props her up against one. "Stay here, Mom; I gotta get the others out."

The other wolves that braved the portal move over to guard her. Madison returns to the two cages, finding a young dragon and another wolf, each barely conscious. Speaking quietly to the dragon, knowing they often react first, she explains as best as she can that she is here to help. Opening the cage, she carefully drags the teenager into her arms and carries him back to her mom, placing him down next to her.

On the third trip back, just as she is releasing the wolf, Landon and his witch Vespera step through the portal. Vespera screams at the sight of her sister's dead, her red eyes blazing as they turn to Madison, her arms full of an unconscious wolf. "Well, Shit."

Landon growls at her. "What have you done?"

"Now, that depends on what you are talking about. Her sisters, I didn't touch. The cages, I did."

"How did you get free? You were chained in silver with wolfsbane in you."

Madison places the wolf down at her feet, lifting her arms to look at the manacles and chains dangling from them as she steps away from the innocent. "Still am, actually. Just not attached to the wall anymore. I did mention I command the Ironwood Moon pack, right? Or did you miss that tidbit of information?"

Landon stalks towards Madison, his rage growing within at the fact that this woman is destroying years of carefully laid plans. All in a matter of a week. "I heard you, but you will be my Luna!"

"That's fucking Alpha to you." She sidesteps to the left, not wanting to include the others in the fight she knows is going to happen. She catches the witches bolt out of the corner of her eye heading her way, feeling the power behind it. Madison draws on her fey magics to shield herself, instinctively knowing her magic is not bound by runes out here in the open. She staggers back as it strikes her, returning the favor and sending a bolt back at her, taking the witch off her feet. "I can play that game too, witch."

Landon watches the bolt sink into her shield, roaring in anger at the fact his witch is targeting Madison. "DO not harm my Luna!!!"

Vespera returns to her feet in anger. "She killed my sisters!"

Materializing behind Vespera and towering over her, the Shadow Walker wraps his arms around her. "Noooss, shhhee diiidn'ts, buuttts I diiiddss." He kisses her on the cheek and fades away with her just as Ironwood's elites walk through the portal.

Madison breathes a sigh of relief as she spots her warriors, knowing they are safe. She sinks to her knees, finally allowing the gravity of the situation to sink in.

Landon charges toward her, only to get pounced on by her protectors before reaching her. She watches as they swiftly contain him, her eyes moving to the ones approaching the captives. Her captain approaches and assists her to her feet. "Alpha."

"Captain Jacques. Thank you for finding us so swiftly."

"Thank the witches. They guided us to your location."

"I will. Did the others find Aurora?"

"I haven't heard."

Back in Silvermoon, the group breathes a sigh of relief that Ironwood arrived in time. All but Lucian turn their attention to Caden and Brittany approaching the pack house in Duskrunner. He can read the weakness Madison is clearly hiding now that the fight is over and her adrenaline is fading. Wanting nothing more than to pull her into his arms after he scolded her for her actions. A flicker of movement behind her draws his attention, seeing the Shadow Walker appear, hearing the grating sound of his voice, and not liking it one bit.

"Prrinncesss, I haave a giiifftt."

Madison closes her eyes, the deep sense of dread filling her, and turns around to face the Shadow Walker. Stuffed in a large bag is a child, eyes wide open and looking around. "Aurora!" Her eyes find the creature's, giving it a nod of appreciation, and reaches out to take the bag. He starts to hand it over, only to grab her wrist instead and pull her in close to him. "Mooove annnds shees ennds upps likkesss themesss."

They freeze in place, watching as he places the bag down gently. The Shadow Walker's hands move over Madison carefully, causing Madison to shudder. He stops at her bra and dips his fingers into her shirt, earning a furious slap from Madison.

"What the hell?"

He pulls the pin off and drops it at her feet, then fades from the clearing and takes Madison with him.

"NOOO!! MADISON!!"

The rest all turn to the screen, seeing the view on the monitor, the Ironwood elites staring in shock at a baby. One of them picks up the pin and looks it over. He pulls his phone out and texts the preset group between them all.

> ♦Beta Clarice, we have a problem. A Shadow Walker just traded a baby for Madison and took her away.♦

She texts back, her eyes moving to Lucian, who has dropped to his knees and is clutching his chest.

> ♦We saw. She released it from the cells. Finish the mission. We will have to find Madison after. Alpha Xandor and Alpha Davis are still unaccounted for. Collect their computers, laptops, journals, papers, anything that might incriminate them. The witches will create a portal here so that you can send the baby and the captives through first. I will text when we are ready for Landon.♦

> ♦Understood.♦

He tucks the phone away, looking at those cowering in the corner.

"Everyone over here. There will be a portal soon that will take you to safety. Our Beta Clarice will be waiting."

Victor moves to Lucian. "What's wrong Lucian?"

"I can't feel her. It's like they ripped her from me."

Iris moves over to Lucian and pulls his shirt aside. "Your mark is still active. She's not dead. Therefore, she's in another realm. My guess is theirs, and no one knows how to access it but them."

Lucian growls softly, closing his eyes and taking a few deep breaths, reaching to the mark that bound them and rubbing it softly. "Please come home in one piece, Maddie."

"She is strong. She will figure a way out. Have faith in your bond. Now, we need to get those others here." The four create a shimmering silver portal to the token that Jacques holds, with a mixture of leaves and fire burning around the edges.

Jacques collects the baby and hands her over to one of the stronger wolves as he guides them through the portal. A few of the freed wolves carry the barely conscious ones through, landing in the room in Silvermoon.

Paige gasps as she recognizes her daughter. "Faeloria!"

Lucian lifts his gaze and looks at the dragon in shock. "Haku?"

Victor moves over to collect the baby. "Aurora, will your parents ever be happy to see you?"

D'andre looks over at the newcomers. "Alright, everyone, I know you are probably exhausted. You are safe here. I will have my Gamma Ethan show you to some rooms. I cannot contain you, but I ask that you not contact anyone and that you stay in the pack house until our mission is done. There are other groups out there beside Alpha Madison who saved you, and I don't want them placed in jeopardy."

He makes sure they all agree, the youngest wolf asking quietly. "Will she be alright? We told her not to free it."

D'andre looks over at Lucian, struggling to his feet to approach the dragonling. "She will be fine. It was a rescue mission and her job was to rescue everyone. She did the right thing. I am certain she will play that card if it comes down to it. I have found her very resourceful and clever."

"I thought I was going to die there. Can I stay until she comes back?"

"Of course. You are all welcome to stay as long as you like. Now, I am certain you will like some rest. Food and drink will arrive in your rooms within twenty minutes. I think Haku and Faeloria should retire as well, and you two can talk to them after."

Paige frowns at D'andre, but realizes he is correct. "Lucian and I will assist them to their rooms. Then we will come back and finish the mission. The faster we do that, the faster we can find Maddie. Please let Caden know. It might motivate him to move faster."

Clarice's gaze remains on her father's monitor, seeing him stagger as he reads the text and responds to D'andre. "He knows. Jacques sent it to the group text. Pierce's men will know as well."

Caden and Brittany approach the pack house with their four guards, seeing the wolves moving around as normal, doing their routine. A few of them look over at them with curiosity in their eyes. As they are about to enter, Caden hears his phone beep and pulls it out, staggering back as he stares at the text, a growl escaping from his lips.

Brittany glances his way, "What's up?"

"A Shadow Walker took Madison, one she released in the cells. We need to move so that we can focus on getting her back."

Her brow furrows, trying to determine why a Shadow Walker would take Madison and that she would even release a creature that was a risk factor. "Right then, let's get inside the pack house, deal with Davis, and figure out why she let it go, only to have it take her. My sisters may have an idea."

Caden tucks his phone into his pocket and steps up the stairs, entering the pack house as if he owns it, only to have guards step out and block him. "Where are you going, Professor? You are not welcome in the pack house."

Caden growls, rolling out his Lycan aura. "I will go where I damn well please. Now, take me to Davis."

"Of course, Professor." They bow and bare their necks in a submissive gesture, fighting the confusion within as they know he doesn't have a wolf, and yet, here he does. They rise and lead their way to the office, stepping aside for him to enter.

Caden pushes the door open, his dark gaze landing on Davis. "Alpha Davis, you are under arrest. For extortion, kidnapping, attempted murder, among many other things that I am certain we will find when we confiscate your books. Caden gestures to his guards. "Arrest him!"

Davis rises to his feet, laughing at the audacity of this human. "What? Do you seriously think a human has the power to arrest an Alpha? Good luck, Professor. It seems you are missing your mate? You just made this so much easier to make sure that Landon gets his mate." His eyes darken dangerously as he gestures to his Beta and the guards behind them. "Kill him, and kill Victor as well."

Brittany smiles coldly and dispels the magic upon them, causing Davis to stagger back in fear and the guards to back away in fear. "Go ahead, Alpha, challenge the Lycan King. I would love to see it defeat him."

"KNEEL." Caden roars in anger, cowering everyone in the near vicinity. He turns to Brittany. "Bring in the others and arrest the whole BLOODY Pack!"

Brittany nods, calling forth a portal to where the King's guards waited, watching them file through the portal and begin moving through the pack house and grounds, arresting all the wolves they can find.

Gamma Ethan, along with Paige and Lucian, lead the rescued down the hall to a group of rooms. Each with fresh linens, a private bathing chamber and a variety of clothes folded on a dresser. "The clothes are for you. Please feel free to soak, shower, rest, whatever you need. Just ring the bell, and the staff will assist you. Food will arrive in about twenty minutes. If you are too keyed up to rest, you are welcome to watch the mission or visit the games room further down the hall. As Alpha D'andre said, we ask that you contact no one and do not leave the pack house until our operation is complete." Once they are all settled in their rooms, He, Paige, and Lucian return to the conference room.

D'andre watches as they walk away, mind-linking a few more guards to come to the conference room. *'One prisoner incoming. Take him to the dungeons for now. Lock him in silver, both arms and legs. ALL prisoners are to have legs bound now too.'*

'Yes, Alpha.'

He turns to Clarice. "Guards are on their way for Landon. Send him through."

Clarice nods and types into her phone.

♦Send Landon through.♦

Six guards step into the room at the same time Landon does. Two of them grab him and drag him down to the dungeons as he screams obscenities at Silvermoon, but most especially at Madison, and her obstinance about not wanting to be his Luna. D'andre shakes his head, realizing that perhaps Landon is not entirely sane, and hopes he does not plead insanity at his trials.

Nineteen

The Shadowveil Sanctuary

LSEWHERE, ON AN unaccounted-for plane, Madison fights against her captor, who suddenly lets her go. She stumbles slightly but spins, backing away slowly, her legs taunt as she prepares to fight. The Shadow Walker shifts before her eyes, the darkness fading from him as a humanoid form appears. Or rather, a very striking male elf with emerald green eyes and long ash blonde hair. Dressed in blue silk robes with an overlay of light armor over it. "Princess Madison. I will not hurt you."

Her eyes scan the landscape, noticing that she is standing in a circular grove, a variety of symbols etched into stone and placed around them. Tall trees with purple bark and blue leaves surround her. Green flowers with red stems bend in the light breeze, and the sweetest smell she has ever smelled fills the air. Like a mix of vanilla and mango, encouraging her to breathe deeply of the scent. She sways slightly at the intoxication filling her, knowing she shouldn't, but finds the scent irresistible. "What have you done, and where am I?"

"You are in our realm, the Shadowveil Sanctuary. I was sent to yours to find you, but found myself captured instead. You have freed me, and so now, I am in your debt. Thank you."

"To find me?"

"Yes, Princess, you."

"How do you know I am a princess?"

"It's in your blood and aura. We can see the auras of all that we look at. Now, your father awaits."

"Wait, my father? Davis is NOT My father." Madison hisses in anger at him and backs up another step.

He nods, a slow smile crossing his lips. "We are aware of that. Your father is Jean Claude, and he has been looking for you."

"I don't understand."

"You will Princess. Come. This way."

Madison chews on her lip, weighing her options as she looks around at the new realm, realizing even if she ran, she has no idea where to even run to. She sighs softly and steps in behind him, wishing she could just curl up in Lucian's arms.

"You think of your mate. He is worthy of you."

Madison's gaze snaps up, rubbing her arms at the chill in the air and the wolfsbane in her system. The chains rattle at her wrists. "How do you know that?"

"It's in your aura, Princess. He will be fine."

"What do you mean by that?"

The elf man laughs, eyeing her carefully. "Princess, you read too much into my words."

She mutters softly. "You would too if the dreaded Shadow Walker kidnapped you."

He chuckles. "Only in your realm, Princess. It is a curse placed upon us a long time ago that we have yet to break. We have twenty-four hours in this form outside our realm; then, we turn into the beast. And we do not harm the innocent or those with pure auras, even in beast form."

"Not what I have heard."

He stops suddenly, catching Madison as she stumbles in shock. "And yet, you still opted to free me. Why?"

Madison sighs and looks up into his emerald eyes before down to the arms that held her, suddenly feeling very tired of fighting. "I was on a rescue mission. Every one of Landon's prisoners was to be freed. You were there, and therefore, one of my objectives."

"How did you get free, Princess? I heard them bring you in chains, and I could smell the heavy dose of wolfsbane in your system from my enclosure.

Still can, actually."

"I was trained by one of the best, Victor Martinez."

"Indeed, you were. I am grateful. I will have to meet this Victor, Princess."

She nods, suspecting that he was going to no matter her decision.

"Come, Princess, the sooner we get you to your father, the sooner we can get you home."

"Wait, I am not a captive?"

He reaches up to caress her cheek lightly, smiling at her flinching back from his touch. "No, Princess." He dips down and lifts her into his arms, carrying her across the landscape at a quicker pace.

Madison stiffens in his arms, her fists clenching at the thought of another carrying her this way. After a few minutes though, the exhaustion creeps into her body as it shakes in shock of all that she has just seen. She closes her eyes, feeling surprisingly comfortable in this man's arms, not in the lover sense, but more in a Delta sort of way.

The Shadow Walker smiles as she relaxes in his arms, looking down at her beautiful face, the thick lashes that framed her closed eyes, the freckles that dotted her face, and her soft pink lips. He felt an admiration for this woman, knowing most would barely even be moving with the poison in her system, and yet she fought her way out. And fight she did. He can hear a soft hissing sound from her lips, a deeper, gravelly voice. "Don't even think about it. We have our mate."

He laughs at the spunk of her companion. "You must be her dragon, as I can feel her wolf still sleeping."

"Damn right. We are all off-limits. Keep your hands to yourself."

"Indeed. No one will dare to touch her here, Dragon."

"They better not!"

He smiles gently. "What's your name? Or hers, for that matter?"

"Somoko. And if you want her name, ask her. Yours?"

"Welcome to the family, Somoko. I am her older Brother, Zed."

"WHAT? Since when?"

"Since before she was born, I suppose."

Somoko growls softly. "You are playing with me."

"No Somoko, I am not. I have spent many hours searching for her and cannot answer your questions. Another will. Now, we are almost at our destination. Please, just rest." He continues to carry her through the woods before stepping out into a small clearing. Set in the middle of it was a two-story mansion with white and aqua coloration. A small pond sat to the left of it, glistening in the light, despite there being no sun in the sky. Strange animals floated happily upon it, looking much like a cross between a duck and a squirrel. An aquamarine cobblestone walkway leads to the white door, with flower beds on either side of it. Zed's emerald green eyes glow softly as the door opens before him and closes after him as he steps inside. Closing his eyes, he senses through the mansion and finds their father in the study. He heads upstairs, down a long corridor, smiling at the fact that his search is finally over. He adjusts her gently in his arms and knocks quietly.

"Enter."

The door opens as Zed steps in, offering a bow to his father. "Father, I have found her."

The man sitting in the chair rises, standing taller than even Zed, looking over the girl in his arms. Long brown hair is braided at the sides and pinned together in the back, leaving the rest to cascade in waves behind him. His skin is pale, like Zed's, but unlike Zed's green eyes, his are aquamarine like Madison's. His eyes darken in anger as he looks over at the pair. "Why are there chains on her wrists and wolfsbane in her system?"

"I will leave that for her to explain." Zed moves over and places her on the couch, startling her awake.

She pushes herself up, her eyes finding first Zed's, then gasping in shock as she stares at her own eyes standing across from her. The scent of cedarwood fills the surrounding air, soothing her much like Lucian's pine scent did. She scans him quickly, from head to toe, noticing the rich robes that indicate wealth, tied to a clear air of authority. Suspecting, at the very least, he is the Alpha here in this house. She drifts her gaze to Zed at his side and sees the family resemblance, finding herself instantly curious. "Let me guess, you would be my father?"

The man moves forward and places a hand beneath her chin to study her carefully, seeing the fires fill her eyes at his touch as she pulls her chin back. "Indeed. Jean Claude. And you are?"

"Alpha Madison Martinez."

He chuckles. "Madison. I like it. Martinez is new, though. Married name? I see you are marked."

"No, Marzire will be my married name when we get there."

Flickers of a frown cross his lips before he schools his expression, wondering if this is the reason his searches have been fruitless. "But Evenstone was your mother's name."

"Yes. It was mine until they banished me. I took up my adoptive parents' name."

"Your mother would not banish you. What are you talking about?" His eyes move to his son questioningly.

Zed shrugs his shoulders. "I am sorry Father. I cannot answer that. Witches captured me. She freed me as a walker."

Jean Claude looks back down at his daughter in surprise. "You freed my son? In his beast form?"

"Yes, he was a prisoner and my mission was to free all. I made him agree to not kill me before I did though."

"Your aura is bright and strong. He would not have."

"I didn't know that. I have heard the stories and hoped he, not that I knew he was a he, was a creature of his word. Though he did get a bit handsy when he kidnapped me." She sends a scowl Zed's way.

"It was necessary, Princess. You had a witch's magic on you."

Jean Claude glances at Zed, knowing his son well enough to know it would be an innocent search. "You work with witches?"

Madison returns her gaze to her father. "Yes, not all witches are evil. Some work with light magic. They were the ones helping with the rescue mission."

"And who were you trying to rescue, exactly?"

"My brother's baby and my birth mom."

"Faeloria? Is a captive?" Jean Claude feels an undeniable rage at whoever had imprisoned his mate.

Madison feels the anger that radiates in the man before her, not understanding why. He's the one that left her mom there, not the other way around. "Was. She's free, and so is Aurora, thanks to your son... my brother." She rubs her temples, the silver chains rattle softly, feeling a headache creeping in. "Why does it even matter? You left her with Alpha Davis. A man who forced her to be with him."

Jean Claude sits on the couch beside her. "Because she is my mate, and I had to. We can only survive twenty-four hours in your realm in this form. I was on borrowed time before the beast took over. I was also not carrying the gateway token that allowed me to bring her with me. I returned to my realm and needed to tend to matters here. When I went back to her, she was gone. I did not know I had a daughter out there, or I would have searched for you sooner. I only found out when you entered our realm and stayed in a cave, but you were untouchable, no matter what we tried."

"Wait... Are you saying I came here when I fell? You were who I felt watching me?"

"Fell?"

"Yes. I had lost my dragon and wolf after the pack banished me, and I rejected it back. I just drove until I no longer could. Then it felt like the floor was yanked out from beneath me, and I fell into darkness. There was a cave, but I could sense something in the shadows watching me."

"Yes, your walker side did. But yet, you maintain your form over there and do not bear the same curse as us."

"Perhaps it's because mom is not. I take after her fey heritage, and my great grammy's heritage in having both a wolf and a dragon."

"Interesting... We might need to look into this further. Now, you said your Mother is free?"

"I hope so. They were with my elite forces when I was stolen."

Jean Claude sighs softly. "I prefer the term borrowed. Can I not want to meet the daughter I never knew I had?"

Madison studies the man before her, shifting her fingers to the back of her neck and pressing in to quell the pain, feeling the weight of the shackles on her arms. "Sorry, I am just tired. It was a stressful mission to run without a wolf, and I know she's gonna be pissed at me when she wakes up. And now I don't even know if we succeeded."

Zed speaks gently. "I suppose it depended on your mission. You saved all the captives; I killed all the witches and left the one Alpha for you to deal with. And I found the baby you were seeking. What else was there?"

"Two other alphas and their conspirators."

"Then I cannot say. And by now, the mission will be done."

"Perhaps. It's probably still in progress."

"Sorry, Princess, it will be done. You have been here for about forty minutes, which means three and a half days have passed in your realm."

Madison jumps up and glares at Zed. "WHAT the hell do you mean by that?"

Jean Claude sends a dark look Zed's way. "What your brother is trying to say is... time passes differently here. When I said I tried to go back to your mother, I did. Several times. Here, it has been seventy days. There... Over twenty-three years have passed. We knew there was a time anomaly, but it never mattered before, not until I started hunting for my mate. Shortly after we sensed you, I sent Zed to look for you. He was not to return until he found either you or your mother. He has been gone for fifteen days."

She could feel her anger rising at the two of them. "Why didn't YOU come for us then? Why send him if you care that much?"

"Because, my daughter, he is the best choice. I am the King here, and I cannot just leave for that amount of time."

Madison's eyes snap to Zed. "Princess, you were calling me that, not because I am the Lycan princess, but because I am YOUR princess. Well, Princess or not, I can't stay here. Sorry, but I am the Alpha of one of the largest packs in my realm. I have a mate, two mothers, and a father waiting there. Plus, that shit disturber D'andre who is like, now my best friend somehow, and his lovely mate Erica, who clearly has more patience than I do. She's sooo sweet. She even put on a festival just for me!"

"Madison, we are not keeping you here. I realize you have a life there, and that I am new to your life. It is my hope, though, that we can get to know each other better. Now, come, let's get those shackles off you. We should also give you a detox to assist with the wolfsbane. It is not good for the pup."

"Pup?"

Jean Claude arches a brow, glancing at Zed for a second, who shakes his head. His brow furrows as his gaze returns to Madison's. "You did not know?"

She backs away a step, her hand going to her stomach, glaring at the pair. "Oh no, you can't know. I DIDN'T Know! It's been One night! Last night! And this morning perhaps. There is NO Way!"

Zed blushes softly. "It's in your aura, Princess."

"What the hell? Is there anything else you just might want to tell me that's in my aura?"

"No, Princess."

Jean Claude reaches out to take her hand. "Perhaps not the best way to break the news. You still need to detox, or it will affect your pup." His eyes glaze over as if mind-linking someone. "It is getting made. I will admit, it is foul-tasting, but it works. Now, after we remove your bracelets, I would like to look over some maps of your territory. I truly wish to speak with my mate and bring her home. She belongs here with me."

Madison laughs wryly. "That will be a hard sell. She's destined to rule the Lycan Kingdom, especially now that the King and Queen found her. They lost her when she was eight in a rogue attack. Besides, where is the mother of Zed? I am certain my mother will not share willingly since she already suffered at Davis's hand with his betraying the mate bond."

Sadness flickers momentarily across his gaze. "Saji was my chosen mate.

She was killed just after Zed was born. As for your mother, she is my fated mate. I need to try."

"I'm sorry, I did not know."

"You couldn't, and it's not something I wish to discuss at this moment. Perhaps at a later date."

Madison sighs as her thoughts move to Lucian at the discussion of mates and what he is thinking or feeling right now. She rubs her mark, knowing it is there, that the bond is still intact, despite not feeling it. Her eyes drift to the King, her Father, seeing the pain and sincerity in his actions. She closes her eyes, doing her best to stabilize her emotions. A pup! She had a pup already. How was that even possible? *'Somo? Did you know?'*

'No Maddie. I would not have agreed with the mission. Wolfsbane is a risk to pups.'

'Do you think they are right?'

'They do appear to have powers we do not. They have no reason to lie about that.'

'Damn it. Do you think our pup will be alright?'

'I do not know Maddie.' Madison opens her eyes, feeling the agony in her heart that she might have caused their pup injuries with her actions. She can feel the pain in her wrists and hands, suddenly feeling confined and wanting out of the damn shackles. "Shackles first. They are really beginning to hurt."

Jean Claude nods and leads her out of the study. They travel down to the basement of the mansion, where a variety of tools lay. He motions for her to sit on the chair and place her arms on the tables beside her. She fights against the apprehension within, but does so and closes her eyes, breathing deep to calm her nerves. She opens her eyes, feeling the gentle touch at each of her wrists as they work to pry the shackles apart. She leans back in the chair, struggling against the urge to sleep, knowing time is precious, and sleep would come when she returns home. She can feel one shackle pop, seeing the King looking over her wrists, then at the shackle, following down the chain to the pin that attached them to the wall.

"Impressive that you pulled them out of the wall."

The corners of her lips lift, her gaze moving to the pin he holds. "It's a little trick I learned in training exercises, and Somo helped."

"Somo?"

"Her dragon." Zed answers automatically, his focus still on breaking the second shackle.

Madison scowls his way. "Does that show in my aura too?"

"No, Princess. She scolded me for looking at you when you drifted off to sleep. Told me to keep my hands to myself despite the fact that I was using both to carry you. Informed me, you were ALL off limits because you have a mate." Zed wedges the pins in, hearing the snap of the release, and gently pulls it off, frowning at the burns on her hand and wrist.

Madison chuckles. "That would be Somo for you."

Jean Claude takes the other chain and tosses them in a scrap metal bin in the corner. He turns and offers his hand to her. "Alright, time is ticking. I will take you to the war room where your drink is waiting. There I have maps of your lands. I would like to know more about where you reside so that we might visit."

Madison rubs her wrists carefully with her burned hands, knowing they will not heal as fast as she wants because of Zuri being asleep. She looks at the hand offered, debating it a second before placing hers in it, deciding if she could accept Caden as a Gran-Pappy, then she could accept this man as her father.

He leads them back up upstairs, this time leading down another passage to a large room, the walls covered in maps, not just of her realm, but others as well. She releases his hand and wanders around looking at them, pausing at their realm, and smiling at the fact that it is outdated. But then if time passed so slow here, it would be hard to keep up on pack territories and who owns what. She reaches up to caress her pack, missing her home, as the King moves to stand on one side of her, with Zed on the other.

"That is your home?"

"Yes, though it is much larger now." Tracing a pattern on the map,

lighting it up with her fey magics. "This is my pack, the Wildfire Crescent."
She follows it down to Whispering Pines. "This is the Royals and where
my mom comes from. If as much time has passed as you say, I suspect she
will have returned home with her parents, King Caden and Queen Paige.
My grandparents." Pointing to Silvermoon, a smile graces her lips. "Alpha
D'andre was the one to help us and keep us safe from these three packs.
The Howling Oak, Duskrunner, and Nightshade Howlers. The Alpha's
Xandor, Landon, and Davis were in on kidnapping innocents, draining
their souls to feed their magic into tokens and selling them on the black
market."

Jean Claude moves to the East edge of the map. "Here is where I found
your mother. On a beach, alone and crying. I knew at that moment we
were mates, and so did she, which only seemed to make her cry more. I
left my guards and went to her, where we sat and talked. Hours later, we
were in each other's arms for an afternoon of bliss. I had no idea she would
conceive the one time we were together, which clearly is a family thing. If I
had, I would have found some way to keep her safe. When I returned, she
was gone."

Madison furrows her brows. "That is a long way from the pack house.
She must have fey-stepped."

"Fey-step?"

"Yes, it's much like a portal or teleport, or your ability to walk through
shadows. It's our own way of traveling."

"That might also explain why I did not find her. I searched the coast and
its towns, thinking she lived close by."

Madison sighs, her voice laced with sadness at all that was lost; her Mom,
her, all the trauma that Davis caused. "The pack house is over a day away
from those shores. I am sorry you didn't find her."

"Perhaps this is the way it is meant to be. If I had, you would have been
born here with the curse and never met your mate."

Her eyes lift to his, reading the sincerity in them. "Perhaps... I will need
to return to D'andre's. Something tells me that my mate is still there."

"Then that is where we will go." He moves to the glass sitting on the table nearby. "Now drink. You will need it."

Madison accepts the cup, her nose wrinkling in distaste at the pungent smell emanating out of the cup. "Ugg, it smells horrid."

Zed chuckles. "It tastes just as bad. Drink it fast."

Back at the Duskrunner pack house, Caden's army quickly arrests all those nearby, seeing some shaking at the sight of him, others sobbing, with a lot looking around in confusion as guards place cuffs upon them. "By my command, shifting of this pack is off-limits until I decree it." He watches them all nod stoically, turning as his men bring more to the pack house from the outskirts. "Is that all of them within the community?"

"Yes, Sire. Even the ones at the gate. Two of our men are there in case any arrive."

"Great. Brittany is in the office now, going through the paperwork and computers there. So until then, we wait." He pulls out his phone and texts his daughter.

> ♦Duskrunner captured and on lockdown until you say so. Have you found Madison?♦

He taps the top of his phone, his eyes narrowing on the ones that glare at him, knowing those are the ones remaining in chains. Within a minute, he receives Clarice's texts back.

> ♦Just waiting on Alpha Pierce's confirmation with Landon's people. Ironwood is approaching Xandor's pack house as we speak. Nothing on Madison yet, but we have Luke's pup.♦

He growls deeply, causing a few of the wolves near him to shiver, knowing it is never good to have the King angry with you, and yet, here they are. Caden narrows his eyes, a storm brewing in them as they land on Davis, who appears to match his glare. A slow smile crosses his lips. "If you think Landon is saving you, then you are more of an idiot than I thought.

He's already captured and languishing in silver chains. His witches are all dead too, just to squash all hope you may have. You, Xandor, and Landon are never seeing the light of day again."

Davis growls and fights against the chains that bind him and the two guards specifically assigned to him. "You can't do this. You have no proof."

"On the contrary, we have all the proof we need. It seems Madison is skilled at what she does, what with being an Ironwood elitist." Caden smiles coldly as the color drains from his face. "Oh, Landon didn't tell you. Yes, her Delta is none other than Alpha Victor Winterbourne. Imagine my surprise when he walked into the meeting at Silvermoon. A man I have been hunting for twenty years, hiding as Madison's Delta and my daughter, her Beta. In plain sight no less. That was an interesting encounter, to say the least."

"Shit." Davis's shoulders sink, recalling how confident Madison was when she returned, and understanding why. It was a confidence she didn't have before she left, and had hoped to use that to his advantage with Landon. The idea was sound, but damn it all, she had to end up in the wrong place. A place that made her strong. A kink in all their plans. Plans he knows are ending as he kneels before the Lycan King.

"That's right, Davis; shit is the operative word. Both because you are done, and because I am pissed this all happened in my kingdom. Duskrunner, Howling Oak and Nightshade Howlers, are finished. Now, which one of you is Luke Evenstone?"

"I would be Luke." One off to the left spoke up, kneeling near a petite she-wolf.

Caden looks over the two, immediately noticing the puffy red eyes hidden behind a layer of makeup on the female. He grimaces, understanding what it is like to lose a pup, for in reality, he lost two. Faeloria when she was stolen by rogues and Clarice when she ran away. "You may rise with your mate. We have your pup at Silvermoon." He looks at one of the guards. "Atticus, remove the chains off that couple."

"Oh my goddess, thank you, Sire." Rosa bursts into tears at the news, as does Luke, both of them grateful that somehow, someway, their pup is safe. Luke pulls Rosa into his arms once they remove the chains and holds her tight as she sobs gratefully against him.

Caden turns, slightly shocked that he heard a gasp of relief from Davis, and narrows his eyes, wondering at the reason for it before turning his attention back to the grateful couple. "It will be a few hours before you can see her. We need to wait until we contain the other two packs, then we can portal you to Silvermoon, where she will be waiting."

"Understood, Sire."

"Now, if you can access the computers the same way Madison does, I ask that you go assist Brittany in the office. The faster we get the information, the faster we can reunite you."

Luke nods. "Is Madison alright?"

Caden hesitates, his eyes moving to Davis. "It seems Madison was exchanged for your daughter."

Luke feels a fear fill him. "What does that mean, exchanged?"

"Well, we took a chance that Davis knew Landon stole your daughter and that you would get her back only when he had Madison. We allowed Landon and his witch to take Madison when we arrived earlier, pretending to fight in the bar as her mate and Delta. She wore a magical necklace to distract from the tracker on her, which monitored her movements, as well as ours. All of which are being watched, recorded, and stored at Silvermoon. It seems there was a Shadow Walker in the dungeons that she freed along with the others, as was her mission. He returned with Aurora and took Madison."

Luke staggers under the pressure of what happened. "No, please no! She was finally back. They kill everything."

Caden moves over and places a hand on his shoulder. "He didn't kill her when she freed him. Your sister is clever. She will hold that against him and return to us. Have faith."

"Yes, you're right, she is clever. Thank you for saving Aurora, Sire." Luke half smiles, a sadness within his eyes at Madison having to suffer again.

"Don't thank me. Thank Madison when she returns. She's the one that discovered all this."

Davis growls softly at the thought that his daughter caused this, or rather Faeloria's daughter as he knew the second she was born, and she opened those elfin eyes, that she was not of his blood. This is her fault, and he is going to end her himself, despite knowing that once you are in the Lycan prisons, you never escape.

Xandor sits on the steps of his pack house, his head tucked on his knees, hearing the chatter within the mind-link of his pack getting arrested. His heart sinks, knowing none of this is their fault and that he alone caused it. For trusting Landon, for putting faith in his childhood friend. He should have seen it. Get rich quick schemes never ended well, and now he will lose everything. He lifts his gaze as wolves dressed in black surround him, his eyes drifting to the road his Luna drove away as he raised his hands slowly above his head. "Please don't hurt my pack. They are innocent in all of this."

"Alpha Xandor. By the King's decree, you and your Howling Oak pack members are under arrest."

Xandor bows his head and nods. "The pack didn't know, including my Luna and pups. Only my Beta and Gamma knew. Everything you need to know is open on my computer."

"They will take that into consideration." They snap chains on him and take him to where the others are. Jacques pulls his phone out and texts the group.

◆Howling Oak contained.◆

Frostbite Syndicate glides gracefully through the clouds, shrouded in magic, towards the Nightshade Howlers pack, understanding that even rogues are to be captured. They fan out and surround the pack borders, with a small elite force heading straight for the headquarters. Once they land, they do an immediate take of the situation and quickly contain those in the vicinity, and work their way out. They meet at those closing in from the borders, and within the hour, Nightshade members are contained and moved to the central pack house. A few dragons do a sweep along the shorelines, catching sight of two boats speeding away, suspecting these are ones tied with Landon. They swoop down and lift them out of the water gracefully, boat and all. The occupants growl in surprise, unable to see the invisible dragon as they lift higher into the sky, panic beginning to set in. They carry the boats back to the headquarters and drop them in an empty space where the guards quickly swarm over them as they try to run.

"Found these escaping by water Beta Granite."

"Got it. They smell like rogues."

"Yes, and will be punished as rogues when the King arrives."

One of them rips a necklace off, knowing that a rogue receives only death, hearing the growls of the others beside him. "No, I am not a rogue." He tosses the chain to the ground as his scent changes. He growls back at the others. "I have a mate and two pups! One of which Landon has as a prisoner somewhere. I am not dying because of him. I just want my pup back." Another speaks up, pulling his chain off too. "He has mine as well." The rest growl menacingly at the two of them.

Granite chuckles, "Well, now we know who Landon's loyalists are." He pulls out his phone seeing a few text messages have already come in. His face drains of color, hearing a few of the loyalists snickering.

"What, did Landon get his Luna? You won't find her until it's too late if he does. He plans to mark her immediately as his."

Granite growls at them, seeing them flinch in fear. "No, Landon's in chains and locked up. Duskrunner and Howling Oak also contained. It's a successful takedown." He quickly types into the messages and awaits the King's orders.

♦Nightshade contained.♦

Gamma Thorne mind-links Granite. *You got pale fast, Granite, enough so that they noticed. What happened?'*

'A Shadow Walker took Lucian's mate.'

'Hell no. He just got her.'

'Exactly. We need to let Pierce know, as he's not in this group text.' He texts his Alpha, keeping him abreast of the situation, that all the packs in question are contained, and they were waiting for further instructions. He turns to the two bowing before him, two that proclaimed their pups were prisoners. "It sounds like Alpha Madison released about fifteen prisoners, and they are safe at Silvermoon. If, in fact, your pups are there and both you and your pup testify against Landon, I am certain the King will consider a lenient punishment. Now, chain them all. We wait until he arrives."

The three groups work diligently throughout the day and well into the evening, sorting, containing, imprisoning the packs and going through the records and information obtained. Those that are questionable remain in the pack's prisons while the rest are portaled to the Lycan's cells, deep beneath the castle. Only to see the light of day for their trial, where they will either be executed for treason or sent back into the cells to serve out their time. Caden and Paige place a figurehead at each of the packs until a decision is made regarding them, knowing they can wait until they find Madison. Those that are to testify are reunited with their pups and placed under lock and key at Wildfire Crescent with Ironwood guards to keep them safe.

Thalia and Brittany call in other covens, each magically searching for Madison, but finding nothing. After a few days, they decide to take a rest, knowing that wearing themselves to exhaustion is not helping her. D'andre and Erica offer their pack house for as long as they want, hoping that if Madison gets free, she will fey-step here. Caden and Paige take Faeloria back to the palace to rest, while Alpha Pierce arrives to return Haku to his family. He tries to convince Lucian to return home but understands why Lucian opts to remain in Silvermoon. He clasps his shoulder, giving it a squeeze, and teleports out with the teenager. Clarice and Victor remain at Silvermoon, trusting in their Gamma to keep Wildfire defended. Each day that passes brings forth the very real possibility they may never see her again.

Twenty

Between Realms

⁕

MADISON CHUGS THE drink, nearly bringing it back up as it hits her stomach, but clamps her mouth shut as the cup falls from her grasp. Closing her eyes at the pain within, she wonders if they just poisoned her and she fell for it. Feeling darkness closing in around her, she struggles back through their conversations for anything that showed they intended to harm her. She sinks to her knees, feeling hands on either side of her, steadying her. She squints at them, trying to focus on the blurriness before her. "What have you done?"

"Shhh Madison. You will be fine. It's just the detox kicking in. You have more wolfsbane in your system than we have ever seen. Now, we need to get you to your mate. He is the one that is needed now."

The room spins before her, feeling herself being picked up and carried. She drifts in and out of lucidness, feeling almost as if she imagined what being drunk would be like. She starts to giggle, before full-out laughing and at the purple trees with blue leaves. "Whys you haves puuurple twees. Them's suuupose to be bruns and gweens."

Jean Claude chuckles, grateful that the detox is kicking in. "Are they not better in purple?"

"Weelllls." She pouts, struggling to focus her thoughts. "Themsss is prettiersss butts notss wights."

"Shhhh Madison. Just close your eyes and rest. Zed and I will have you home soon." Jean Claude watches as she closes her eyes and grows limp against him, her lips parting as she slips into sleep. The three of them travel quickly, heading to the gateway that allows them to travel between realms.

Once they step into the circle, he looks to Zed. "Do you know where Silvermoon is?"

Zed shakes his head. "No, I believe we were in Howling Oak by her words."

"Right, that could pose a problem if it's more than twenty-four hours away."

A soft voice escapes Madison's lips. "Wake her up, and she can fey-step you there."

Zed smiles. "Thank you, Somoko."

"You're welcome. Now get us home to our mate."

Zed chuckles as he activates the runes, arriving in the same location they left. Zed looks around, noting the bodies of the witches are gone, the cages hanging in the wind, and the runic pattern beneath their feet destroyed.

Jean Claude looks down at Madison as Zed shakes her slightly. "Madison, you need to wake up."

"Nooos." She grumbles and tucks her face closer to Jean Claudes' chest.

Zed takes her hand gently. "Yes. If you want to get back to your mate, you need to fey-step us."

Madison struggles to open her eyes, her voice quiet and tired. "I's casntss sstwepss acrosses pwwanezz."

"We are not on our plane anymore, Madison. We are back on yours."

She closes her eyes, instantly feeling the link to Lucian snap into place, and the three of them blink out, arriving in the foyer of D'andre's pack house. She struggles to get out of Jean Claude's grasp, only to sink to the floor as her strength wanes. "Wucy, pweaaseess."

Lucian staggers as Madison returns to the plane, suddenly overwhelmed by her scent of coconuts. He closes his eyes, his hands grasping the railing, feeling Victor's hand on his shoulder.

"What's the matter, boy?"

"She's here." He lifts his gaze, certain he heard her voice, and bounds down the stairs, landing at the bottom. He takes in the two elf creatures, each bending down to Madison, who sits on her knees, wolfsbane radiating from her system and burns all over her hands and wrists. A deep purple bruise on one cheek as tears flow from her eyes. "Madison! WHAT Have you done?" Rhydian forces forward in anger stalking the two that appeared to have hurt his mate.

"Rhysesss, Noooss, I wantttess Wucy." Madison crawls forward. "Pwweasees."

Rhydian growls in warning, before withdrawing and allowing Lucian forward, who drops and kneels before her, pulling her into his arms. "Oh my goddess, Maddie, I thought I lost you again."

Madison closes her eyes, allowing Lucians pine and snow scent to fill her, his arms bringing her comfort. "Pweases dwwon't beeess mwadess Wucy."

"I am not mad, Maddie. I love you."

"I wovees wou tooes." Madison curls up in his arms, listening to his heartbeat, finally allowing sleep to take her away.

Victor follows Lucian down the stairs, watching the situation take place, noticing the wounds are still on her as well. He shifts his attention to the two elves, knowing they are not true elves but uncertain what or who exactly they are. "And who might you be, that you bring my daughter back in this condition?"

Clarice moves forward to where Lucian kneels, pulling Madison's hands out to look them over, seeing the blisters and burns all over them. "What's wrong with her?"

Jean Claude turns his attention to the two that arrived. "I am Jean Claude, King of what you call the Shadow Walkers. This is my son, Zed. He is the one she rescued. She is also my daughter, and Faeloria, her blood mother, is my mate. What she is suffering through right now is a detox, as she has high levels of wolfsbane in her system and it is not good for her and the pup."

Lucian gasps. "Pup?"

Jean Claude chuckles. "Yes, she was quite shocked as well, but it's written in her aura. He will be a powerful dragon."

Lucian pulls her tighter, kissing her forehead. "A pup..."

Clarice scowls. "Why is she just detoxing now? If you knew she had a pup in her, why wait nearly two weeks?"

"Because only a few hours have passed in our realm. It is a half-hour walk to the gateway each way. We talked, had her shackles removed, and gave her the detox. Then we returned here. All she needs right now is her mate's touch and sleep. Now, we only have twenty-four hours before the curse of the beast strikes us, and I would like to see Faeloria. Is there a way to get to her?" He turns his gaze to the other hallway, seeing two more running into the foyer, their eyes landing on Madison wrapped in Lucians' arms, on the floor.

D'andre glances towards Lucian and Clarice sitting on the floor. "Madison?"

"She's fine." Exasperation entering Jean Claude's voice. "Faeloria please."

Clarice nods and pulls out her phone, texting Caden.

⊠Father, Madison's back with Faeloria's mate. You may want to return to D'andre's. ASAP.⊠

She glances at the elves, studying them carefully. "I texted him. I am certain he will get here as soon as he can, as Madison is his granddaughter. I am Clarice, and this is Victor, her adoptive parents. And that is clearly her mate, Lucian. Walking in right now are D'andre and his Luna, Erica." She turns to D'andre. "This is Jean Claude, King of the Shadow Walkers and his Son, Zed. Father of Madison, and mate to Faeloria."

D'andre arches a brow and shakes his head, suddenly laughing. "Damn! To think, I almost turned her away."

Jean Claude's brow furrows, his back stiffening as the tone of his voice chills. "Why would you turn her away?"

"Because I didn't know who they were. An Alpha, a Delta, and a human at my gates, asking for asylum. Who knows what was chasing them? And I had a pack to think about. But my guards said she looked pretty broken. Then to find out while she was in our pack hospital, that she is *the Ruthless*

Madison Martinez that everyone fears. The best damn warrior I have ever seen. It was a shock to find out that she was a Lycan, and could hold her own against King Caden, only to add a princess title to that and now she's a second princess. Damn. That girl is blessed."

Zed places a hand on his father's arm. "Father... She did state that, what was it she used exactly... Somehow the shit disturber D'andre has become her best friend. I am certain he is simply making fun."

"Wait! She called me that?"

"Yes, and that your lovely mate clearly has more patience then she does." Zed turns to Victor and approaches him, offering a hand, smiling as Victor hesitates before taking it to shake. "Victor, you trained my sister well. Thank you. And thank you for sending her in to save us all. Most would have left me to rot in those cells."

"She said I trained her?"

"Trained by the best, as a matter of fact, and watching her work, I have to agree."

A blush stains his cheeks at the praise. "Well, as D'andre said, she is blessed and tries to believe the best in everyone. Her mission..." He sends a slight scowl to his wife. "...Not that we were privy to it, was to get captured and rescue all the prisoners. Which she succeeded at. But you did have us concerned when you stole her."

Jean Claude steps up beside his son. "I prefer the term borrowed."

Victor growls softly. "Borrowed implies that we knew she was being returned. We were not, ergo, stolen. So what happens now?"

"Well, I hope to convince my mate to return to our realm, and continue to find out how to break our curse so we can visit for longer than twenty-four hours. I would love to get to know my Daughter better, as an hour was not long enough."

At that moment, a portal opens into the foyer, and an impressive looking Lycan steps through, followed by his Queen, her daughter, and a witch. Caden surveys the situation quickly, narrowing his eyes on Madison, unconscious in Lucian's arms, burns still adorning her body. He takes in that everyone seems to be fine with the condition she is in, so expects it's already been explained. "Clarice, You texted?"

"Yes, Father, I did."

Jean Claude turns, feeling his mate's pull as she steps through the portal, love in his eyes as he looks her over, noticing that she has aged since he last saw her. His voice is soft, a smile gracing his lips as he drinks in the sight of her. "Loria."

Faeloria gasps in shock and runs from the portal, straight into his arms, wrapping hers around him tightly. "JC!"

Jean Claude kisses the top of her head, wrapping his arms tightly around her. "I came back. I looked for you. As often as I could, but I could not find you. I swear. I tried to keep my promise to come back, but I was too late."

She shakes her head, tears springing to her eyes. "No, Davis bound me to the pack house after that. I couldn't get back to the beach. And you are here now. You fulfilled your promise."

Zed turns, his eyes taking in the new party as the scent of grapefruit overwhelms him. He steps to the side and looks past the pair to the witch behind them, meeting her gaze intently. "Mate."

Brittany shakes her head, feeling the undeniable pull of his emerald green eyes, his scent of ginger calling to her. Her legs shake as she resists, wanting to go to him, but knowing she is bound by the King.

Caden growls deeply. "Could someone PLEASE explain what's going on, and who these two elves are."

Clarice sighs at his impatience. "Father, here is my understanding of the situation. This here is Jean Claude, King of the Shadow Walkers and Zed, his son. Faeloria is his mate, and Madison is their daughter. It also looks like Brittany is Zed's mate, so you might want to release her from service. Apparently, time travels differently between the realms. Madison has only been on their plane two hours, hence her condition, but ten days have passed here. They removed her shackles and detoxed her, but it seems to have knocked her out. They have twenty-four hours here in our realm before a curse takes them over and they turn into the beast that Madison freed. Which I gather was Zed." She looks at the King, her sister wrapped in his arms. "Did I miss anything?"

"I want to take my mate home with me, to my realm, to be my Queen. Madison said it would be a hard sell, but I will pay whatever you request in a dowry to make it happen."

Caden runs fingers through his hair, having just got his daughter back, and now, possibly losing her again. It is not something he wants, but she clearly loves him by the way she ran straight into his arms.

Paige moves forward and places an arm on his, seeing very much the same thing. "She is to choose, Caden. If she wishes, then we let her go, but we make the demands in the dowry that they return to visit as often as they can. The same with Brittany. She has a coven here and her duties to us, but Zed is her mate. Perhaps having a witch in their realm can help break the curse and they can stay longer than twenty-four hours."

Zed smiles sadly, his eyes looking over his father and his mate, pain striking his heart at having to leave his own behind. "We only brought one gateway token with us. As I did not expect to find my mate, I will need to return for her, but at least I know where to find her. We were looking for my father's mate in the wrong place. Now that I have seen this foyer, I can gate-way right to it, but it will be at least five days before I can return if she accepts me."

Brittany moves forward, taking in the man who claims her as a mate. She watched the footage, seeing him take away the witch, claiming to have dispatched her sisters. He made it look easy and despite standing as an elf; he had power radiating off him, much like the unknown power she could feel on Madison, but kept silent about. She smiles up at him and offers her hand. "If the King frees me from my duties, then I accept."

Caden growls deeply, his fists clenching at his side as he struggles to control his rage. "Bloody Hell. I am losing two of you in one day."

Brittany turns, her hand tightening on Zed's. "It sounds like I have five days, Sire. I will get one of my sisters to take my place so that you will still have a witch. The coven will need to replace me to keep it balanced, but I can assist with that. If I cannot, then I am certain Madison can with her access to the dark web."

"Wait, you advertise on the dark web?"

Brittany laughs softly, feeling a strange happiness engulfing her at being near him. "Of course, Sire, humans cannot know genuine witches exist."

"Fine, you may go. In five days and not a second before. Understood?"

"Yes, Sire."

Zed smiles, pulling on Brittany's hand, and draws her into his arms. "Once we have my father's mate in our realm, I can take the token and return here."

Caden turns to his daughter who was crying happily in Jean Claude's arms; a man who is desperately clinging to her like Lucian is doing with Madison. "Faeloria?"

Faeloria looks up at her father, and smiles, leaning her head on Jean Claude's chest. "He came back, Father. I will visit, I promise, but my place is with him."

"Damn, I knew you were going to say that. Right, well, we have twenty-four hours to get to know who's taking two of my family members away. Lucian, I would suggest you take my granddaughter up to bed. She looks like she needs rest, and D'andre, get a healer in here to check on her."

Lucian lifts Madison into his arms and rises, heading back up the stairs with her slowly. He adjusts her slightly, hearing her grumble in his arms about not to move, as he opens the door. Once inside, he kicks it closed and carries her to the bed. Placing her in it gently, he curls up beside her and draws her into his arms. He breathes in deeply, feeling her wrap around him, his body shaking as the stress of the week leaves him. "Never again, Maddie. I know I said it before, but this time I mean it. You will never leave my side again."

She mumbles softly and curls up closer, slipping back into sleep.

D'andre nods and mind-links a nurse to arrive at the pack house, as he leads the group off to the conference room and settles them into it before heading back to greet Natalie. "This way. She will probably be sleeping so do what you can."

Lucian kisses her cheek gently and closes his eyes, following her off to sleep, unaware of the nurse that enters the chamber with D'andre, who does her best to tend to Madison's wounds. She draws some blood and does a quick screening on her, before turning to her Alpha. "With the amount of wolfsbane still in her system, she will need a few days of rest. After that, she should be good to go. Once her wolf wakes up, she will heal faster. And he looks as if he hasn't slept in a week. Perhaps you should lock them in this room, D'andre."

He chuckles, looking down at the pair. "I will inform the King and he can command it."

Natalie smiles. "If she takes a turn for the worse, let me know. I will return immediately. I am surprised she is even functioning with this amount in her."

"Yes, and this is after a detox, apparently. She is pretty damn impressive."

"I would be curious to know what they used."

"I will ask, and if they have a recipe, send it your way."

"Thank you, Alpha." She leaves the room taking her bag with her.

D'andre stands and watches the pair sleep, smiling at the fact that she is his friend, enough so that she calls him a shit disturber to essential strangers. He chuckles softly, as he turns and strides from the room, closing the door quietly after him. Knowing this Yule is going to be one he never forgets, despite all the stresses tied to it. D'andre meanders back to the conference room and steps inside as all eyes shift to him. "Madison will be fine. She just needs rest. They are both sleeping, so I expect we will not see them till morning."

"And the pup?"

"Pup?"

"Yes, apparently she has a pup growing in her."

Jean Claude smiles. "Will be fine. Its aura is strong."

D'andre arches a brow. "Impressive. You can see that so soon. Especially if only a few hours passed for her. That would have been yesterday, by my reckoning."

"Yes, that's what she implied when we mentioned it to her. Believe what you will, it's there plain as day."

D'andre sits at the table, studying the two of them. "So these auras, how do they work?"

"They allow us to see who a person is beyond what they show to the world. Whether their soul is good, neutral, or tainted."

D'andre looks at Caden, knowing there were still a variety of prisoners from each pack still to be interrogated. "So you could look at a prisoner, and tell us if they worked for Landon or not?"

Zed rubs his temple gently. "Why do I get the feeling you are about to put us to work with our answer."

D'andre smiles. "I wouldn't know what you are talking about. What is your answer, by the way?"

"Yes, my dear shit disturber, we can." Zed chuckles, understanding completely why his sister liked this man. "Landon's men have shadows throughout their aura, with no light. Unlike the lot of you, though your King has a shadow tarnishing his, it is not an evil shadow. Just a hint of something he has done wrong and is suffering because of it."

Caden growls at Zed, sending a dark look his way. "I would rather not discuss it."

Zed smiles. "I meant no disrespect, just explaining your aura. And where your thoughts just went only increased the shadow, so you know what I am talking about. Can I tell you what exactly it is? No, but it has something to do with Clarice and Victor, as matching shadows just flickered within them at his growl."

D'andre laughs, his eyes moving between the three of them, before landing back on Zed. "Tell me, what does the King's aura do when I mention the fact that his granddaughter th…"

"ALPHA D'andre! Enough!" Caden growls in warning.

"You really are a shit disturber."

"Gotta earn my title somehow! Soo?"

"Oh, it changed dramatically, despite the fact that you never finished the sentence. Now I am curious though. What did my sister do to earn those emotions?" He turns to Caden and studies him carefully.

"She threw me across the room... Twice. If not for Clarice's intervention, she likely would have defeated me."

Zeds looks over the King in shock, being that he is twice her size. "She did. Whatever for?"

"I was beating on Victor."

Zed glances to Victor, knowing his skill at having trained Madison, and back to the King. "Why?"

"Long story, not getting into it. Let's just say I was really mad at Victor, and she put me in my place fast."

D'andre laughs heartily. "Yes! And what a sight it was to see. The King sailed through the air as if he was nothing but a rag-doll."

Erica places a hand on D'andre's arm. "D'andre, hun, you are baiting the King and know it. I would like to point out that Madison is not here to defend you should the King decide to pick you up and toss you like a rag-doll just to ensure you know what it feels like. I also will not stop him if he does and this time, I will have my phone recording it."

Zed chuckles, understanding Madison's comment about the patience his wife must have to deal with her mate. "I see. I don't expect many would survive if someone tossed our King through the air."

Caden mutters softly. "Not here either. She's lucky she has supporters in her corner."

Paige sighs, placing a hand over Caden's. "And you are lucky she does too, or I suspect I wouldn't have a mate. Somoko was beyond pissed and meant to end you. That much was clear with the condition in which she left the room."

Zed coughs slightly. "You provoked her dragon? I got spoken to about keeping my hands to myself when I frisked her for the witch's token. Then again as I was carrying her back to the mansion. That was enough warning." He turns to Paige. "What did she do to the room?"

Paige smiles. "I suspect you will find out at breakfast, as D'andre here covered the table in resin as a reminder."

D'andre laughs at her comment. "Indeed, I did, AND I had Somoko sign it!"

Erica rolls her eyes. "Of course you did." She sends a look to the King and Zed. "Please forgive my husband. Madison is correct in her description of him."

They both chuckle. "We can see that."

Brittany glances up to Zed. "How did you know she had that pin? It was magically concealed."

Zed smiles down at his mate. "We see all auras and can separate them. I could read Madison, and see it for what it was, but others blended with hers. Two, in fact. One of her sons and one of another, not tied to anything in her, therefore external. It meant she was being tracked with magic of some sort. As it didn't surround her completely, it needed to be an object upon her. I just needed to zero in to where it was located and then I removed it."

"I was with Caden locking down Duskrunner when my sisters watched you find it."

"So they are locked down, then? Her mission completed? Because she was quite concerned about it. More so about it, than herself."

"Yes, all three packs are done. We are still sorting prisoners and determining who is innocent, and who is not."

Zed reaches out to brush a strand of hair off her face. "She will be glad to know that when she wakes."

Hours pass as the group gets to know each other better, with Jean Claude and Zed explaining their home world to them, and what they know of the curse that turns them into beasts after a day. Not just in this realm, but in all the realms they step to. Caden and Paige, in exchange, explain about their kingdom, with everyone filling in what happened to cause Madison to go on a rescue mission. Dinner arrives and passes, with the group separating to their rooms in the evening. D'andre leads Zed and

Brittany to a room, placing Jean Claude and Faeloria into a set of rooms next door. "These will be yours for the night. I will have a maid wake you in the morning and guide you to the breakfast room. Maddie and Lucian should be there too. After breakfast, I am hoping you could do a scan on the prisoners and perhaps at the royal prisons. It would make ending this so much faster."

Jean Claude steps forward, shaking his hand. "It's the least we can do for letting us stay. We shall see you in the morning."

D'andre returns the hand shake, gives each a nod and strides up the stairs to where he knows his Luna is waiting.

Madison opens her eyes to darkness, a pounding in her head and an unsettled feeling in her stomach. She can feel Lucian's arm around her and pushes it off, running for the bathroom, and bringing up the contents of her stomach. She gags again at the smell, the mix of the foul smelling drink mixed with a heavy dose of wolfsbane emanating from the toilet. Resting her head on the bowl, she groans, feeling Lucians hand on her shoulder as he kneels next to her.

"You alright, Maddie. Is it the pup?"

She shakes her head as another wave of nausea strikes her, emptying what's left in her stomach. She grabs a towel and wipes her lips, tears slipping from her eyes. "That shit is just as foul coming back up."

Lucian pulls her into his arms, the scent of wolfsbane filling the bathroom. He closes the lid and flushes the toilet in hopes the air around them clears. "It's hard to tell, as it's lingering in the air, but I can't smell it on you anymore. You are back to coconuts. Is Zuri there?"

Zuri answers Lucian's question in her mind. *'Yes, Maddie, I am here. That detox absorbed all the wolfsbane like a sponge and you just removed it. We are good.'*

Madison smiles weakly. "Coconuts huh? You are pine and fresh snow. And yes, she answered. She's here."

"My favorite scent. When you were gone, I used to order pina coladas, just to remind me of you."

Madison grimaces against him. "Ugg, I don't think I could eat or drink anything right now."

"You don't have to, Maddie, it's three in the morning. You should get more sleep."

She nods and struggles to her feet. "I will meet you there."

Lucian assists her, his brows furrowing slightly at her comment. "I can..."

"Lucy, I need to use the ladies' room. Get out!"

Lucian chuckles, giving a nod and leaves, closing the door after her. Moving over to the bed, he sits on the edge, waiting for her return. He smiles as he sees her stagger out a few minutes later, rising to assist her to the bed. Crawling in next to her, he caresses her face gently. "I missed you, Maddie. I was so scared."

"I'm sorry, Lucy. We had to keep it a secret. I wanted to tell you, but I knew you would stop me."

"You're right, I would have, but it doesn't matter now. It's done. You are safe and here in my arms. That's all that matters."

Madison nods, curling back up against him. "I love you, Lucy. I missed you too, even if it was only a few hours for me."

"I love you too, Maddie, more than I can ever imagine. Now sleep. You need more rest."

She nods, a yawn escaping her, feeling his touch, hearing his heartbeat and breathing in his scent, each bringing her comfort as she slips back into sleep.

Lucian watches her sleep, running his fingers through her hair gently. She was his, and no one else's. This bundle of amazement that is so soft in his arms yet fights better than any warrior he has seen. With the amount of wolfsbane in her system, she should have been out for the count and yet he watched her free prisoners. He saw techniques he has never seen used before, accepting burns to her hands to free people she didn't know. And as much as he is loath to admit it, he knows Clarice will not have placed her in the situation if she couldn't handle it. He smiles as he lies back down on the pillow, pulling her closer, his thoughts drifting to the pup. A pup, already. A dragon pup, even. He kisses her gently on the forehead, allowing sleep to take him again, as dreams of a family creep into his mind.

"Twenty minute warning for breakfast." A knock on the door wakes Madison, as she blinks in confusion, hearing the voice outside her door. It sinks in what she said as a growl escapes her lips.

Lucian chuckles, and opens his eyes. "Why so cranky, my love?"

She mutters under her breath. "You would think they would give a bit more than a twenty minute warning."

"We could save time and shower together."

A blush crosses Madison's cheeks. "I am pretty certain that will not save time."

"No, perhaps you are right. We would indeed be late."

"Lucy! You are so bad!"

His eyes darken in desire. "What, I love you, can't I want..."

Madison places her fingers to his lips. "Shh, Lucy. We have twenty minutes." She kisses his cheek and rolls out of bed, running for the bathroom first. Turning the shower on, she steps out of her clothes and drops them on the floor. Stepping in, she breathes a soft sigh of delight at the warm water on her skin. She closes her eyes and tilts her face up against the shower, just as she feels an arm wrap around her waist. She turns her head, her gaze lifting to Lucian. "Lucy, Wh..."

Lucian's eyes gleam, placing a finger against her lips as she did. "Shh, Maddie. Just shower. I am not ready to leave you unattended just yet."

Madison reaches up to caress his cheek. "Alright." Picking up the bar of soap, she scrubs herself down, including her hair. Doing her best to wash away any taint of wolfsbane and Landon that might linger on her. She pauses at the mark on her wrist, looking it over, as she tries to rub it away, making a note to speak to her Brother about it. Once she is certain she is clean, she hands the bar over to him, her fingers lingering on his as a warmth fills her.

Lucian groans as her arousal fills the shower stall. "Rinse and get out,

Maddie. Or we are not making breakfast."

"Right." Madison blushes and rinses quickly. She grabs a towel and wraps it around her, leaving the bathroom. She moves to the clothes and pulls out a set, dressing quickly in tights and a hoodie. Once dressed, she sits at the table and runs a brush through her hair, tying it in a loose braid. She turns as Lucian steps out, the scent of pine and snow fills the room. His skin glistened slightly from the water running off his damp hair. She chews on her lower lip, feeling a heat pool inside her, suddenly desiring his touch all over her.

Lucian growls softly. "Madison, I will turn you over my knee when we get back upstairs for such thoughts when we need to get downstairs."

Her already flushed cheeks deepen in color. "Sorry, Lucy. I can't help myself."

"Trust me. I understand. But I suspect that your father and brother are still here and will want to see you downstairs. I know Victor wants words with you for planning a mission without his knowledge. Then clearly coming home drunk after said mission, ten days later, which, by the way, was adorable."

"I was not drunk. It was that toxic drink."

"You were drunk. Called me Wucy... several times. Even let Rhy have it when he pushed forward. He was less than impressed that you wanted me."

Madison mutters, averting her eyes as Lucian gets dressed. "Still mad at Rhydian."

Lucian pulls on slacks and a Henley. He moves over to kneel in front of her and takes her hand before rising. "It's fine, Madison. He will get over it. Now, we should get downstairs. After you passed out in my arms, Caden arrived with Paige, Faeloria, and Brittany, who is apparently Zed's mate. The King is not happy he is losing both his daughter and his witch to your family."

Madison rises with him, pulling him into his arms and hugging him tight. "Thank you."

"You're welcome. Afterward, I guess we need to have a serious talk about that pup in your belly."

Madison moves her hand down and nods. "I don't know how they can know already."

"They are magical. I guess we will find out."

"Are you alright with it Lucy, if it's true?"

"I am more than alright with it, Maddie."

She nods, a smile crossing her lips at the thought of mini Lucians running around. "Right, let's go." Pulling the door open, she is surprised to see a guard standing there. Giving him a nod and a smile, she bounds down the stairs, her dragon senses finding D'andre in the main chamber. She glances back at Lucian and giggles, running to the room just to see if he would follow. She catches the soft growl behind her, feeling Lucian's arms wrap around her waist, just as she reaches the door. "You do run!"

"Told you I am not ready to let you out of my sight." He whispers in her ear. "And I would chase you any day, my dear."

Madison blushes at the promise in his voice, and mumbles under her breath, before hearing D'andre's chuckle.

D'andre and Erica look up from where they sit talking quietly, seeing Madison and Lucian together in the door. He smiles at the blush staining her cheeks at something Lucian whispered, low enough that even their wolf hearing couldn't catch it. "And here I would have thought you would be the last one to arrive."

Madison scowls slightly at D'andre, despite the humor dancing in her eyes at her friend. "D'andre. It's good to see you too, and why would I be last?"

"Oh I don't know, new mate bond and wolfsbane in your system. That being said, I can't smell any radiating off you. That detox sure cleansed you fast."

"Yes, it's wretched shit, Tastes just as bad coming back up."

"Too much information, my dear. Especially as we are about to have breakfast. But I am curious about that recipe. I will have to ask your blood father about it. Meant to last night, but we got distracted with other chatter in the conference room. Though he wasn't much of a talker. Zed did most of it. Your father only seemed to have eyes for the princess."

Madison moves forward and settles herself next to D'andre, with Lucian to her right. "I heard that Gran-Pappy was upset that he was losing two of his people to the Shadowveil."

A loud gasp drew people's attention to Caden, standing in the doorway, staring at Madison in shock.

She looks down at her hoodie in confusion, running a hand over her hair, shifting under his stare. "Am I missing something?"

Paige places a hand on Caden's arm. "No honey, you just called him Gran-Pappy. He wasn't expecting it."

Madison frowns, trying to recall her last words, realizing that she had, in fact, addressed him as such. "Well he is my Gran-Pappy."

"Yes, he is. Does this mean you are no longer mad at him?"

"Well Somo still is 'cause I can feel her bristling inside me, but I am not mad. He played a good Lucian."

Paige laughs. "Yes, I heard all about it from Brittany, but I informed her it was fine. I didn't feel any mate bond betrayal, no matter how much you snuggled, or that he kissed your forehead several times."

"She was a great scowler, just like Victor."

Victor growls quietly behind them. "Just because he is your mate, Maddie, does NOT mean his hands could wander."

Madison jumps up and runs into Victor's arms, drawing Clarice into a group hug. "Vic! Clary. It's sooo good to see you both."

Victor hugs her and steps back, looking his daughter over. "What brought that on lass?

Clarice laughs. "Oh Vic, you are so clueless at times. She's sucking up, so she doesn't get *the* lecture from you."

"MOM! I thought you were on my side."

"Oh honey. If I have to suffer through the lecture of keeping secrets from him, so do you." Clarice touches her cheek gently, before moving to sit next to Lucian.

"Damn!"

"That reminds me, I have a lovely bar of floral scented soap with your name on it when we get home."

"Seriously, Mom?"

"Yes, I do believe I will make it part of the next mission."

Madison growls softly as she stomps back to sit beside Lucian, causing both Caden and D'andre to chuckle. She favors each of them with a scowl as well. "I just did a mission and won! I get to sit the next one out. Them's the rules."

Clarice smiles at her adopted daughter's antics. "Indeed, perhaps the next two missions, then."

"That's not fair, Mom!!"

"Life's not fair, dear. Get used to it."

Faeloria walks in on the arm of Jean Claude, taking in the banter between those at the table. She sits next to Caden and Paige, her true parents. Introduced to her after a day of rest here at D'andres' pack house. And a sister apparently who had somehow instinctively taken in her daughter. Her gaze lands on Madison, whom she hasn't seen in thirteen years, a pout and scowl on her face, despite the humor dancing in her eyes. A daughter who came looking for her at her own risk and rescued her from Landon's men.

Faeloria's grip tightens on Jean Claude's arm, her memories unwillingly going back to the day that Landon appeared at Davis's pack house. Not that Landon wasn't a regular at the pack house she was bound to with an Alpha's command. No, this time he came with a witch in tow, one with accusations of her using glamor. She cast a spell and apparently removed it, but looking in the mirror, didn't see any difference other than the mirror didn't seem to have the same shroud around the edges. They did though, or so they said.

Davis, who was already angry with her, was furious and handed her over to Landon to get her out of his sight. It was the last time she saw him, her daughter or her son. It was not until she arrived here, talking to Caden and Paige, that some of her memories returned. Happiness filled her when she found out Faeloria was her true name, one she preferred over Megan that her other parents gave her. She had even given JC that name, which, thinking about it, would also explain why he couldn't find her if he asked around for Faeloria.

She shifts her attention to Clarice, her Sister. While growing up with her family, she often asked about her sister, but each time, they could not answer her. They just stated they found her on the beach and no one claimed her as missing, but they still loved her as if she was their own. And she loved them. They were gentle and loving to a girl they found. Caden, though, was less than impressed with the news, and they drove out to see her parents with her, wanting to know why they kept her when he was missing a daughter.

After hours of discussion, they informed Caden they had posted notices. When no one came forward, they assumed rogues killed her parents. Especially as the doctors they brought in only confirmed that memory loss was often a result of trauma or a head injury. They brought out the family album, which held pictures of her glamoured form of deep brown eyes, and almost black hair, compared to the ash blonde and green eyes that she truly had. So since they couldn't seem to have kids, they took her under their wing until Alpha Davis saw her outside and fell in love with her. He even arrived the next day with a dowry so large, her parents would have been idiots to decline it.

Faeloria looks down to her lap as her thoughts roll around in her mind, recalling the car ride to the pack house, the adoration that he had for her, their first night together when he said he was going to mate mark her, whatever that meant. That she needed to bite him back in order for it to be binding, and she complied. Her brow furrows, recalling when her wolf Mystic arrived on her true eighteenth birthday, somewhat of a surprise at hearing another voice in her head. Her parents had been uncertain if she was human or wolf, so had remained silent on the matter as well.

She still felt the anger of fighting for days with Davis after Mystic informed her he had tricked her into marking him. That their true mate was out there somewhere and he took it away from them. She asked to be released from the binding, but Davis denied her, saying not until she provided him with a male heir, as that was the contract made with her parents. It was after this, her wolf Mystic taught her she could fey-step and so in her free time, she stepped out, finding a love of the ocean waves crashing against the shore on the other side of their pack.

She lifts her gaze to Jean Claude, catching his eyes watching her intently, and smiles at him. He looked exactly as she remembered him, walking down the beach with two guards in tow. How Mystic raged inside her, that this was her fated mate and they needed to get out of the bond with Davis. She recalled how their eyes met, and every detail they talked about on the shores, before making bittersweet love with his promise to return to her. When she returned to her pack house that night, Davis struck her. It was the first and only time, and she didn't understand how he knew. Well, it didn't take long before she felt the betrayal pains herself, as he returned what she had granted him.

How many nights she cried herself to sleep in pain? Waiting for the return of her mate. Only to be forced to the realization that he was not returning or keeping his promise. It was not long after she discovered she was pregnant, which brought Davis around again, for he desperately wanted a son. When a girl with aquamarine eyes was born, life took a turn for the worse, with Davis returning to her bed only once after that in a drunken state. Luke, the boy he wanted, conceived that night. With her dignity in shreds, she put her time and effort into raising her children, only to end up sold to Landon when they were ten and eight. A wry smile crosses her lips, recalling Landon wanting to mate her as well, only to deny him, as she knew her true mate was out there. Not that she told anyone. Upon her rejection, Landon traded her to the witches, where she swapped Alpha chains for magical cages. Drained her of her fey magics, time and time again. She had hoped, as she languished in the cages, that Davis was treating her children right, only to find out the opposite.

Madison watched her mom Faeloria, seeing her lost in thought, recognizing the flickers of pain in her features. "Mom Faeloria?"

Madison's voice snaps her out of her thoughts as looks across the table, catching everyone's eyes on her, including Zed and Brittany's who she didn't even see enter. "Sorry, I drifted into the past."

"It's all good, Mom, you're allowed. Landon, Davis, they can't hurt you anymore."

"I know. Thank you for coming to save me."

"I'm sorry it took so long, Mom. I had always hoped that you ran away with another, but as I got older, I knew that wasn't the case."

Jean Claude places an arm over her shoulder. "If I had my way, Madison, she would have. I just wish I had known about the fey-step sooner and that she went by Megan. I would have looked inland instead of just along the coast."

"You have her now, that's what matters." Madison smiles, glad that her mom has finally found her mate.

"Indeed, I do."

"Is there room at the table for us? I heard my long-lost sister has returned for a second time and Aurora is dying to see her. You know, despite the fact that she's the reason Aurora got stolen in the first place."

Madison spins in shock at the sound of her brother's voice, seeing him walking in with Rosa, carrying one little bundle of joy. She jumps up and draws Luke into a tight hug. "Luke! How are you here?"

"Can't breathe, Maddie."

Madison releases him. "Right, sorry."

"It seems a text came in from Nathan last night that you had returned and suggested we make the drive over for breakfast. Something about important things to discuss."

Madison turns to look at D'andre. "D'andre?"

Caden coughs slightly. "That might have been me, Madison. We have three packs with no Alphas. Lucian said you had a plan?"

Madison stares at Caden in shock. "But you are the King. It's your choice."

"Aye, I am the King. Next in line for the throne is my daughter Faeloria, but it seems she is going to the Shadowveil Sanctuary, so being her first born, that leaves you. It's about time to make some decisions regarding it."

She shakes her head. "Can I respectfully decline the throne?"

"Excuse me?"

"Sire... Gran-Pappy... Caden. I am Alpha of Wildfire Crescent. I am not a queen and don't want to be in all honesty. Clary and Vic are my Beta and Delta, so to speak. I mean, I suppose Clary could be next, and her pups, and I am not deciding on her behalf, but both your Daughters have been missing in action for a long time. Really, I believe your son Felix should ascend the throne. It's what he's been training for, right?"

Caden looks over at Clarice, who nods in agreement with Madison. "Sorry, Father, but I am with her. Felix is the best choice for the throne."

Caden runs his fingers through his hair and starts laughing. "You know, a lot of kids vie for this kind of power, and here I have three declining the position I am offering them."

Madison smiles. "I have my power with Wildfire. One I can manage, and one I will leave to my pup."

Caden looks at his wife, Paige, who smiles back at him. "Fine. I am still making you decide what to do with the packs. This was your discovery and, ultimately, your mission."

Madison nods, turning to look at Luke. "Lucian and I already talked about it. I would like to offer Duskrunner and Nightshade to Luke, who will rename them and step in as Alpha." She turns to Luke and Rosa. "If you do not wish it, and would like to move to Wildfire, then you will be welcome with open arms. I will give you time to think about it."

Luke turns to his mate, and both smile at each other. "We wish to join Wildfire, Maddie. While Duskrunner has some wonderful memories, it holds a lot of bad as well. If Mom is going to the Shadowveil with Jean Claude, then she only needs to visit one place to see all of us. Though we ask that Rosa's parents be accepted as well."

Madison beams in delight. "Fair enough. They are welcome too." She turns back to the King and smiles. "Then I grant all three packs to D'andre."

D'andre rises suddenly. "WHAT?"

Madison turns to her friend. "You housed us here, you kept us safe, you helped plan a mission. They are all together and I have faith you can incorporate them easily enough under the Silvermoon banner. It will be work and take time, but I think you can do it."

"What did I do to make you hate me so much, Madison?!"

She laughs at his comment. "I told you I would get you back. And in doing this, you might actually be the second largest pack out there, after me, of course. Frostbite might give you a run for your money for second position though and technically, they are tied to me, cause Lucians my mate!"

"Hey wait, we have an alliance agreement to be drawn up, so I am tied to you too!"

"That's true. Hand me a piece of paper and I will draw it up now."

"Seriously?"

"Sure, why not?"

D'andre mind-links a maid, who arrives in a few minutes with lined paper and a couple of pens.

She accepts the paper and places it on the table, taking a seat in front of it, her pen moving carefully across the paper.

I, Madison Martinez, Alpha of the Wildfire Crescent pack, do hereby agree to an alliance with the shit disturber, D'andre Camdon of the Silvermoon pack. Well, actually, I agree to the alliance with his Luna, Erica Camdon as she's the more sensible and patient of the two and can keep him in line. Within this alliance, we agree to be friends forever more, to stay in regular weekly contact, and to come to each other's aid when needed. It is also agreed upon that we shall descend in mass numbers, children and all, to D'andre and Erica's pack house every year for the winter festival they will put on. Only Luna Erica will be allowed to complain when we take over the pack house for a week because this is somehow D'andres fault, even if it's not. If it is heard that D'andre complains, he will face Alpha Madison in a scenario of Victor's choosing, or Princess Clarice in a snowball fight. Included in the takeover is everyone sitting in the room at the very moment, and their family, even new members that arise. Listed are as follows.

King Caden and Queen Paige Sylvanax. King Jean Claude and Princess Faeloria. Head Witch Brittany, Prince Zed, and her Coven sisters. Alpha Victor and Princess Clarice Martinez. Alpha Luke, Luna Rosa Evenstone and their daughter Aurora. Myself, Alpha Madison Martinez, soon to be Marzire, and my mate Alpha Lucian Marzire and our pup, not named yet. Lucian's brother Alpha Pierce Marzire and his family, who are not in the room presently, but are included in the list. Oh, and the phone wolf, Nathan and if he has a mate, her too.

Alpha Maddie Martinez.

Once she is done, she signs and dates the bottom of it and hands it over to him. "Sign it and print me a copy. I want it before I leave."

D'andre reads the parchment and laughs, signing the bottom immediately and handing it over to his wife. "Agreed, Madison. Though

I will still have one hundred lawyers look over it for loopholes. Thank you for making this winter one to remember. Now let's eat, so we can get Prince Zed and King Jean Claude to look over the prisoners before they need to return home."

Madison turns to Zed and scowls at him, pulling her hoodie sleeve up. "Speaking of which, Brother. You bloody well marked me! How do I get rid of it?"

Zed smiles at his sister. "You don't Princess. It is the Royal mark of King Jean Claude Vyndell and is there for life. Consider it a connection to our plane and family. One that will warn any creatures of our realm not to touch you or their life will end immediately. It will also allow us to feel and connect with you. For example, if you are in trouble, it allows us to find you at any time or any place."

"You bloody well put a dog tag on me?"

"Essentially, if that's the way you want to look at it. I have one, and your mom Faeloria does now, for I can feel her in the family. Brittany will too if she accepts it."

She glares at him. "At least they got a choice!"

"Princess, I was a captive for four years when I was supposed to be looking for you. You found me, and I recognized you right away. I was not letting you slip through my fingers again. If you truly wish it gone, your father can remove it."

Madison turns her gaze to her father, seeing the concern in his features seconds before he schools his expression. She sighs gently. "No, it can stay."

Jean Claude's shoulders relax at her words, as a smile crosses his lip. "Thank you, Madison."

Caden grins at them, his eyes moving to the paper in Erica's hand. "Right, Luna Erica, please hand over the contract. I wish to approve it and place my signature on it as well." He accepts the agreement from her, and chuckles as he reads it. "Impressive, Madison. I, King Caden, accept the terms of this contract under Kingdom law." He signs the bottom below both Madison's and D'andre's signatures.

D'andre mutters under his breath. "At least that saved me one hundred lawyers' fees." Which earns laughter from everyone in the room as they read the contract that is handed around.

The group laughs and jokes amongst themselves, partaking in a fine breakfast of bacon, eggs, pancakes and waffles. The maids enter and refill the coffees, teas, and juices as necessary. Each of them enjoying the fact that they succeeded in their mission, saved the innocents, and stopped the three packs behind the disappearances. Because of that, the group has a bond that cannot be broken.

After breakfast, Caden rises, glancing at the group. "Right, we only have a couple of hours before Jean Claude and Zed must return. I would like to hit all the packs, and go through them as D'andre suggested, if that's alright? If you can do what takes us hours, then I would feel better releasing those that are actually innocent faster."

Zed and Jean Claude nod, rising in their seats. "Agreed. Madison went on a rescue mission to free innocents. We cannot have them languishing longer than necessary."

Caden smiles. "D'andre, since you are taking over the packs, you shall join us so they know who their new Alpha is. There will be an official swearing in ceremony within the month."

"Understood, Sire."

"The rest can stay here and relax."

Madison rises, and moves over to hug her mother, father and brother. Knowing they will probably just phase back home before returning here. "I will see you all when you return."

Zed's eyes lock on to Brittany's. "Yes, in five days."

Madison follows his gaze and nudges her brother. "Think you can handle her, Zed?"

He chuckles, nudging her back. "I am going to find out."

"Good. Thank you for helping Gran-Pappy."

Caden grins. "Still can't get over the fact that I am now accepted as Gran-Pappy. Now, let's go. Brittany portal us to Nightshade first."

Brittany draws on her magic, as golden lights surround her, creating a portal to Nightshade Howlers pack house, waiting until those attending step through before following. They immediately take in a blend of Frostbites and the King's men patrolling the grounds as they head downstairs to the overcrowded dungeons. It doesn't take long for Zed and Jean Claude to go through the pack, pointing out the innocents based on their auras, detaining and moving the guilty to the Lycan cells to await their trials.

Caden leads the freed wolves upstairs to where D'andre waits with Faeloria, talking with some wolves out there. Caden points to the courtyard. "Please stand there. Now, you are free because you are innocent. Nightshade Howlers no longer exist and are formally stricken from the books. Any that cling to the name will end up in the stocks. You now fall under the banner of Silvermoon, and Alpha D'andre. Within the month, there will be a swearing in ceremony, where you WILL swear allegiance to him. Is that understood?"

A murmur moves through the courtyard, before one raises his hand to speak.

D'andre turns to him. "Speak."

"What happened?"

D'andre's gaze turns to the King, who nods. "Well. Long story short. We arrested Alpha Landon for kidnapping, trafficking of wolves and other supernatural creatures to dark witches, attempted murder, as well as many other things. He will never see the light of day and it's unlikely his men, who were portraying themselves as rogues, will either."

The young wolf contemplates his words, offering him a smile. "Thank you. None of us understood why we were all suddenly arrested."

"I'm sorry. It was better to arrest the whole pack at the time due to the fact that Duskrunner and Howling Oak were also in on this. There were several things happening at the same time."

"But we are free now? To return to our homes and such."

"Yes. Pack life will continue as normal. I intend to build a new central pack house within the next year. There is still a lot to do and it will be work to integrate four packs together, but we WILL do it."

He drops to his knees and bows to him. "Thank you, Alpha D'andre."

Caden watches the group accept the fact that D'andre is their new Alpha and looks to Jean Claude and Zed. "Thank you, a few more packs to go."

"You're welcome."

Much the same happens at Howling Oak and Duskrunner, though at Duskrunner, Jean Claude and Zed take time to walk through the pack house, where Madison and Faeloria lived. Jean Claude pulls a family photo off the wall and looks it over, sadness filling him at the time he missed with his family. He smiles at Faeloria as he tucks the picture into his robes and follows Caden and Brittany to the Lycan prison.

Jean Claude and Zed travel through the cells, looking over the ones already convicted, and bound in silver chains around both ankles and wrists, as well as locked in a cell. They nod in agreement to everyone except one. Both of them pause at Alpha Xandor's cage, his aura giving mixed signals, studying him carefully. They speak in a language between them for a few minutes before turning to Caden. "This one has an overall good aura, but shadows encase it. Dark magic also surrounds him, magic like the ones my son killed. There is confusion and fear within his aura, but not for himself, for another. The rest in the dungeons do not contain this within their aura."

Caden looks at Xandor, hanging in his chains, his head down, a clear aura of despair hanging over him. "What are you saying?"

"I am saying he is not dark. Unlike Landon, who has the darkest aura we have ever seen. This one has a magical compulsion on him and if you remove it, his aura is bright. It cannot take away from the crimes he partook in, but he did not do it of his own free will or consciousness. He will forever carry the shadow of the guilt of what's happened because you cannot take those memories away. The choice is yours."

"What would you do?"

"Free him to be with whoever he is concerned about. I am guessing his

Luna and children. Perhaps serve time outside the cells somehow. Strip him of his title and position and post him where he can be monitored. But I think you will find he will be a model citizen."

Caden nods at his words. "Done. Brittany, can you and your sisters free him."

"We can try, Sire."

Jean Claude looks at his hands, seeing the nails elongating. "Perfect. Zed can confirm it when he returns to collect Brittany." He reaches out to shake Caden's hand. "Thank you for hosting us in your Kingdom. Now, we need to go. I can feel the change happening."

Brittany's brow furrows as she quickly hugs Zed. "I will be waiting. Madison has Caden's number. Just call and I will find you."

"I will... Five days, look for me..." Zed kisses her gently, and steps back, as the three of them fade from the realm.

Twenty-One

Epilogue

MADISON FRANTICALLY RACES around the bedchamber, madly rummaging through her dressers to pack her clothes, having already packed their three pups' clothing. She pulls out a handful of shirts and tights, sorting through what matched before running them back to the suitcase on the bed.

Lucian watches his wife's frenzied pace, smiling as he knows it doesn't really matter what time this afternoon they arrive. "Maddie, it's D'andre. He's not going to care that we are late."

Madison scowls his way as she throws clothes into the suitcase and on the bed. "He's not, but I will. Besides, I am certain Clary and Vic are already waiting downstairs."

"They are, I can sense them. Luke and Rosa just arrived with their kids as well."

"Of course they are." She groans and runs to the bathroom, gathering all of her toiletries and stuffs them into a small bag. She returns to the bedroom and places them in the corner of the suitcase, turning to face Lucian as he approaches her.

Lucian wraps his arms around her. "I love you. They love you. A few minutes isn't going to kill them. Take your time. Relax and breathe. We have gone through this every Yule for the past ten years and will continue to do so for the next ten or more."

She leans against him, feeling his pine scent overwhelming and soothing her. Closing her eyes, she stands still, letting the calmness of him travel through their bond, knowing he is right. And it was not like they had to catch a plane or they would definitely be missing that flight. She sighs softly. "I know Lucy. It's just I hate being late."

Lucian chuckles and holds her close. "No stress, Maddie. Remember. This is a vacation that you committed us too."

She relaxes against him. "It seemed like a good idea at the time."

"It still is a good idea, Maddie." He caresses her cheek gently, before cupping her face and kissing her softly.

"I know. Thank you Lucy."

"Anytime, my love. Now, close the suitcase. If there is something you are missing, you can fey-step back and get it."

She swats him with the shirt in her hand. "That's not the point, Lucy. We are there on a holiday. We don't come home in between."

"But I promise, I wont tell anyone and neither will Pierce nor Violet."

Madison mutters under her breath as she stuffs the rest of the clothes into the suitcase and zips it closed. She moves over, slips her boots on and collects her cloak. Pulling it over her shoulders, she fastens the bobbles at her neck. "Right, let's get the pups." She closes her eyes, drawing on her draconic senses to locate them. "I got Jess. She's in the kitchen with her nanny. Owen is in the training barracks, watching the warriors. Looks like Oliver is already with Oma and Opa waiting."

Lucian kisses her cheek. "He's always there. Takes after his mother."

"Perhaps."

They head down the stairs where Madison drops her suitcase off at her parents' feet. She races to find her child, with Lucian heading outside to the training grounds. Madison stops and watches her daughter help roll out pastry dough, the flour covering the shirt she had just put on her ten minutes ago. She sighs inwardly, watching her daughter's aquamarine eyes sparkle in delight as the cook pounds her own dough in front of her. "Jess, sweetheart, time to go."

"Ok, Mama." She brushes her blonde hair aside just like her father's and runs into her mother's arms.

Lucian steps outside into the brisk air, heading to the barracks. He spots his son hanging on the railing, watching the men train. Smiling, suspecting that were he not dressed to go to Auntie Erica and Uncle D'andre's, he would be in the ring with them. He had yet to defeat the warriors or parents in the ring, but he certainly gave it his best effort. "Owen, Mom's waiting."

"Just another minute, Dad."

Lucian chuckles and walks over to stand beside him, watching Ironwoods elites wrestling in the ring. He ruffles his son's blonde hair, something all three of his children inherited. "Now... I am sure you can watch D'andre's warriors tomorrow."

Owen's blue eyes roll at his Father. "They are not as good as ours."

Lucian laughs and picks his son up, the split image of him when he was his age. "You're right, but they have other skills you can learn from. Come, your brother is already waiting with Oma, Opa, Uncle Luke, Auntie Rosa, and your cousins."

"Yes, well, he's a nerd. He would be ready."

"He differs from you, but he is still your brother. Be nice."

"I know, Dad. And I love him, but all those sciencey books bore me."

"Hey, watch it! Your father is a science nerd."

"I know. That's why I am gonna be like Mom. She's at least cool!"

"Yes, that she is."

Within five minutes, they each return with a kid hanging off their hip. Madison smiles at the group waiting patiently with their eldest son, Oliver. She shifts the luggage in between them as they form a circle around it. "Ready?" Once they all give a nod, she fey-steps the group of them, luggage included, to D'andres' new foyer. Madison turns as Erica greets them.

"You are two minutes late, Madison!"

Madison laughs and moves over to hug Erica with one arm. "Sorry, next year, I will be on time. I promise."

"I think you promised that last year. It's a good thing you didn't put a time in that contract of yours." She pulls Jess out of Madison's arms and sits her on her hip.

Madison groans. "I would be in breach every year! The little ones take far too much time to pack for."

"Don't I know it? I am glad mine are older now. Now come, I will place you in your rooms. JC and Zed are already here with Brittany and Loria. They are in the games room duking it out with D'andre. At least you beat Caden and Pierce."

"YES! I am sooo not late then!"

Oliver smiles up at Erica. "Auntie Erica, is Cousin Archer around?"

Erica nods. "Yes, sweetie, He is in the games room with Mila."

Oliver turns to his Mom. "Can I go play with him?"

"Yes, you can. Take your brother and cousins Aurora, Jade, and Silas with you."

"Aww Mom!"

"Don't you aww Mom me, or I will send your sister with you as well."

"Right, let's go everyone." He grabs his brother's hand and pulls him towards the games room at a run, with the others trailing after him.

Madison chuckles, watching them take off, her eyes turning back to Erica doting on their little girl. "Did you put us in the same rooms as last year?"

"Of course, they were built for you. D'andre said it is an unwritten rule in the contract."

Madison laughs. "Of course he did. I will drop our luggage off in the room and meet you and the others in the games room."

Erica winks at her. "Don't get lost now that you have a break from the kids."

Madison blushes, her eyes straying to Lucian. "Never! If I was not here to greet him, Gran-Pappy would NOT let me hear the end of it."

A portal opens into the hall, and Caden steps through. "Hear the end of what, Madison?"

She mumbles softly, her blush deepening. "Nothing."

Erica laughs, giving a slight bow to Caden. "Her getting lost again in this pack house."

Caden chuckles, moving to hug his granddaughter first. "Like last year and the year before you mean. You would think the pair of them were freshly marked with how they behave." He hugs his daughter and Rosa next before shaking Luke's hand. "The kids?"

"Gran-Pappy!" Madison feels a blush staining her cheeks.

Luke points down the hall. "You're late. They are already in the games room."

"Oh, Maddie, you know it's true! Now, you are safe to run away and get lost. We are all here. The rest of the sisters will arrive in the morning. They have things to do apparently for JC and Zed."

Madison catches Lucian's chuckle. "You're NOT helping!"

Lucian shrugs his shoulders. "What? I like getting lost with you."

She growls softly at him before moving forward to Paige and hugging her. "Gran-Mama. Hope everything is well."

Paige smiles at her granddaughter. "It is, and you?"

"Busy! How would you like three kids for a month now that you are retired and Uncle Felix and Auntie Alexis have taken over?"

Paige laughs softly. "Don't ask questions you don't want the answers to, my dear. I would happily take them for a month, and you know it."

Madison nods. "I know. I would miss them too much."

"Perhaps we can come stay for a month?"

"That would be fantastic! I will have rooms done as soon as we get home!"

Pierce chuckles and moves to hug his brother's wife. "You know, if Lucian gets too much to handle, you can always send him home. No need to bring the Monarch in to look after him."

Madison hugs him back. "You better watch it. I might just do that. Kid free, mate free, ah, it sounds like heaven. I would need to get rid of the parents and brother though too!"

Victor growls softly. "NOT going to happen, lass. Said it before, you are stuck with Clary and I."

Violet laughs, following her mate in hugging Madison. "For about four hours, dear, then you will be bored out of your mind. Trust me. I know!"

Madison drapes an arm around Victor and rests her head on his shoulder. "Fine, Vic. How about the four hours that Violet offered? Could I at least have that?"

Clarice smiles, winking her way. "I will keep him busy for four hours, dear."

"Ewww Mom! Too much info!" Madison glances around, realizing they were missing some offspring. "Speaking of which. Violet, where are Theo, Kai, and Angelica?"

"With their mates this year. They are all grown up now."

"Wow, that's hard to believe."

Erica smiles. "Well, Archer is nineteen already and has yet to find his mate. He's planning to pack hop this year. Perhaps I will send him to Wildfire first, just to torture my husband. He is waiting for Victor's payback with Mila and her mate, being that she's almost at that age. Next year, she will be eighteen and get her wolf."

Victor chuckles. "I cannot wait! I will be the devil on her shoulder, just as he was for Maddie."

She laughs. "I fully expect it. He deserves it." Erica calls in a few maids to take their luggage up to their rooms as they make their way to the games room. Madison runs over to hug her father and Zed. "It's so good to see you, even if it's just for twenty-four hours."

"Actually, about that, Maddie, Brittany and her sisters have worked their magic. We now have a week before we shift into the beast. They are hoping by next year they will have the curse lifted."

"That is the best present a girl can ask for!" Her eyes travel to her mom. "Mom, I certainly hope JC is still treating you like a Queen."

Faeloria smiles and hugs her daughter. "Always!"

"Perfect... Brittany, thank you for doing this for them."

"Anytime Maddie. Don't tell them, but it's one hundred percent a selfish reason. This way, I get to spend longer than 24 hours on this plane, as Zed is a touch possessive."

Madison giggles. "I might have got that impression." She turns around to face their host. "There is the shit disturber! D'andre!"

D'andre steps forward and draws Madison into a tight hug. "Madison! What are we doing this year? Taking over Whispering Pines? Dethroning Felix? It's been ten years since we had an escapade! I am bored!"

"Oh D'andre. Didn't you know, we are taking over Silvermoon! Absorbing them into Wildfire Crescent."

"Damn, and here I heard they put on this fantastic winter festival that kept them off Wildfires' radar."

Madison steps back to stand beside him, looking over all the family that had gathered. The laughter and love that fills the room within the close-knit group. Erica at the snooker table with Archer, challenging Zed and Brittany to a game. Paige and Lucian watch Caden wrestle with the children, Oliver, Owen, and Silas on the mat as they do their best to take him down. Jean Claude at the poker table with Victor and Luke, while Faeloria and Clarice play with the three girls, Aurora, Jess, and Jade. Rosa and Mila standing in the corner making tea and chatting. Even Nathan and his mate Kelly duke it out at the console, with their two pups, Steph and Zoe avidly watching. "Yes, D'andre. They certainly do. Every year it gets better and better."

D'andre drapes an arm over her shoulder and follows her gaze. "Yes, it does. Thank you, Maddie, for showing up in my pack ten years ago."

She turns and kisses his cheek, hearing Lucian's soft growl through their bond. "Thank you for accepting the strays at your gate, D'andre."

He chuckles. "Powerful strays. That I even get to keep, according to my wife. Now, on that note, I see Victor at the poker table. It's a tradition; I need to take that stray's money and keep him up all night."

Madison laughs. "You better not keep him up too late, D'andre. Clarice is here."

"Right, I forgot about her. Perhaps half the night then." He winks at her and strides over to the poker table, joining the others in the game of chance.

Lucian watches D'andre leave and moves to step beside his wife. "My love, kissing another man. In front of me, no less."

"Bah, you know who I love, Lucian."

He pulls her close, trailing a hand gently down her cheek. "Yes, my dear, that I do. Clearly D'andre!"

She smiles and kisses his cheek too. "You might just have to share."

"Never." He whispers softly, staring into her aquamarine eyes before capturing her lips with his. "You will always be mine, Maddie. You, Zuri, and Somo belong to Rhydian and I forever more."

She sighs, feeling the flood of emotions through their bond. "Yes... yes, we do. I love you Lucian Marzire."

"I love you, Madison Marzire."

......*THE END*.....

And they all lived happily ever after.

(All except Landon and Davis that is.)

Twenty-Two

People of the Realm

Alpha - Leader of the pack

Luna - Leaders Mate

Beta - 1st guard of the Alpha

Gamma - 2nd guard of the Alpha

Delta - Personal guard of the Luna

Warrior - Other guards

Omega - Working class, smaller wolves

Hierarchy

Lycan is top dawg! (King and Queen)

Alpha and Luna (Think Baron and Baroness)

Dragon, Wolf, Fey, Vampire Shifters, Witches, all battle it out below Lycan (Think Nobles)

Rogues - Wolves with no pack, either banished or disowned. (Think Rebels)

Whispering Pines

Lycan King - Caden Sylvanax

Wolf - Sterling

Lycan Queen - Paige Sylvanax

Wolf - Venus

Princess - Faeloria

Princess - Clarice

Wolf - Lycine

Prince - Felix

Princess - Phoebe

White Witch - Brittany (Coven - Eclipsia Enclave)

- Sisters - Thalia, Fiona, Dallas, Iris

Kings Guards - Orion, Atticus, Jasper and Adrian.

Epilogue - Ten years

Alexis

Wildfire Crescent

Alpha Madison - Evenstone (Martinez) Fey touched (Aquamarine eyes, brown hair, freckles)

Dragon - Somoko

Wolf - Zuri

Delta Victor Martinez (Brown hair, Brown eyes)

Former Alpha of Ironwood Moon pack as Victor Winterbourne

Wolf - Zion

Beta - Clarice Martinez

Wolf - Lycine

Children - Cole, Amelia, Finn, Logan.

Gamma - Cole Martinez

Former Alpha - Gregory

Epilogue - Ten years

Oliver - 9.5

Owen - 7.5

Jess - 4

Duskrunner

Alpha Davis Evenstone

Luna Megan Evenstone

Luke Evenstone

Rosa Evenstone

Aiden Warner - Captain of Football team

Sasha Minckler - Gossip monger

Mathew Parkers - Warrior Mate to Sasha

Martin Lopez - Secretary

Professor Lucian Deplois (Blonde hair, blue eyes)

Dragon - Rhydian

Receptionist - Stephanie

Humans towns in pack territory - Newport

Epilogue - Ten years

Aurora - 12

Jade - 10

Silas - 8

Frostbite Syndicate

Alpha Pierce Marzire

Luna Violet Marzire

Beta - Granite

Gamma- Thorne

Epilogue - Ten years

Theo - 25

Kai - 23

Angelica - 20

Silvermoon

Alpha D'andre Camdon (Short brown hair, hazel eyes, goatee)

Luna - Erica (Blonde, hair, gray eyes)

Children - Archer and Mila

Beta - Terrence (Light brown hair, green eyes)

Gamma - Ethan

Nurse - Natalie

Omega Maid - Vivian

Omega Maid - Maria

Nathan - Phone liaison (Fake Stormfang contact)

Mate - Kelly

Spy/Traitor - Alaric

Human town in Pack territory - Bourke

Epilogue - Ten years

Archer - 19

Mila - 17

Steph - 11

Zoe - 8

Nightshade Howlers

Alpha - Landon Tack (Black hair, green eyes)

Luna -

Beta - Marco Vinyx

Gamma - Garrick

Witch - Vespera (Coven - Blood Moon Sisters)

Sisters - Lydia, Circe, Malvina, Damara

Spy - Issac

Spy - Caleb

Spy - Noah

Howling Oak

Alpha - Xandor

Luna - Monica

Stormfang

Alpha Darian Ravenwind

Luna - Willow

Beta- Kieran

Daughter - Zara

Nathan Wilson

-Wife Diana

-Daughter Zoe

The Shadowveil Sanctuary

King Jean Claude Vyndell

Chosen mate - Saji

Son - Zed

Time anomaly - Shadowveil Sanctuary to Wolf realm

720 hours - 10 years (divided by 24 is 30 days)

360 hours - 5 years

72 hours - 365 days

6 hours - 30 days

3 hours - 15 days

2 hours - 10 days

1 hour - 5 days

½ hour - 2.5 days

15 mins - 1.25 days

Wolf Packs

Starfall

Wildfire Crescent

Thunder Paw Alliance

Whispering Pines

Amber Claw

Frostbite Syndicate

Stormfang Clan

Silvermoon

Howling Oak

Duskrunner

Nightshade Howlers

Twenty-Three

Portraits

Madison Martinez (Evenstone)

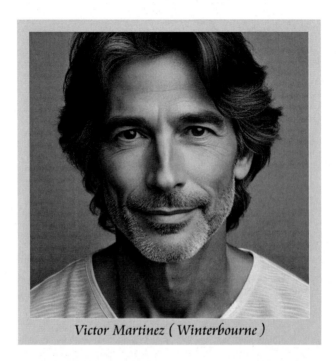

Victor Martinez (Winterbourne)

Proffessor Lucian Deplois (Marzire)

Davis Evenstone

Landon Tack

D'andre Camdon

Erica Camdon

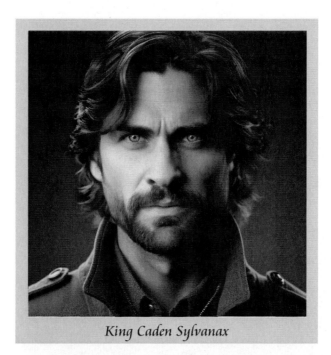

King Caden Sylvanax

Queen Paige Sylvanax

Clarice Martinez

Faeloria Evenstone

Twenty-Four

Age Chart

Davis	27	30	36	44	49
Megan	20	3	9	17	22
Madison	1	4	10	18	23
Luke		3	9	17	22
Rosa		3	9	17	22
Aurora					2
Lucian	11	14	20	28	33
Victor	25	28	34	42	47
Clarise	18	21	27	35	40
Felix	15	18	24	32	37
Landon	29	32	38	46	51
D'andre	10	13	19	27	32
Erica	7	10	16	24	29
Archer				4	9
Mila				2	7
Caden	45	48	54	62	67
Paige	43	46	52	60	65
Xandor	28	31	37	45	50
Monica	21	24	30	38	43
Pierce	15	18	24	32	37
Violet	13	16	22	30	35

Twenty-Five

About the Author

About the Author

Randi lives in Victoria, BC. Canada. She is a dog groomer by day and a writer/gamer by night. She loves to read and write fantasy and has been for years. She taught medieval dance for just under fifteen years and partook in the SCA. Since 2004, she attended the Faerieworlds festival yearly, keeping fantasy alive in her heart until they closed it down in 2022. She hopes her book draws you away from the modern world and into a land of intrigue and fantasy where magic, dragons, wolves and kings roam the lands.

Twenty-Six

Contributers

Thank you to everyone that helped with this book !

Cover Design - R Dey.

Bing Portraits - Edited by R Dey and layered into the cover with Impact.

Beta readers - M Verronneau, N Doyle.

Arc reader - T Street.

Editors - T Street, N Doyle.

Editing Programs – Google Docs, ProWritingAid, Impact, Atticus.

Contributors - A Henderson. M Harris.

Author Portrait - G Woodward.

Twenty-Seven

Additional Information

———❧———

Thank you for taking the time to read my stories and I hope that you enjoyed them.

If you like this, here are other books released or upcoming.

Please feel free to follow me on the pages for the books, or add me via Goodreads or Facebook,

Also, reviews are important to self published authors, so please take the time to leave one. Thank you.

Social media: www.facebook.com/AuthorRandiAnneDey

www.goodreads.com/author/show/45347028.Randi_Anne_Dey

The King's Mystic: Oct 2023

www.facebook.com/kingsmystic

Madison's Web: Mar 2024

www.facebook.com/madisonswebbook

The Dragon's Mystic: May 2024

www.facebook.com/dragonsmystic

Chahaya-Five Swords of Power:(Five book series) Eta 2025

www.facebook.com/chahayadurmada

Royal Deception: Tails Scales and Tiaras Anthology - (short story) Summer 2024

Bloodbound Echoes: Eta 2024 (Dark Fantasy) (Co-written)

Cantara's Mystics: Release Unknown

Manufactured by Amazon.ca
Acheson, AB

12923807R00179